Fangs? Okay. This wasn't a joke.

Somebody was seriously messing with her, and maybe they wanted her hurt. She couldn't explain the eyes and the fangs, so this had to be bad. This guy was obviously capable of inflicting some real damage. His eyes morphed again to the electric blue, and somehow, he broadened even more, looking more animalistic than human.

"I don't understand," she said, her voice shaking as her mind tried to make sense of what her eyes were seeing. "Who are you? Why were you unconscious in a coma? How did you know my name?"

He breathed out, his broad chest moving with the effort. The fangs slowly slid back up, and his eyes returned to the sizzling aqua. "My name is Ronan Kayrs, and I was unconscious because the shield fell." He eyed her, tugging her even closer. "I know your name because I spent four hundred years seeing your face and feeling your soft touch in my dreams."

Also by Rebecca Zanetti

Vampire's Faith

Rebecca Zanetti

LYRICAL PRESS
Kensington Publishing Corp.
www.kensingtonbooks.com

LYRICAL PRESS BOOKS are published by
Kensington Publishing Corp.
119 West 40th Street
New York, NY 10018

All Kensington titles, imprints, and distributed lines are available at special quantity discounts for bulk purchases for sales promotion, premiums, fund-raising, educational, or institutional use.

Special book excerpts or customized printings can also be created to fit specific needs. For details, write or phone the office of the Kensington Sales Manager: Kensington Publishing Corp., 119 West 40th Street, New York, NY 10018. Attn. Sales Department. Phone: 1-800-221-2647.

Lyrical Press and Lyrical Press logo Reg. U.S. Pat. & TM Off.

First Electronic Edition: June 2018
eISBN-13: 978-1-5161-0745-2
eISBN-10: 1-5161-0745-4

First Print Edition: June 2018
ISBN-13: 978-1-5161-0749-0
ISBN-10: 1-5161-0749-7

Printed in the United States of America

This one's for Baby Whitman. Welcome to the world, little one. It's a much better place with you in it.

Acknowledgments

We've headed back to the Dark Protectors! I have many people to thank for getting this book to readers, and I sincerely apologize to anyone I've forgotten.

Thank you to Big Tone for the support, love, kisses, flowers, and Panera on demand. I like you and I love you forever.

Thank you to Gabe and Karlina for being such amazing human beings. Being your mom is my biggest blessing. You went from toddlers to teenagers way too quickly, and I'm truly excited to see what you do next.

Thank you to my hard-working editor, Alicia Condon, whose class, intuition, and dedication are an inspiration every day.

Thank you to Alexandra Nicolajsen, whose ingenuity in this business is only matched by her incredible kindness.

Thank you to the rest of the Kensington gang: Steven Zacharius, Adam Zacharius, Lynn Cully, Vida Engstrand, Jane Nutter, Lauren Jernigan, Lauren Vassallo, Arthur Maisel, Kimberly Richardson, and Rebecca Cremonese.

Thank you to my wonderful agent, Caitlin Blasdell, whose support, clear thinking, and wisdom have provided very much needed guidance for me as an author.

Thank you to Liza Dawson and the entire Dawson group, who work so very hard for me.

Thank you to Jillian Stein for the absolutely fantastic work and for being such an amazing friend.

Thanks to my fantastic street team, Rebecca's Rebels, and their creative and hard-working leader, Minga Portillo.

Thanks also to my constant support system: Gail and Jim English, Debbie and Travis Smith, Stephanie and Don West, Brandie and Mike Chapman, Jessica and Jonah Namson, and Kathy and Herb Zanetti.

Finally, thank you to the readers who have kept the Dark Protectors alive all of these years. It's because of you that we decided to return to the world of the Realm.

CHAPTER ONE

Dr. Faith Cooper scanned through the medical chart on her tablet while keeping a brisk pace in her dark boots through the hospital hallway, trying to ignore the chill in the air. "The brain scan was normal. What about the respiratory pattern?" she asked, reading the next page.

"Normal. We can't find any neurological damage," Dr. Barclay said, matching his long-legged stride easily to hers. His brown hair was swept back from an angled face with intelligent blue eyes. "The patient is in a coma with no brain activity, but his body is...well..."

"Perfectly healthy," Faith said, scanning the nurse's notes, wondering if Barclay was single. "The lumbar puncture was normal, and there's no evidence of a stroke."

"No. The patient presents as healthy except for the coma. It's an anomaly," Barclay replied, his voice rising.

Interesting. "Any history of drugs?" Sometimes drugs could cause a coma.

"No," Barclay said. "No evidence that we've found."

Lights flickered along the corridor as she passed through the doorway to the intensive-care unit. "What's wrong with the lights?" Faith asked, her attention jerking from the medical notes.

"It's been happening on and off for the last two days. The maintenance department is working on it, as well as on the temperature fluctuations." Barclay swept his hand out. No ring. Might not be married. "This morning we moved all the other patients to the new ICU in the western addition that was completed last week."

That explained the vacant hall and nearly deserted nurses' station. Only one woman monitored the screens spread across the desk. She nodded as Faith and Dr. Barclay passed by, her gaze lingering on the cute man.

The cold was getting worse. It was early April, raining and a little chilly. Not freezing.

Faith shivered. "Why wasn't this patient moved with the others?"

"Your instructions were to leave him exactly in place until you arrived," Barclay said, his face so cleanly shaven he looked like a cologne model. "We'll relocate him after your examination."

Goose bumps rose on her arms. She breathed out, and her breath misted in the air. This was weird. It'd never happened in the hospital across town where she worked. Her hospital was on the other side of Denver, but her expertise with coma patients was often requested across the world. She glanced back down at the tablet. "Where's his Glasgow Coma Scale score?"

"He's at a three," Barclay said grimly.

A three? That was the worst score for a coma patient. Basically, no brain function.

Barclay stopped her. "Dr. Cooper. I just want to say thank you for coming right away." He smiled and twin dimples appeared. The nurses probably loved this guy. "I heard about the little girl in Seattle. You haven't slept in—what? Thirty hours?"

It felt like it. She'd put on a clean shirt, but it was already wrinkled beneath her white lab coat. Faith patted his arm, finding very nice muscle tone. When was the last time she'd been on a date? "I'm fine. The important part is that the girl woke up." It had taken Faith seven hours of doing what she shouldn't be able to do: Communicate somehow with coma patients. This one she'd been able to save, and now a six-year-old girl was eating ice cream with her family in the hospital. Soon she'd go home. "Thank you for calling me."

He nodded, and she noticed his chin had a small divot—Cary Grant style. "Of course. You're legendary. Some say you're magic." Faith forced a laugh. "Magic. That's funny." Straightening her shoulders, she walked into the ICU and stopped moving, forgetting all about the chart and the doctor's dimples. "What in the world?" she murmured.

Only one standard bed remained in the sprawling room. A massive man overwhelmed it, his shoulders too wide to fit on the mattress. He was at least six-foot-six, his bare feet hanging off the end of the bed. The blankets had been pushed to his waist to make room for the myriad of electrodes set across his broad and muscular chest. Very muscular. "Why is his gown open?"

"It shouldn't be," Barclay said, looking around. "I'll ask the nurse after you do a quick examination. I don't mind admitting that I'm stymied here."

A man who could ask for help. Yep. Barclay was checking all the boxes. "Is this the correct patient?" Faith studied his healthy coloring and phenomenal physique. "There's no way this man has been in a coma for longer than a couple of days."

Barclay came to a halt, his gaze narrowing. He slid a shaking hand through his thick hair. "I understand, but according to the fire marshal, this patient was buried under piles of rocks and cement from the tunnel cave-in below the Third Street bridge that happened nearly seven years ago."

Faith moved closer to the patient, noting the thick dark hair that swept back from a chiseled face. A warrior's face. She blinked. Where the hell had that thought come from? "That's impossible." She straightened. "Anybody caught in that collapse would've died instantly, or shortly thereafter. He's not even bruised."

"What if he was frozen?" Barclay asked, balancing on sneakers.

Faith checked over the still-healthy tone of the patient's skin. "Not a chance." She reached for his wrist to check his pulse.

Electricity zipped up her arm and she coughed. What the heck was *that*? His skin was warm and supple, the strength beneath it obvious. She turned her wrist so her watch face was visible and then started counting. Curiosity swept her as she counted the beats. "When was he brought in?" She'd been called just three hours ago to consult on the case and hadn't had a chance to review the complete file.

"A week ago," Barclay said, relaxing by the door.

Amusement hit Faith full force. Thank goodness. For a moment, with the flickering lights, freezing air, and static electricity, she'd almost traveled to an imaginary and fanciful place. She smiled and released the man's wrist. "All right. Somebody is messing with me." She'd just been named the head of neurology at Northwest Boulder Hospital. Her colleagues must have gone to a lot of trouble—tons, really—to pull this prank. "Did Simons put you up to this?"

Barclay blinked, truly looking bewildered. He was cute. Very much so. Just the type who'd appeal to Faith's best friend, Louise. And he had an excellent reputation. Was this Louise's new beau? "Honestly, Dr. Cooper. This is no joke." He motioned toward the monitor screen that displayed the patient's heart rate, breathing, blood pressure, and intracranial pressure.

It had to be. Faith looked closer at the bandage covering the guy's head and the ICP monitor that was probably just taped beneath the bandage. "I always pay back jokes, Dr. Barclay." It was fair to give warning.

Barclay shook his head. "No joke. After a week of tests, we should see something here that explains his condition, but we have nothing. If he was injured somehow in the caved-in area, there'd be evidence of such. But... nothing." Barclay sighed. "That's why we requested your help."

None of this made any sense. The only logical conclusion was that this was a joke. She leaned over the patient to check the head bandage and look under it.

The screen blipped.

She paused.

Barclay gasped and moved a little closer to her. "What was that?" Man, this was quite the ruse. She was so going to repay Simons for this. Dr. Louise Simons was always finding the perfect jokes, and it was time for some payback. Playing along, Faith leaned over the patient again.

BLEEP

This close, her fingers tingled with the need to touch the hard angles of this guy's face. Was he some sort of model? Bodybuilder? His muscles were sleek and smooth—natural like a wild animal's. So probably not a bodybuilder. There was something just so male about him that he made Barclay fade into the *meh* zone. Her friends had chosen well. This guy was sexy on a sexy stick of pure melted sexiness. "I'm going to kill Simons," she murmured, not sure if she meant it. As jokes went, this was impressive. This guy wasn't a patient and he wasn't in a coma. So she indulged herself and smoothed his hair back from his wide forehead.

BLEEP
BLEEP
BLEEP

His skin was warm, although the room was freezing. "This is amazing," she whispered, truly touched. The planning that had to have gone into it. "How long did this take to set up?"

Barclay coughed, no longer appearing quite so perfect or masculine compared to the patient. "Stroke him again."

Well, all righty then. Who wouldn't want to caress a guy like this? Going with the prank, Faith flattened her hand in the middle of the guy's thorax, feeling a very strong heartbeat. "You can stop acting now," she murmured, leaning toward his face. "You've done a terrific job." Would it be totally inappropriate to ask him out for a drink after he stopped pretending to be unconscious? He wasn't really a patient, and man, he was something. Sinewed strength and incredibly long lines. "How about we get you out of here?" Her mouth was just over his.

His eyelids flipped open.

Barclay yelped and windmilled back, hitting an orange guest chair and landing on his butt on the floor.

The patient grabbed Faith's arm in an iron-strong grip. "Faith."

She blinked and then warmth slid through her. "Yeah. That's me." Man, he was hot. All right. The coming out of a coma and saying her name was kind of cool. But it was time to get to the truth. "Who are you?"

He shook his head. *"Gde, chert voz'mi, ya?"*

She blinked. Wow. A Russian model? His eyes were a metallic aqua. Was he wearing contacts? "Okay, buddy. Enough with the joke." She gently tried to pull loose, but he held her in place, his hand large enough to encircle her entire bicep.

He blinked, his eyes somehow hardening. They started to glow an electric blue, sans the green. "Where am I?" His voice was low and gritty. Hoarse to a point that it rasped through the room, winding around them.

The colored contacts were seriously high-tech.

"You speak Russian and English. Extraordinary." She twisted her wrist toward her chest, breaking free. The guy was probably paid by the hour. "The jig is up, handsome." Whatever his rate, he'd earned every dime. "Tell Simons to come out from wherever she's hiding." Faith might have to clap for her best friend. This deserved applause.

The guy ripped the fake bandage off his head and then yanked the EKG wires away from his chest. He shoved himself to a seated position. The bed groaned in protest. "Where am I?" He partially turned his head to stare at the now-silent monitor. "What the hell is that?" His voice still sounded rough and sexy.

Just how far was he going to take this? "The joke is over." Faith glanced at Barclay on the floor, who was staring at the patient with wide eyes. "You're quite the actor, Dr. Barclay." She smiled.

Barclay grabbed a chair and hauled himself to his feet, the muscles in his forearms tightening. "Wh—what's happening?"

Faith snorted and moved past him, looking down the now-darkened hallway. Dim yellow emergency lights ignited along the ceiling. "They've cut the lights." Delight filled her. She lifted her voice. "Simons? Payback is a bitch, but this is amazing. Much better than April fool's." After Faith had filled Louise's car with balloons filled with sparkly confetti—guaranteed to blow if a door opened and changed the pressure in the vehicle—Simons had sworn vengeance.

"Louise?" Faith called again. Nothing. Just silence. Faith sighed. "You win. I bow to your pranking abilities."

Ice started to form on the wall across the doorway. "How are you doing that?" Faith murmured, truly impressed.

A growl came from behind her, and she jumped, turning back to the man on the bed.

He'd just *growled*?

She swallowed and studied him. What the heck? The saline bag appeared genuine. Moving quickly, she reached his arm. "They are actually pumping saline into your blood?" Okay. The joke had officially gone too far.

Something that looked like pain flashed in his eyes. "Who died? I felt their deaths, but who?"

She shook her head. "Come on. Enough." He was an excellent actor. She could almost feel his agony.

The man looked at her, his chin lowering. Sitting on the bed, he was as tall as she was, even though she was standing in her favorite two-inch heeled boots. Heat poured off him, along with a tension she couldn't ignore.

She shivered again, and this time it wasn't from the cold.

Keeping her gaze, he tore out the IV.

Blood dribbled from his vein. She swallowed and fought the need to step back. "All right. Too far, Simons," she snapped. "*Waaaay* too far."

Barclay edged toward the door. "I don't understand what's happening."

Faith shook her head. "Occam's razor, Dr. Barclay." Either the laws of physics had just changed or this was a joke. The simplest explanation was that Simons had just won the jokester title for all time. "Enough of this, though. Who are you?" she asked the actor.

He slowly turned his head to study Dr. Barclay before focusing back on her. "When did the shield fall?"

The shield? He seemed so serious. Eerily so. Would Simons hire a crazy guy? No. Faith tapped her foot and heat rose to her face, her temper stirring. "Listen. This has been fantastic, but it's getting old. I'm done."

The guy grabbed her arm, his grip unbreakable this time. "Did both shields fail?"

Okay. Her heart started to beat faster. Awareness pricked along her skin. "Let go of me."

"No." The guy pushed from the bed and shrugged out of his gown, keeping hold of her. "What the fuck?" He looked at the Foley catheter inserted into his penis and then down to the long white anti-embolism stockings that were supposed to prevent blood clots.

Faith's breath caught. Holy shit. The catheter and TED hose were genuine. And his penis was huge. She looked up at his face. The TED hose might add a realistic detail to a joke, but no way would any responsible medical personnel insert a catheter for a gag. Simons wouldn't have done that. "What's happening?" Faith tried to yank her arm free, but he held her tight.

Dr. Barclay looked from her to the mostly naked male. "Who are you?" he whispered.

"My name is Ronan," the guy said, reaching for the catheter, which was attached to a urine-collection bag at the end of the bed. "What fresh torture is this?"

"Um," Faith started.

His nostrils flared. "Why would you collect my piss?"

Huh? "We're not," she protested. "You were in a coma. That's just a catheter."

He gripped the end of the tube, his gaze fierce.

"No—" Faith protested just as he pulled it out, grunting and then snarling in what had to be intense pain.

God. Was he on PCP or something? She frantically looked toward Barclay and mouthed the words *security* and *Get the nurse out of here.*

Barclay nodded and turned, running into the hallway.

"Where are we?" Ronan asked, drawing her toward him.

She put out a hand to protest, smashing her palm into his ripped abdomen. "Please. Let me go." She really didn't want to kick him in his already reddening penis. "You could've just damaged your urethra badly."

He started dragging her toward the door, his strength beyond superior. A sprawling tattoo covered his entire back. It looked like...a dark image of his ribs with lighter spaces between? Man, he was huge. "We must go."

Oh, there was no *we.* Whatever was happening right now wasn't good, and she had to get some space to figure this out. "I don't want to hurt you," she said, fighting his hold.

He snorted.

She drew in air and kicked him in the back of the leg, twisting her arm to gain freedom.

Faster than she could imagine, he pivoted, moving right into her. Heat and muscle and strength. He more than towered over her, fierce even though he was naked. She yelped and backpedaled, striking up for his nose.

He blocked her punch with his free hand and growled again, fangs sliding down from his incisors.

She stopped moving and her brain fuzzed. *Fangs?* Okay. This wasn't a joke. Somebody was seriously messing with her, and maybe they wanted her hurt. She couldn't explain the eyes and the fangs, so this had to be bad. This guy was obviously capable of inflicting some real damage. His eyes morphed again to the electric blue, and somehow he broadened even more, looking more animalistic than human.

"I don't understand," she said, her voice shaking as her mind tried to make sense of what her eyes were seeing. "Who are you? Why were you unconscious in a coma? How did you know my name?"

He breathed out, his broad chest moving with the effort. The fangs slowly slid back up, and his eyes returned to the sizzling aqua. "My name is Ronan Kayrs, and I was unconscious because the shield fell." He eyed her, tugging her even closer. "I know your name because I spent four hundred years seeing your face and feeling your soft touch in my dreams."

"My—my face?" she stuttered.

His jaw hardened even more. "And that was *before* I'd accepted my death."

CHAPTER TWO

Ronan kept a tight grip on the woman while moving out of the room into another area: A corridor of sorts with no windows. Why were there no windows? Was he underground? Only dim yellow candles glowed from the ceiling. "Where are we?" he asked, choosing a direction at random and moving.

She pulled back, digging in her heels.

He paused, not wanting to harm her. "Stop fighting me." They had to get away from this place with smells that burned his nostrils. What was that stench? Why had his cock, head, and arm been hooked up to those objects? "We must go." To have her in his hands after he'd given up the dream of her was too much. He needed to acquire safety and regroup. To find his people. Perhaps she could help him do so. "You're one of the Enhanced. Take me to your king."

She jerked her arm, nearly freeing herself. "King? Are you nuts?"

He blinked, looking down at her. She was smaller than she'd seemed in his dreams when she had whispered her name to him. Long black hair, olive-colored skin, stunning amber-colored eyes. Brown with a glow much brighter than in his dreams. She wore dark boots, blueish pants, a pink shirt with a white overcoat. "Nuts? No." Perhaps her king was dead. "Your father, then. Let's seek him."

Her chin lowered while her dark eyebrows rose. "Seek? All right, crazy man. Release me, now."

Why wasn't she cooperating? He stood to his full height. "I am Ronan Kayrs of the Kayrs ruling family. Obey me, woman."

She snorted.

He gaped. What had happened to the world he'd protected? A chill swept down his back, and he looked around. The floor was comprised of odd tiles, and boxes with blinking colors covered a raised table-like area. His heart thumped. "When am I?"

She kept her gaze on his face. "Excuse me?"

"Year, woman. Give me the year." He'd learned the hard way that time was fluid and felt different in other places. Other realms. "Or just a century. Give me that."

"Twenty-first century," she said, her voice softening along with her eyes. "Please let me get you some help. You're hurt."

He looked down at his mostly naked body. The holes in his head, arm, and inside his cock had already healed, but his knees still trembled. He wasn't at half-strength yet. And the long white material on his legs appeared ridiculous. "Are these the fashion of the day?"

She patted his arm, leaning toward him. "No. Those are to prevent blood clots, since you were lying in a bed."

Blood clots? "My blood doesn't clot." He bent, shoved the offending garments off with his free hand, and kicked them aside. He looked around. "I require clothing."

The tall man from earlier ran around a corner with two other men, these wearing brown garb with what appeared to be weapons at their belts. As soon as they came into sight, the first man drew back and let the other two with weapons slowly approach him.

"Don't hurt him," Faith said, holding out her hand to partially ward them off. "He's sustained extensive head trauma."

Truth be told, his head did hurt like a motherfucker. "Leave us," he ordered, not surprised when they continued advancing. "What the hell has happened to the world?" he muttered.

"Amen, buddy," Faith said, her body tensing. "Release me, and let's figure this out."

He looked around, his gaze catching on a drawing of himself lying on the table. "Did you draw that?"

She frowned and followed his gaze. "That's a picture of you. They probably put it on the news to see if you have any family or friends."

"The news?" His mind worked rapidly to catch up despite the headache. "That drawing was taken away and shown to others? Publicly?" How big was the world now? "When?"

"I don't know when," she said, pulling against his hold once more.

Pain flashed through his palm, burning up his arm and right into his heart.

She gasped and tried to jump back.

"Sorry," he said, wincing. It wasn't much of a surprise, though. "Did I burn you?"

Her eyes wide, she slowly nodded, her scent of wildflowers filling his head. "How did you…ah, do that?" Her hand was still up toward the advancing soldiers as if she was trying to keep control of the situation.

"It's the marking," he explained, facing her but tracking the men out of the corner of his eye. "The mating marking." How could she not be aware of the phenomenon?

"Huh?" she asked, her body tensing again.

What was happening? The two soldiers were getting closer, so he released her and held up his palm to show them the design. "Here. I am Ronan Kayrs. This is my marking, and this is my mate. I don't know to whom you align, but please take your leave."

The duo stopped.

Faith slowly backed toward the tall table. "Head injury," she said to the soldiers as if by way of explanation. "We need to get him to a room in the north wing." Then she studied his hand. "Nice tattoo."

Tattoo? "No. Marking." He looked at the jagged edges of his family marking with the K surrounded by fierce lines. "It appears when we find our mate. Surely you've dreamed of me."

"Right." She edged farther down the counter, her voice a little too high. "We're going to get you some help. I promise."

He turned his attention to the soldiers, seeking their vibrations. "You're human," he said, glancing instantly to his woman. "Why are human soldiers guarding you?" None of this was making sense, and it was time to go. "Faith?"

"Listen, buddy," the taller of the two men said, his gaze remaining on Ronan's face. "My name is Joe. I'm security, and I've been hit in the skull before. I know how you're feeling. How about we take you to the north wing so you can meet with a nice head doctor there and get some clothes?"

Ronan tilted his head to the side to study Joe. The man appeared to be about thirty years old with blond hair and earnest blue eyes. He looked fit and his hand rested lightly on a square-shaped contraption. "I do not wish to harm you, Joe." Even though Ronan was weak from the fall, he could overpower a couple of humans. Ronan checked out the other man. This guy was at least fifty, with a neatly trimmed gray beard and bushy hair. "Nor you, elder."

"Elder?" the guy asked, looking toward his friend. "All right." He drew a barrel-shaped weapon from his belt and pointed it at Ronan. "Enough talk."

"Agreed," Ronan said. Apparently, the soldiers weren't going to listen. He hated fighting naked. Nor would he attack two humans without further provocation.

"Joe?" the elder said.

"No—" Faith protested, just as Joe pushed something on the box. Two wires sprang out, landing on Ronan's chest. Lightning shot through him, zipping painfully. He gasped, looking down at the twin metal squares. His innards protested, but he couldn't help but smile. Delight mixed with the pain. "You've learned to harness lightning." He yanked the offending wires out of his body and tossed them back at Joe. "Very impressive." He nodded at Faith. "Lightning. I never would've thought it."

Her chin dropped. "How are you still standing?"

Oh. "The weapon is probably meant for humans, sweetheart." His heart rate was slightly elevated, but it still clutched as a horrible thought hit him. "Tell me my people still exist." Of course they did. What a ridiculous fear. Vampires and demons couldn't be banished, even though he'd felt two of his brothers die. He just didn't know which two. Yet.

"Ah," she said, looking toward the soldiers. "Was that thing charged?"

"Yes," the elder said, moving to the left and pointing the other weapon at Ronan. "I don't want to shoot you, but I will."

Ronan sighed. "I do not particularly wish to be shot." The lightning had hurt and no doubt this was a bigger weapon. If they kept attacking him, he would never regain his strength. "What does that release?" Might it be fire? That could harm a vampire-demon hybrid.

"What's he on?" Joe asked Faith, looking down at his box.

"Undetermined," Faith said, squinting to study Ronan. "The tox report came back clear, but obviously..."

The air changed. The hair rose on the back of Ronan's neck. He inhaled, searching for a scent. "Faith. We must go." The drawings of him had called attention to his location. "Now." He moved toward her.

The elder fired.

Something exploded and pain ripped into Ronan's shoulder. Instinct took over, and he leaped across the space, grabbing the elder by the neck and throwing him into the wall. Before Joe could move, Ronan punched him squarely in the jaw, tossing him back several yards to land on the floor, where his head hit with a loud thump. The elder dropped to the ground, also unconscious.

Ronan rushed and grabbed the weapon from Joe before reaching for Faith. "I did not want to hurt them." But at least they'd live.

She cringed away, her gaze on the blood pouring from his shoulder. "You've been shot. Please let me take you to the surgical wing." Her fear was palpable, and the animal he kept bound deep inside began to stir in protest.

He looked down at the hole in his flesh. A metal of some type was embedded inside him, and he mentally shoved it out—but nothing happened. He was too weak. He tried to send healing cells to his wound, but it didn't close. Damn it. He required sustenance to rebuild himself.

Faith tried to back away.

"We have to leave," Ronan said, grasping her arm again. "Where is the exit to this place?" He looked around, seeing large doors at the opposite end of the hall. Perfect. The guards had arrived from the other direction. "Please don't fight me." His temper was finally starting to boil, and he needed time and space to figure out this new world. So, he started moving.

Faith hit him in the other arm and struggled, but he didn't stop this time. He'd have to explain everything to her once they were out of danger. It was coming closer and his breath quickened.

Those doors opened.

"What the hell?" Faith breathed, focusing on the enemy.

Ronan's chest settled. The metal object fell out of his shoulder, and his wound began to heal. He'd been too slow to get her to safety. "Apparently, your picture of me reached faraway villages."

"What in the world is he supposed to be?" she asked, her voice trembling.

"He is one of the Cyst," Ronan said, grateful she hadn't encountered them before. So, it wasn't known she was his mate. Good. Stretching his hands, he allowed weak power to clash through him. "Have you ever teleported?"

"Jesus," she muttered, shaking her head. "You're freaking crazy."

He drew on the elements of time and dimension, trying to make the jump.

Nothing.

"My powers haven't returned yet." Not a surprise, since he'd apparently been unconscious for quite some time. Well, he would have to fight, full power or not. It had been too long. "Stand out of the way, woman." He released her.

"Gladly." She turned in the other direction just as another Cyst soldier emerged through the doorway, standing guard on the other side of the downed human soldiers. "What the fuck?"

His woman had a mouth on her. Had she been shown no discipline in her life? That was about to change.

The first soldier moved forward, studying him. Apparently they had updated their uniforms through the years, from long black robes to black pants and shirts with matching boots. Their skin was a pasty white, their teeth yellow, and their eyes a blood purple. Only one strip of white hair ran down the middle of their heads, braided down their backs. Most Kurjans had red hair with black tips or black hair with red tips, but the Cyst, the special ones—they had white hair. Freaks.

Ronan growled.

The soldier moved closer, withdrawing a sword. "It is you. The Butcher."

Finally. A weapon Ronan recognized. Since they'd only sent two soldiers, it just must be a scouting party. Good. His hands itched with the need to do violence, although his body wanted to shut down. "I'd hoped the Kurjans had died out," he said, tensing his back leg.

"You tried." The Kurjan hissed and charged, swinging the sword in an arc. Ronan pivoted away from Faith and ducked. Then he turned quickly and kicked the Kurjan in the chest. The soldier fell back and then rushed forward again, his movements graceful but not nearly fast enough. He sliced down and Ronan dodged, striking the Kurjan's neck with the blade of his hand.

Bones shattered.

The Kurjan shrieked and fell back.

Ronan kicked him in the gut, spun, and claimed the sword. This male was barely trained. So, they hadn't trusted that picture and hadn't believed it was him. Or they would've sent a force. Thank the gods they hadn't. The Kurjan grabbed his neck, his eyes morphing to a pure red.

Ronan swung and cut the enemy, but he didn't have the strength to decapitate. "Your death will have to wait." He kicked the Kurjan beneath the jaw and bones snapped.

Faith screamed and looked frantically around.

Ronan turned toward the other soldier. He was speaking into his wrist. But he didn't move. Somehow, he must be calling for backup. Ronan snarled, wanting nothing more than to decapitate both monsters. But he had to get Faith out of there and center himself.

She stared in shock at the Kurjan. "You killed him."

"No." Ronan reached her and wrapped an arm around her waist, lifting her and running toward the exit. She started to struggle. An open doorway to his right caught his attention, and he moved inside a closet with what appeared to be clothing on the shelves. Blue and flimsy.

"What are you doing?" she hissed, pushing against his side.

He set her down, keeping his body between her and the door. Then he grabbed some pants and pulled them on before yanking a shirt of sorts over his head. The pants fell just beneath his knees, and the shirt pulled tight across his chest, constricting his upper arms. "What are these?" The material was unfamiliar but not uncomfortable.

"Scrubs." She tried to move past him to freedom.

He easily picked her up again and rushed for the exit, kicking open the doors with one bare foot and hurrying outside.

Fresh air hit him first, along with the darkness of night. A full moon glowed down, adding illumination to an area already lit by tall, odd candles. Different sized and colored boxes, some sleek, filled an area next to a sign that read STAFF PARKING LOT. Grass and trees were dotted throughout. One box came to life and he stiffened, growling. Lights sprang alive on its front, and it propelled itself toward them, turning at the last minute and swinging around the building.

"Teleporting devices?" he asked, awed by the thought.

"No. Cars, you dipshit," Faith muttered, kicking his side as he held her aloft. "They transport."

Ah. Fascinating. Horses had been replaced. "Which one is yours?" he asked.

"Fuck you." She kicked him again.

He sighed and shook her. "More Cyst will be arriving soon." Very soon, if they had some of these transport machines. "We have to go." He pointed Joe's weapon at her rib cage, not having a choice. "Take me to your machine, or I'll shoot you and find it myself." He'd never harm her, but apparently she didn't know that. "I don't want to kill you, Faith. But I will."

CHAPTER THREE

Faith couldn't breathe. The arm banded around her waist was unrelenting, and she couldn't get the right leverage to take out Ronan's knee. Her lungs seized and she looked frantically around the quiet parking lot. The last car hadn't even seen her. She opened her mouth and tried to draw in air.

Ronan's hold tightened. "Don't scream."

The gun hurt her side. She looked again. There was nobody around. "Fine. It's the red Volkswagen." She pointed. If she could get him to a more public place, she'd find help.

He instantly moved toward her Touareg and set her down.

She opened the passenger-side door and gestured him inside. He pushed her in with one broad hand. Swearing, she moved across the car to the driver's side, noting her purse on the floor. She'd forgotten to take it inside again. There was a canister of mace in there.

Ronan sat and shut the door. "Go. Now."

She put her foot to the pedal and pressed the ignition button before carefully backing out of the spot. The police station was about ten miles from the hospital, and at this time of night, there wouldn't be too much traffic. She drove around the hospital and headed for the main road.

"Extraordinary," Ronan said, examining the lights on the dash. He kept the gun pointed at her side.

She swallowed, trying to calm her nerves. The guy was crazy and an amazing fighter. "Where did you learn to fight like that?" He'd dispatched the weird-looking guy with no problem. And what about that bullet hole? Was he still bleeding? How was he even conscious? "Kill like that?" Her voice trembled.

He sighed. "I'm sorry you saw the violence. I'll protect you better in the future."

Future? Her stomach rolled over and settled hard. "Ronan, you really need help. Please let me go, and I'll make sure you get it." She pulled out into the main thoroughfare.

He gasped and looked around at the other vehicles and then at the buildings on either side of the avenue. "This is truly amazing."

She frowned and switched lanes. "Why were those freaky guys after you?" At first, she'd thought somebody was messing with her or wanted to harm her. Or make her go crazy. Now it seemed that this was some sort of weird cultlike thing with Ronan. "Who are you, anyway? Is this some sort of role-playing game? What are you involved in?" Something seriously creepy and wrong was going on. Had those security guys been in on it?

"I told you." He gaped at the fifty-story building they passed. "I am Ronan Kayrs, I'm your mate, and I'm mostly a vampire."

She coughed, her body revolting. "You think you're a vampire." The fangs and weird eyes. She hadn't figured out how he'd done that, but movie props made anything possible these days. "And those Cyst guys—they're vampires too." This was taking role-playing way too far.

"Kurjans. The Cyst are the religious leaders of the Kurjan empire. Similar to monks, but evil. They are good fighters," Ronan answered absently, still watching the world outside. "I hope you're taking me to your father."

Anger started to burn through her fear. "My father has been dead for well over a decade."

"Oh." Ronan's voice softened. "I'm sorry to hear that. Then please take me to your guardian."

She gave him a look and took another turn. "Listen, asshole. I think everyone has a right to live their lives any way they want, so long as it doesn't hurt other people. But this freaky role-playing cult thing you've got going on isn't okay. You killed that guy." Just how delusional was Ronan? And those other guys? What was happening to society?

"He was going to kill us, and he should be well in a few minutes," Ronan said reasonably. "I am sensing you do not believe me. You're not aware of my people."

Okay. He was crazy. Fear rose in her again, this time with thick dread. She exited the freeway and drove farther downtown, pulling into a spot right outside the police station.

He looked around. "This does not appear to be a home."

She turned toward him in the sudden quiet of the vehicle. "No."

He lifted the gun again, pointing it at her temple. "Take me to your abode, or I'll use this weapon against you."

She faced him. "No." Taking an armed man to her apartment held a lot more danger than sitting here. Everyone knew not to take an abductor to a remote or isolated location. "If you're going to shoot me, it'll have to be right here and now." Drawing in a breath, she planted her hand on the horn as hard as she could. The blare quickly punctuated the silence.

"Damn it, Faith," Ronan snapped, even as his eyes filled with pride. He looked around and grabbed her purse, quickly shoving himself from the vehicle. He tossed the gun on the seat. "We are not finished."

Cops started jogging out the front door of the station.

Ronan dodged behind a car and then ran off into the night.

Faith released the horn and sagged, panting several times. A uniformed police officer knocked on her window. Tears filled her eyes, and she shoved open her door, getting shakily to her feet. "My name is Dr. Faith Cooper, and I was just kidnapped."

Shuddering now, going into shock, she pointed toward where Ronan had escaped. "He went that way."

* * * *

Ronan kept to the darkness, dodging between the mammoth buildings, ignoring the glass and rocks digging into his feet. Where were the horses? Grass? Trees? Just these hard surfaces surrounded him, and he kept running through the night to find something—anything—that was familiar.

He saw other people in the shadows—unwashed, hiding, hunched-over people. They ignored him and he did the same. His body needed to rest, but his mind was on fire.

Ultimately, he came to a treed area with benches. The scent of the foliage grounded him and he stopped running, finally allowing his body to relax. Ignoring the seating areas, he stalked deeper into the trees and slid down the rough bark of a pine, stretching out his legs and sending healing cells to the cuts on his feet.

The world had changed too much. How would he ever find his people? Were his brothers alive? He rubbed his chest, reaching out with all of his senses to find them.

Nothing.

He knocked his head back on the tree trunk, trying to focus. Then he stared at the myriad of scars on his left hand. Slashes upon slashes to create what he'd become. And now his right palm held his marking.

Very well. He was a warrior and he knew his path. This was a strategic offensive, and the first directive was reconnaissance. Information on the world around him was imperative.

A sound emerged from the bag he'd taken from Faith's Volkswagen.

Slowly lifting, he turned the bag over, shook, and dumped the contents on the grass. Shiny material in tubes, something called a tampon, a brush, another smaller bag that matched the bigger one, and a flat device making noise. He picked the device up and shook it.

The thing grew silent.

He blinked. "Make that noise again."

The thing was dark and shaped like a rectangle, but it remained quiet. He gripped it tighter, his thumb pressing in.

The accoutrement glowed.

"How can I help you, Faith?" a woman's voice asked.

What the holy hell? His hands shook. "I am not Faith," he whispered.

"I don't know what that means. If you like, I can search the web for 'I am not Faith,'" the woman said.

He looked wildly around for danger and saw only trees and the night. "Who are you?"

"I'm Siri. But enough about me...how can I help you?" She had a pleasant voice.

Was there a person in this device? "Where are you?" he croaked.

"Right here," Siri said.

He coughed. This world was crazy. Reconnaissance was often tedious. Not in this new time, apparently. "I need to find Faith."

"I'm sorry," Siri said. Then she was quiet.

He tried to focus. "Okay. Where am I? Do you know?"

"You're in Denver, Colorado," Siri said. Suddenly, the glow turned into what appeared to be a map.

Oh, Lord. This was amazing. Siri knew where he was. He tried again. "Do you know where Faith is?"

"Which Faith?" Siri asked, and a list for three Faiths came up on the device.

"Faith Cooper," he said, finding his Faith. A drawing, or maybe one of those *pictures*, was next to her name. He pressed on her face.

Siri beeped and then brought up the picture with other drawings. "Here is the contact information for Faith Cooper."

What was all of this? "Can you take me to her?" he asked.

"Uh-oh, Faith Cooper doesn't seem to have an address. Tap the name below if you'd like to add one," Siri said.

His heart sank. An address? Maybe Faith had one in her possessions. He searched through the smaller bag, finding flat cards, currency, and some coins. A picture caught his eye, and he pulled out another card. This one had her picture, birthdate, and...an address. The Saints were with him, finally. He gave the address to Siri and a map came up on the screen.

How spectacular. But how could one keep investigations private if all information was this easily accessible? "You are of extreme help, Siri," he murmured.

"I don't really like these arbitrary categories," she replied.

Oh. New vernacular. Interesting. Besides discovering the changes in the world, he needed to build alliances. He gathered Faith's items and replaced them in her bag, turning to follow Siri's directions to Faith's address. "Siri? Are you an ally?"

"I don't know the answer to that question," she said.

He sighed. "Sure? Are you my friend?"

"What a question! Of course, I'm your friend," she said.

It was comforting to have found a friend in this odd world. His strategic plan was coming together. "Have you heard of the Seven?"

"Interesting," she said.

He nodded. She hadn't heard of them. Good. So, it wouldn't make sense to ask her who'd died. He'd felt their deaths, piercing and painful, while in the shield. Grieving had taken place alone, and wondering who was gone had nearly driven him mad. He had to find whoever was left.

Light was filtering over the looming dwellings, finally bringing dawn. Thank God. The sun killed the Kurjans, so they'd have to find cover for the day. Unless that had changed as well. Hopefully not.

His heart lightening, he moved out of the trees per Siri's directions, pausing at one of the hard streets. "Siri? I require footwear."

"Not a problem," Siri said, and more maps appeared on the device. "Here are some nearby stores."

"What is a store?"

Lights spun across Siri's surface. "A store is a retail establishment that offers a range of consumer goods," she said.

Stores? He'd have to borrow some of Faith's currency. Once he found her with Siri's help, he'd find a way to repay her. Surely his family had invested his holdings throughout the years. "Siri? Do you know the Kayrs family?"

"I'm sorry. I'm afraid I can't answer that," she said.

"I figured," he muttered, running across the tough surface. One thing at a time. First, shoes. Then, Faith.

After that, he'd continue reconnaissance and then construct a strategy.

CHAPTER FOUR

Faith finished packing clothes in a bag, her work phone on speaker mode on the bed table. The lunatic had stolen her personal phone. "I'm fine, Louise. Stop worrying." Truth be told, Ronan had actually handled her rather carefully. Except for the kidnapping and gun to the ribs part. "The guy even left the gun with me."

"While stealing your purse." Louise's voice exploded through the speaker loud enough that both rescue cats jumped off the bed and made a beeline for the kitchen. "He has your address."

Faith zipped the suitcase shut, only packing two pairs of leather boots and two sketchpads. Her biggest weaknesses: footwear and creating the perfect landscape. "I don't think this guy could figure out a wallet, much less a driver's license. But I've had two uniformed cops at my door all night just in case." She wasn't stupid, for Pete's sake.

"I'm glad," Louise sniffed. "I can head home right now if you need me."

Faith sighed. "I'd forgotten you had that convention in Baltimore, to be honest. Just stay there. I'm going to the cabin and the sun is finally out, so it'll be a nice drive. If I leave in an hour, I'll arrive right before it gets dark."

Louise made a sound of approval. "Good. You're due a vacation, anyway. And the cabin can't be traced easily to you, so that's the perfect place for you to relax until the police catch this guy."

Which was exactly why Faith was going there. "Agreed."

"Just please don't adopt any more animals. Let somebody else rescue a couple."

Faith grinned. "You like that puppy I found for you."

"Hmm. Speaking of dogs, was your kidnapper really that hot?" Louise asked.

Faith paused, remembering the hard planes and strong muscles of Ronan's body. His stunning eyes and fierce jawline. "Yeah. The guy looked airbrushed. Twelve-pack and all."

Louise sighed. "Why do the sexy ones always have to be nuts? Or brain injured?"

"Amen, sister." Faith needed a break and it was time to head to the cabin. "Would you please check in with the women's shelter when you get back? We had a couple of new intakes—one young and pregnant." She volunteered at the battered women's shelter every week.

"Of course. Do you need me to check in at the pound too?"

Faith grinned. "No."

"That's because you probably already adopted another cat," Louise said. "You're a softie."

Faith winced. "His name is Dick and it totally fits. He already ate two of my shoes."

Louise chortled. "It's lucky you have an apartment, or you'd have a million pets."

Probably. Faith took a deep breath. "Okay. Good luck with your presentation. You'll do great."

"Thanks. Love you."

"You, too." Faith smiled as she clicked off the call. She and Louise had been assigned as roommates her freshman year in college, and they'd both majored premed and gone to medical school together. While Faith specialized in neurology, Louise had become a thoracic surgeon. Faith had two sisters in life, Grace and Louise. Someday maybe she'd be able to heal Grace so she could have a life again too.

Faith turned and called out for the cats. "Come on, guys. It's time to load up." A hissing came from the other room. Jeez. "Give me a break, Dick," she muttered, taking her suitcase and lugging it into the small living room. Her eye caught on the photograph taken by her sister of the mountains during a rainstorm.

God, she missed her sister.

She shook off the sadness. "It's time to go, cats." The animals were hiding in the sparkling-clean kitchen to the far left. She hadn't been able to sleep, so she'd cleaned all night. Now it was time to seek haven.

Stepping farther into the room, she paused. Instinct rose. She pivoted toward the balcony doors, her body going cold.

Two of the white-faced, black-uniformed lunatics stood there, even their heads covered. They'd both tossed hefty black umbrellas to the side and out of the way. One held a green gun pointed at her.

She gaped. The door was closed behind them. "How in the world?" she breathed. She was five floors up from the ground. How had they climbed that far, and why would they need umbrellas? The sun shone down without a cloud in the way. She edged toward the front door. Were the cops still out front?

The first guy pushed the covering off his weird head. "We don't want to hurt you, Faith Cooper." His voice was gritty and harsh.

She swallowed, chills skittering along her exposed skin. "What do you want?"

"Just information about Ronan Kayrs. The Butcher. Where is he?" asked the second guy, also pushing his hood off to reveal those weird purple contacts.

She set her suitcase down in case she needed to run. "Okay, guys. You're taking this game or whatever it is way too far. You get that, right?" How many nutjobs were involved in this role-playing world? Ronan had killed one. It was too real. Unless somehow it had all been staged. She just didn't know. "I think I saw Ronan kill your cohort. He's sustained a head injury of some sorts, and he thinks this is genuine. That the threat is real."

The first guy kept his gun trained on her. "The prison world has shattered? Ronan. It was really him?"

She shook her head. Prison world? "Guys. Come on. Knock it off."

"He's not here," the other guy spat. "I can't sense him. Where has he gone?"

So, they were going to continue with the delusion. Maybe this was some sort of illicit game where it was okay to kill. Her legs stiffened and adrenaline pumped into her system. If so, they might murder her. She edged closer to the door.

"Stop," ordered the man with the gun.

She halted. "Listen," she burst out, her stomach heaving. "I left Ronan in the middle of town last night, and I have no clue where he went. He's gone. I can't help you to find him."

The gunless guy tilted his head. "You're Enhanced. I can feel it."

Oh, man. "Nope. No enhancement." That must be part of the game.

The other guy nodded. "The report said that the vampire had created a full Kayrs marking on his palm."

Her mind scrambled for a way to somehow reach them so she would survive. Maybe play a part in their delusion. It couldn't hurt. "I'm already mated. Ronan must have some other...um... mate." Whoever had written this game should just be bitch-slapped. *Mated.* Come on. She swallowed. If she screamed, would the guy shoot her? Or would they run? She was going to have to make a choice and take the chance. "Would you just leave? Please?"

"You misunderstand," the armed man said. "The Butcher is dangerous in ways you can't imagine. He shouldn't be free from the prison containing him. Help us and we will protect you."

Faith coughed, searching for an escape.

"We should take her with us," the unarmed man said.

Her head went back. Before she could scream, the balcony doors burst open, striking both men, shoving them forward. Ronan stood there, fury darkening his face.

The first guy rolled and came up quickly, grabbing her. She went into fight mode, clawing down his face and kicking at the same time. "Sorry about this. No choice. Have to get you to safety." He grabbed her by the throat and yanked her down, cutting off her ability to scream. His bony hand was incredibly strong. She struggled, fighting with her knowledge of anatomy but not succeeding, her vision going dark.

Suddenly, he was ripped away.

She rolled over, coughing, trying to suck in air. Tears slashed down her face.

The sound of rapid punching penetrated her consciousness and then...nothing. It was all over in a matter of seconds.

"Faith?" Gentle hands turned her over. "Are you all right?"

She blinked, her vision focusing to find Ronan's hard face set in concern. "Ah, shit."

"We really must work on your propensity for vulgarity," he said, his full lips compressing into a white line. His face was pale and sweat dotted his upper lip.

She snorted. This was unreal. "You're nuts." The entire world had gone crazy. He frowned, making the sharp angles of his face look even more forbidding. Deep aqua eyes watched her. Man, even struggling, he was good-looking. Rugged features, sharp eyes, rigid jaw. Why did the hot ones have to be crazy? She sat up, taking in the two unconscious white-faced guys. "Tell me you didn't kill them?"

"No." He assisted her to stand. "Though these are also just scouts. I am not at full strength and must recuperate before I take on any trained soldiers. It is imperative."

She looked closer at the nearest guy and then moved toward him, crouching down to feel his pulse. His head was angled oddly. Nothing. His chest wasn't moving, either. He was dead. Dots impaired her vision and she quickly cleared it. "You broke his cervical vertebrae and must've damaged his spinal cord."

Ronan nodded. "Yes, but he's not dead."

She slowly stood and then backed toward the balcony. Were the cops out front? The fight had been fast, but shouldn't they have heard something? Could she survive a jump from the fifth floor? Probably not.

"Faith? I need something to cover their mouths. Do you have a cloth that would work?" Ronan asked, watching her carefully.

The spit in her mouth dried up.

Blood had arced across his scrubs, making him look murderous. Even with huge, sparkly, multicolored size-sixteen shoes on his feet.

He caught her gaze. "They were the only pair in my size. I was told they were the...what was it... the rage?"

Her throat hurt and her breath was wheezing out. But she could still scream. It was her only chance. Just as she sucked in air, the dead body moved.

She jerked.

The dead Cyst groaned and moved his head. Bones loudly popped back into place.

No. He was dead. She'd felt for a pulse. She was a doctor, for goodness' sake. "I...this can't be...no."

Ronan sighed, walked forward, and kicked the Cyst beneath the jaw hard enough to kill. The man's head flew back, his neck breaking loudly and no doubt injuring the spinal cord. Again. The body went silent.

Faith shook her head. Her knees trembled. "No. I mean, that's not. No."

Ronan looked around and walked into the kitchen, yanking open drawers. He frowned and pulled out duct tape, pulling a piece off. "Excellent." He circuited the kitchen island and strode forward to quickly tape both of the Cysts' mouths shut.

The dead guy started to move again.

It was too much. Faith opened her mouth to scream and Ronan rushed her, clamping his hand over her mouth.

How had he moved so quickly? That was impossible. She lifted her gaze to his, and his eyes changed from the sparking aqua to the fiery blue again. A whimper escaped her. This wasn't right. Wasn't possible.

He leaned down several inches until his face was much closer. "I know you are having difficulty believing reality right now, so I am going to prove something to you. I am very sorry about this." He winced, removed his hand, and slapped tape over her mouth.

She sucked in air, shocked, and struck out.

His mouth tightened and he wrapped the duct tape around her wrists, effectively binding her.

She struggled, kicking at his legs.

"Do not make me bind your ankles," he said, looking down at the roll in his hand. "This material is amazing." He gently pushed her into her pin-striped blue chair. "Sit here and just watch. The Kurjans and their Cyst cannot survive the sun."

The doors outside were still open, showing the sun shining down on her wicker furniture. Ronan grabbed both soldiers by their braids and pulled them out into the sun. He quickly divested them of their clothing, leaving both in matching gray boxers, their skin bizarrely pale in the day.

As the sun hit the bodies, fire instantly ignited along their skin.

Faith gasped from behind the tape, her brain sparking. How was this happening?

Ronan stood back, away from the burning masses, watching impassively.

The bodies burned hotly, not awakening, quickly dissolving into piles of ash. Faith shook her head. That was impossible. Human bones didn't burn.

Of course, those weren't humans. Couldn't be. Bile rose in her throat and she gulped it down, terror slashing through her.

Ronan moved inside and gently—oddly—shut her damaged door. "Are you believing me now?"

She watched him, trying to make sense of what she'd witnessed. She'd seen a white-faced monster come back from the dead, twice...and then be burned by the sun. Vampires. Occam's razor. Sometimes the simplest explanation was the truth.

Ronan dropped to his haunches and gently removed the tape from her mouth. "I am sorry about this. Your guards are still at the front of this abode, and I could not allow you to scream." Then he slowly unwound the tape from her wrists.

Her body refused to move.

He gently brushed her hair back from her face. "You are in danger now, and you cannot stay here." Stress cut lines into his mouth and fanned out from his eyes. "I need to get away from . . . this." He swept his arm out. "From the cars, the tall buildings, all the people." Vulnerability glittered for the slightest of moments in his intriguing eyes. "Is there a place we could go? Where I could start a search for my people?"

She swallowed, her throat still aching from the Cyst's attack. "Vampires. The sun kills them." Jesus. Urban legend was actually true. She calculated everything she'd just seen. Yeah. True.

"No." He frowned and gently rubbed a red mark on her wrist. "I am mainly a vampire. We are fine in the sun. It only kills Kurjans and their Cyst sect."

A vampire. She gasped as electricity shot from his soft touch. "Why do they call you the Butcher?"

He winced. "They are my enemy. We fight to the death."

This was crazy. "I don't want to be a vampire." Would he bite her and change her? She tried to think through all the movies she'd seen as a teenager. Oh, crap. Would he want to take all her blood? "Ronan?"

His lip curved. "You will not become a vampire."

"Promise?" she asked, having no choice at this second but to trust him. A little.

"Yes. We are just a different species from humans. You cannot become a different species." He helped her to stand and drew her over to the kitchen, where the cats were huddled against the far cupboard. "Do you believe me now?"

She looked up well over a foot to his face. "I'm trying not to, but I don't see any other possible explanation for this craziness."

"Understandable." He took a knife from her block.

Her stomach dropped. "What are you doing?"

"Finishing the proof." He slid the blade against the inside of his wrist. "For some reason, you are unaware that vampires exist. My people must have decided to go dark when society grew. Here is your proof." He sliced his wrist before she could stop him.

"Ronan!" She grabbed a kitchen towel to stem the blood, and he prevented her with a hand on her arm.

Then the wound stopped bleeding. As she watched, his skin slowly stitched itself together and then healed, leaving his wrist perfectly healthy. He swallowed, growing a little paler. "That should not have cost me any energy, and yet it has. I need time to rebuild."

She reached out and ran a finger over his skin. "That's incredible." Just think of the specialized cells that allowed him to do that. Could they somehow be mutated to help humans? To assist coma patients to regain consciousness? To help Grace? The thoughts zinged so quickly around Faith's mind, she couldn't grasp just one. Well, maybe one. "I believe you." About the vampire part, anyway. But what had the Kurjan meant about a prison?

He nodded. "Good."

She looked at the marking on his palm, where a K was surrounded by jagged lines. "What exactly is that?" Tingles winged through her abdomen.

He looked at the design. "This is a marking that appears on our palms when our mate is near." He pulled his arm back and set the knife in the sink.

"Mate?" she asked, her voice breathless.

"Yes." His eyes morphed to the sizzling blue again. "You, Faith. You are mine."

Whoa. That he belonged to a different species was one thing… the whole mating thing another.

"That's nuts."

"We can mate Enhanced humans such as yourself. You must be empathic? Psychic? Telekinetic?"

She gulped. Her weird ability—the one she'd always had and then had honed after her sister had gone into a coma. "No…"

"You are denying it. How odd," he murmured, his gaze hot. She shook her head. "That marking supposedly appears when a vampire meets his mate?" There had to be a logical and scientific reason that had nothing to do with a sexy word like *mate*.

He lifted a shoulder. "Well, no. Vampires actually do not have a mating mark. They just mate with a good bite and sex. I am primarily vampire, because we Kayrs males only take one true form." He sighed. "However, I am part-demon. Demons have a mark."

She blinked. Once and then again. "You—you're a demon."

He grinned, his fangs sliding down again. "Just half."

CHAPTER FIVE

Ronan finished reading the vehicle manual as Faith drove off the busy interstate. Finally, trees and nature began to appear on either side of them. "Fascinating," he said again, setting the manual down. "Engines. What a lovely concept." Yet he did miss his horses. "Thank you again for trusting me and telling the police officers that you were leaving for a vacation." Ronan had slipped off the balcony without their being the wiser.

Faith kept her attention on the road ahead. "With your ability to heal, I think you can help my sister. Also, thanks for giving me time to settle my cats with a neighbor instead of just kidnapping me again." She glanced his way, her pretty eyes covered by what were called sunglasses. So clever. "You know my sense of reality has completely been skewed, right?"

He nodded, fully understanding. His had taken a direct attack as well. Perhaps they were both on a reconnaissance mission at the moment. "I'd hoped the hour driving with perfect quiet, except for that radio, would assist you to comprehend." This new way of speaking with contractions, as evidenced by the people on the radio, intrigued him. It made speaking go much faster.

"I appreciate the time to think." She slowed down as she came upon a battered truck going very slowly on the old road. "I do have questions."

No doubt. "Please ask them, and I will answer. Then perhaps you can return the favor." He needed to know her better before he could woo her.

She breathed out, her gaze on the truck ahead of them. "How many species are there on earth?"

Perfect beginning question. He smiled. His woman was brilliant. He'd always liked intelligent women. "We have vampires, demons, witches, shifters, Kurjans, fairies, Enhanced, and humans."

She blinked. "You're kidding me."

"Nope." He'd caught the slang from the radio and he liked it.

"Okay." Her delicate throat moved as she swallowed.

His fangs tingled, and he had to banish thoughts of her being his mate. Somehow. After centuries, to be so close to her and not touch her was torture. But there was no doubt he'd have to ease her into the reality of what they were to each other. He was a patient male, after all. "You said you are a doctor. A healer. Why did you choose that calling?"

Her head tilted just a little. "I always liked science in school, and the human body, especially the brain, fascinated me."

There was more to her reasons, but she was wise not to give her trust so easily. "What else?" he asked gently.

She shrugged. "I don't know. The brain and how it works intrigues me, so I went into neurology. But I didn't start researching and working with coma patients until my sister was injured two years ago." She kept her voice level, but a thread of pain wove through the undercurrents.

Ah, his woman was a sweetheart. He let her compose herself. "Your next question?" he asked.

"What makes the immortal people different species? It must be a chromosomal difference. How old are you?"

He blinked. "I'm fourteen hundred years old. We're all just different. Vampires are strong and deadly, demons are calculating with extra abilities like teleporting, witches harness the elements and can make fire; shifters change into feline, wolf, bear, or dragon, Enhanced are special, like you, and can mate immortals, and humans are just human."

Her eyebrows lowered in a very cute line. "What about fairies?"

"Oh, they're crazy. They mostly live outside Dublin—at least they used to—and everyone steers clear of them." Maybe fairies were different these days, but he doubted it. He asked the question he'd been trying not to agonize over. "Why are you not married or betrothed?"

She glanced at him, her eyebrows lifting. Amusement glimmered in her eyes before she turned back to the road. "I've been rather busy raising my sister, attending med school, and becoming a neurologist." She grinned. "The world is a bit different these days from what you're obviously accustomed to."

That was clear. Yet her amused confirmation that she was unattached filled his heart with the first peace he'd experienced since awakening.

Her voice softened. "Why are you here now, Ronan? What happened? What is this about a prison you escaped?"

He sobered, his chest hurting. "I am the first prong of the shield surrounding a prison, and my world failed."

She put on her blinker and pressed on the gas pedal, zipping around the slow truck. "I don't know what that means," she said.

He swallowed. "Of course." How could he explain this to somebody who was unaware of his world? "Is there another instruction manual I could read? Maybe one on buildings or life? Something about world history?" Surely there was a book he could read that would help him explain.

"Sure. It's called the Internet." She drove past quaint-looking buildings. Offices. She had said similar structures were called *businesses*. "When we get to the cabin, I'll hook you up with my laptop."

What did that mean? He was accustomed to being smarter than most people in his vicinity, yet he couldn't follow her words. "That would be very kind of you. I'd like to be, ah, hooked up." Then maybe he could figure out what the hell was going on.

"How about you give it a try? Explain to me who you are?" she pressed.

He sighed. "Yes. For you, I shall make the attempt." Truth be told, much of the dimensional physics weren't clear, even to him. "There are seven of us. We make up the shield."

She nodded. "Okay. Seven of you make a shield."

"Yes. You have seen my back: That is not a marking or a tattoo. My torso has been fused so it is impenetrable."

She stilled. "Excuse me?"

"The ritual of the Seven." He wiped a hand across his eyes. "We thought it would make our bodies immortal and unbreakable, but we were wrong. It only made our torsos harder than diamonds. Our hearts are protected, while our necks are not."

Her shoulders stiffened, but she kept her gaze on the road. "Um, all right. Forgetting the break in reality here, if you're immortal, why protect your heart?"

"It can be ripped out." It was his favorite move in battle, actually.

She paled a little bit. "Whoa. Why were you wrong about the ritual?"

He stiffened and his breath chilled. "Let us just say we were mistaken. For now." He did not want to tell her all the details of the ritual. Some of it might be considered unforgivable.

"That's fair," she said easily, speeding up to pass a small blue car. "Seven of you are a shield."

"The Shield," he corrected quietly. "We're called the Seven. The shield is in place to protect the world from a Kurjan: the Cyst, Ulric." How could one explain pure evil to somebody as sweet as his mate?

"Ulric is the bad guy, huh?" She moved back into the right-hand lane. "What's so terrible about this Cyst, and why didn't you just kill him?"

Excellent questions. He loved how quickly her mind worked. "Ulric is shielded head to toe, not just his torso, and he has the power to kill off Enhanced humans. All of you."

She slowly turned to look at him. "You're kidding."

"Um, no." How could that be said in jest? "His ritual was more complete than ours. He's unkillable."

"Well, that sucks," she said, her tone slightly flippant.

It must be difficult hearing these odd words. "In the year 1000 AD, we employed the strongest elements of physics we knew to create...well, other spheres, using the most powerful of blood—the blood of the complete Seven. We made three other spheres with Ulric in the middle one. I inhabited one sphere and it apparently shattered. I do not know how. My brother is in the other sphere. The other part of the shield." He couldn't tell her all of the details, but this should suffice.

She brushed her hair off her forehead. "Okay. So Ulric is unkillable, and you guys basically created a prison for him with you and your brother as prison guards."

"Yes." How nice that she quickly grasped his meaning. "You are very bright."

"I'm a Trekkie, baby," she murmured. "Kirk and Picard would've had a field day with this. Not to mention Spock."

What was a Trekkie? "Huh? Are these friends of yours?"

"No." She chuckled. "Long story. One more question: How does Ulric have the power to kill so many people? All of the Enhanced? I'm not buying that one."

The phrase was unfamiliar, but he understood the meaning. "I imagine it would be difficult to comprehend." He sighed. "For now, until I get hooked up and can explain better, just believe me. In Ulric's blood is a threat to all Enhanced." With this new world, there were probably advanced mechanisms for ending the Enhanced. He had to gain knowledge and now.

She shook her head rapidly as if trying to dislodge a crazy thought. Then she settled. "All right. Now I'm back to thinking I've been drugged and you're insane."

He settled more comfortably in the seat. Did these come in bigger sizes? Surely there were males his size around. "Perhaps after you hook me up, I'll be able to explain better." The vernacular of the day was just odd. Truly strange.

She ran a hand through her thick hair, making his fingers itch to touch it himself. "All right. A couple more questions, and then we'll be at the cabin." She turned down a narrow road.

The coolness of the forest surrounded him, settling in his chest. There was water near. He could smell it. "Is this cabin secure?" he asked.

She slowed the vehicle down to drive around a pile of brush. "Yeah. Secure. Speaking of which, those Kurjan guys found my apartment. Exactly how much danger am I in since they found me so easily?" Her lips tightened a bit.

"You are in no danger," he growled before he could stop himself. "I'd never allow my mate to be harmed. Surely you must understand that." He wanted to touch her so badly it hurt. Just to offer comfort. "I know I'm not at full strength, but I'll do everything possible to prepare to fight. I just need time." And probably food. A lot of it.

She frowned. "Okay. A couple of things. First, you fought off two white-faced crazy guys today and won. This is you at half-strength?"

Oh, she truly didn't understand. He nodded. "Those Kurjan Cyst members were young and just scouts. Not seasoned soldiers. They didn't know I'd be with you." They were strong enough to take a human like her. Definitely not a hybrid like him. However, the fight hadn't ended nearly as quickly as it should have. A niggle of doubt tried to creep into his mind. Just how long would it take for him to regain his powers?

"Second—" Her voice trembled just a little. "This whole mating business. You know I'm not going to mate you? Right?"

Of course she was. He took a moment to find the right words. "My people have many beliefs when it comes to mates. Some believe it's fate, some believe it's biology, some believe it just is. But when we touch or come close to our mate, the branding appears on our hand."

She bit her lip. "You just came out of a coma. Maybe the shock created it."

He grinned. "I've dreamed of you. Through the years, when I believed I'd never leave the shield world and had accepted that as my death . . . I still dreamed of you."

She shifted in her seat and turned to look at him. Awareness cascaded from her.

He could read her body, even if he couldn't get inside her mind. Yet. The woman was interested. Cautiously so. He liked that about her. "When an immortal mates an Enhanced human, she lives forever as well."

She slowed down and took another turn through the forest, looking back at the road. "Immortality, huh?"

"Yes. Except for beheading, removal of the heart, or death by an inferno," he confirmed, amusement bubbling through him. The woman didn't believe him. Not at all. How extraordinary. He'd convince her, but first he needed to get his feet planted solidly on this ground and in this time. Then he had to find his people to prevent Ulric from being released, if he hadn't been already. "What is the security at this cabin?"

She took another turn and drove to the back of a dwelling made from rough-hewn logs. A beautiful and peaceful lake spread out on the other side. "One of my doctor friends inherited the cabin and land on Shadow Mountain Lake. Six of us were friends in medical school, and we pay the property taxes and expenses equally for the right to use it whenever we want." She sighed. "None of us uses it enough."

"So it cannot be tracked to you, even by Siri?" he asked, opening the door and standing. He tuned into the environment and heard only wildlife and wind. Perfect.

She moved from the vehicle and walked toward the cabin. "No. We're safe here—even from Siri." The last was said with a bit of amusement. Turning, she eyed him up and down, taking off her sunglasses. Her smile turned her cuteness into beauty. "I'll get you settled in here, and then I'll run to town to buy you some clothes. You look ridiculous."

He glanced down at the tight scrubs and very colorful shoes. Yes. He probably did. Humor took him and he looked up, meeting her stunning gaze. Awareness passed between them with a heat he could feel inside his chest.

Her smile faltered.

His widened.

"Ronan," she whispered, bewilderment crossing her expression.

"Yes. Ronan." The woman might as well get used to saying his name. "All in good time, Faith. I promise."

By the widening of her eyes, she might've taken that as a threat. So be it.

CHAPTER SIX

Faith awoke to the sound of gentle lake waves and the smell of fresh pine trees. She'd actually slept the entire night. How crazy. With a vampire-demon hybrid in the cabin, one would think she might've tossed and turned.

No.

Though the dreams she'd had about him, about his magnificent body...well, now. Whew.

But she did believe him. So her reality had changed, as people's perceptions of the world had changed many times over when new discoveries were made. The world wasn't flat after all.

She turned on her side to see the picture of her and Grace taken during Grace's college graduation. Her sister's hazel eyes were full of fun, and she looked stunning in her blue graduate gown. There were tons of people around, all of them Grace's friends. Everyone loved Grace, because she loved the world. Loved living and exploring every day. She'd always looked outward, while Faith had focused inward.

God, Faith missed her sister. They'd drawn together the second they'd found out their parents were dead, even though there was a five-year difference between them. They'd been best friends and confidantes.

For the first time in months, now that she knew there was immortal blood that could heal seemingly fatal injuries, she felt hope. Could she finally break through Grace's coma with assistance from the sexy vampire in the other room?

Man, he was hot. Those dreams still lingered.

She shook herself from her thoughts and moved into the attached bathroom to prepare for the day. Her hair was an easy brush-through, and she spent the normal amount of time on lip gloss. Several swipes, mixing colors, ending with a sealer.

Yeah, she had a weakness for lip glosses. That and boots. Well, and chocolate-fudge ice cream.

She paired her jeans and silk top with her brown calfskin boots from Saks. They were flat but stylish, and she felt centered in them.

Steeling herself, she kept her head up and walked into the comfortable main room of the cabin. It was decorated in warm plaids with a sofa, two chairs, coffee table, desk, and a stone fireplace. One of Grace's photographs of the lake, in contrasting black-and-white, was set above the mantel. Everything faced the wide windows that showed the peaceful lake. There she stopped short at seeing Ronan still at the computer desk, typing away. "Have you been up all night?" she asked.

"Yes." He turned, the sight of him unbelievably sexy in the black T-shirt and jeans she'd bought him the day before. Dark scruff covered his masculine jaw, making him look even more dangerous than usual. His stunning aqua eyes added intrigue to the hard ridges and angles of his face. His dark hair reached his nape, and the ruffled look did nothing to diminish the fierce planes of his body. Which was broad and muscled and incredibly...fit. "I've learned so much."

"Really?" Her body flashed wide awake and alert, and her skin became sensitized. Tingles exploded in her abdomen. She had to get this under control. Yes, he was hot. Yeah. So what? Pretending a nonchalance she didn't come close to feeling, she moved past him to the updated kitchen.

"Yes. I made a list and plan to master one subject a night, beginning with technology, since that seems to be the biggest change since I left. At first, I studied Siri and how she could be in your phone." He chuckled. "Artificial intelligence is just brilliant."

Faith nodded. "What else?"

"The history of computers was fascinating. Then I read about quantum physics, string theory, bubble theory, engineering, and so on. I believe the prison spheres we created are just other dimensions. Then I spent time on the dark web and didn't like it there."

She turned around to face him with the granite-topped kitchen island between them. "You explored the dark web?"

He shrugged. "Yes. Then I studied hacking and did that for a while."

The man had learned to hack computers in a night. "Uh, okay." She shook her head. "Why the heck did you go to the dark web?"

"I couldn't find anything on my family, vampires, or the Cyst anywhere on the Internet. So I discovered the dark web and tried there." He stretched his arms and his T-shirt pulled across the muscles in his chest.

She bit her lip and tried not to sigh. This was crazy. She felt all electrified being near him. When was the last time she'd had sex? Way too long ago. Now, that just wasn't healthy. But he was a freaking vampire-demon. They could probably go forever in bed. But…no. Absolutely not. She would not lead him on like that. The guy thought they were destined to be mates forever. She just wanted an orgasm. Or three. "Did you find anything?" she asked, thinking of the pocket-rocket in the other room. It was more than capable of creating an orgasm.

"Not really." His chest settled nicely. "There was a cached article about what sounded like Kurjans, but the author, a Sarah Pringle, called them vampires." He rolled his eyes. "No follow up, and I couldn't find anything else on her."

Maybe it was just somebody writing a book. She shook herself out of sexual thoughts. "Anything else?"

He nodded. "A series of articles about beings with extra chromosomes that had been deleted from the Internet. Written by a woman named Olivia Roberts. She also disappeared."

Faith swallowed, connecting the dots. "If these women had discovered the truth, would your people have killed them?"

He breathed out. "I hope not. We can contain humans without killing them. Perhaps they were Enhanced and found mates." He shook his head. "But that's all I could find. My family is too smart to let information get out there, so I'm not surprised. But I did find the name of a bar in a place called Chicago that might be owned by one of the Seven. I created an email account with a fake name he'd recognize and have, as one would now say, reached out."

Her lips twitched. "You've been learning modern vernacular."

"True that," he said, returning the smile.

She chuckled as warning bells clanged through her head. He was sexy and smart and funny. No wonder her body was all awake and tingly. He was also a very bad idea. "What else?" she asked, intrigued.

"Well, I joined Mensa."

She coughed out a laugh. "You did."

"Yes." He rubbed his scruffy jaw. "They had a test and I thought it'd be fun. Passed it and they said I could join. I, of course, used a false name."

Of course. He was also brilliant. Nice to know. "Sounds like a busy night."

He frowned, those dark eyebrows slashing down. "One thing confused me, though."

Thank goodness. "What was that?"

"The Kardashians. Who are they and why are they news?" His puzzled expression nearly made her burst out laughing.

"It's a modern mystery," she murmured, not wanting to like him.

His face cleared. "Oh. All right. And I investigated you."

Warning ticked down her spine. "Is that right?" She bent and looked for a bowl on the shelf to start mixing eggs. Why had he looked her up?

"Yes." His voice sounded closer and when she stood, he was right across the counter. Her breath quickened. "Most doctors or scientists go into the field because they're cerebral. Smart. You're very intelligent."

She relaxed. "Thanks."

"But you're all heart," he said softly, towering over her even across the granite. "Sketches you've drawn were in your laptop bag. Drawings of people, some elderly, their faces lined with experiences I could almost touch. I could feel their laughter and their tears. Their lives and loves."

She straightened. "You looked at my sketches?" Her heart stuttered. She never shared those with people.

"Yes. I loved the one of the child on the swing. His eyes showed every emotion he was feeling right that second." His gaze warmed. "There's a lot of depth to you, Faith Cooper."

His proud tone should give her pause. "Not really."

One of his dark eyebrows lifted. "Yes." He swept his hand toward the photo above the fireplace. "I see the same eye for detail in your sister's photograph."

Faith caught her breath. "How did you know Grace took that picture?"

"She signed the bottom right corner."

Oh yeah. Faith grinned. "I forgot we made her do that." Warmth spread through her. "You really see a resemblance between Grace's picture and my drawings?" That was beyond sweet.

He nodded. "I do. You both look deep and see beyond the obvious. I'd know you were Enhanced females without even meeting either of you. I hope you can trust me with your gift at some point."

She swallowed, oddly compelled to share with him. "It's not a gift. I mean, it's just strange. I don't really want to explain it." Trust didn't come easy to her, and she disliked not understanding her abilities. Somehow she could get inside minds and communicate…a little. She'd done so before studying coma patients, but experience had honed her skill.

"That is acceptable. Soon I will earn your trust." The heat of his gaze could melt chocolate.

He did seem to know a lot about her. Or had taken some serious time to figure her out. "You're trying to learn about me," she murmured.

"Of course," he said, his warmth reaching her even over the counter. "I'm gathering intel and preparing to adapt my strategy. Knowing you is step one."

Her eyebrows lifted. "Step one? What am I, a military coup?"

He grinned. "Yes."

Speech deserted her for a moment. He was cute...and serious. "What's step two?" she croaked.

"Well..." He seemed to warm to the subject. "Step two is moving into strategy mode. One establishes a line of communication, builds alliances, and develops a safe base."

Holy crap. He really was serious. "And the next step?" Her stomach tingled a little.

He studied her. "In a military campaign? The final step is to go on attack and win the objective."

Her mouth dried up. "I am not an objective." Now it was a mite insulting.

He didn't answer.

Well, that was an answer. "Ronan?" She tapped her nice boot on the floor.

"I've learned more. You're kindhearted in many ways. You have a history of giving medical care around the world, often without compensation. You pay your sister's medical bills and have her stationed at your hospital. The woman who's been in a coma for two years."

Grace had missed two whole years of her life and would turn twenty-five in just a few weeks. "I'm going to bring her back," Faith whispered, her throat clogging, forgetting all about military campaigns. "Can you help?" Immortal blood should have some side benefits.

His eyes softened. "No. Not if her brain doesn't function," he said, reaching out to run a knuckle down the side of Faith's face, his gaze tracking his hand.

The gentle touch slid through her, warming her, igniting every nerve. Her eyes widened on him.

He nodded. "Yes. Us."

She backed away.

He slowly lowered his hand, his eyes sizzling with green instead of blue. "I will not force you to trust me right now, but—"

The computer dinged.

He paused, gave her a look, and crossed to read the screen. Then he straightened and faced her. "Have you ever been to Chicago? We must leave in an hour."

CHAPTER SEVEN

Faith's world tilted yet again. "Chicago?" No way was she leaving town. "Um, no." She kept her voice low and reassuring.

He straightened. "No? What's wrong with Chicago?"

"Nothing." She pushed the bowl away. So much for breakfast. "I understand you need to go and hopefully find your family, but I'm remaining here." Yes, she'd like to stay in touch with him—even study him. Surely he was wrong and there was a way to use his blood to save her sister. To save other people. "We can remain in contact."

He just studied her, those brilliant eyes revealing nothing.

She fought the urge to shuffle her feet. He was just too appealing, too sexy; she needed some time and distance away from him. To come to grips with this new information that had altered her perception of reality: Vampires existed. "I want you to find your family and friends. I really do." He'd need help fighting the Kurjans—the fact that they were real nauseated her.

He looked down for a moment, as if gathering his thoughts. Then, smoothly, gracefully, he moved around the island and toward her like a jaguar stalking prey from a dangerous ledge. She stepped back instinctively until she stood flush against the counter and had nowhere else to go.

Her breath quickened and her body tensed. Wasn't he still supposed to be in information-gathering mode? This felt more immediate.

He reached out, sliding one broad hand through her hair to cup her nape. The strength in the gentle move was obvious. "I know this is immense," he murmured, his eyes a deep blue now, his tone a hoarse rumble. "Probably too much."

Every nerve she had flared wide awake and on alert. Heat ignited with a low pull in her abdomen.

He stood over her, so wide and warm, strength in every hard-cut line. She swallowed, trying to think. But her gaze rose to his lips, and she lifted her face. His eyes flared and green sizzled through the blue. Then he lowered his head, brushing his mouth across hers.

It was like being burned by a live wire. Her mouth opened on a gasp and he pressed in, his body overwhelming hers with sheer size. Then he kissed her.

Firm and fast and deep. Passion engulfed her, taking her away from every thought she'd ever had. There was only right now and this. Nothing else existed in the universe but his mouth, his body, his hand. *Him.*

He growled, and the sound vibrated down her throat to land in her abdomen. A pulse set up between her legs, and she became all feeling. Kissing him back, she rose to her toes, pressing against him. Taking all she could get. She flattened her palms against the impossibly hard ridges of his chest, her skin sensitizing as he swept his tongue into her mouth.

It was a penetration she felt throughout her entire body. More than a kiss. More than just a touch. A sound of need came from somewhere inside her. He softened the kiss, the hand at her nape relaxing. Then he slowly released her mouth, lifting back up.

Dazed, she could only look at him. Reality slammed into her with a cold slap. She pushed him, panicking.

He stepped back.

"What was that?" she murmured, her shaking hand moving to her tingling mouth. Where had she gone? What had just happened to her? It was like being drugged.

"We're mated," he said simply, taking another step away as if knowing she needed space. "Or we will be."

Self-preservation kicked in. "Whoa. Okay. Wait a minute." She was a doctor, for goodness' sake. Not some fourteen-year-old having a first crush with the cool guy on the football team. Or the intriguing bad boy hanging out behind the bleachers. "Do all vampires kiss like that?" Maybe it was a biological thing.

He blinked. "How should I know?"

"You've never kissed one?" Her mind was still fuzzy and she tried to clear it.

"Oh. Did I not mention that vampires are male only? We only make males." He twisted his lip. "I like women. So, no kissing of other vampires."

Male only? An entire species? That should not make her knees all wobbly. Darn it. Her knowledge of genetics clashed with this new information. What she wouldn't give to study a vampire's blood. "I see." All right. She cleared her throat. "I need a few minutes."

He gave a short nod. "That is allowable. You should pack for a week."

She hadn't agreed to go with him, but she didn't mention that fact and instead moved past him to the bedroom. His scent, wildness and woodsy male, followed her. This was beyond insane. Her body felt empty and cold, and a part of her—one she didn't like much—wanted to turn right back around and tackle him to the ground. She'd seen him naked, and truth be told, he was impressive. But she'd been in doctor mode then. Now she was all woman, and that was a hell of a man.

She shut the door behind her and sagged against it. Okay. What in the world was she going to do now? She'd have to be dead to not want to explore that kind of sexual attraction. He'd nearly brought her to orgasm with one freakin' kiss.

Her phone buzzed and she leaped for it, thankful for any interruption to her thoughts.

"Cooper," she said, her voice an octave too high. She cleared her throat. "Dr. Cooper here."

"Faith, it's Jordy Wallace." Excitement filled Jordy's low voice. "We've had a development with Grace. She opened her eyes and tracked movements."

Faith froze. Jordy Wallace was an excellent neurologist and Grace's primary doctor. "Are you sure?" Her sister had been in a coma for over two years, and during that time, there had been no change. None.

"Yes. The minute we spotted an improvement, we captured her on a cell phone. I'll send you the video," he said. "We already think she's a miracle."

Yeah. Grace's body hadn't broken down during the coma as normally happened. Nobody understood why.

Faith leaned back to watch the screen. Her sister's eyes opened, which wasn't uncommon for a coma patient. Then she watched a nurse walk from one end of the room to another. Jordy's voice was audible, and her sister turned slightly toward where he stood in the room. Then her eyelids shut again.

Jordy came back on the line. "It's progress, Faith."

Yeah, it was, astonishing progress. Her mind scrambled. She didn't believe in coincidence—never had. "Has anybody visited Grace in the last two days?"

"Not that I know of," Jordy said. "You need to come down here. This is significant."

Definitely. "Jordy, listen to me. Have you seen anybody... well...odd in the vicinity? Role-playing groups or people just dressed up? Big guys?"

"Of course not. What is going on with you?" Jordy asked. "You're acting strange."

That was probably an understatement. Ronan had been with her all morning, so he hadn't been able to influence her sister's health.

But he had friends and enemies out there. And a whole lot was going on that Faith didn't understand. "I need your help," she said.

"Anything," Jordy answered. They'd been friends since medical school. "What do you need?"

She breathed out. "Security. I was kidnapped the other night, and I'm fine. I'll tell you all about it when I get there. But please have security meet me at my car, and post them at Grace's door and along the corridor." This was definitely not a coincidence, but at the moment, the only thing that mattered was her sister. "Please."

Jordy was quiet for a moment. "You were *kidnapped*?"

She brushed hair away from her face, a sense of urgency making her hand tremble. Grace was getting better? Was it possible? Even if this was some sort of crazy immortal trap, she didn't care. It was time to see her sister. "I'll be right there." She clicked off the phone.

Now. What the heck should she do with the vampire in the other room? She bit her lip. He was big and strong...but what was going on? He wasn't the one who'd helped Grace.

So who had?

She shook her head. Ronan had been adamant that she travel to Chicago with him. Like her, he'd suspect Grace's recovery was a trap, and he might try to stop Faith from going to the hospital, even though she'd taken precautions.

But this was family, and she'd do anything for her sister. Jordy would have the floor blanketed with security by the time she arrived there. She couldn't take the risk that Ronan would stop her and kidnap her again.

Quickly writing him a note, she scrambled for her purse. As quietly as she could, she moved to the bedroom window and slid through, wincing as the sticker bushes outside pricked her jeans.

Then she ran for her SUV.

* * * *

Ronan stood beneath the tree by the lake cabin, his gaze on the dirt settling along the road. She'd left him. Jumped out a window and had just taken off. Betrayal cut through him for the briefest of moments before he regained control of himself.

The last day surely had been overwhelming for Faith. She'd learned of vampires, of the Cyst, and of her enhancement.

And he'd kissed her.

If she'd felt half the reaction he had, she was probably frightened and cautious. His body still rioted with a hunger that troubled him. He'd never wanted a woman this badly. The marking on his palm cut deep with a pain that demanded appeasement, and only transferring it to her flesh would ease him.

He'd courted her too strongly and she'd bolted.

Perhaps she'd just gone to town again, needing to be free of him. He rubbed his chest and turned to go back into the cabin. In his healthier days, he could've chased down the vehicle and probably caught her before she reached the end of the long, deserted road. But now? He wasn't even close to being able to do that.

When would his strength return? What if it didn't? He'd been in the other dimension, the prison shield, for more than a thousand years. Surely that could cause some bodily damage.

What should he do?

He wiped a hand across his eyes and stepped inside, his gaze going to the computer. *Think, damn it.* Years ago, he would've commanded an army. He would've been able to find her and make sure she was secure. Now? At the moment, he had nobody. Not even his mate. What if his people hadn't survived? What if he had no family?

The idea was too painful to contemplate, so he shoved it away. He was a Kayrs. That meant something. Hell. It meant everything. His family would've survived somehow. He just needed to find them.

He sat at the computer and reached out to his contact in Chicago, typing quickly.

There has been a delay. I will be in touch soon.

An answer came immediately. *No delay. Plane arriving at private airport for you in one hour. Be there or we go dark.*

Enough of this. He clicked a couple of buttons and ignited the webcam software. A blank screen came up with his face on a smaller screen in the corner. He typed his message: *I am Ronan Kayrs of the Seven, and I demand to see who is there. Face me, you coward.*

The screen remained dark. Then slowly, a face took shape. One Ronan did not know. The male had mid-length blond hair and piercing blue eyes. "I'm here. Be careful who you call a coward, asshole," he said.

Ronan studied him. There was something familiar about the male's jawline. "Who the fuck are you?"

The male's left eyebrow rose.

A hammer slammed into Ronan's gut. He knew that look. "You're related to Igor. Where is he? I must see him."

"I'm Ivar." The male's chin dropped and his eyes sizzled with a dangerous glow. "Igor is dead. I named a series of bars across the country after him. Igor was my brother."

Ronan dropped into his seat, pain slashing cold fingers through him. Igor dead? There was one of the deaths he'd felt while in the shield. "He was one of my best friends." One of the Seven. "I'm sorry to know he passed on." Jesus. Igor was as tough as they came. "What happened?" Who could've killed Igor?

"War happened," Ivar said simply.

Ronan coughed. War? What all had he missed? "You've taken his place?"

"Yes. I survived the ritual and am one of the Seven," Ivar said.

"*Cad iad na Seacht?*" Ronan asked quietly, holding his breath.

Ivar studied him for two beats. "*Bráithreachas a rinneadh i bhfuil.*"

Thank the gods. He knew the code. "Where is everyone else?" Ronan asked. "What's going on? Has my brother, Quade, returned to this plane? What about my brother, Jacer?" Jacer had been one of the five to remain on this plane and handle the world of humans. "Who else died? I felt it happen."

Ivar shook his head. "I don't know you, friend. Yes, you gave the right code. But that doesn't mean anything. You come here, meet me in person. Prove you are Ronan Kayrs. Then we'll see."

He couldn't just leave Faith.

A ruckus sounded and Ivar's chair was shoved away. A broad face was lowered to the camera. "Ronan? That you?"

Relief and hope rushed into Ronan so quickly he couldn't breathe. "Benny?" he asked, leaning toward the computer. "You are alive, my brother."

Benjamin Reese smiled widely, his rough face transformed. "Ronan. Fuck, man. It's really you." He yanked a chair into place and dropped his huge body into it. "I mean, it's great to see you, but that means the entire system is falling." He sobered instantly. A sight most people never saw. "We're in trouble, right?"

Weren't they always? "Where are my brothers? Either of them?" Ronan looked around for the large black boots Faith had bought for him. "We must begin to plan."

Benny coughed. "Listen, man. It looks like you and I think you are you, but I can't be sure until we're in the same room. Get on the plane and I'll tell you everything when I see you." He rubbed his chin thoughtfully. "If you're you, I mean. If you're not you, if you're somebody else, then I'll have to kill you. Whoever *you* are."

Jesus. Benny was still slightly nuts. Or his sense of humor had just skewed to the point of really messing with people. Ronan had never been sure. "I have experienced a delay."

Benny leaned back. "Define *delay*."

"I may have lost my mate," Ronan said, frowning. "She left me."

Benny sighed, his metallic eyes sparkling. "You Kayrs men always were terrible with the ladies. No finesse. No charm."

Ronan growled. His old friend wasn't helping.

"Does she have a phone?" Benny asked.

Of course she did. Then the question hit home. Ah-ha. Ronan had researched Siri and phones the other night. "Yeah," he said softly.

"Then you can track her," Benny said reasonably. "Track her GPS, get her, and be here now. We have work to do." He clicked off.

Ronan sat back. Good plan. When he caught up to his mate, they were going to have a little talk. He had tried to be reasonable and ease her into this odd new reality. And she'd jumped out a window and run away from him.

This time, he'd try something else.

CHAPTER EIGHT

Faith rushed to her sister's room, taking a moment to appreciate the security personnel on the floor. Two armed guards had escorted her from her car to the door, and nobody had tried to intervene. She reached the door and moved inside, seeing Jordy near her sister's head in the small private room. Monitors beeped behind him.

He looked up and grinned. "She's back out now, but it was real, Faith."

"How is she scoring on the Glasgow?" Faith asked, moving toward the quiet woman on the bed. Grace's brown hair curled around her shoulders, and her skin was pale from being inside for two years. "Jordy?"

"Better than last week," Jordy said cheerfully, his brown eyes earnest. At about thirty and newly married, he was usually in a good mood. And he was brilliant. Faith had requested him to be Grace's doctor since she couldn't treat a family member. "I have some rounds to do. Why don't you stay here and talk to her? See if you can get her to focus. To maybe squeeze your hand."

Faith pulled up a visitor chair and sat. "Are you sure she hasn't had any odd visitors?" None of this was making sense.

"Not that I know of and nobody signed in," Jordy said, walking toward the door in fresh tennis shoes. "I checked after you called."

He patted her shoulder and kept striding for the hall. "I'll be back in thirty minutes to hear all about your kidnapping."

Faith nodded and reached for her sister's hand. All of this crazy immortal stuff might explain why Grace's body was still healthy and hadn't lost muscle tone. If Faith was Enhanced, maybe Grace was too? "Gracie? Can you hear me?"

Nothing.

She tightened her hold. "If you can hear me, please squeeze my hand."

Nothing happened.

She sighed and closed her eyes, trying to enter Grace's consciousness. "Gracie?"

Nothing. Inside Grace's mind, there was no place to settle. These things took a lot of time. But still. Grace had tracked with her eyes. That was huge. How did it happen? Ronan had said he couldn't save Grace, so it hadn't been him. But should Faith have brought him anyway? Would he have come, or would he have just kidnapped her? She couldn't take the chance.

"Grace?" she whispered again, trying harder, her mind spinning. There had to be an explanation for all of this.

As usual, her sister didn't respond. Faith lowered her head to the bed and closed her eyes. For some reason, she remembered another time Grace had gone silent.

It was the first day of junior high, and Grace was only twelve. Her long brown hair curled around her shoulders, and her greenish-brown eyes had been serious. They'd had to move to live with an elderly aunt just the month before because their parents had died. The school in Denver was much bigger than the one they'd attended in Iowa. She hadn't talked all day and that was weird for Grace.

"What's going on?" Faith asked, looking up at the imposing brick building. The high school was just around the corner, and she had to get going for her first day there. "Grace?"

"What if they don't like me?" Grace whispered.

Faith held her hand and leaned in until their foreheads touched. "Who are we?"

Grace snorted. "The Cooper girls."

"That's right." Faith had rocks in her stomach for both of them. What if the kids at the high school didn't like her? She was seventeen and totally alone. But Grace came first. "Everyone is going to love you. You know why?" She leaned back. A reluctant smile tilted Grace's pink lips. "Because I'm lovable?"

"Yes." Faith squeezed her hand. "You're the best person I know in this whole world. And I'm ridiculously smart." Her dad had said that to her through the years with great fondness.

"And I'm ridiculously adventurous," Grace said softly. "I miss him. And Mom."

Tears threatened Faith, and she batted them back. "They're watching over us. Let's show them how much we can live."

Grace steeled her shoulders. "Yeah. Let's live."

One of the security guards poked her head in to the hospital room, yanking Faith back to the present. "Ah, Dr. Cooper? You have visitors. Homeland Security agents are here. Well, one and a half, anyway."

Faith stiffened and stood, turning toward the door. "What?"

A man strode inside. He stood to at least six-foot-seven with long black hair and eyes hidden behind refractive glasses. Tight muscle filled out his dark suit, and his skin was pale against it. He flashed a badge. "Dr. Cooper? I'm Dayne Walls from Homeland Security."

A tall boy of about seven hopped behind him, peering around the agent.

Dayne sighed. "This is my son, Drake. He's out of school for the day, and my wife had to work."

Drake nodded politely. He also had black hair and pale skin, but his eyes were a deep green. "Doctor," he said, looking around and heading for another chair in the corner. He dropped a backpack off his shoulders and reached inside, quickly losing himself in a video game.

She looked at him, her instincts humming. "What's going on?" Did Homeland Security know about vampires? Probably? Or was she caught up in some weird *X-Files* thing? At this point, who knew? "Agent?"

Agent Walls moved toward the bed, looking down at Grace. "She's Enhanced, you know."

Faith stopped breathing. Then she began backing toward the door. If she screamed, the security guy would come running. "You know about Enhancements? Our government knows? Humans know? Is this for real?"

He turned toward her, his body relaxed. Slowly, he drew down his glasses to reveal bright purple eyes. "Humans don't really know."

She took another step back. "You're not with Homeland. Or are you?" Maybe the agency was made up of these guys.

He smiled, revealing even white teeth. Even though he was unnaturally pale, he was rather good-looking. Hard jaw, glimmering eyes, intriguing features. "No. The badge is fake but appears genuine." He held up a hand when she opened her mouth to yell. "We won't hurt you. We just want to talk."

She blinked. Her chest hurt, giving signs of an impending panic attack. She hadn't had one of those in years. "I don't—"

"I know," he said, his gaze intense and his tone gentle. "We helped your sister. *I* helped her."

"You did?" she breathed, looking around until her gaze landed on Drake.

The kid glanced up and nodded. "Yep." He went back to his game.

Confusion blanketed her and she struggled through it, focusing back on Dayne. "Why? How?"

He glanced at the woman in the bed and then turned to fully face Faith. "I gave her a little of my blood. We're immortal, just like vampires and demons."

We? The purple eyes. She shook her head. "You're part of the Cyst?" Had he dyed his hair?

"No. I'm a Kurjan. Their leader, actually." He appeared relaxed and his hands hung loosely by his side. "The Cyst are like our religious sect, and it's not their fault they appear as they do. It's a genetic mutation." He shook his head, the movement sad. "They're good and kind, and yet the vampires have hunted them through the centuries. You don't judge on looks, do you?"

She blinked. "No." There were several human genetic mutations that led to pale skin and an aversion to the sun. Perhaps the Cysts' mutations led to even stronger reactions to sunlight.

"I helped your sister because I could, and because I wanted to get your attention," Dayne said, his cheek creasing. "Did I?"

Were all immortals arrogant? She nodded, breathless. "Yes. Can you heal her?"

He studied her. "No, but I know somebody who can. We have doctors who could help."

"What do you want?" Might as well get to the point. She'd freak out later about all the different immortals she'd had no clue existed.

"I want the Butcher." Dayne's eyes narrowed and changed to a brighter purple. "He was convicted of killing many of my people centuries ago, and we had him locked up in a prison far away from here. In another dimension. Yet he broke free."

Wait a minute. "You're saying Ronan is the bad guy here?"

The kid snorted from over in the corner. "Bad guy." He shook his head, his concentration remaining on the game. "Like the devil is merely bad."

Dayne nodded. "Don't tell me. He gave you the epic story of him being the hero."

She faltered. "Well, yeah." Thinking back, she realized the Cyst guys hadn't threatened her. Oh, they'd asked about Ronan, but they hadn't said they'd hurt her. Until the one guy had started choking her to make her unconscious. He'd apologized first. What did that mean? She'd never know because Ronan had dragged them both into the sun to fry. "There's a marking on his hand." Heat infused her face.

Dayne paused. "Oh no. Don't tell me. He gave you that bullshit about the Kayrs marking and that you're, what? His mate?" Dayne pressed his lips together as if he was trying not to laugh. "He used that one centuries ago. If I remember right, he could even shove some heat into it to shock a lass."

The warmth intensified in her cheeks. That was a trick? Yeah, she'd fallen for it. Like some damsel in a rom-com movie looking for adventure. Man, she was an idiot. But wait a minute. This guy might be lying too. "So I'm not Enhanced," she murmured.

Dayne lost the smile. "Oh, you're definitely enhanced. I can sense that as well as any vampire could."

"What does that really mean?" she asked.

"You can mate an immortal," Dayne said. "There's no marking or anything like that. It takes a bite and sex and something more… something forever. But the marking is just a prop Ronan created to seduce women." He growled. "When he wasn't butchering innocent monks, that is."

This was so damn confusing. Ronan kissed like a god, but Dayne had actually tried to help Grace. Of course, he could be manipulating her. And while the two men had opposite stories, they agreed there were immortals out there and that she was Enhanced. Which meant she could mate an immortal and—what, become one? She chewed on her lip, trying to figure out this mess. "Why can't you give my sister more of your blood?" she asked.

He nodded as if in approval. "Our blood is dangerous to most humans. I could give her a little because she's Enhanced, and it did help her. But if I give her any more, it would kill her."

"I'd like a sample of your blood," Faith said instantly. Maybe she could isolate its healing properties.

He straightened. "We're prohibited by law from giving our blood to humans. All immortal species have that kind of protection in place. We can't have you all knowing about us. Just think of the outcry and scramble to control us. We'd have to harm humans to defend ourselves."

She kept her gaze on him, her shoulders going back. "I will arrange a meeting between Ronan and you if you heal my sister and give me a sample of your blood." Was she making a deal with the devil? Or had she kissed one in the cabin? Or were they both bad? Either way, if anybody could help Grace, Faith would take it. "What do you say?"

Dayne breathed out, his wide chest moving with the effort. "All right. I can take you to our doctor, and she can explain how to save your sister."

"She?" Faith asked.

"Sure. Humans aren't the only species with intelligent females," Dayne said, amusement in his eyes.

Whatever. "There are female Kurjans?"

Dayne frowned. "Of course. Why wouldn't there be?" His gaze cleared. "Oh, man. Is he still using that one as well? That vampires are *male only*?" His voice lowered to a dramatic whisper on the last. "Why do women fall for that?"

"I..." She truly didn't have an answer for that question. There had been something intriguing, maybe even sexy, about an all-male badass species. And she *had* fallen for that concept.

Dayne studied her for a moment as if trying to peer inside her brain. As if he was measuring her.

Did he think she was a moron? She barely kept from shuffling her feet. Yeah, she'd believed Ronan. But this guy was telling just as crazy a story. Yet he'd offered to help Grace when Ronan had said she couldn't be helped. "Listen, Dayne. You've all altered my perception of reality, and I need time to process all the new information. But how about this? You bring your doctor here, and if she can heal Grace, I'll help you meet with Ronan."

Dayne shook his head. "Our doctors are protected. Carefully. She won't travel here and be exposed, especially with the Butcher free again. He had a fondness for torturing Kurjan females."

That didn't sound like the guy who'd worn the too-small clothing, goofy shoes, and sweet smile. The vampire who'd studied the computer all night. Ronan didn't seem like the type of man to hurt a woman.

The quiet beep of a monitor was the only sound for a moment. What should she do?

Dayne gestured to his son. "Come on, kiddo. It's time to go." The kid grabbed his pack and shoved the game in, straightening his jeans when he stood. "This is your choice, Dr. Cooper. Come with us or not." He waited until his son had reached him and then turned for the door, striding gracefully toward the hallway.

"Are you a soldier?" Faith blurted.

Dayne paused and looked over his shoulder. "No. I'm more like a diplomat. But I get the job done." His smile was charming. "Remember my phone number in case you want to reach out to me." He recited the digits for her.

Faith took note of the number and followed him into the hallway. She nodded at security guards posted outside the door. "Please keep security on this room until further notice. Twenty-four hours."

The taller guard nodded.

She hustled after Dayne. "There has to be a way for me to meet your doctor."

"There is," Dayne said easily, turning a corner and heading toward the elevator. "We parked in the underground parking lot, and you're more than welcome to join us."

Yeah, but she'd be an idiot to just climb in a car with a Kurjan she didn't know. She definitely didn't trust this guy, but she couldn't lose an opportunity to help Grace. "This is crazy," she muttered.

"I'd imagine it must seem so," Dayne said cheerfully as Drake followed dutifully behind him.

They'd almost reached the elevator when a supply-closet door opened and a broad hand grabbed Dayne's hair and jerked the Kurjan inside. A large snap echoed. His neck breaking?

Faith pivoted instinctively to protect Drake, and the kid shoved past her, diving into the closet. She scrambled to stop him and was yanked inside as well.

Ronan shut the door, securing them all inside. Dayne lay in a heap on the floor, his neck at an odd angle. Faith gulped and pushed Drake behind her, backing them away from the vampire blocking the exit. "You killed him," she whispered, fear tightening her throat.

Ronan rolled his eyes. "Not yet, I haven't."

"You won't," Drake burst out from behind her. "I'll kill you first."
Faith angled herself to keep the kid behind her. "You need to leave now, Ronan. I mean it."

The vampire crossed his arms, and only the bulging vein in his neck showed any emotion. If she had to guess, and she did, he was seriously pissed. "Go out to your car and wait for me. I'll be finished here in a moment," he ordered.

Finished? What? Her lungs compressed and then whooshed out air. "You are not going to kill them."

"They're Kurjans," he said slowly, as if explaining to an idiot.

Fire raged through her. He couldn't seriously be considering killing a child. And Dayne was a diplomat, not a soldier. He didn't stand a chance against Ronan. "So what? You're prejudiced, Ronan. You really are. Just because they're Kurjans doesn't mean they're bad."

He blinked twice, incredulousness wrinkling his eyes. "Yes, it does." He studied her as if seriously doubting her intelligence.

She swallowed rapidly, trying to think of a way to save the child behind her. Even if the Kurjans were evil, he was just a kid. This close to Ronan, her body hummed again. What was up with that? It didn't make any sense. Maybe there was something biological going on. "I won't let you harm this boy," she said, her voice shaking.

Ronan sighed. "Fine. You come with me now, and I won't kill them or any of the guards on this floor. You scream, and I won't be responsible for the carnage."

That's why they called him the Butcher. Her knees shook, but she couldn't let anything happen to Drake. He was just a child.

What choice did she have?

CHAPTER NINE

Ronan parked Faith's car near the end of the small and very private airstrip where a plane waited. The woman had complained when he'd insisted on driving, but he hadn't given her a choice. He was still immensely irritated that two Kurjans had gotten so close to his mate.

And she'd protected them.

He kept calm only through force of will as he eyed the small jet. The sight of the plane made his gut ache. He wasn't ready to fly. Vampires and demons weren't meant to fly. If they were, they'd have wings.

Faith continued to ignore him from the passenger side, conducting searches on her phone.

"What are you looking for?" he asked. Again.

She cut him a sharp look. "Any research on pheromones."

Pheromones? He scrolled through his mind for any information he might've gleaned about them while searching the net. The definition flashed quickly before his eyes. "The word comes from ancient Greek and refers to a secreted chemical factor that triggers a response in somebody else." Then he mulled it over and barked out a laugh. "Wait a minute. You're trying to find a scientific reason for the attraction between us?" For the first time that day, his heart lightened. There was something sweet about her intellect.

She hunched her shoulders. "You're a bad guy, Ronan. At the very best, you're just the bad-boy type. At the worst, you're the Butcher. I should not be attracted to you."

Yet she was. He grinned, even though she'd called him the Butcher. The Kurjans had given him that nickname after a particularly bloody battle. One they'd started, by the way. "All right." He opened his door and gestured her out of the car. "Did you text your friends?" He'd made her do so before leaving the closet, threatening her with the murder of Drake.

She glared at him, while also somehow looking bewildered. "Yes. I've let the hospital know I'm on vacation still, asked my neighbor to continue watching the cats, and I emailed Louise and told her I was heading out for a spa week. Nobody will worry about my disappearance."

He nodded. "Have you flown in an airplane before?"

She stepped onto the concrete and slammed her door a little too forcefully. "Of course."

He moved around the car and took her arm. "Please give me your phone."

She jerked free. "No."

"Yes." He didn't want to engage in a tug-of-war with her. "I tracked you by your GPS, and I have no doubt the Kurjans will do the same." Everything inside him rioted with the need to go back and end Dayne. Breaking his neck hadn't been enough.

Her mouth tightened, and she put her phone behind her back.

Man, she was cute. "We both know I could take it from you, Doc." It was the first time he'd used the nickname and he liked it. He held out his hand. "Either give it over, or…"

Her pretty eyes blazed. Then, being an obviously intelligent woman, she slapped the phone into his hand. "You're a dick."

Yeah. He probably was. "Thank you." He slipped the phone back into the car and turned, keeping her arm and striding toward the waiting plane. Two males stood outside, neither armed, both watching him carefully. He tuned in his senses. Vampires. Pure vampires—no demon blood. He nodded.

They both wore tan cargo pants, white shirts, and brown boots. Both were tall, but one was at least six-eight. He nodded. "We're your pilots."

Pilots. "I hope you know what you're doing." Ronan eyed the narrow steps leading into the belly of the plane. He gently set Faith in front of him and then followed her up the stairs. The plane had several plush leather seats, with two on either side of an aisle for five rows. A large television took up a wall in the front.

Faith moved and chose a chair by the window, so he sat next to her, extending his feet and crossing his ankles. His palms grew damp, so he flattened them on his dark jeans. His stomach felt like a tremendous hand held it in an inflexible grip.

The pilots jogged up the stairs and into the plane. One of them instantly headed up front, while the other one secured the stairs and shut the door. Without a word, he too disappeared up front.

Ronan felt a change in cabin pressure in his ears. A sealed interior? He cleared his throat and rolled his shoulders.

Faith put her back to the window and faced him. "Scared to fly?"

He cut her a look, keeping his face stoic. "Of course not." What kind of idiot *wasn't* afraid to fly? Again...no wings. "Are you still mad at me?"

The engines flared to life.

His heartbeats increased in number and his ribs ached.

The pilots set the plane in motion.

Jesus. They were going to die. He stiffened.

"Ronan. As soon as we're in the air, you can use the laptop and learn more about the world." Faith slipped her hand beneath his and entwined their fingers. "Flying is much safer than driving a car."

Her hand was cool and delicate in his, so he lightened his hold.

"Good. Now relax your entire body. One thing at a time," she said, her voice soothing.

He breathed in and followed her instructions. The plane sped up and slowly lifted into the air. His gut dropped to his feet. A ringing set up between his ears.

"Breathe," Faith said calmly.

He breathed. In and out. More. They kept climbing and finally leveled off. His entire body felt like he'd gone over a waterfall. "I'm all right," he said, turning toward her. She must be a hell of a doctor. She'd helped him calmly and gently. His heart thumped hard for her. "Thank you."

"No problem." She withdrew her hand, making his fingers ache for another touch. Her light brown eyes were veiled. "Just didn't want you going into a panic attack and ripping apart the plane." Good point. Was that all, though? She'd very naturally offered comfort, when she still didn't trust him. "You're a sweetheart, you are," he murmured.

Spirit flashed in her eyes. "Don't count on it."

He smiled, wanting nothing more than to ease her mind. "All right. Let's review whatever that Kurjan said to you."

She arched one eyebrow. "Take everything you said to me, make it the opposite, and there you go."

He frowned. "Could you be a little more specific?"

"Sure." Pink filled her cheeks as her temper spiked. "You're the Butcher and you have killed many of the Cyst."

He drew air in through his nose, wanting to give her the truth. "They do call me the Butcher, and I have killed many of the Cyst." In ways a woman like her could never imagine and he would never express to her. "What else?"

She swallowed. "*You* were the one contained in a prison dimension, there *are* female Kurjans and female vampires, the Kayrs marking on your palm is just a way to seduce women, and the Cyst are good guys. Monk-like."

Man, she was pretty when riled. Then her words caught him. "Good guys?" He couldn't help the low chuckle that rolled up his throat. "Wow. What a load of crap." He'd learned the expression the previous night, and right now it really fit. "And good ole Dayne brought his kid with him to disarm you." As a strategic move, it was smart. When had the Kurjans gone from being desperate fighters to using subterfuge?

This new world might hold more than a couple surprises.

He focused first on his mate. "I told you the truth. There are no female vampires or Kurjans, but there are female demons, shifters, and witches. The Kurjans do call me the Butcher because I'm good in battle. The Cyst are bad guys, really bad guys, as are the Kurjans as a whole."

She stared at him, clearly not believing a word. If anything, she looked even angrier when he finished talking.

He sighed and held up his palm. "This is the Kayrs marking, and it appears when our mate is near. Period."

Her eyes narrowed.

He leaned in, appreciating it when her pupils widened again. "Do you really think I need to lower myself to using stunts in order to seduce a woman?"

* * * *

Faith stared into his somber eyes, noting the color change once again. The blue and green had melded together into a sizzling and intense mixture. The guy had a point. He was big and strong and handsome in a way that promised multiple orgasms. Would he need to use any sort of ruse? Probably not.

He took her hand again, sending sparks of electricity up her arm, through her chest, and much lower. The ridges of the marking heated against her skin. "Faith. I would not lie to you."

Okay. She tried to reconcile her instincts about him with the knowledge she'd gleaned in the last few hours. "What if neither of you are lying?" she murmured.

His upper lip quirked. "Impossible."

Maybe. "You've been gone about a thousand years, right?" Her mind quickly sorted facts into place.

He nodded.

"Things change and species evolve. What if there are female Kurjans and vampires now?" She leaned toward him, warming to her subject. "History gets changed daily, whether we like it or not. Maybe the Kurjan history is one where you were the bad guy. Where you were the one put in prison and not, um, what's his name?"

"Ulric," Ronan all but growled.

"Right. What if Dayne was taught a different history?" Ronan's hand was warm—too warm. It was hard to concentrate with him touching her, and she had to get a grip on herself. "What if the Cyst have evolved and become true religious leaders? They didn't threaten me or really harm me the other day, if the one was telling the truth about trying to get me out of danger. And you just killed them." At the thought, her skin chilled. She shivered.

Thoughts crossed his rugged face, but they were difficult to read. "That is insane," he said, rather mildly.

"You maintain there are no female Kurjans or vampires?" That was a verifiable difference in their stories. "What if there are both now?" Maybe their species had evolved in the thousand years since Ronan had been on earth.

His eyes lightened.

"What?" she asked.

He glanced down at their entwined fingers. "There's a prophecy. A very old one—ancient. That one day a female vampire will be born, and her choices will dictate our survival. Whether vampires will become extinct." His voice was almost reverent.

Another shiver took Faith. "So it's possible?"

"Just the one female vampire," he said, looking back up at her face. "That's it. No female Kurjans and no other female vampires. Dayne lied to you."

Probably. But she needed to examine what she'd been told from every angle. "The rest of it is possible."

"And this?" Ronan released her, and the marking on his hand almost glowed. "Do you believe him?"

She looked at the marking and tingles exploded again in her abdomen. What was it with that thing? "Say for a second that you're telling the truth, and that's a mating mark. What if the Kurjans have heard an alternate history? That the marks don't really exist?" If the two groups were truly enemies—and there seemed to be no doubt about that—it was totally possible their views of history and of each other were skewed. "Maybe Dayne told the truth as he knew it."

Ronan slowly shook his head. "Not a chance. The Kurjans are evil and always will be. You can't change the nature of a being, sweetheart. They've just begun using lies as well as swords and knives. Maybe."

"He said he was a diplomat," she countered. But she remembered that Dayne had moved gracefully, like a soldier.

Ronan's lip twitched. "He told you he was a diplomat? The leader of the Kurjans?"

She nodded, not liking his amusement. "Yes."

Ronan laughed out loud this time. "Man, he is good. That guy was pure soldier, and now I understand better."

"Understand what?" she asked, goose bumps rising on her arms.

"How I so easily broke his neck," Ronan said, his gaze warming again. "It was an act for your sake. So you'd think he was harmless." He shook his head. "Nice. It was a risk, because I could've killed him. But he banked on the fact that I wouldn't. Or that you would stop me."

What about Drake? He seemed like such a nice kid. So she gathered her courage and met Ronan's gaze evenly. There had to be an explanation that worked for everyone and also let her off the hook for this ridiculous physical reaction to him. He couldn't be evil. "Were you or were you not imprisoned in a different dimension?"

"Yes," he said, his chin lifting. "We created three worlds. The prison one in the middle and two on either side, containing it. My brother and I sacrificed our lives—agreeing to exist in the outside spheres—to make sure Ulric never escaped by fortifying the walls every damn day. Morning and night. He was the bad guy and still is. Period."

"Then how are you here?" she asked, truly wanting to understand.

His gaze moved around as if he too sought an answer. "Somehow my dimension, or sphere, or world—failed. I am unaware of the events leading up to the failure of that world. And I don't know if Quade's broke as well as Ulric's. We have to find those answers, Faith. We must."

He seemed so earnest. So truthful. Maybe a little lost. She cleared her throat. "Even if everything you say is true, you know I'm not going to mate you just because there's a marking on your hand. Right?"

A light she couldn't identify burned in his eyes. "Right."

She swallowed as her throat tightened. "How does it work, anyway?" Darn her curiosity.

He ran his finger along her palm. "Sex, a bite with fangs, and the transfer of the marking. Immortality would be yours."

Immortality? Now, that was appealing. Sort of. "Then I'd never see my parents again."

He shrugged. "Not true. We all die at some point. Some of us just get a few thousand years first. Who wouldn't want that?"

"Have you ever mated before?" she asked, truly wondering what kind of woman would appeal to him. Besides a modern-day doctor.

He gave a slight shake of his head. "Oh. No. One mate only. That's all we get."

Her eyebrows rose as she tried to comprehend. "Seriously? For thousands of years? That must make for a lot of infidelity."

He cocked his head to the side, his gaze searching her face. "No. None. A mate can't touch another member of the opposite sex for any duration without succumbing to a terrible rash. It's called the mating allergy."

Back to crazy-town, apparently. "That can't be true."

Tension rolled off him, filtering around her. "Mate me and find out."

CHAPTER TEN

The landing had been smooth, but Ronan was certainly more relaxed on the ground. Acutely aware of the immortal at her side, Faith sat back in the luxurious town car as they navigated the gridlock of Chicago to a sketchy area of the city. Upon landing, the pilots had ushered them right to the car, which had already been running. The privacy screen was up, so she couldn't get a read on the driver. Couldn't see if he'd help her. "This is kidnapping, you know," she muttered, crossing her arms.

"Aye," Ronan said, craning his neck to look up at a skyscraper. "Incredible."

Aye? "What are you, Irish?" she asked.

"Part of me is, and I spent a lot of time outside of Dublin long ago." He turned away from the window to face her. "Thank you for the use of your laptop on the plane. I studied modern weaponry and security measures. The amount of knowledge available to everyone on the Internet is truly awe-inspiring. In my wildest dreams, I wouldn't have imagined the weapons humans would create. Nuclear and biological warfare concern me."

"As they should," she said. "Stop changing the subject."

"Are you a prepper?"

She frowned. "A what?"

"A prepper. Somebody who preps for doomsday. With hidden food, weapons, medicine." He scratched his head. "I watched a video of some people prepping, and they were training themselves with guns in a forest. Guns may be new to me, but I have to tell you, those men were doing it wrong."

She rubbed her aching temple. "No. I am not a prepper."

He nodded, approval in his gaze. "That is good. You have no need." He looked outside again at the buildings flying by. "I have a concern about privacy in this new paradigm. For now, anyway. Satellites are impressive. Cameras are everywhere."

"For now?" Her head was starting to hurt from her frown, and it didn't seem to be intimidating Ronan, anyway. "What do you mean?"

He faced her fully, and she could actually feel his gaze deep beneath her skin. His scent wrapped around her and even now, she couldn't exactly describe it. Woodsy and comfortable and on edge. The scent was just...him. Intelligence shone in those otherworldly eyes. "It's all temporary. You understand that, true?" he asked.

She shook her head. "What do you mean?"

He swept a broad hand out. "This. The buildings, the cameras, the technology. It's a blip in time. All this won't be everlasting—especially with humans creating such weapons. Land and family and ties and blood last forever. That's all."

"Maybe, maybe not," she said quietly. "I have faith in the future."

"As do I, but we might see the future differently," he said, his gaze wandering her face. "You're still angry. Would you like me to get your sketch pad? Drawing might help you to relax."

She hated that he'd figured that out about her. At the moment, she was more likely to stab him with the pencil than to draw anything interesting. "No. How about you don't ever kidnap me again? Then I'll feel nice and relaxed."

"I couldn't exactly leave you alone since the Kurjans had already found you. You're my mate."

"No," she burst out, "I'm not, damn it. Get that out of your head right now."

His eyes darkened to a glint of green color on battered bluish steel. "I'm a patient male, Doc. But finding you in the presence of the Kurjan leader—if that's who he really was—has greatly depleted my stores. Not to mention the unholy act of flying we just endured. I suggest you hold your tongue."

Hold her tongue? Anger raced through her so quickly her head rang. "Just who the hell do you think you are?" she snapped.

"Your. Mate." He spoke through gritted teeth. "I'm allowing you time to learn what that means and to adapt to this new reality."

"Or what?" She poked him in the chest, telling herself his audacity did nothing but piss her off further. "What exactly is your course of action here, oh-so-patient one?" She poked him harder. "You can't mate the unwilling."

He moved before she could blink.

One second she was in her own seat, and the next she was perched on his lap. One broad hand spread across her upper chest, above her heart, securing her against the muscled arm along her back.

She couldn't move her upper body.

So she kicked out, her boots bouncing harmlessly on the vacated leather seat.

He leaned down until his face was merely an inch from hers.

She stopped breathing.

"Do you really think you'd be unwilling?" he growled.

A tremor started in her lower abdomen and spread out, sensitizing her entire body. "Release me," she whispered. This close, she could see the blue rim around the aqua of his eyes.

"No," he whispered back just as softly. "You need to learn when to stop pushing."

She was so out of her league right now she couldn't see straight. "You can't force me to mate you." How crazy was her life that she was even using those words?

"Force?" His gaze warmed now. The hand across her chest—her entire chest—moved up, and he ran his knuckles along the edge of her jaw. The touch heated her with an electricity that had to be unnatural. Her blood pumped faster through her veins, and the air in her lungs burned. "I would never force you."

Her breasts grew heavy.

He twisted his wrist and slid his thumb across her lower lip.

She could turn her head, but her body's reaction to him kept her immobile. With just his soft touch, she turned into one throbbing mass of need. Nerves she hadn't known existed pulsed and ached. Demanded. Him. There was certainly something between them. Unless all vampire-demon hybrids caused this reaction in women. It was possible. "Pheromones," she muttered.

He smiled, his eyes clearing like the sky after a brutal storm. She stopped thinking, fully entranced.

The car rolled to a stop.

He sighed. "We'll discuss this later." Opening the door to an alley behind a long, dilapidated brick building, he stepped out with her still in his arms and then gently set her down. He shut the car door. "Stay behind me, and if I tell you to run, you do it."

The car took off down the alley, spraying water on each side.

She shivered. The alley was chilly and damp, and mud puddles dotted the entire stretch. In front of them was a gray metallic, very battered, heavy door. Other back doors were visible as well, but most of those at least had a business name above them.

This one was blank.

Ronan scanned the entire area and then focused on the door. He strode forward and grasped the handle, pulling. The door opened with a loud creak.

"This is a bad idea," Faith said, backing away.

Ronan held out a hand. "I can sense vampires inside. No Kurjans."

That was supposed to be comforting? She shook her head.

Ronan's gaze leveled on her. "Come, Faith. It's safe."

She swallowed and looked down the long alley. It was so far to a main street.

"You won't make it," he said, echoing her thoughts. "Now, Faith."

Getting tackled in an alley held little appeal to her. No way could she outrun him. Maybe there'd be help inside the business.

It wasn't as if she had a choice. Glaring at him, she moved closer, ignoring his outstretched hand.

He sighed and clasped her hand anyway, pulling her inside an unlit room. The smell of bleach and booze assailed her.

The door clanged shut, and complete darkness fell.

A gun cocked.

Ronan set her behind him and backed up until she was pressed between his hard body and the door. "Show yourself, vampire," he growled.

The lights came on. The room appeared to be a small entryway with shelves of paper towels, toilet paper, and cleaning supplies on each side. Faith peered around Ronan's huge torso.

Two men stood near the far door, both holding green guns. They were each well over six-feet tall and tough looking. One guy was blond with blue eyes, and the other had sparkling metallic eyes and longish brown hair.

The guy with metallic, colorful eyes studied Ronan and then lowered his gun, rushing forward for a hug that sounded like a tackle. "It's you. Shit. It's really you," he said, clapping Ronan on the back hard enough to echo throughout the entire room. "I'm glad to see you, but…"

Ronan hugged the guy back and then pushed him. "Benny. I never thought I'd see you again."

The emotion in his tone caught Faith around the throat. She sidled out from behind him.

Benny's eyebrows rose. "You brought a girl."

"My mate." Ronan grasped her hand and slowly drew her forward. "Dr. Faith Cooper, please meet Benjamin Henry Reese. One of my oldest friends."

Benny held out a hand the size of a dinner platter. "Mate? No kidding. Hi."

Faith accepted the handshake that swallowed her up to the wrist, grateful the giant was gentle. This close, the metallic colors in his eyes turned green and black. Fascinating. "Um, hello." Now probably wasn't the time to dispute the whole mate issue.

Benny looked her up and down while pumping her hand. "Wow. It's nice to meet you. A mate. Man, you have a lot to explain, Ronan." He grinned.

Ronan gently pulled her away. "As do you."

Benny sobered. "Yeah. Good point." He jerked his head toward the blond guy. "Ivar Kjeidsen. He was Igor's brother, and we swore him in as a Seven upon the Viking's death. He lived through the ceremony. I'm thinking there must be something genetic about it, since more than a couple of you have had family members survive."

A real Viking? And wait a minute. Survive? "How many people live through your Seven ceremony?" Faith asked.

Benny faltered. "Not many. Bad percentage. Talk for later, actually. Anyway. Ronan, Ivar."

Ronan reached to shake Ivar's hand. "My condolences on your brother's death. He was a fine warrior and an even better friend." Raw emotion lumbered in his voice.

"Thank you," Ivar said, his tone low. "Igor spoke highly of you. Very."

Benny and Ivar shared an odd look.

"What?" Ronan asked, taking Faith's hand. She allowed him to keep it, glad of an ally in this odd new world. These guys were freakin' huge, and there was an energy all around that she could feel. Definitely odd and… what? Supernatural?

Benny sighed. "Let's get you all caught up on the world as it is today."

"I've been researching on the Internet but have much knowledge still to seek." Ronan's tone was a low rumble. "I must find my family."

Benny opened the far door. "Yeah. We're gonna need vodka for this talk. A lot of it."

CHAPTER ELEVEN

Ronan ignored the unease prickling down his back and took a seat in a booth at the far end of the dark establishment, settling Faith inside against the wall. Tables were strewn throughout, and many bottles lined mirrored shelves behind a long, handcrafted wooden bar. At this early hour, only a couple of hunched-over drinkers sat toward the door, so no threats loomed near. The place smelled of alcohol and sweat. Just like the taverns of his youth. "Nice place."

"Thank you," Ivar said, sitting across from him and next to Benny, motioning for a waitress.

A young lass hurried over with a bottle of Tsarskaya Gold vodka, narrow glasses, and a plate of pickled cucumbers next to small open-faced sandwiches.

Ivar poured four shots and handed them out. "Many of my family were Russian—distant family, really. Vodka is a good way to celebrate and plan." He held a glass up. "*Za zda-ro-vye.*"

"To your health," Ronan replied automatically, tipping his head back and downing the alcohol while the others did the same. Delicious. Ah, he'd missed alcohol. Then he took the traditional piece of pickled cucumber and bit in, his focus narrowing, and his heart already aching with the sure pain to come. "Give me the bad news, Ben. I felt deaths through our connections, and since they're not here..."

Benny kept his gaze, his eyes somber. "Jacer died in 1710."

Hearing the words was like a boot to the gut. His biological brother—the middle one. The one they'd left on earth along with four other of the Seven. Ronan absorbed the pain and allowed the rawness to cut into every nerve. He'd been grieving for centuries, but hearing the confirmation was like slicing open an old wound and letting it bleed again. Somehow, even though he hadn't wanted to admit it, he'd known Jacer was one of the fallen. "How did he die?" The words came out hoarse.

"War," Ivar said simply, pouring four more shots. "One of many between the immortal forces. He was killed by the Cyst general, Omar, who we've been seeking since. Even though the Cyst didn't participate in the last war, Omar came hunting us. Used the war and confusion to get to us. The fucker has gone underground."

Just the name sent Ronan's fury into a raw burn. "I should've killed him before entering the shield." He'd fought Omar's troops more than once, and he'd wanted nothing more than to cut off the head of the snake by killing the Cyst general. He wasn't the leader, but he was the head soldier for the Cyst. The bastard was pure evil and enjoyed the killing.

Ivar shook his head, anger burning in his gaze. "Timing was too important, as I've learned. We will find Omar. I give you my word."

"Agreed," Ronan said, studying this Viking descendant he'd never met. One who'd also lost a biological brother in addition to shield brothers. Igor had been a good warrior. Ronan took his shot of alcohol. The time to grieve would have to come later. "To fallen brothers. All of them."

Ivar lifted his chin, sharing the pain in his eyes. Grief filled the air around them. "Our brothers."

They drank again.

Faith tipped back her drink, watching quietly. Beneath the table, she took Ronan's free hand, her soft touch settling him. Easing his pain just enough that he could breathe again. "I'm sorry about your brother," she said. "And yours." She nodded at Ivar.

Ivar smiled. "Thank you."

Jacer dead. The idea was unthinkable. "My line has died out here?" Ronan asked quietly. There were no Kayrs members protecting the world?

"No," Benny said. "There's a shit-ton of you assholes running around." Then he grinned the smart-ass smile Ronan remembered well. "Jacer had two kids who died in the last war. But one of his sons, Hunter, had five boys before moving to the great beyond. The oldest, Dage, is King of the Realm now."

Five boys? Hope leaped into Ronan's chest. He had family. Thank God. Jacer would live on in his descendants.

Benny's eyes twinkled. "They live on a lake in Idaho."

Ronan straightened. He didn't care where Idaho might be. "Are they good warriors?"

"Of course," Benny said, pouring more shots. "Was there ever a doubt about that?"

Excellent point. Ronan downed his next shot, noting that Faith was wobbling a little after her third. "You don't have to keep up, sweetheart." Russians never left a bottle with alcohol in it, and if Ivar wanted to drink the Russian way, they'd drink until it was empty. Those Vikings always could drink, and Ivar seemed in his element. "Slow down," Ronan murmured to his mate.

She just blinked.

Okay. So he had family. He adjusted his current strategy accordingly as he gathered more knowledge. Now was for intel. Fighting would come later. "What about the second shield or dimension? Since mine shattered, we can assume Quade's will as well. Then the prison shall fail—and Ulric will return."

"Could've already happened." Benny shook his head. "We didn't even know yours had broken until you sent that message, and here you are."

Ivar poured more drinks, leaving Faith's empty this time. "I have a line on a couple of physics experts. It's time we figured out exactly how the ritual created those other dimensions, and why they broke. I'll take care of that issue. You two deal with the others."

"Others?" Ronan asked.

Benny sighed. "Besides Jacer and Igor, we lost Zylo Kyllwood in the last war. The Seven is still down two members, and we need to get up to full speed."

Having the shield brotherhood complete had to be their top priority. "Did Kyllwood have progeny?" Ronan asked, his heart taking another hit. Too many of his brothers had died while he'd been trapped in another damn dimension.

"Three nephews," Benny said. "One is leading the demon nation, so he's out. The middle one, Sam...is destined for something else. I'd like to have the youngest one, a hell of a fighter and rather gifted. Name is Logan." Benny tipped back another shot. "Best friends with one Garrett Kayrs, who has a power I've never seen before. Has barely come into it. I want them both to round out the Seven."

Kayrs? Ronan straightened. "You want someone else from my family?" Hadn't his family sacrificed enough for the Seven? Perhaps it was time to protect Jacer's descendants.

"Yes. Garrett is involved in Realm business and has ties to every other species on the planet. He's intelligent, well trained, and tough as I've ever seen." Ivar sat back, his gaze earnest. "Even among immortals, he's something unique. Special. He should be part of the Seven. I feel he'd survive the ritual."

Then he would be in the minority. "If he's a Kayrs, he should be surrounded by family right now as we speak," Ronan countered. "The existence of the Seven isn't known to anybody else, and we have to keep it that way." He wasn't going into details with Faith there. Sometimes values had to be sacrificed for the end result. Whether one liked it or not.

"I'm sure the kid can keep a secret," Ivar countered. "He's been through a war already."

Benny poured yet more shots. "I have dossiers on Garrett and Logan, as well as several other candidates, and we can vote until we agree on who to invite and who might want to risk their lives by joining us. Or attempting to, anyway. We have to get them in place now that the child has been born."

Ronan stopped breathing. He sat back. "She's been born? The female vampire?" Were the legends really true? Was it possible?

"Yeppers," Benny said, throwing his head back for another shot of vodka. "Name is Hope Kayrs-Kyllwood."

Heat and then chills swept Ronan. His heart thudded. Hard. "She's a Kayrs?" he whispered reverently. Not once had he even considered the possibility. The prophesied female vampire, the one and only, shared *his* blood?

"Yes," Ivar said, remaining perfectly still, much as his brother always had. "Her birth must've somehow triggered the destruction of your dimensional bubble. Correct?"

A female vampire. That would do it. "Possibly," Ronan said, his belly warming from his seventh shot of vodka. "I truly do not know." Nor did it matter. She was alive. Legends were true.

Benny poured yet another round, this time including Faith again. Apparently the vampire thought she'd had enough of a reprieve. She sat quietly, watching and listening, her eyes a little unfocused. "Hope is a cute little thing too. Turned seven years old just a few months ago," Benny said.

The special one was just a child. Ronan shook his head to regain his bearings. "This means we can take down Ulric. Finally." So far, the prophets had been correct. A female vampire had been born. Were there any updated prophesies since she'd become a reality? Ronan blinked again. The vodka was taking effect, and he still had not acquired all the details. "Have you found the Keys?"

"No," Benny said shortly. "But since the female vampire is alive, so are they. We will find them."

Faith finished her shot and sagged a little against Ronan. "Keys are alive? How is that? Huh?"

Good lord. He'd let her get blotto. Gently, he removed the shot glass from her hand. "Yes. They're women with Enchanted blood, and we must find all three of them." He tugged her close, and she let him, closing her eyes. Raising his glass, he looked at his friends. He had expected to be dead when Ulric escaped. Destiny had other plans, apparently. "It's time."

Finally.

CHAPTER TWELVE

Faith awoke slowly in a comfortable bed, her brain fuzzy, her temples aching. Vaguely, she remembered heading upstairs and taking a hot shower. Her hair had dried and she blew it out of her face. She stretched against the smooth sheets and halted quickly. Something hard and hot was at her back. Her eyelids flipped open as she came fully awake.

She was tucked into Ronan's body, her butt to his groin, her back to his chest. One of his heavy arms was banded around her waist, and his nose was pressed against her nape as he slept. Even fully relaxed behind her, he felt like solid rock.

Surrounded by lava.

Man, he gave off heat. She couldn't remember a time she'd been so toasty warm.

She didn't recall coming to bed. So much for trying to go toe to toe with vampires when it came to drinking. Or demons. Or hybrids. Whatever Ronan was, he could outdrink her. Not much of a surprise. At least she still had on her T-shirt and panties. Wait a minute. She looked around an antique-riddled bedroom to see her bra, jeans, and shoes on a settee. He'd taken off her bra.

She reached for his arm to push it away and his hold tightened. "You're awake," she muttered.

"Humph." He snuggled closer into her, his lips pressing against her sensitive nape.

"You removed my bra," she said, trying not to shiver. Nope. A shiver took her, right from her neck to her toes. How did he *do* that?

"Figured you shouldn't wear it to bed," he murmured sleepily, his lips moving against her skin. "I didn't look."

Need rolled right through her, just from his mouth, and she tamped it down. He didn't look? Really? Right. "Then how did you get it off?"

"I snapped the ties at your shoulders and pulled it down with your jeans. Broke it."

"That's not okay." She jabbed an elbow back into his rib cage.

"Woman," he protested, pulling her closer into his impossibly packed body. "No hitting in the morning."

Desire caught her around the throat and slid through her veins. She had to get away from him. "Let me go." She started to struggle.

He sighed and released her. "You were a great deal more pliable last night."

"Last night I passed out," she countered, scooting to the other side of the bed. The sheets chilled her and she curled her knees up.

"Yeah. You were quiet and nice. I may feed you vodka more often." Amusement filtered through his tone.

She rolled over to face him, ready to give him hell. One look and the words froze in her mouth. A shadow covered his angled jaw, and sleep had tousled his black hair. His eyes had turned an intriguing greenish-blue, adding a mystical element to his hard-cut features. The sheet had been pushed to his waist, revealing his bare and muscled chest.

Her mouth started to water. It just wasn't fair. Nobody should look that good in the morning. Ever.

He watched her, not moving, a predator completely at home in his own skin. "I'll buy you a new bra."

"With what?" she ground out, her skin way too tight all of a sudden.

"Turns out my friends invested my holdings through the years," he said. "I can buy you anything you desire."

The word *desire*. Hearing it from his lips sent her system into overdrive. She shifted, just a little, and her thighs rubbed together. Sparks shot through her lower body. A moan almost escaped her, but she shoved it down. How was this possible? She was a doctor, for goodness' sake. Sure, there were pheromones, but this was over the top.

This was unreal.

His nostrils flared and the green turned to blue in his stunning eyes. "Faith." He slowly reached out and slid the hair off her cheek. "So pretty."

She couldn't breathe. For years, she'd taken care of her sister after their parents had died. She'd worked hard, she'd gone to school, she'd become educated and strived to be the best in her field. Financially, she was independent. But here, in this bed with him, she felt...feminine. Female and somehow *not* in control.

His thumb caressed her cheekbone. "Stop thinking so hard," he rumbled.

"I'm a scientist. A doctor," she said.

"I know." He caressed down to her jawline, his gaze following his warm fingers.

Such a simple touch, yet it stole her ability to think clearly. But she tried anyway. "I don't believe in fate or coincidence. In soul mates or even...mates." It all contradicted her entire belief system.

A smile played on his generous mouth. "I do believe in fate and soul mates. Definitely in *my* mate." He cupped her jawline with warmth and gentle strength. "There's probably a scientific explanation for all of it, and I'm sure you'll figure it out at some point. Maybe in a thousand years or two."

Was he laughing at her? She pulled her face away and studied him. She read amusement and indulgence in his expression. "I could figure it out," she answered evenly, meaning every word. "Doesn't mean I'll choose to do so." However, one thing had been eating at her since meeting with Dayne. "I think you can help my sister, and if you will, I'll do whatever you want." It was an easy deal to make.

His head lifted and his eyes flared. "I'll not blackmail you into mating me, Faith Cooper."

"Then help my sister."

"If her brain is injured to the point that she cannot consent, she cannot be helped." His wrist twisted, and he grasped her chin between his thumb and forefinger. "You will choose to mate me, and it will be for no other reason than you want to be *my mate*."

The audacity of the man. "Want to bet?" she burst out.

"Absolutely," he said instantly. "Whoever wins gets to name our firstborn."

Her breath heated. "You're impossible." An image of a cute little boy with curly dark hair and bright greenish-blue eyes flashed through her mind and then disappeared. Now she was becoming fanciful. She lifted her arm and dislodged his hold on her chin.

His hand dropped to the bedspread. "Just because you can't explain something doesn't mean it isn't true." Then he grasped her wrist and tugged her slightly toward him, flattening her palm over his thorax. "You feel my heart. For centuries, even when I thought I'd sacrificed my life, this has beat for you. Every second, of every minute, of every day, of every year…I was trapped in that bubble."

His heart pumped steadily beneath her palm. A part of her, *waaaay* deep down, wanted to believe him. To fall right into his fantasy. But he really believed this, and it didn't make sense. Would she be taking advantage of him by pretending? Just for a minute?

"Ah," he murmured, tugging her closer. "You're tempted. I can see it."

Of course she was tempted. He was the sexiest thing in this or in any other dimension, and it made sense that he was something other than human. But the fact that she was tempted didn't mean anything more than he was hot…and she was aroused. "Ronan. I don't want to hurt you," she murmured.

He paused. His head lifted. Those sexy lips parted slightly. "Explain."

Warmth infused her face. "I'm attracted to you, and you're incredibly alluring. But I don't believe in your ideals, and I don't want to, um, lead you on."

"Lead me on," he repeated. "I am unfamiliar with this idiom."

Her blush intensified until her cheeks ached. "I don't want you to read emotion into this situation. To think or believe there's more here than there is."

"What is here?" he asked, his lips twitching again.

"Attraction," she burst out. "I know you feel it too." Right? Man, she hoped so.

His wide hands encircled her biceps, and he pulled her while rolling onto his back. She landed easily on top of him, and his heat pushed right into her muscles. "I believe I understand," he said.

Her mouth gaped open. It was like lying on a solid rock that had been warmed by the sun all day. A rock with an obvious erection. "Ronan, I think I've confused you."

His smile made him look years younger. "You're the one who is confused." His command of contractions in his speech was becoming evident.

Only her thin panties and the boxer briefs she'd purchased for him separated them. Her knees naturally fell on either side of his hips, and she balanced herself with her palms on his muscular chest. "I'm not confused," she countered, her mind fuzzing despite her words.

He flattened his palm above her knee and caressed up her thigh. "I believe what you are saying is that you'd like to explore this attraction we have without causing me heartache?"

Was that her intention? Why did she suddenly feel like she'd walked right into a trap? "I'm admitting there is an attraction," she murmured, her panties getting damp. "I'm not agreeing that we should act on it." Right? Man, she couldn't think. He was just too…male. Yeah. Too male.

"Hmm." His other hand went to her other knee and traced a similar pattern until he clasped both her thighs. "I've been trying to ease you into reality."

Forget reality. Those hands were heating her legs and entire lower body. A pulse set up between her legs. If she moved just a little, she could rub against him. But then it'd be over. She'd be lost and she knew it. "I don't need easing," she said, trying to track the conversation.

"I'm beginning to realize that," he agreed. His eyes cleared. "You think I'm simple."

She blinked. "No, I—just—"

He chuckled, his body moving deliciously against hers. "You do." Wonderment now filled his voice. "This is truly unexpected."

"No, you're not simple," she rushed to say, not wanting to hurt his feelings. "It's just, to believe in fate and magic and all of that." He was from a time long ago, when they probably still thought the world was flat. "There's an innocence to such beliefs."

He coughed, paused, and then laughed out loud. The rich sound warmed the entire room. "Innocence? You believe me to be innocent?"

She couldn't find the right words, so she just started babbling. "No, it's just the mating thing and all this talk of one true love. I mean, have you waited for your mate?" She couldn't take advantage.

His eyebrows rose. "Have I waited?"

"Yes," she whispered, feeling his dick pulse between her legs.

"For sex," he said slowly, his gaze penetrating hers.

She nodded.

He had dimples. Who knew? "No, Faith. I lived for nearly four hundred years before sacrificing myself into the shield. I did not wait."

She breathed out. All right. "I don't want to ruin anything for you, Ronan." Sure, he was mistaken about a lot of things, including the Kurjans, probably. But he'd just discovered that his brother and a couple of good friends had died. "You understand that the physical aspects of being together don't always include an emotional component?"

His eyes softened. "Yes, Doc. I understand that we can fuck like rutting wolves without professing undying love."

There was something indulgent about his gaze now. "You're making fun of me."

"No." He lost the smile. "Most people were afraid of me. Or at least cautious around me. To find a woman who's worried about my, ah, long-gone innocence is different. I do like your sense of freedom around me, and yet, your naïveté concerns me."

Her naïveté? If anybody was naive, it was the vampire. "My eyes are wide open," she said. "You don't have to worry about me. I can take care of myself."

"It's as if we are speaking two different languages using the same words," he murmured.

"I don't understand." Her nipples hardened beneath the T-shirt even as she tried to have a normal conversation.

His gaze caught sight of her breasts and his eyes flared, turning a startling green.

Whoa.

He lifted his glowing gaze to meet her eyes. "You believe your view of the world is correct, and I believe mine is."

She nodded, her body rioting in a craving that actually hurt. "Agreed."

"My view has existed for several thousand years," he said, his hands tightening. "Your view, that of modern science, has existed for how long? Maybe two hundred years?"

He might be making some sense.

"How about we reach an agreement. We can explore this attraction, as you put it, without trying to influence each other about our worldview? Once?" he asked.

She tilted her head. "Once?"

He nodded. "Yes. I can give you once, if you like. With no talk or expectation regarding the future."

"Then what?" she asked, already imagining what it would be like with no clothes between them.

He studied her, obviously searching for the right words. "I'm a Kayrs. A leader of two species more dangerous than you can possibly imagine."

She stretched against him, unable to help herself. "What's your point?"

"When I want something, Faith, I get it. Always." He pushed her thighs back, upsetting her balance, and she fell flat on top of him. Faster than a thought, he rolled over until she was trapped beneath him.

She opened her mouth in surprise and he swept in, taking her mouth hard. Fast and deep, he kissed her, stealing every objection she might've made.

Her body went from slow heat to full burn in seconds.

He lifted up, his gaze intense, his huge body bracketing hers and pressing her into the mattress. "Say yes," he ordered.

Oh, hell yes. Just once. As she opened her mouth to agree, an explosion ripped through the morning, blowing a hole in the entire wall.

She screamed.

CHAPTER THIRTEEN

Ronan went from playful to deadly in a second, wrenching Faith to the side and leaping between her and the gaping hole in the wall. They occupied a guest room on the third floor, so he had not expected an attack from the east.

Bricks crumbled down and wires hung haphazardly. What the hell had happened? Smoke billowed through, and he moved closer to the devastation, looking down. Rain blew in to cover his legs. The alleyway below was quiet and empty. He moved closer, searching for the threat through the smoke and dust. What had blown a hole in the building?

"Ronan!" Faith jumped from the bed, landing hard against him in an attempted tackle.

He caught her and instinctively leaped away from the window, where she wanted him to go. "What?" He swung her around, putting himself between danger and her.

Something clinked on the floor, shot from the building across the street.

"Run," Faith bellowed, fighting to climb off him. "Grenade!"

He tucked her closer and lunged for the door, bursting into the hallway and running down the stairs. Their room exploded and heat flashed against his back. He kept running, nearly slamming into Benny on the second-floor landing.

"They're coming through the front," Benny said tersely, handing Ronan a gun. "Point this and squeeze the trigger."

Ronan shifted Faith from his front onto his back. "Got it." He'd researched weapons the night before after having put Faith to bed, not only on the Internet but on private Realm websites. Immortal guns shot lasers that turned into steel upon impact. "Is it the Kurjans?"

"Dunno," Benny said. "Follow me." He was bare to the waist but had obviously yanked on some jeans and boots. He hustled down another set of stairs, leading them into the bar, where Ivar was waiting by the bottles of liquor with a shotgun in his hands. He lifted a divider and kicked open a door near the cash register. "Let's go."

The front and back doors blew open, and soldiers wearing all black rushed inside, guns pointed. At least three from each entry point fanned out, with more running boots sounding from outside. They'd brought an incredible force.

Ivar hit a lever beneath the booze, and metal-enforced walls dropped from the ceiling, blocking both exits and preventing more soldiers from entering.

Smart.

Ronan ran for the bar and set Faith behind it, pressing the gun into her hand. She appeared fragile in her thin T-shirt and panties, her long legs bare and vulnerable. Fury gripped him. What he wouldn't give for his ability to teleport her to safety before returning to fight. Then he turned and vaulted over the bar, tackling two of the enemy to the ground. Their faces and heads were covered with black material, leaving only their eyes visible.

Gunfire pattered and bottles exploded, sending glass in every direction. Faith screamed.

That sound settled Ronan into killing mode. It had been centuries since he'd really fought, so he went silent inside and let training and instinct rule.

The first guy punched him in the neck, and Ronan clipped him on the wrist, sending the weapon spinning beneath a table.

Then he lifted a knee and kicked the other soldier's weapon just as the guy was beginning to rise. The guy kicked Ronan beneath the chin, and he flew back to smash into a barstool. Pain crashed through his shoulder and his temper exploded.

Growling, his fangs sliding down, he straightened to his full height.

Benny fought two guys at the back door, while Ivar battled the two near the front.

These assholes were his to take care of. He rolled his neck and steeled his shoulders, moving forward.

The first guy rushed him, removing a knife from his waist and striking out. Pain slashed down Ronan's left arm. He pivoted and ducked, throwing the soldier over his shoulder with a hard push. The soldier spun in the air, careening into the metal barricade and denting it with a loud bang.

The second soldier yanked a gun from his pocket, and Ronan kicked it away with his bare foot before it could fire. His knees weakened and he growled again at his lack of strength. The soldier attacked, wrapping Ronan in a bear hug and taking him down to the floor. Fury lit sparks behind Ronan's eyes and he clapped both hands against the asshole's ears. The guy snarled, his protective mask remaining in place.

The punch to the jaw came from out of nowhere and Ronan saw stars.

Something battered the front protective wall, and it cracked.

"We have to get out of here," Ivar bellowed as the sound of the fight continued.

The guy on Ronan grabbed a knife from his back pocket and lifted his arm. Ronan punched up, nailing the guy in the throat. Then he struck again, sweeping out, and rolled them over. Several hard punches, and Ronan broke the guy's throat. Temporarily.

He staggered to his feet.

An explosion ripped from the back, and the rear shield began to crumple.

Faith yelled and Ronan turned to see her hitting an attacker with a serving tray. Her face was fierce, and in her limited clothing, she looked both fragile and determined. She grabbed a bottle of vodka, smashing it against the soldier's head. Glass cut into her bare thigh and blood spattered.

Fury lit him and he ignored his waning vision, leaping across the space and taking the attacker down. Faith followed him, shattering a bottle of rum against the guy's ear. The mask took most of the brunt, and the male punched up, hitting Ronan in the mouth. Blood burst from his lip.

Damn it.

He drew on his remaining strength and punched down with all his might, crushing the guy's larynx. The injury would only keep him down for a minute or two, but it was long enough.

Shoving himself unsteadily up, Ronan grasped Faith's liquor-covered hand and pulled her through the doorway with Ivar and Benny on their heels. The door shut behind them, and Ivar ran forward, taking the lead. They reached stairs and started running down. Ronan released Faith so he could balance. His vision was black now, and he was making his way by sound alone.

The air cooled.

"Where are we?" Benny asked from behind Ronan, his boots loud on the concrete.

"Safety tunnels," Ivar said as it became pitch-black.

Benny coughed. "You fuckin' think of everything, Ivar."

That was true. Ivar was apparently the planner in the group. Good. They needed one. Ronan kept his senses tuned into his mate. She kept pace in her bare feet, not complaining, her breath a series of soft gasps.

She'd bounced back incredibly well from being kissed to having the world explode around her. Pride swept him, even though his feet had gone numb. Fate had chosen well for him. Faith Cooper was an incredible woman.

Ivar held up a hand. "All stop for a second."

They came to a halt, everyone breathing heavy.

Ivar fumbled around loudly and something creaked. Light ignited and he handed back a flashlight to Benny and then a couple to Faith and Ronan. "Stay right behind me. These tunnels are old, and I've altered many of them through the years as escape routes. The paths twist and turn, and if you go the wrong way, we won't find you. There are also some booby traps along the way."

Of course there were. Ivar's planning abilities were impressive. Igor would be proud of this younger brother of his.

The air was damp and musty, and something skittered in the distance.

Faith pressed against Ronan. He took her hand again. "It'll be okay, Doc. Trust me."

She shivered.

Anger took him and he shoved it away, needing to concentrate. They'd dared to attack his mate. "Who were they?" he asked, launching himself into motion behind Ivar.

"Kurjans, not Cyst," Ivar replied tersely, speeding up. "Could you not sense them?"

"No," he said quietly, keeping his flashlight pointed to the uneven ground. His voice echoed off old rock walls. "I'm not at full strength for anything right now." Something pounded above them on the tunnel door. The sense of urgency took him. "How did they find us?"

"A million ways," Ivar replied, taking a sharp left turn. "Probably satellite. Followed the plane and then your car. Chances were they had to wait for satellite pictures and didn't locate us until this morning."

Satellite. He was really starting to hate human technology. "They know who we are. The Seven."

"They know you and probably now Ivar," Benny returned, his voice hushed. "And of course, Quade in the bubble."

"What about Adare?" Ronan asked, tucking Faith closer, increasing his speed. Why wouldn't his eyes work? "Have you called in the Highlander?" He'd love to see his old friend, who'd descended from a dangerous line of demon hybrids in the Scottish

Highlands. He had talents nobody else on the planet could imagine, and he was needed until Ronan regained his full strength. Hell. Adare was always needed.

Ivar took another sharp left turn. The sounds in the distance dissipated. "We haven't worked with Adare in four centuries. He disappeared after losing his mate in one of our worst wars."

The news was a blow to the chest. "He was mated?" Ronan whispered, and even the words hurt. The pain of losing a mate was incomprehensible. Unimaginable, really.

"More like betrothed and not mated yet," Benny returned, his voice grim. "Kurjan invasion two wars ago. Devastating."

Ronan's ears rang. The cut on his arm wouldn't heal. He swayed.

"Ronan?" Faith asked.

Ah, shit. Darkness completely descended across his vision. "I'm fine. Just experiencing residual vision problems."

"You took several hard impacts to the cerebral cortex area of your brain." She kept his hand and ran in front of him. "I can see to follow Ivar." Her voice was brisk and determined. Somehow soothing.

Aye. His mate. A healer, a fighter, a sweetheart. She'd almost become his lover before the wall had blown apart. For that interruption alone, he'd kill the Kurjan soldiers.

He let her lead him, keeping his still-working senses tuned in for threats. The ceiling rippled with an explosion. They were coming.

His bare feet scraped rock and he winced. Good. The feeling was coming back. But his heart slowed. The ringing between his ears intensified and his temples began to pound with a rabid pain that had him wincing.

He fumbled and tried to regain his footing. His feet slipped out from under him, and he released Faith so he wouldn't pull her as he went down. Hard.

Then...nothing.

CHAPTER FOURTEEN

Faith sat on an opulent sofa and smoothed the hair back from Ronan's strong face, her hand trembling now that she was coming down from the adrenaline rush. Ronan's boxers were torn and bruises covered his torso and one leg. They both needed clothing. She tried to tug her T-shirt down to cover herself and gave up.

Benny huffed in the corner of the perfectly decorated living room, rolling his neck back and forth after having carried Ronan through the tunnels and up an elevator to a luxurious penthouse. He'd grunted and complained the entire time, asking nobody in particular if Ronan had been eating bricks in the shield world.

"Are you sure they can't follow us?" she asked, her skin chilled.

Ivar glanced over from the wide wall of windows that looked over the Chicago skyline. "I'm certain."

She swallowed. Several times he'd somehow moved walls of solid rock with his palm print, and they'd shifted back into place the second it was clear. The guy had created an impressive series of escape routes, and he looked so much like a Viking from days gone by. His mind would be fascinating to study. "This is your penthouse?"

"No. It's in Adare's name," Ivar said, overwhelming a floral settee as he sat down. "Even though he dropped off the Earth, we invested his holdings for him. The Cyst don't know he's one of the Seven, so many of our warehouses are in his name as well."

That made sense. She rubbed a bruise on her arm and leaned up to examine Ronan's head. "I don't see a contusion."

Benny glanced at Ivar. "He's not okay."

"No." Ivar turned from the window and crossed his arms. Mottled bruises covered the right side of his face, and he was favoring his left leg. "He essentially died when he sacrificed himself, and who knows the kind of damage that could do to a guy? While immortals can usually heal anything, sometimes an injury lasts."

A bullet hole in Benny's bleeding neck slowly closed. "Especially when we're dealing with dimensional travel and physic-altering rituals. Who knows what the witches did to create the shields and the prison world."

Faith rubbed Ronan's arm, unable to stop touching him. "He still fought those two guys off."

Benny grinned and cracked open his split lip. He winced. "Aren't you sweet, defending him?"

She frowned.

"He'd be a hell of a lot stronger if he mated," Benny said, not losing the smile. "Just sayin'. That would speed up the process."

Heat flew into Faith's face. "You are a rogue, Benjamin Reese," she murmured.

His smile widened. "You are not the first to call me that, lady."

"I wasn't one of the original Seven, but I've heard the legends about Ronan." Ivar sighed and moved forward to sit on a matching chair. "A thousand years ago, he would've plowed through those attackers like a bowling ball. Ripping off heads and limbs."

Benny nodded fondly. "We could've sat in the corner and toasted him each time. Man, I miss those days."

Ivar's nostrils flared. "He'll regain his strength—he has to for the fight to come. Maybe we should start feeding him protein. A lot of it."

"That would help to rebuild muscle," Benny said thoughtfully. "It's the power I'm worried about. Where is it? He's shown none, which is odd for a vampire. Even an injured one."

"I could take both of you assholes," Ronan said evenly, opening his eyes and shoving himself to a seated position.

Faith scooted down to give him room. "How are you?"

"Apparently being discussed," he said, giving Benny a look. "I'll be fine—and protein is a good idea, as is mating. I'm starving... for both." He rubbed at the cut on his arm, coating his hand with blood. "I require a shower. Are you sure we're safe here?" His coloring was still pale, but his eyes burned a deep green. Tension emanated from him.

"Why do your eyes change color?" Faith asked.

He blinked. "They always have. Vampires normally have two eye colors. One normal and the other for extreme situations. I've always had three. Blue and/or green, normally."

"And the other color?" she asked, her breath catching in a funny way.

He lifted a shoulder. "If you see it, you see it. Might be gone. Who knows what changes happened to me in that shield world." Grunting, he moved to his feet. "Ben? Order food, would you? Ivar? Please reach out and fucking find Adare. We need all of us in one place to plan. The enemy is coming for us and they'll be searching for the Keys, so it's time to go on offense instead of defense."

Faith turned to him. "I think we should move my sister somewhere else. I have security on her, but..."

Ronan's chin dropped. "There was a time I could order an army to her bed. Before I became one of the Seven." He looked toward Benny. "You?"

Benny shook his head. "The one downfall of going dark and being in a secret society."

Faith paused. "Why are you guys secret?"

Tension rolled through the room, coming from all three of them. And silence. Not a word.

Finally, Benny cleared his throat and continued his thought. "I have no army, although I do have family and some friends. I could reach out and get your sister security for a limited time, but nothing long-term."

"Then we'll need to fetch her. It's too early to reach out to possible allies." Ronan wobbled slightly and then looked around, his frown darkening. More bruises began to purple along his neck. "Shower?"

"I'll take you," Faith said, standing in case he needed assistance. "Benny showed me around while you were out."

Benny looked up. "After your shower, we'll go to headquarters. We've created one for the Seven when the time came."

"The time has definitely come," Ivar said soberly, cutting a look toward Benny. His ribs loudly snapped back into place and he winced. "We'll figure out how to fetch the doc's sister from there."

Ronan ignored them and looked toward the door, where a hallway extended in either direction.

Faith moved ahead of him, resisting the temptation to put a shoulder beneath his good arm. The vampire might try to break it off. She'd dealt with tough-guy patients before. Part of this was ego and the other part a fear he'd probably never admit. What if the damage to his body was permanent? Would their mating really heal him? Man. No pressure there.

She led the silent immortal down the hallway and into a guest bedroom with en suite bath decorated in calm blues and greens. "Why do they call you a vampire instead of a demon?"

He paused inside the bathroom, looking around.

She moved into a stone-tiled shower with no door and turned the corner, flipping the faucet to hot and avoiding the spray. Then she stepped out as he was dropping the boxers. Heat infused her face, and she worked very hard to keep her gaze above his chest.

He rubbed a bruise across his ribs. "It's faster to say than vampire-demon, and I'm more vampire than demon. Each immortal only has one true form." Then he shrugged. "They could say *hybrid*, but that's the nickname we gave Quade, for some reason."

"That makes sense." She itched to help him into the shower but knew better.

He sighed. "Also, I look more like a vampire than a demon. Purebred demons have very blond hair and black eyes. The males appear deadly and the females beautiful. My mother was stunning." His eyes darkened.

It hit her then. Although his loved ones had passed on centuries ago, he'd just learned of their deaths, so it was all fresh. "You haven't had a chance to grieve," she said softly.

He quietly scoffed. "There will be no time until we find the Keys and destroy Ulric for good. We must discover if he's free yet." He cracked his neck. "And if Quade is free, and if he survived."

There he was, back to his strategic plan. It made sense he was worried about his other brother. She ran a hand down his good arm. "You survived the shield collapsing, so there's no reason to believe that Quade won't be all right. We'll figure out a way to track him down. First, you need to get your strength back."

He studied her. "How?"

"I don't know." She forced a smile. "But I'm a doctor, a good one, and this is just another physical mystery. I deal with those all the time, and I'll discover how to help you." It probably would just take time and rest, which they didn't have right now. "Trust me."

"I do." His eyes morphed into the mingled blue and green, somehow darkening in his pale face. Then his gaze dropped to her shirt. "You have blood on you."

She glanced down. "Right." It was his blood, probably. "I'll need a change of clothing."

"How about a shower?" Tension of a new sort rolled from him.

A soft humor struck her. "That sounds a little intimate."

"Yes," he agreed.

"Neither of us is in a state to get physical. Getting naked and taking a shower with a man is very intimate, and we're not there, Ronan." Their brief moment of the morning was long over. She tried to soften the rejection with a smile.

"Male," he said.

She frowned. "Huh?"

He brushed the hair off her shoulder. "I'm a male. Not man. Not a human, remember?"

As a distinction, it did carry a whole bunch of impact. Desire tried to mingle through the exhaustion of coming down from the fight. Prompted by one simple touch from him. "Okay. Male."

"And this male is more than ready to get to that state," he rumbled, a slight grin playing on his mouth. "I promise I could get you there with one kiss. Maybe two."

The teasing side of him, after all the danger and fright, was a little too appealing. "Ronan."

He sobered. "I know you don't believe in mates, but I do. No male would let his female stand covered in blood while he washed himself. It's impossible. So either you go first, or you let me take care of you like I want. Like I need."

This earnest side of him caught her off guard, scattering her words. He needed to get under the warm spray and now. But even injured and not at full power, he was stronger than her, and no way could she force him.

He moved to the side. "Please shower and I will fetch you clean clothing."

She grabbed his arm. "You shower. You need the heat to fix that bleeding arm." Probably. Who knew? Somehow she figured it'd help. "I can wait. I'm not injured."

There was no warning. One second she was trying to be reasonable with him, and the next he'd manacled her arms, turned, and deposited her right under the spray. She opened her mouth to argue and sucked in water, leaning over to cough uncontrollably.

His sigh echoed off the tiles, and he gently patted her back. "You are a handful."

She stood and moved to the side, turning to face him and away from the spray. Her hair hung wetly against her face, and her soaked T-shirt plastered itself against her body. "I can't believe you did that."

"Believe it." He turned to step out of the shower, revealing that wicked tattoo across his back and an equally impressive butt.

"Fine." She grabbed his arm and pulled him back. In her years as a doctor, she couldn't count how many naked bodies she'd seen. This could be clinical. "We can share the shower, but nothing intimate. No kissy-kissy. Keep your mouth and your hands to yourself."

He turned, triumph in his gaze. "Except for your hair. It would ease me to be able to wash that mass. I've wanted to dig my hands into those wild curls from the first moment we met."

Ease him? "Did that line work on the ladies a million years ago?"

His dimple winked at her when he grinned. "I've never used it. Did it work now?"

A little bit. She pushed him toward the spray, surprised when he moved for her. "When you healed yourself before. How did you do that?"

He turned as the spray sliced over his side. "We have healing cells, and we can send them where we wish. It's just like your brain telling your foot to kick or your eyes to focus."

How freaking fascinating. There had to be a way to duplicate those cells and help humans. To help Grace. For now, Faith had a vampire to cure. "Okay. Close your eyes and let the heat into your skin. Allow it to go deep, and then try the mojo with those healing cells." The wound on his arm continued to bleed, mixing with the water and turning the bottom of the shower red. "Go slow and just concentrate on that one task. Let everything else wisp away."

He turned back into the spray and shut his eyes.

Odd tingles popped in the air around them, mixing with the steam. "Cool," Faith murmured.

He breathed in and out, but the bleeding didn't stop.

She frowned and moved closer to him, setting her hands against his back—at the bottom of that crazy tattoo. Ribs and jagged ink. "You can do this. Trust me."

His body settled beneath her touch. The steam turned electric and then began swirling around. She leaned to the side to check his arm. The bleeding slowed and then stopped. The wide gash began to mend together, creating a long scar, and then disappearing. Absolutely amazing. The air even felt different around them. Just what kind of power did a fully healthy immortal hold?

He straightened and turned around, his eyes a fathomless blue. "Thank you."

She began to step back and he stopped her, his hand on the hem of her T-shirt. When she didn't protest, he pulled the wet material gently over her head. Like a gentleman, he kept his gaze on her face as she tossed her panties outside the shower. "Tell me how you're feeling," she whispered, flushing hot.

His lip curved.

She chuckled. "Okay. Not that. After healing. During healing. I want to help you."

He tugged her closer and then reversed their positions, setting the back of her head beneath the spray. "Close your eyes."

She did so, and he moved away, only to return to rub coconut-scented shampoo through her hair, his touch reverent. Even his left hand was rough. She reached for it, studying the crisscrosses of scars on his palm. "What in the world?"

"Ritual to become a Seven. Cuts and blood."

"Oh." She released him. "Tell me about healing."

He cleared his throat. "Healing felt good, but slow. It feels as if there are thousands upon thousands of bees inside me, all stinging and trying to get out. My essence is—split. Uneven."

Adrenaline? Maybe something with the adrenal glands or thyroid? Did immortals even have the same organs? The thoughts zinged through her head and then settled into bliss as he washed the shampoo out and kneaded her shoulders. She groaned and opened her eyes.

"For immortal beings, we're rather uncomplicated," he said, washing her shoulders and arms, his gaze intense. "Food, exercise, and sex usually fix what ails us."

She grinned. "That's a heck of a come-on."

His grin matched hers. "You think? How about this?" His hands curved over her shoulders and he moved in, his mouth settling on hers.

This kiss was different. Smooth and gentle, he coaxed a response from her, seducing instead of challenging. Her heart speeded up, and desire flowed fast and warm through her blood. She leaned into him and his erection brushed her stomach, weakening her knees.

Somebody pounded on the bathroom door.

Ronan growled and lifted his head. "What?"

"The plane landed and is waiting for us. We want to stay under the radar, so we need to go. Now," Benny yelled.

They had to fly again? Faith sighed.

Ronan dropped his forehead to hers, his body vibrating. "I think this new world is trying to kill me."

Faith gulped and tried to quiet her rioting body. "You and me, both."

CHAPTER FIFTEEN

Ronan awoke as the private plane landed with a hard thump. He sat up, his gaze searching instantly for Faith. She sat next to him by the window, her head on his shoulder, her breathing even. After eating a huge meal of several loaded pizzas, they'd both dropped off into sleep. His body felt better. Not invincible, but definitely better than before.

Benny glanced up from a stack of papers. "Hey. Getting stronger?"

"Yes," Ronan said, glancing toward the front of the plane, where Ivar was serving as copilot. His injuries had healed, and he could actually feel his strength returning. Power flushed through his veins. "Thank you for letting me sleep."

"You needed rest."

Ronan eyed this brother of his. They'd been bonded for centuries, and it felt good breathing the same air again. "I really did miss you, Benny."

Benny sobered—a rare sight. "I missed you too. I wondered about you. Went by the stones we used to haunt and would talk to you sometimes. Tell you what was happening in the world."

Peace filtered through Ronan for a brief moment. "I used to talk to you too." He looked outside at the trees filing by the taxiing plane. "The days were empty and lonely, so I created stories. About us and about what we might be doing." He gestured around the plane. "I had no idea about this."

Benny smiled again. "I'm glad you're back, brother."

Ronan returned the grin. "As am I. Where are we? Denver?"

The plane rolled to a stop, and Benny stood, stretching his massive body. "No. Wyoming."

"Where is Wyoming?" Ronan asked, careful not to jostle Faith.

The plane powered down, and Ivar moved back into the cabin. "It's somewhat of a central location where we could build a headquarters into a mountain. We built it and have left the place alone except for updates through the years so nobody can trace us to it."

"What about satellite tracking us today?" Ronan asked, glancing toward the still-sleeping woman. She had been through so much already, and there was more to come.

"We're fine," Benny said as he pushed a button and the door opened. Cool air rushed in. "We took several underground routes to the private airport and then entered through a basement. There's no way to trace us. Or shouldn't be. Unfortunately, nothing is truly secret these days."

Ronan scanned the area. The enemy was strong and smart. Not once would he allow himself to relax. He stood and gently lifted Faith into his arms, striding for the door and easily maneuvering the steps. The plane was parked inside a sprawling metal building where a black Chevrolet waited. He moved to a window and looked outside.

Mountains and fresh air surrounded them. His chest settled. No more concrete and imposing buildings. "This is perfect," he murmured.

"Yep." Benny gestured him toward a closed door. An office?

Faith stirred and looked up. "Ronan?"

He smiled down at her, enjoying the feel of her in his arms. All his. Although she had clothing now, he still needed to acquire sketch pads and charcoals for her. "We're in Wyoming."

She blinked and looked around. "Huh." She gave a slight struggle.

He reluctantly set her on her feet and held her arms until she regained her balance. Benny had procured tight, faded jeans and a deep blue T-shirt for her, but he'd forgotten a bra. Her breasts were nicely outlined against the cotton, and Ronan struggled to keep his gaze on her face.

He'd borrowed a pair of Benny's jeans and a green T-shirt, which fit perfectly.

Her hair had been allowed to air dry, and it curled wildly down her back. She pushed a strand away from her face and glanced down, sighing at the plain white tennis shoes. Then she shook her head and looked back up at him. "What about my sister?"

"Let's get to safety, and we'll talk." Benny opened the door to what looked like a supply closet. Paper, towels, and cleaners lined a shelf.

Ronan frowned and moved in behind him with Faith and Ivar. The door closed. "I do not enjoy small spaces."

Benny grinned and flattened his palm in the center of the far wall. It slid open to reveal a wide box. "Come on and I'll show you." He stepped inside and Ivar pushed past Ronan to follow. Faith held back.

Ronan frowned. "I do not like this box."

"Just wait," Benny said, his eyes sparkling.

Sometimes Benny was shit-assed crazy. Ronan took Faith's hand and led her into the room. The door closed. Benny hit a button, and they plunged down.

Ronan bit his tongue and tightened his legs to stay upright. They came to a rather gentle stop, and the doors opened to a rock cavern.

He walked out of the box and looked around. "It's just rock."

"Not so," Benny said, moving forward and pressing his palm against the rock. Another door slid open, this one revealing a cavernous round room with massive screens on the front wall and tables of computer equipment throughout.

Faith whistled. "Holy bat cave."

Bats? He hated bats. So he took the lead, keeping her behind him.

"Ivar created this place." Benny pointed to a far doorway. "Living quarters are that way. At the far end, there's another elevator that will take you to the surface, which is a valley between two mountains fully protected from satellite surveillance. I'll explain all the details later."

Ivar moved toward the nearest console and typed on a keyboard. Three of the screens lit up with images of the earth. He pointed to the far left of the globe. "Allies. Vampire, demon, shifter, and witch headquarters and large groupings."

Benny nodded toward the middle screen. "Known enemy encampments across the globe. Kurjan and Cyst—our data isn't the best since the last war took so many out. They've been hiding and rebuilding."

Ronan moved toward the screens. Modern technology would make war so much easier. He glanced at the third large screen, which had pink dots all over the globe. "And that?"

"Possible Keys." Benny bent down and typed, focusing on a couple. "We've traced Enhanced women the best we could to keep track of them. The lineage of those first three Enhanced females has gone in many directions, and we're hopeful we have them all here. We must find the three Keys."

Faith rubbed her eyes and then looked at the screen. "Wait a minute. You said the three Keys could take down Ulric, and you had three Keys in Enhanced females way back when? So why couldn't they take him down at that time?"

Excellent question. Pride warmed Ronan's chest. "If the first three were alive today, which apparently they are not, then they would be needed."

"They are not alive and have not been for centuries, I'm very sorry to say," Ivar said, turning toward Faith. "At the time we created the prison world, we required more than the three Keys."

She frowned. "Is that just a designation for these women? Or are they real keys to something?"

Damn, she was smart. "Real keys," Ronan confirmed. "Which means we had to wait for a lock."

Benny typed again, and the middle screen cleared to make way for a picture of a very pretty seven-year-old girl with blue eyes and brown hair. Her intelligent eyes blazed from fragile features. "Meet Hope Kayrs-Kyllwood."

Ronan breathed out, his chin dropping. For years, he'd wondered about finding the female vampire. The prophesied one. "The Lock."

* * * *

Hope Kayrs-Kyllwood finished the spatial-relation game on her console and snuggled down in her comforter, her eyes heavy, happy she didn't have to practice her piano lessons. They were so boring, and her fingers didn't get the notes right. Her mama had tucked her in and gone to the other room, worry on her pretty face. Vampires didn't get sick, and yet Hope had a cold.

Just a little cold, but her nose was runny and her throat hurt. Her daddy had come home from work to feel her forehead and kiss her nose, telling her she'd be fine.

But his dark green eyes hadn't smiled.

She didn't know how to reassure the grown-ups in her life that she was okay. Lots of human little girls got colds. She was more human than they knew. More than she could tell them.

So she hugged her stuffed dinosaur closer to her chest and closed her eyes, falling into a light nap. Before long, she wandered near the ocean in her special world, entranced by the bright blue birds flying around. "Drake?" she called.

He stepped out of the forest near the beach and kicked off his shoes, walking in the sand. "Why is your nose red?"

She grinned, revealing a lost tooth.

He blinked. "Your tooth. You're missing the front one."

She nodded. "Yeah. I'm hoping the tooth fairy gives me five dollars for this one. It was a big tooth."

Her friend lifted one of his bony shoulders. He was only seven, like her, but he was a lot taller. They'd been meeting in this dream world for almost six months, and he seemed to get more serious each time. "I didn't know vampires did the whole money thing for teeth. Like humans."

"My mama was a human before mating my dad," Hope said. "Wasn't yours?"

Drake rubbed his chin and looked over the quiet waves of the dream ocean. "She was human but could never be a Kurjan. Doesn't have the power." He sighed, and his shoulders hunched. "Why can't mates get powerful? They just get immortal, and sometimes that's not enough."

Hope reached for his hand and took it, enjoying the sand between her toes. "I don't know, but she had to be Enhanced, so that must be good." Hope hopped over a puddle. "Did you tell your mom about this world?"

"No," Drake said, stopping and facing her. "You and me are supposed to be enemies. At least, our people are enemies. I don't think we should tell anybody that we're friends."

Probably a good plan. For now, anyway. Someday they'd have to tell in order to fix the world, she was pretty sure. "Yeah, you're right."

Drake looked around at the trees and the wild birds. They flew up above, wide and powerful, swooping down to the ocean and then flinging themselves back up. "Do you know where we are? How we're here in this, um, dream world?"

Hope bit her lip. "It's just a dream world. My mommy and daddy met in one until they were grown-ups, but my mom had to break it in order to stop the world from exploding. I don't think she knows about this one." Mommy and Daddy had met just like Hope and Drake were meeting. Sometimes people were just meant to be friends. "Can you get in here without me?"

"No," Drake said, eyeing the end of the beach where the sand fell off. "Only you can do that."

Well, she was a prophet, whatever that meant. Someday she'd find out. "What have you been doing?"

His chest puffed out. "Working with my father."

Wow. Work. "Doing what?"

He let go of her hand to scratch his elbow. "I can't tell you. It's Kurjan business."

She pouted. "You could tell me a little bit."

He grinned, his green eyes sparkling. "One of those big birds could land on your lip."

She snorted. "Whatever." The dream got hazy. "Oops. I hafta go. See ya later." The entire world disappeared and she woke up in her room.

"Hey," giggled a high voice.

Hope opened her eyes to see her best friends in the entire world sitting on her bed. They were both seven years old, just like her and Drake. "Hey," she responded to Liberty, who had her blond hair piled into two pigtails. Libby was a feline shifter who hadn't been able to shift yet, but she would someday.

Paxton stood beside the bed, his silverish-blue eyes worried. "Your mama said you were sick. How can you be sick?" He had a doughnut in his hand but seemed too concerned about her health to eat it.

Hope sat up, eyeing the doughnut. Pax's daddy had told him to stop eating so much sugar because he was turning roly-poly. Hope wasn't sure what that meant, but it hadn't sounded good, and Pax's daddy had been frowning in a dark way. When a vampire frowned in that way, it looked kind of scary. Any vampire. "It's just the sniffles." She held out her hand.

Pax reluctantly gave her the doughnut and then licked all the glaze off his fingers. His black hair curled over his nape and had a little sugar in it.

She reached out and brushed it away. "It's okay, Paxton."

"Did you practice your piano? I've been working on my guitar. We could play together," Pax said, looking around again. "But don't tell my dad."

Why didn't his dad like the music? That male didn't seem to like much. "I won't tell," she whispered. "But I didn't practice since I had to nap."

Libby leaned in, her brown eyes sparkling. "Did you see *him* in the dream world?"

Paxton moved closer. "Shhh," he warned, looking back toward the bedroom door. "We'll get in trouble."

It seemed like Pax got in trouble a lot, and Hope didn't want to add to his problems. So she whispered really quietly. "Yes, I saw Drake. He said he's been working with his dad."

"Wow," Libby said, her eyebrows rising. "Working already?"

"Yeah," Hope said. That Drake was awesome, just like the boys on television shows.

Pax eyed the doughnut but didn't try to take it back. "What kind of work?"

Hope shrugged. "I don't know. But Drake's good, so it has to be good, right?"

Libby nodded vigorously.

Pax bit his lip. "Says who?"

Hope sighed. "My mommy and daddy met in a dream world and they saved everybody, remember? So there has to be a reason Drake and me are meeting there." She rubbed her hand down the dark blue prophesy marking on her neck. "It's probably something about me being a prophet when I grow up." There were three prophets alive at any time, and they were the religious leaders of the Realm. She'd been born with the marking on her neck, making her one of them. When she thought too hard about it, her stomach hurt. So she pretended the marking wasn't there sometimes.

Paxton patted her shoulder. "You don't have to be anything you don't want to be," he said softly.

Libby bounced on the bed. "That's true. We can all be what we want. Maybe we should invent something really cool and get rich. And buy tons of ice cream."

Pax grinned. "Yeah. Let's invent something."

Hope snorted. What could they invent? She wished there was a way to take Pax and Libby into the dream world so they could meet Drake. Someday she wanted them all to be friends. "How about ice cream that doesn't melt?"

Libby giggled again.

Pax shuffled his feet. "Good idea."

Hope sniffed, her head hurting a little bit. "We hafta find a way for you to come into the dream world with me."

Libby's eyes widened. "Yeah. Let's do that."

Pax shook his head. "No."

Hope frowned. "Why not?"

Paxton looked at her, his round face vampire hard. "We're vampires, and I start training to be a soldier next week. Drake is a Kurjan. We can't be friends."

Pax was wrong. Someday, she'd prove it to him.

CHAPTER SIXTEEN

After a dinner of steak and potatoes, Faith finished checking in with Jordy, who'd reported that Grace hadn't tracked voices that day, and her blood pressure was slightly low. But she was safe and there were security guards still in place. Should Faith tell him Grace was going to be moved soon? Maybe not. It would just raise more questions, and she didn't have answers.

She hung up the specialized glowing phone that Benny had assured her couldn't be traced. She looked around the large bedroom with attached bath. There was a king-sized bed, two bed tables, and a reading chair set strategically on a thick white area rug. A small desk also sat over to the side, piled high with manila files she'd taken to reading about the mating process.

There was a feeling of security being so far underground, encased in natural stone. A plasma television took up one wall, showing scene after scene of lakes and oceans. Even a sunset or two.

She reached for her wineglass and finished the very good Chardonnay, letting her body go a little numb. They'd polished off a couple of bottles before the immortals had moved on to more vodka, several hours ago. At that point, she'd excused herself and headed to the bedroom to read her files and make her call to Jordy.

The door opened and Ronan stepped inside, lines fanning out from his eyes. The peaceful air became charged—electrifying.

"It's after midnight," Faith said, studying him. "You're not going to heal if you don't get some sleep."

He looked around the room. "I had to catch up on the dossiers Benny has compiled. On my family, the leaders of the world, and my enemies. Then I got on the computer and researched the history of all the species."

"You did?" How odd that must be.

"Yes." His eyes gleamed. "Humans landed on the fucking moon. Can you believe it? The moon!"

She chuckled. "Yes. I did know that. We're starting to slowly explore other places too."

"I know. I hacked into several NASA files, but had to stop when I grew tired. My eyes feel like they're about to pop from my head."

She swallowed. "What about my sister? Are plans in place?"

"Not yet," Ronan said, holding up a hand to stall her protest. "We shall devise a plan tomorrow. Benny called in a couple of favors and has security of the vampire and demon sort watching the hospital, as well as her room. Two younger males he wants to recruit for the Seven. She's safe for now."

Faith's shoulders relaxed. "Then we'll get her tomorrow."

"Yes." Ronan leaned back against the door. "I wish we could heal her."

"We can." Faith started to move toward him and then stopped herself. "Dayne's blood helped her, so why not try yours?"

"Too much will kill her," he countered.

Okay. She remembered now that Dayne had said something similar, but there had to be a way. "She's in a coma from a brain injury. Your blood can cure injuries. You said she's Enhanced, like me. Can't she mate somebody?"

He crossed his arms. "There's no decent immortal in the world who would mate an unconscious woman. That'd be rape, Faith."

She shook her head. "I'm not talking about intercourse. I've been studying the information you have on the mating process. The bite and brand cause a physical reaction in the female that does something to the chromosomal pairs, increasing them and consequently leading to immortality. The sex seems to just be part of the bonding process. I think a mate could save her even without sex."

He blinked. "Even if that crazy scheme worked, and I don't think it would, she'd awaken mated to a vampire for life."

Faith chose her next words carefully. Just being this close to him thrummed her nerves to life. "Not necessarily."

Ronan lifted his head. "Excuse me?"

She pointed to the stack of manila files. "Apparently, there's a virus that negates the mating bond. It's fairly new, and it has only been used with widows who've lost a mate years ago. But it's a chance."

He straightened, power in his gaze. "There can be no negating of the mating bond."

"Welcome to the twenty-first century," she said softly. How the heck was he dealing with such incredible changes in a world he hadn't thought he'd see again? "Science has progressed."

"That is a bad progression." He shook his head. "Mates are forever."

Again with the sweet. Not simple, but sometimes his view was classically sweet. The urge to touch him, to ease him, was overwhelming. She studied him for a moment. "How are you feeling?"

"My arm is fine." A veil drew down over his eyes.

"That's not what I meant." Now she approached him carefully, sensing the turmoil going on within him. It matched the turmoil she felt, but hers was more clear-cut. Need and want. His was need and hurt. Not a good combination. "You've lost so much, and you have to be concerned about Quade." Hopefully Ronan hadn't lost another brother. "I'm sorry for your loss."

"Loss is a part of being a soldier," he said, almost automatically. "Thank you for your concern, but I'm quite well."

"That's not true." She slipped her hands over his forearms, electricity shooting up her wrists. "If you need to talk, I'm here for you."

He stiffened, his emotional facade cracking. "You're here for me, but you don't believe me. About mates, about the Kurjans, even about you. About fate."

"I believe in science and fact," she said softly, her heart starting to beat faster.

"Do you?" he asked just as softly. "I've read your sister's medical reports. There's less than a zero-point-five percent chance she'll ever awaken, and even if she does, she won't have cognitive function. Yet you're still trying to find...a miracle. How is that either science or fact?"

The words stung. "Science progresses every second, so a zero-point-five chance can turn into a real chance with the right research," she said, letting go of his arms and taking a step back. Cool air surrounded her and she refrained from hugging herself. "You and I don't have to agree on everything to be friends."

"Friends?" His lip twisted. "I assure you, I do not want to be your friend."

She exhaled. The man, or rather *male,* seemed put out she didn't agree with his view of life. Or he was just grieving and not doing a very good job of it. "I think you need a friend, Ronan."

He began to turn.

She stopped him by grabbing his wrist, unable to just let him go. "I believe you should talk."

"The last thing I want to do is talk," he muttered, color sliding across his high cheekbones. "There has to be a way to go for a run in these mountains. I shall go do that."

She stepped right up to him. "I'm tired of dancing around this and you. Tired of not saying the right thing or wondering what you're thinking."

"Then stop talking or wondering," he countered, his hands going to her biceps.

"All right." Good enough. She rose up on her toes and kissed him, sliding her mouth against his firm lips.

He drew in a breath.

Whatever there was between them was just getting stronger. She wasn't a woman who waited around for something to happen. This…she wanted. She nipped his bottom lip a little harder than necessary.

His eyes darkened to deep blue with no green. "What are you doing?"

"Giving up on the talking." Pressing her body against his, she kissed him again.

With a low growl, he kissed her back, taking over. Her mind spun and settled, going quiet as her body flashed wide-awake and heated.

* * * *

So many thoughts bombarded Ronan that he couldn't catch just one. Her soft lips were beneath him, and her stunning body was flush against him. She'd put herself in his hands. On purpose.

Another growl shook him and he kissed her harder, sweeping his tongue inside her mouth. She tasted of wine and woman, an irresistible combination. This was a mistake—he wasn't fully in control—but he didn't give a shit.

She'd kissed him.

He slid an arm around her waist, lifting her off her feet and bending her back. She moaned, and the sound slid down his throat and landed in his groin. Hard. Rock-fucking-hard. Keeping hold of her, he moved easily toward the bed, warning bells clanging in his head.

The marking on his hand burned hotter than ever before.

He set her down at the edge of the bed and released her mouth, trying to engage his mental faculties.

She snagged hold of his shirt and tugged it up, all but forcing him to duck his head or be choked. The shirt flew across the room.

Her smooth hands caressed his chest and she murmured something in approval.

He shot both hands into her hair, tangling his fingers and drawing her head back. "Faith. Wait a minute."

She blinked, her pupils dilated and her lips a rosy red from his. "What?"

His mind blanked. Her scent, woman and wildflowers, wound around him. Through him. "I'm not in control."

"Good." She smiled, a siren's image. "No control here. Just feel."

He'd wanted this since the first second he finally touched her after all these years, but he wasn't making himself clear. "I'm not a casual male. Not with you. Ever."

"I understand," she said, running her hands down his abs. "But we're not mating, so keep your brand to yourself. This is just us and just tonight. All right?"

He'd tried to explain, and he wanted tonight more than his next breath. More than any breath. "I understand. I just hope you do." He released her hair and caressed her breasts through her shirt, grabbing the bottom and lifting it over her head.

Her breasts sprang free. Full and firm with pretty pink nipples. He touched her, rolling them, leaning in to take her lips again. Finally. Faith here with him. He deepened the kiss, wanting to be gentle, but craving her to the point of insanity. She fumbled with his jeans and released his zipper, sliding her hand inside to caress him.

His knees nearly buckled. He grasped her hips and lifted, tossing her back on the bed. She landed with a soft chuckle, using her elbows to inch her way to the top. Keeping her in his sights, he shucked his jeans and then pressed a knee to the bed, moving up her until he could remove her jeans.

Then he took a moment. "You're beautiful," he said, running a hand across her abdomen. "Everything I could've dreamed and more." Her skin was soft and supple with strength beneath.

She breathed out and reached for him, sliding her hands over his shoulders. "You're amazing. So much strength."

If she only knew. Soon, he'd regain his full power, and then she'd see all of him. For now, he'd be gentle with her. This first time had to mean something, even if it was only to him. He kissed beneath her jaw, licking and nipping, moving down her slender neck to pay homage to her breasts.

He sucked one hard nipple into his mouth, enjoying the soft sounds of pleasure she made.

His cock pounded in pain and he wanted to be inside her. Now.

Yet he took his time, playing with her other breast, tapping his fingers down to her sex. She was wet and ready for him. Tight. He slipped one finger inside her, and she arched against him with a small gasp.

God, she was fucking perfect. Never had anything in his life been sweeter.

She dug her nails into his chest, pulling him toward her. "Now, Ronan. Get the edge off. We can play later."

Play? Hell yeah, he'd play later. For now, he moved to appease her. Bracing himself with his elbows, he positioned himself at her sex, trying to push in. The woman was tight.

He'd prepared her and she was wet and willing. But her body was so much smaller than his. He had to slow himself, working in very small increments to get inside her. The strain to his control threatened to overwhelm him, but he would not hurt her. Ever.

Finally, her body allowed him entrance.

She widened her legs and wrapped her fingers over his shoulders, her eyes dilating.

He paused. For his entire life, for as long as he still had a life, he'd never forget the sight of her. Deep chocolate eyes, hair spread over the pillow, delicate features. So soft and sweet. Passionate. "I never thought I'd be here. With you," he rumbled. "After I agreed to the shield, I thought this—you—were out of my grasp."

Her eyes softened. "I'm right here."

Yes, she was. He pushed deeper inside her, taking his time, allowing her smaller body to adjust to him. She moved against him, urging him on, her soft gasps echoing in his heart.

Finally, he eased all the way in, coming as close to ecstasy as a killer like he would ever reach. She was hot and wet…and she surrounded him. He was finally home. His body rioted with the need to move until his biceps shook with the effort, but he held still, savoring the moment.

She kissed him gently, sliding her tongue along his lips.

The growl that rumbled up from his chest was a sound he'd never made before. Ever.

CHAPTER SEVENTEEN

Faith could barely breathe as Ronan kissed her, his tongue playing with hers. He was inside her, all of him...somehow. So much of him surrounded her that he was everywhere. His cock stretched her in ways she hadn't imagined, melding pain and pleasure, touching nerves she hadn't realized existed. And she was a doctor.

Even so, the look in his eyes. . . possession and promise.

Her heart caught and she paused. No. This was just here and now. A way to get them both out of their heads. She kissed him back, pushing worries away.

Then she ran her hands down his chest, around his ribs, and over his lean back. His body was truly amazing. Beyond human. "Ronan," she murmured against his mouth, lifting her knees on either side of his hips. "Now."

He smiled against her mouth, and the feeling wandered down to her heart and tried to take hold.

Then he rose up, grasping her hips and gaining leverage. Taking his time, he withdrew and then pushed back in, igniting every nerve she had along the way.

Never in her life had she imagined such completeness. He overwhelmed her with sheer size and strength, and she couldn't help but revel in it.

A knock sounded on the door.

No, no, no. She grabbed his arms, trying to keep him inside her. "Ignore it."

He nodded and pulled out to shove back in. Electricity zapped through her. She gasped and arched against him, taking more. Her nails dug into his skin and she scraped, enjoying the low growl that rumbled from his chest.

An immortal's growl was the sexiest thing ever.

Or so she thought until he drove deeper inside her. He started to move faster, harder, keeping a tight hold on her hip to give him access.

She arched her neck and his mouth was instantly there, fangs lightly scraping over her jugular. The decadent feeling almost pushed her into an orgasm. She moaned and turned her head, granting him better access. What would it be like to be bitten—

His fangs slid in, somehow hitting a nerve connected to every other nerve in her body. Fire lanced through her and she jerked.

The knock came louder. "Ronan? We have a problem," Ivar called.

The fangs retracted and Ronan licked the wound clean. "Fuck, fuck, fuck." He pulled out of her and rolled off the bed, frowning when she gasped in protest. No. "What?" he bellowed, standing next to the bed fully aroused, fury lining his face.

"We're not secure. There are signs that the area has been scouted lately. I've been surveying the perimeter, and we have to get protections in place right now. I need your help."

Ronan grabbed his jeans from the floor and yanked them on, wincing when they hit his dick.

She sat up, still panting. "You can't seriously be thinking of leaving right now." She was two seconds from a phenomenal orgasm, and her body was starting to hurt. Her stomach even ached.

"Security comes first." He shot a hand through his hair, brushing it back. Arousal and anger combined on his high cheekbones, making him look deadly.

She was never going to get laid. "I don't believe this. I really don't."

He sat on the edge of the bed and began pulling on his boots.

"Oh, God." She shook her head. "Wait a minute. I mean, I didn't even think. I'm a doctor, for Pete's sake."

"What?" He laced up the first one.

"Protection," she whispered, as if saying it any louder would make her worry too real. "We didn't even think about protection." While it was doubtful a centuries-old vampire who'd lived alone in a different dimension had contracted any sort of disease, there was still the concern about conceiving a baby. Thank goodness they'd been interrupted. "We didn't protect against pregnancy."

"Oh." He looked at her over his shoulder, his gaze lightening. "Vampires can only impregnate our partners after being mated. You're safe."

Relief filled her. Then irritation. So from her point of view, there was no reason to stop. "Ronan. You're going to get blue balls." She felt like she had blue balls. That everything down there was blue. Frowning, she sat up and clutched the sheet to her chest.

He turned around to lace up his other boot. "It'll be worth it in the end. You're everything I hoped, Faith," he said.

She sobered, her gaze on his bare and tattooed back, his words somehow making her feel vulnerable. When he'd been inside her, she'd felt taken over and safe. Now, struck with his size and strength, she felt small. Delicate. Human.

"I apologize for the interruption—again. This is getting tedious," he growled as he finished the laces and stood.

"No kidding," she muttered, her clit throbbing.

He turned toward her, caressing her cheek and rubbing his thumb across her bottom lip. "I wonder," he mused.

"What?" she whispered, focusing on his eyes, which were a deep green now.

"You keep yourself so distant normally. It is nice to see beneath the shields," he said thoughtfully. "You lost your parents young, and then your sister was injured. Is that why you keep yourself apart? Afraid to lose again?"

Okay. He was seeing way too much. She shook her head. Her body *hurt*, damn it.

"How did your parents die?" he asked, his fingers gripping her jaw.

"Car wreck after bowling one night. Grace and I were at home," she said. Maybe there was a good showerhead in this place that could befriend a girl.

"And Grace?"

She swallowed, a familiar ache grabbing her chest. Her body started to relax and let go the hope of an immediate orgasm. "Two years ago, a burglar broke into her apartment and attacked her. She fought back, but she didn't win."

Ronan stilled. "Is he dead?"

She bit her lip. "No. The police never found the guy. I check with them every month or so, and nothing. If she wakes up, then she can tell them who it was. Or at least describe the guy." Her stomach hurt.

"I will find him," Ronan said, his voice low. "I give you my word."

She couldn't help but grin. "I think your plate is full with finding your family, taking down Ulric, locating the Keys, and securing the Lock." Her body still throbbed for him.

He didn't return the smile as he grabbed his shirt off the floor and pulled it over his head. "Yet I will avenge you and your sister. On my life."

Surprising tears pricked the back of her eyes. What the heck? She wasn't the type to get all mushy about a guy making promises. For so long, she'd taken care of herself. Nobody had even thought to offer her protection.

"Hey." He wiped a tear from the corner of her eye. "It's okay to be fragile, Doc. I won't allow anything or anyone to break you. Right now, I'm going to go make sure this base is secure." He kissed her nose. "You're in my heart, in my blood, whether you want to be there or not." He smiled as he leaned back. "I shall return shortly to finish what we started."

Her body couldn't take another unfulfilled night. "Bring a big lock and something to bar the door," she muttered.

"You have my word."

* * * *

Ronan finished scouting the outside of the compound. Ivar was correct. Footsteps lined the edge of the property. But perhaps the interloper had just been a lone hiker who'd come upon the area by chance.

Or…the Kurjans had found the base. It wasn't impossible to believe they'd been looking for years. Now they might be waiting to strike. The evidence wasn't conclusive, so he followed Ivar's directions and set land mines in designated areas.

Faith was still sleeping in their bedroom, and his cock was still hard. To have been inside her without reaching completion was a torture he'd never imagined.

Grumbling, he walked to the end of the hall and rode the elevator up to the top. It opened onto a wide valley of grass, trees, and a rushing stream under a full moon. The purity of nature hit him, and he breathed in, his entire being unsettled. He wanted to return to bed and take his woman. Several times.

"For a guy who just got laid, you look cranky," Benny said from a wooden table hidden in shadows beneath a couple of tall pine trees.

"Almost laid." Ronan turned toward his friend.

Benny winced. "Shit, man. That sucks."

Ronan snorted. It had been so long since he'd talked to another person, he couldn't quite remember the right way to begin. Maybe just with the truth. "I'm struggling."

"No shit, buddy. I just finished setting traps on the north side and decided on having a drink before starting on the security system." Benny gestured toward a seat on the other side of the table. "Have a seat." He pulled a bottle of tequila across the table and held it out. "Don't tell Ivar. He gets pissy if anybody takes a small break. Fuckin' Vikings."

The grass caressed Ronan's feet as he strode toward Benny and grabbed the bottle, taking a healthy swallow and handing it back. "Fuckin' Vikings," he agreed.

Benny tipped back his head and drank, then handed back the bottle. "Sit."

Ronan dropped into the chair and stretched out his feet, allowing the moonlight to calm him. "It is good to drink with you again."

"Ditto. What was it like in the shield, anyway?" Benny's eyes pierced the darkness.

"Lonely. I was alive, but not living. As I told you, I talked to you often." Ronan rubbed the back of his aching neck. "There was a day and a night like here, but several moons in the sky. In the morning, I performed the ritual to keep the shield strong, and in the evening, I repeated the same ritual—moving to the poles of the place every two months or so." There were rocks he would configure and reconfigure that somehow polarized the shields, or magnetic fields, and kept the prison world secure. It was monotonous...but something to do, at least.

"That kind of blows," Benny said, gulping down a healthy portion of the tequila. "Did the shield ever come close to shattering?"

"Not until it did," Ronan said. Was Ulric free? Somehow, Ronan thought he'd feel the infusion of evil into this realm. "I do not like this new world."

Benny chortled. "It's the same world you left. Just older and wiser."

There was nothing wise about the world he'd seen so far. "We immortals are a secret, the Keys are lost, Adare is missing, and my mate doesn't want to be my mate, although she'd like an orgasm." Ronan took a deep drink, and the sharp alcohol landed in his gut and heated him throughout.

"Ah." Benny reclaimed the bottle. "Maybe you suck in the sack."

Ronan fought the urge to smack his oldest friend in the face. "I do not suck."

"Maybe that's the problem."

Ronan snorted and half-heartedly punched Benny in the jaw.

Benny laughed out loud. Then he sobered. "You need to find yourself, my friend. Get centered."

No shit. "Exactly what do you mean?"

Benny rested his elbows on the table and stared out at the darkened trees on the other side of the meadow. "The Ronan I used to know, the guy I shared a calling with, never would've left a Kurjan alive. You would've torn off his head and left his blood burning a hole in the floor as you walked through it."

"Dayne back at the hospital in the closet?" Ronan sat back, studying the rock formation behind the trees on the other side of Benny. "Yeah. I know."

"So?" Benny asked.

Ronan exhaled, reaching for the bottle again. "He had a kid with him. His kid."

"Again...so?" Benny shook his head. "A Kurjan kid grows up to be a Kurjan warrior who tries to kill us. Or tries to force Enhanced women into matehood."

Ronan took a healthy swallow and warmth spread through him again. "I'd hoped maybe that had changed. That they had...evolved."

"No. No evolution." Benny's gaze narrowed. "And hope? You weren't a guy who had hope."

Maybe that was the problem. "I figured my life was over when I entered the shield," he admitted. "Now, I have returned to this plane. I've lost one brother, maybe both of them, and I've found my mate. I know my duty and I'll do it, but how can there not be hope now?"

"Speaking of which. Your mate is here, you just had a night because I can smell her all over you, and yet you're not mated. That's not like you, either."

Ronan pushed the alcohol toward Benny. "Like I said. This world has changed. She doesn't want to be my mate, and the old ways of negotiating with family, of arranging these alliances already decreed by fate, no longer exist. I am employing strategy as always."

"Huh?" Benny took another drink, nearly emptying the bottle. "The taking of mates has not changed. You're just not on your feet yet, or you would've already taken care of business."

Probably also true. "This is like any campaign. I have been gathering intel, and now we've created a home base."

Benny paused. "Are you serious?"

"Yes."

Benny chuckled. "You're treating your mating like a military strategy."

"Of course." It was all he knew.

"Man, you're a moron." Benny held up a hand. "This is going to backfire. I know you. You gather intel, create safety, and then attack. But you can't just take her over."

"I might have to at some point. The woman doesn't know how to trust. She's been alone too much of her life." A gentle and steadfast approach would be best with Faith, but it might not be enough in the end. For now, he had the patience to ease her. "Earning her acceptance will take time."

"You don't have time," Benny said bluntly.

Tonight had been a good start. Those walls around Faith's heart had started to crumble. Finally. "I'm aware," Ronan agreed.

"Enough talk about your crazy plan." Benny leaned back. "Tell me more about the shield world. I'm so curious."

"It was empty of people," Ronan said. "It was a dimension with animals and water and peace. A lot of quiet. I could eat and sleep and explore and reconfigure the stones to protect the magnetic field...but that was all."

Benny blew out air. "That does sound lonely."

"It was."

"How did you go on, even speaking to imaginary me? Day after day after day?" Benny asked.

Ronan shrugged. "There was no alternative. The world was tied to my energy, so if I died, it ended. The shield was needed to contain Ulric in his dimension, so I did my job."

Benny lifted his head. "There's more."

Ronan looked up at his old friend. Many people thought Benny was crazy, but in truth, it was an act. Mostly. The guy was incredibly insightful when he wanted to be. To know that one fact was to be Benny's family. "Yeah. There's more."

"Well?"

Ronan eyed the bright moon. "Faith. I saw her in my dreams. Felt her touch. So I thought, maybe...that the shield world wasn't the end for me. I tried not to hope, and I did my job, but thinking there might be something else someday helped me go on."

"And now she won't mate you."

Ronan barked out a laugh. "Yeah. Exactly."

Benny snorted. "Stop being such a romantic. She's obviously willing to sleep with you. Next time, bite her and mark her. Then it's a done deal."

Sometimes Ben was a moron. "Right. Because who wouldn't want to spend eternity with a mate who's been forced into matehood?" Ronan asked drily. "Especially an independent, educated woman who has put her trust in science and has no fear of the immortal world?"

"Jesus, Ronan. You can't shield her from reality like that."

Sure, he could. That was his job. "I won't allow her to get into danger. When I need to mate her to protect her, I will." Her response to him showed she'd be more than willing. When it came to life or death, saving her trumped all other considerations.

The elevator door opened and Ivar crossed into the moonlight. "We have another problem."

Ronan shoved to his feet. "Well?"

Ivar gave him a look. "Satellite feed came up, and there's movement toward Denver by the Kurjans. Or Cysts. Or both. They're coming from Arizona and should land in about an hour. It's an impressive force."

Ronan's body chilled. The Kurjans were going after Grace. He'd thought it would take them longer to create a plan. This new world was just pissing him off now. "How far away are we?"

"Thirty minutes by helicopter." Ivar held the door open. "The armory is on the other side of the communications room."

Ronan jogged for the elevator. "I need one of you to stay here and cover Faith. Please."

"Not me," Benny said, right behind him. "I would love a good fight."

Ivar sighed. "I'll cover comms here and keep you updated. But Ronan, you're putting yourself in a helicopter with Benny flying. Sure you want to do that?"

Benny grinned as the elevator doors closed.

Ronan paused. He hadn't gotten to all vehicles yet in his study of this new world. "What exactly is a helicopter?"

CHAPTER EIGHTEEN

It had to be early morning. After a very quick shower with rather chilly water to quell her still-aching arousal, Faith drew on her jeans and shirt, surrounded by quiet. The entire world was silent so far underground. She moved into the attached bath and tied back her damp hair, brushing her teeth. Her body was empty. Aching. Her arms chilled. Where was Ronan?

The mountain pulsed around her, giving an aura of safety. Odd. She flashed back to the scene of a waterfall she and her family had climbed to while on vacation. She had been ten and Grace had been five. Their dad had carried Gracie part of the way, and the girl had chirped on about birds the whole time, her eyes sparkling.

Their mom had pointed out fauna, her pretty eyes alight with fun. Faith had held her hand and pretended to touch poison ivy, making her mom laugh, the sound gleeful. She'd already memorized all of the local trees and fauna, but it was fun listening to her mom, so she didn't say anything.

The day and the surrounding area had been safe. Secure and beautiful.

Faith returned to the present and looked at the stone walls around her. Ronan made her feel the same way. Mountains and safety. Just like when she'd been young and her whole family had been alive and well.

She walked into the hallway and followed the passage to the communication room. Lights glowed from the ceiling, making the trek easy.

Ronan stalked out of a room on the other side wearing full combat gear. Black cargo pants with pockets, gun strapped to his thigh, knife strapped to his calf. The bulletproof vest widened his already huge chest, and he had a pair of what appeared to be night-vision goggles in one hand.

Wow. Just holy wow.

Benny walked behind him in similar attire.

Both men stopped at the sight of her.

Benny smacked Ronan on the arm. "I'll go help Ivar get the helicopter ready. It's been a while since we flew it." He nodded at Faith, his usual smile absent.

Her legs went weak. "What's happening?"

Ronan moved toward her, looking like an ancient warrior about to jump into battle. His hair was still damp from a shower. "We've spotted Kurjan movement toward your sister, and we're going to fetch her. She'll have to be moved sooner than we'd hoped."

Faith's stomach dropped. They couldn't just move her sister. The woman had been in a coma for two years. "Let me get my shoes. I'll be ready in a second." She turned to run back to the room.

"You are not coming."

She halted and turned. Her chin dropped. "Of course I'm coming. Don't be ridiculous."

He stood there, so tall and broad, his expression veiled. An impenetrable wall. "I understand you believe the Kurjans might be good guys, and that's sweet, but I can't allow you to discover the truth the hard way. You can have all the freedom you want except when it comes to immortal fights. Those are mine. You are staying here."

She went to him then, having to tilt her head back to meet his gaze. His scent and heat rushed over her. "Absolutely not. I'm going and that's final. So get out of my way."

He changed subtly. Not in a way she could identify, but tension cascaded from him, overloading her senses. "Faith. I'd prefer you return to bed and catch up on sleep. Alternatively, you may stay in the control room with Ivar and track our progress. I promise I will bring your sister to you." He turned to go.

She grabbed his arm, digging her nails into his skin. "What the heck, Ronan? I'm going."

He turned so suddenly she almost fell over, and only his hand on her arm prevented her from landing on her ass. "I'm not allowing my mate to go into a battle with the Kurjans." His nostrils flared, and he loomed over her with an intensity she could almost taste.

She shoved him and he didn't move a centimeter. "I knew almost sleeping with you would change things."

"You're right." He stepped right up to her, forcing her to tilt her head even more to hold his gaze. "It did change things, but not in this way. Even if I hadn't tasted you, known your touch, I would never allow you to put yourself into a battle with an enemy when I could keep you safe somewhere else. I fight. You do not."

"That is not your call," she said, her back teeth grinding.

"I am trying so hard to be patient and give you time," he returned evenly—maybe a little too evenly. "And I'm willing to continue that path. But this is nonnegotiable. It would've been the same on day one of our meeting—if I had a safe place for you, which now I do. So sit your butt down in a chair and wait for Ivar."

"Or what?" She poked him in the chest, her temper flying free.

He lifted her so suddenly, she lost her breath. A second later, maybe less, her ass was in a chair and he was leaning over her, trapping her in place. "Until now, I have been willing to allow you time to adjust because I had the space to do so. Do not mistake my willingness for weakness. Do not misread me, mate."

Holy shit, had she misread him. Gone was the simple guy waxing on about fate and feelings. This guy had a hardness to him he'd hidden. Or perhaps this was the first chance he'd had to show his real face. "Who are you?" she wondered out loud.

"I'm who I've always been," he said, his eyes burning. "This new millennium is unable to change that."

What in the world did that mean? "Ronan—" she tried to keep her voice level and not start screaming at him—"it's my choice, not yours, to put myself in danger or not. To go and save my sister or not. Surely you understand that."

If anything, he drew nearer to her, caging her. "No."

Her head jerked. Fury caught her. "No? Are you serious?"

"Yes."

Where was the vampire who'd worn goofy shoes and shared his feelings? His concerns? "That's not okay."

He lifted one strong shoulder. "I don't care. Immortal fights are mine, not yours. Especially since you're still human. You can die, Faith. That I will not allow."

Anger rushed through her so quickly she almost choked. "You're saying that if I mated you, if I became immortal, then you'd be just fine with me coming and challenging other immortals?"

"God, no." He leaned back, disbelief crossing his chiseled features. "Are you crazy?"

Getting there. Definitely heading into furious nutjob land. "Listen, buddy. The foreplay was nice and all that, but you have no claim on me. You certainly can't tell me what to do."

His hand was suddenly around her neck. Her entire neck.

Her eyes bugged out in shock. He wasn't hurting her, but the warning was there.

His eyes morphed to a deep blue with a bright green ring around the iris, proving once again he was nowhere near human. "Foreplay and sex should never be *nice*, baby." His mouth took hers, hard and fast, sending flames to burn her nerves. He raised his head. "I'll show you what I mean. Later."

Seconds later, he was out of the room, leaving her mouth tingling, her body wanting, and her temper blowing.

* * * *

Ronan's mind wandered to his furious mate's face—again—and he banished all thoughts of her to prepare for battle. He studied the lights on the dash. Helicopters were much better than jets. Perhaps it was because he was up front with the stick and more in control. "You must teach me to fly," he said through the headset to Benny.

"Affirmative. Just watch what I do for now, and we'll work on planes when we have a chance," Benny said. "This is a modified helicopter. Humans don't have access to anything like this, so rule number one is that if we go down, we blow the entire thing up." He reached over and tapped the console in the middle of a dash. "Let's reach out."

"To whom?"

Benny clicked a couple of buttons, and a face came onto the screen.

Ronan's heart clenched. He didn't know the younger vampire, but the broad forehead was familiar. Jacer had had that same hard ridge.

The kid looked from one to the other of them. "Uncle Benny," he murmured, his sizzling gray eyes curious. "We're still watching the hospital in Denver per your request. Now, are you gonna tell me what's going on?"

"I'm not your uncle," Benny muttered into his headset. "My nephew Chalton isn't related to you."

"Close enough," the kid said easily, his gaze studying Ronan. "Who's your friend? He looks...familiar."

Benny banked a hard left. "Fellow soldier. You can call him Ronan." He glanced at Ronan. "This is Garrett. Kayrs."

Ronan swallowed and hid his emotions. This young soldier was what? His great-great-nephew? The visual proof that his bloodline had survived hit him harder than he would've imagined. He lowered his chin and studied the vamp. "Hi."

The kid gave a short nod and then looked back at Benny. "Why are we in Denver and why is it such a secret, Benny? I don't like keeping secrets from family."

"You two were just screwing around in Vegas," Benny said easily. "You jumped at the chance for an op."

"I didn't say I wasn't happy to help. I just said that I don't like hiding anything from family. My dad would kick my ass and then yours. Twice." Garrett didn't seem overly concerned with the thought. "Why are we here and when are things going to get interesting?"

The camera tilted and another face came into view. Black hair, world-wise green eyes. Demon and vampire features. "Hey, Uncle Benny."

Benny sighed. "I'm not your uncle, either. You didn't even grow up with my nephew, Logan Kyllwood."

Logan grinned. "Meh. Family is family. We're all suited up and ready to rumble, per your instructions." Anticipation lit the young hybrid's face, making him look even more dangerous. "What's going on?"

Kayrs and Kyllwood. These two were uncles to Hope, the Lock. Ronan studied them.

Benny began to lower the craft. "We'll be there in about ten minutes. Several squads of Kurjan soldiers are about to descend on the hospital, trying to take Grace Cooper out. She's in a coma, and we have to get to her first."

"Who the hell is Grace Cooper?" Logan growled.

"My mate's sister," Ronan said evenly, his blood beginning to settle for the battle ahead.

Garrett's gray gaze narrowed. "Why is this a secret? You could use Realm enforcements if the Kurjans have come out of hiding."

"I will explain everything once we have the woman," Benny said. "There's a lot going on, and I'd like for you two to be a part of it. But if you say one word to family, to anybody in the immortal world, your invite gets lost in the mail. You're out before you're in."

Garrett's chin lifted. "I don't like threats."

Ronan's chest filled. The young Kayrs looked just like Jacer. He desperately wanted to get to know this blood relative of his. But after one look, he knew he couldn't put another family member in jeopardy. He couldn't subject either of these kids to the risk of becoming one of the Seven. "We've decided we don't require your help beyond today, and we'd like you to keep that quiet."

Logan's eyes burned a dark green. "I doubt we'll be interested in anything that forces us to lie to family."

"No need to lie," Benny said cheerfully as he set the helicopter down on the grass outside the hospital. "Just don't say anything."

Garrett's eyes widened on the screen. "Benny. You fucking landed on the grass."

"Yep." Benny powered down the machine. "Just got an update. The Kurjans are five minutes out. Go time, boys."

CHAPTER NINETEEN

Faith paced the stone floor as Ivar worked on the computers. How could Ronan get all bossy and assholish on her? When he returned, she'd give him hell. Pausing, she looked toward the elevator to the surface.

"It's programmed only for my hand or Benny's," Ivar said, typing away, his back broad and powerful. "Now Ronan's too."

"Then program it for my hand, damn it." She turned to face him, feeling like steam might be coming out her ears.

He sighed and swung around in his chair. "You can't leave."

She put her hands to her hips and glared at him. His dark blond hair curled over his ears, while his arctic blue eyes glowed. He looked like a Norseman with a kick—definitely a Viking vampire. "I can do as I please. You can't be serious about kidnapping me."

He stretched his muscled arm across his wide chest. "I think it's false imprisonment at this point. You came along willingly, so no kidnapping charge."

"You think this is funny?" she burst out, her hand clenching into a fist. How would the Viking like her idea of a practical joke? She could fill the entire place with glitter that would stick to his long hair for weeks.

"Eh." He gestured toward the vacant desk chair next to him. "Instead of pacing a track in my nice stone floor, why don't you help? We'll need the right medical equipment and supplies for your sister, and if you'd just type in a list, I'll make sure we have what you need."

She eyed him and then moved forward, taking the same chair Ronan had put her in earlier. It took several minutes, but she finished the list and hit *send* on the email. Then she sat back. "This is what we'll need."

He turned toward her, his gaze soft. "You love her very much."

"She's my sister." Faith settled back in the chair. "I promised I'd take care of her when our parents died." She'd failed.

"You are taking care of her," Ivar said. "Tell me about her."

Faith blinked and swiveled her chair toward the immense Viking. Most people didn't ask about Grace—afraid to bring up a painful subject. She smiled. "Grace is so insightful, and she truly likes people. They gravitate to her naturally."

Ivar smiled. "She sounds lovely."

"She is," Faith said, leaning forward. "She's a photographer who was working for the newspaper in Denver. It was a fun job to her, but she enjoyed outdoor photography."

"Someone who sees beauty," Ivar murmured.

"Exactly," Faith said, warming to the big Viking. He really did understand people.

He glanced to the side and read the screen before concentrating on Faith again. "How was Grace injured?"

"Burglar attacked her," Faith said, losing the warmth. She shivered.

Ivar cocked his head to the side. "You sound…uncertain."

Man, he was insightful. And he invited confidence. "I just don't know. She was dating a guy I didn't like much, and I've always wondered." She'd mentioned it to the police, but they hadn't found anything. "It's just a feeling. There was never any evidence that he hurt her."

"Where is he now?" Ivar asked, his gaze sharpening.

"Denver," she said. "He used to try to visit Grace, but I put a stop to that. So I assume he's still in Denver."

Ivar nodded. "You should let Ronan take care of him. He will, you know."

There might not be anything to take care of. Faith frowned. "I don't understand this ancient brotherhood thing you have going on."

He flashed a smile and spun around to his keyboard. "It's hard to explain."

"Try anyway," she muttered, looking up at the twinkling pink lights. The potential Keys. Whatever that meant.

He typed again and then sat back, his gaze on the computer screen in front of him. "I assume you've seen Ronan's back?"

"The tattoo? Yes," she said. "The detail is impressive."

Ivar snorted. "Detail. Man. You two need to talk and not just dance around each other."

She turned more fully toward him. "I don't understand."

Ivar frowned and pivoted his chair to face her. "It's not really my place to say. Except that what you've seen—no tattoo artist did that."

"What?" She tilted her head, truly trying to understand. "Ronan said something like that too, but how can a tattoo not be a tattoo?" she asked.

"Good question. Maybe when the tattoo is bonded with bone and blood." He glanced toward the screen again.

"What the heck does that mean?"

He typed with one hand and then turned back to her. "Forget everything you think you know, Dr. Cooper. You're in the Stone Ages when it comes to physics and the human body. All humans are."

"Then enlighten me, Viking," she murmured. "Speaking of which, you actually look like one."

"I am one. It's not something that just goes away, even if the world does change. Although it has been too long since I laid siege to anything." His grin softened the hard edges of his immortal face. "All right. Here it is: There's a dimension, one only known to us, where the laws of physics are…different."

She narrowed her gaze. Was he messing with her? "The laws of physics are absolute."

He laughed then, the sound deep. "Ah. So cute. Humans." Shaking his head, he turned back to the screen. "They've just arrived in Denver." He watched for a moment, keeping his attention forward. "Even in this place, this dimension, blood and bone are everything. Especially blood, right? It takes oxygen to the brain. It feeds the heart. It can be transferred from one person to another. No blood...no life."

She shivered. "Okay. I'm with you so far."

"There's a ritual performed only by the strongest warriors. One kept secret through the eons. One that protects them in battle." His tone lowered to reverence. "When the rite is performed, when the blood is powerful and pure, it forges unimaginable strength. A shield..."

Her mind flashed to Ronan's tattoo. "The rib cage," she whispered, straightening, her chest filling. "Those were his ribs. They form the shield." How poetic.

"*Ja,*" Ivar said, his accent slipping free for the first time. "We mixed our blood together, all seven of us, and we drank."

"You have it too?" she asked.

For answer, he turned and pulled off his black shirt, revealing the same raised rib and shield marking across his entire back that Ronan had. "Yes. There's more to it, of course...and I can tell you it hurt like hell. Thought I would be one of the ones to die."

She leaned back. "What?"

He shrugged back into his shirt, his eyes blazing. "Only ten percent of us lived through the bonding."

Holy crap. Ten percent? "That's a horrible survival rate," she said, her mind reeling.

"Yes. My brother and the others kept going, soldier after soldier, until seven of them lived. The shield." He cleared his throat. "I replaced my brother after he passed on."

So many of them must've died trying. How was this possible? The marking on Ivar's back proved his tale, but it still seemed crazy. "What could've been so important?"

"The shield," he said again. "To form the prison worlds, it took seven of us who were bonded in such a manner. Even so, we knew the shield would fail at some point, and we thought Ronan and Quade would perish when it did. We got that wrong."

Hopefully Quade had survived as Ronan had. "I'm glad you did."

"As am I. We five who remained were to protect earth and find the Keys to prepare for the day when the prison world shattered. We've tried."

Much of this still didn't make any sense. "You made yourselves nearly invisible, even by immortal standards. Why be so secretive?"

He paused. Then he shook his head. "You'll have to ask Ronan that question."

She would. Definitely. And she'd get an answer this time. "Fine. You said three of the shield have died. How?" she asked.

His gaze hardened. "Our chests and hearts are protected, and our spinal columns are like steel. But as with any power, there's a weakness. Right below our chins, we can be decapitated, and the Cyst have the right weapon to do it."

"The Cyst killed your three shield members?"

"Brothers," Ivar said, his chin lifting. "We're bonded in blood and bone. They killed my brothers."

She leaned forward. "Are you sure this really happened? It was a long time ago. Is it possible they have a different view of history?"

His eyebrows rose. "Hell, no. Not a chance."

"Instead of going through all of this, why not just kill Ulric way back when? Even though Ronan isn't at full speed yet, I've seen him fight. Seven of you going after one guy back then would've been unstoppable."

Ivar's eyes glowed with an ancient wisdom. "I wish that were true. But Ulric perverted the ritual."

She gave a slight shake of her head. "So? Ronan said Ulric's body was fortified. But why not cut off his head?" Then she winced. There was a sentence she'd never thought she'd say. What kind of a world had she entered? How was this all possible?

Ivar tugged his T-shirt back into place. "He can't be decapitated. His ritual was for him and him alone. He doesn't have a brotherhood or a solid frame of support, Dr. Cooper. When I say *perverted*, I mean it. He sacrificed nearly one hundred of the Enhanced to gain his strength."

"He killed a hundred human women?" she asked, her voice hushed.

A muscle ticked in Ivar's jaw. "Yes. He imprisoned them, found the prison dimension, and conducted the ritual. Only he survived—by design. The bastard took the essence of those women, their blood and bones...and he forged them together within himself. He can't be killed from the outside. There is no vulnerability. No weak spot."

From the outside. He couldn't be killed...from the outside. She switched back into doctor mode. "Bone...and blood."

Ivar nodded. "You are smart, aren't you?"

"Yes." She ran through different scenarios, trying to put the pieces all together. "There's something in the blood of the Keys. When he took the blood of the hundred...something happened? What?" She shook her head. "This is unbelievable."

"Yet you believe it," Ivar said. "There's enough *science* there that it seems possible. Even to you." The emphasis had a bit of sarcasm to it.

"I'm not sure." Although an alternative explanation wasn't coming to her. The tattoos. The fangs. These otherworldly men. *Males.* "Tell me the rest of it. Why three women? Three Keys."

"Enhanced women are their own species. You present as human, but your genes are slightly different, Doctor. One of the women he killed was a powerful seer. A prophet...one of the first. She poisoned her own blood, preparing to fight, but creating what would these days be called a plan B."

"Plan B?" Faith coughed. "Seriously. Plan B. With blood."

"Definitely with blood. Gertrude had triplet girls. Already powerful as toddlers. She infused each of them with altered blood, and together, they were able to set the poison free. The poison that Ulric ingested when he killed Gertrude."

This sounded like a freakin' fairy tale. "You're crazy." Just how much of this had the Seven gotten wrong through the years? Was it possible the legend had grown far beyond what had really happened? How was a prison world even possible? How was another dimension really attainable? Her temples started to hurt.

Ivar breathed out. "Stop thinking so hard. Your brain will explode."

She blinked.

He leaned back. "I'm just kidding. Brains can't explode. Jeez."

Wonderful. A joking vampire. Just what she needed. "You're trying to find the triplets?"

"No. The trips are long gone. We're trying to find descendants of each. A special woman—born whenever one is lost. We hope."

Wow. That was a lot of hope. "How will you know when you find one?"

He sighed. "A couple of ways. Power has a signature. We can feel when a vampire is near, when a shifter is near, and so on. The Keys should have their own signature."

"Anything else?" A feeling wasn't much to go on. Even for these rather superstitious creatures.

He leaned over to the computer before her and quickly typed, igniting the screen. "Just this marking. It's a birthmark, and the Keys all have it. Somewhere." A file opened, and a drawing of a key-shaped birthmark came into view.

Faith stopped breathing. The world felt like it held still, ending the constant spinning. Her focus narrowed and she studied the mark.

"What?" Ivar asked.

She swallowed over a lump in her throat. No way would she tell him. Not right now. This was impossible. "Nothing. It's just odd. A birthmark that looks so ordinary."

"It's anything but ordinary." He tensed and then sat back. "They're heading into the hospital."

She barely heard the words. The birthmark was as familiar to her as if it had been on her own body. But it wasn't. The key was upside down and lightly twisted, but it had been on her sister's upper chest, just beneath her clavicle, from the day she'd come into the world.

Grace was one of the three Keys.

CHAPTER TWENTY

Ronan kept low and ran for the hospital side entrance, where Garrett and Logan waited. The power emanating from both was staggering, and pride nearly dropped him to his knees. His brother, Jacer, would be smiling down from wherever he was right now. Ronan held out a hand. "Ronan."

"Garrett." The younger vampire shook, his hold strong but not aggressive. The kid had class.

Logan did the same.

They were young, looking to be in their mid-twenties. While they appeared youthful, both held eons in their gazes. They'd been through some shit, without question.

Garrett studied him, his metallic gray eyes shining with intelligence. "There's something familiar about you. Have we met before?"

"No," Ronan said, seeing his father in the angle of Garrett's cheekbones. His heart thumped hard for a moment. Now wasn't the time to tell his great-nephew the truth. Maybe it could never happen, since the Seven had to remain a secret. "We've never met. I'm just another vampire-demon, like you."

"I'm pure vampire," Garrett said.

Logan leaned around his friend. "I'm a hybrid. Welcome to the club."

"Garrett, you're part demon, dumbshit," Benny said, craning his neck to look up the three stories of the hospital.

Ronan tensed in case Garrett lashed out, but the immortal surprised him again. Garrett just raised one eyebrow. "I have heard rumors to that effect." He grinned, flashing fangs. "Call me a name again, and I'll tear your legs off, Ben."

Benny snorted. "I've always liked you, kid. I'd hate to rip out your throat and eat your larynx."

"The liking is mutual," Garrett agreed.

Logan moved toward the door. "Aren't the Kurjans coming? We can joke around later."

"Who's joking?" Garrett and Benny said at the same time.

Ronan frowned. His brother had had an odd and usually inappropriate sense of humor, which was why he and Benny had gotten along so well. Who knew that characteristic was inheritable? "Enough. Let's get in and out before anybody knows we're here."

A big black helicopter landed on the roof, swooping in from nowhere. It definitely didn't look civilian.

"Too late for that," Benny said, a growl coming from his chest. "The Kurjans have arrived."

Ronan looked up at the night sky. "Does everybody in this new world have a helicopter?" It was unthinkable.

"New world?" Logan asked.

Benny swept the question away with one broad hand. "Later. The Kurjans won't care who they kill, so we'd better get in there and now."

The human security guards wouldn't have a chance. Ronan settled into battle mode. "This woman is my mate's sister—her only family."

Garrett gave a short nod. "Understood."

Logan opened the door. "Which floor?"

"Second," Benny said. "At least she was on the second floor when Ivar sent the information. There's no reason for her to have been moved."

"I studied the schematics in the helicopter on something called a tablet. Amazing device," Ronan said, leading the way into the building and turning for the stairs. "Garrett and I will take the stairs. Benny, you and Logan take the nearest elevators. We'll approach the room from opposite sides."

"Affirmative." Benny tapped Logan on the arm. "I'll lead."

Logan nodded at Garrett. "Stay safe, brother."

Garrett yanked open the door to the stairwell. "Ditto. Remember that Kurjan blood burns."

"Burn, baby, burn," Logan responded, pivoting and jogging after Benny, his hand already at the knife near his waist.

Ronan watched the hybrid go. "Brother?"

"We've fought, killed, and almost died together," Garrett said, pulling a weapon out of his waistband. "His brother mated my sister, and that too makes us family. He's my brother. Period." He ducked his head and started running up the stairs. "Plus, we share a niece. One we've vowed to protect. Regardless of the cost."

The Lock. Hope Kayrs-Kyllwood. "I see," Ronan murmured, following Garrett, his new boots sure on the steps. His strength was returning, and there was no doubt in his mind it was because he had started bonding with his mate. There were so many questions he wanted to ask the young Kayrs, but now wasn't the time.

He caught Garrett's shoulder before the male could bound into the hallway. "I'm lead." Without waiting for an argument, Ronan shoved past him and moved into the hallway, keeping his gun hidden.

A boot to the face threw him back into Garrett. He bounced off, reached out, and yanked the offender into the stairwell. Pivoting, he took the attacker down, ripping off the asshole's mask. Red hair, black tips, purple eyes. Fucking Kurjan.

The Kurjan snarled and punched up, hitting Ronan in the nose. It cracked, broken.

He punched down, aiming for the neck and yanking in his knees to break the Kurjan's ribs. They broke with a loud shatter, and the soldier hissed in pain.

Garrett moved to the side, his gun out. "Finish this."

Ronan nodded. He was trying, damn it. Snarling, he punched down into the Kurjan's throat again. At full strength, he would've hit the floor. This time, bones cracked but stopped him. Pain ripped through his hand, and he growled, lifting it away and stretching his fingers.

Garrett gasped, his gaze on Ronan's Kayrs mating mark.

Ronan reached for his knife. "I can—"

Garrett fired three shots from a green gun into the Kurjan's forehead. The soldier jerked and then slumped, unconscious and not breathing.

Ronan pushed away and stood.

Garrett put his back to the wall and pointed the gun at Ronan. "What the fuck."

Ronan glanced at his bleeding hand and the Kayrs marking. The K and surrounding jagged lines were covered in blood. "Long story. Talk later." He moved toward the hallway.

"Talk now," Garrett countered. "This gun fires lasers that turn into bullets in an immortal's body. It won't kill, but it'll knock you into a deathlike state long enough for me to cut off your head. Who are you and how are we related?"

"We don't have time for this." Ronan sent healing cells to his hand, but nothing happened.

Garrett's gray eyes sizzled into a wild blue. "What's wrong with you?"

"We don't have time for that conversation." Ronan shook out his hand, throwing blood. "My name is Ronan Kayrs, and I'm your great-great-uncle. My brother, Jacer, would've been your great-grandfather." All of a sudden, he felt fucking old.

Garrett frowned, his aim steady. Very steady. "My great-grandfather was an only child."

"Aye. That's the story that was told. Obviously, he was not." Ronan held up his palm and the Kayrs marking. This was a disaster. The existence of the Seven had to remain a secret, and it was too dangerous to indoctrinate this young immortal into the brotherhood. Ronan couldn't lose another family member. What had he been thinking to even consider it? "Believe me about our ties or not, but right now we have an Enhanced woman to save."

Garrett lowered his gun. "We're not finished with this discussion."

Ronan nodded and pulled the door open, sliding out to step calmly into the hall.

Garrett fell into perfect position behind him, close enough that he could keep his gun out. Smart. Definitely smart.

Ronan ignored the nurses' desk and the few patients milling around in gowns and reached the correct room. He glanced down the hallway, not seeing anything. But the hair prickled down his neck. He moved inside and then his muscles tightened into stillness.

A woman lay in a bed hooked up to machines much as he'd been. On the other side of her, near the window, stood a warrior he'd hoped was long dead. "Omar," Ronan breathed. Rage took him and his blood started to heat. Fast and strong.

Omar had partially lifted the mask off his face, revealing his too-pale skin and blood-red lips. He snarled, showing yellowed fangs. "The rumor is true. You survived."

If it was just a rumor, then Ulric hadn't found his way home yet. "I had to kill Ulric first," Ronan said.

Omar smiled, the sight garish. "We both know the Superior can't be killed." He pulled the remaining material off his head, showing the one strip of white hair braided down his back.

Ronan stopped breathing.

Garrett stepped closer and shut the door, leaning back against it. "What in the holy fuck of a nightmare are you?"

Ronan jerked. "He's Cyst. The general."

Garrett's face contorted in disbelief. "What the hell is a Cyst?"

How could that not be known? Ronan slid the knife from a sheath on his thigh. "What do you want here?"

"She's Enhanced, and we're collecting for our future and for Ulric's return." Omar reached for the knife at his waist. "We need more for the ritual he has planned for his homecoming."

Ronan's stomach tilted. That could never happen. "It will be a pleasure to kill you. I've dreamed of doing so for nearly a thousand years."

"Still upset I killed your baby brother?" Omar asked, drawing a sword from behind his back.

Ronan stilled. "You must've used deception. Jacer was a much better warrior than you."

"Yet he's dead." Omar smiled, the sight a parody.

Fury had claws as it ripped through Ronan. "I'm going to enjoy tearing your head off." He took another step closer.

Garrett sucked in air. "Why do I feel like I've stepped onto a tightrope with no net?"

"Welcome to my reality," Ronan returned, moving to the right and away from the fragile human in the bed. Very faint vibrations came from her, telling him she was an Enhanced female, but he couldn't get a strong grasp on them. He could barely sense them. Her coma was complete. His heart hurt for his mate. There was no way to bring back her sister.

Omar moved closer to the window. "This woman isn't worth fighting over. She'd be useless as a mate."

"You're not here for the woman," Ronan countered. "You're here for me."

"I'm here for answers." Omar's eyes morphed to a deep purple. "Where is Ulric?"

Ronan moved closer and angled to the side, noting Garrett guarded the door. Good.

Omar glanced at Garrett and then focused on Ronan again. "Tell me where Ulric is, or I'll blow up this entire hospital. My soldiers have been placing explosives throughout as we've been talking."

"Life is full of hard choices," Ronan said easily, reaching for the knife at his waist. "I'll sacrifice a hospital of humans for you, General. In a second."

Garrett remained silent.

Omar tilted his head toward Garrett. "All right, young Kayrs. You might want to listen to my offer." He put his back to the wide window, and streetlights outside glowed behind him.

"I doubt it," Garrett said, almost sounding bored.

Under different circumstances, Ronan would've been amused and probably proud of his new family member. As it was, his hand twitched with the need to plunge the knife into Omar's neck. But for now, the monster was talking; maybe he'd give something away. Let Ronan know what they were up against. "What's your offer to my nephew?" he asked quietly.

Omar ignored him, his gaze appraising Garrett. "You're not surprised I know of you?"

"Everyone knows of me," Garrett said without an ounce of arrogance. "Killing you would probably just enhance my reputation with the ladies." He locked the door and pointed his gun at Omar.

"No," Ronan said softly. "He's mine."

Garrett didn't move. Or lower the fucking gun.

Omar's smile widened. "Oh, young Kayrs. You don't know the Butcher, but I do. He may have been a Kayrs at one point, but even his family disowned him. Put him in a prison world dimensions away. You've probably never heard of him."

Garrett didn't twitch. "Are we going to talk or fight? I'm missing a rerun marathon of *Friends* right now." He tapped his ear and seemed to listen. "Copy that," he said quietly.

What the hell?

Garrett glanced toward Ronan. "Logan and Benny engaged three Kurjans on the roof. They were planting explosives. We have them now."

There was a communication device in Garrett's ear? How did that work? One thing at a time. Ronan cocked his head to narrow his gaze on Omar. "Kurjans? You didn't bring Cyst?"

Omar sighed. "Garrett Kayrs. Kill this interloper as your ancestors intended, and we guarantee we won't go after the Lock. We'll let her live in peace."

Garrett yawned. "I don't have a Lock."

"You know her as Hope Kayrs-Kyllwood, the prophet," Omar said smoothly.

The room heated. The air popped, and an unreal tension gouged a hole through the oxygen.

Ronan eyed his nephew, adrenaline flooding his body.

Garrett lost any pretense of boredom. "You just threatened my niece."

Omar nodded. "Indeed I did. You have no idea of her importance. Yet I give you my word she will not be touched or even sought if you do as I ask. Kill the Butcher before he kills you. And her."

Garrett snarled. "You don't understand family, freak." Then he charged.

"Now!" Omar yelled.

The window blew open, and four canisters bounced on the ground. Instinct ruled, and Ronan leaped across the room to cover Grace Cooper with his body.

The world exploded.

CHAPTER TWENTY-ONE

Safe in her Idaho home, Hope Kayrs-Kyllwood bolted upright in bed, sucking air as if she'd been drowning. Her body was cold, so she pulled the covers up to her chin.

"You okay?" Paxton asked from the floor.

She fumbled for her pink light with butterflies all over the shade and turned the knob. "Pax?" She blinked sleep from her eyes and looked over by her white desk.

He pushed up from a curled position, his wild black hair messy around his face and his blue eyes almost black. "Yeah."

She scooted over. "What are you doing here?" They lived in a subdivision on an Idaho lake with only immortals nearby. Pax's house was several blocks over from Hope's, and it had been nighttime for hours. Had he walked over by himself in the darkness?

"Your mom said I could stay." He shrugged and stood, pulling up too-big sweats over his round belly. "My dad is on mission, and I was worried about your sniffles. Vampires shouldn't get sick."

"Oh." She lifted the covers back. "It's cold in here."

He ambled over and slid into the bed, leaning back against the white headboard with carved butterflies on it. "I read that shivering burns calories."

She frowned and tossed the covers over him, sitting up next to him, her butt on her pillow. "You're not fat."

"My father says I am." Pax plucked at the covers. "He's right."

"No." Hope patted Pax's arm, her heart hurting for him. "You're perfect. My bestest friend. Ever." She smiled. "And Libby. It's three of us. Always."

He leaned his head back and shut his eyes. "I know."

"I think seven years old is too young to think about calories," she murmured. "Even if we are vampires and learn faster than human kids."

"Vampire-demons," Pax retorted. "My mama was a demon." One who'd died in the last war.

Hope patted his arm again. "I'm sorry she's gone." His mama had been a kind lady. Much nicer than his dad. "Do you want me to ask my mama if you can live here? Be my brother?"

"No." Pax pushed his wild hair away from his round face. "My father wouldn't let me, anyway."

At least Hope's mama had let Pax stay the night. "How did training go yesterday?"

"Don't ask," Pax muttered. "I suck. I wish I could just play my guitar and be a famous musician."

"You'll get better at training," Hope whispered. "As soon as my cold is gone, I'll start training too. We'll work together."

"The real training doesn't start until we're teenagers. But even this early stuff kind of stinks." Pax stretched his legs out under the covers. "If you'd just practice your piano, we could start a band."

"Okay." If it would make Pax happy, she'd be in a band with him. Libby could play the drums. "I promise."

"Good. And I fixed the tire on your bike so your parents wouldn't see you'd damaged it." He yawned, his voice cracking. "But you have to promise you won't try to make that jump over the creek again. You could've broken your arm."

"Maybe." She really wanted to clear that creek. Libby had done it the other day.

Pax sighed. "Tell me about your bad dream. I heard you wake up."

She rubbed her eyes, keeping her voice quiet. "I don't know what I saw. There's a male who's mostly bald but with one braid of white hair down the middle of his head to his back. He has purple eyes. Kind of looks like a Kurjan, but a lot meaner than Drake could ever look."

"This Kurjan sounds creepy."

"He was," Hope said, her voice shaking a little and her stomach hurting.

Pax took her hand. His was warm and bigger than hers, and she held on tight. "What else?" he asked.

"In the dream, he was looking at me. Kind of like he was there," she said, shivering.

"Like in your dream world?" Pax asked, his voice going higher.

She shook her head. "No. It wasn't real like the dream world. But it *felt* almost real. He looked at me and smiled."

"Not a good smile?" Pax asked.

"No," she breathed. "I'm kinda scared to go back to sleep, but I want to go find Drake. He'll help us, Paxton. I know that someday he will make everybody safe."

Pax didn't say anything.

Man, Hope wished they could meet. Then they'd be friends too. It would be the four of them. "You'll see," she whispered.

Pax snuggled down in the bed, yawning. "Fine. Go find him. But if the bad guy shows up, wake me."

"Okay." Hope cuddled down, still holding Pax's hand. It was nice to hold his hand. If she got scared, he would know it. And Pax would do anything for her, just like she'd do for him. They'd be friends forever and forever.

He fell asleep first, breathing lightly.

She closed her eyes and let herself go to the calm place. Then sleep.

For hours, she wandered in the dream world, looking for Drake. She called for him, searching around the beach and forest.

For the first time, he didn't come.

* * * *

Ronan sprawled across the hospital bed, blinked and tried to focus past the incapacitating ringing between his ears. He brushed a woman's hair out of his face and lifted his head, looking down.

Grace Cooper remained untouched, save for a swelling bruise along her cheekbone from the impact of his jaw. Her hair was tousled, but her skin smooth and her expression nonexistent. For a woman who'd been in a coma for two years, she appeared surprisingly healthy.

He rolled off her toward the window, coming up in a crouch to fight.

Wind blew inside, clean air mixing with the smoke. Tiles were broken across the floor, and a ceiling tile hung down, cracked in half. What the hell?

Garrett picked himself up off the ground, his eyes a dangerous gray, blood sliding down his hard face. "Asshole went out the window. Jumped right into a waiting helicopter."

"Are you okay?" Ronan gasped out, inventorying his body.

"Fine." Garrett kicked broken tiles out of his way. "You have glass imbedded in your neck."

So that explained the breath-stealing pain he felt. An inch lower and the glass would've bounced off his shielded torso. "I'm fine." It wouldn't do to let this nephew see a weakness.

Garrett rolled his eyes and moved over to the window, looking down, anger vibrating down his broad back. "They're gone." Somebody pounded on the dented door and he turned, striding forward and opening it. "We're good."

Logan nodded from the other side and whipped a leather square out of his back pocket that had an odd-looking metal badge in it. "I'll take care of it out here. Stand by." He turned and disappeared from sight.

Benny moved inside, bruises across his neck. He tried to close the damaged door and ended up just leaning against it. "Who are we?"

"Homeland Security," Garrett said, spitting blood on the floor. "Logan plays a good agent, and the badge looks real. He'll have the doctors and nurses convinced this was a small matter and that we're already working with the local cops."

So long as nobody got in his way, Ronan didn't give a shit who played what, and he'd already dealt with enough cops or security guys. He stomped on a couple of smoldering pieces of wall. "What was that?"

"Grenade. The live kind," Garrett muttered, looking around. "At least it gives us an excuse to move her."

Benny craned his neck to see Grace. "On that note, I'll go get a doctor to release her into our care. We have the documentation sent by Dr. Cooper." He yanked the door open and didn't seem bothered when it cracked down the middle. "I'll be right back."

His neck freely bleeding, Ronan moved back to Grace's side and settled the bedclothes securely over her. Her delicate jawline was similar to Faith's, and the sight hit him in the rib cage. She was so young. So lost. Was her body still healthy because she had been one of the Enhanced?

Garrett stretched his arm, revealing part of a bone broken through the skin.

Ronan winced. "Can you heal that?"

Sweat dotted the younger vampire's brow and upper lip. "Yeah." He straightened his shoulders and then went still. The bone settled back into place with a loud pop. He growled and dropped his chin to his chest so he could take several deep breaths. His skin slowly mended.

"Nicely done," Ronan said. How proud Jacer would've been of this young male.

Garrett's body remained still, but he slowly turned his head. His shaggy hair fell over his brow, mixing with the blood. "Why don't you heal your neck?"

Ronan took in air and sent healing cells to the top of his spine. The pain worsened.

Garrett straightened and stalked toward him, his black boots crunching the damaged floor. A cut above his left eye slowly mended together, leaving only a small white line. He grasped Ronan's shoulder and turned him. "Shit."

Yeah. That probably summed it up.

"A sizable glass shard from the broken window has sliced you to shit. I have to take it out," Garrett said, his voice hoarse through the smoke. "Brace yourself."

Ronan set a hand on the bed and tried to focus on how similar Grace's cheekbones were to Faith's. Or how different. Faith's were higher and fuller, where Grace's were hollowed out, no doubt from being in a coma for two years.

Garrett tightened his hold on Ronan's shoulder. "One, two—"

Agony pierced through Ronan's entire head, and his fangs dropped of their own volition, slashing his lip. His eyes burned, no doubt changing color.

"Can you heal?" Garrett asked, helping him to stand.

Ronan eyed the two-foot-wide jagged and bloody sheet of glass. "Yes." He wondered if he'd spoken the truth.

Garrett leaned around him to peer at his nape. "You're not. Yet."

Ronan hissed, his head spinning from the pain. "I'll be fine."

"Jesus, you're a stubborn bastard. We really must be related." Garrett shoved him to turn him around, but Ronan didn't move. "Strong, too."

Yet he was about to pass out. "Don't worry about me. We need to transport Grace to safety." So Ronan could hunt down Omar. It was a travesty that the brutal bastard was still living.

Garrett's fangs slid free.

Ronan lifted his head.

Garrett slashed into his right wrist and lifted it to Ronan's mouth, and then started talking before Ronan could object. "Listen. For whatever reason, you can't heal yourself right now. You're wearing the Kayrs marking on your hand, which means we're related. Any immortal blood would help, but family blood, especially mine, will heal you."

Ronan shook his head and pushed the arm away. "You're healing yourself right now. Keep your blood."

Garrett snarled. "I need you at full strength, dickhead. We might face resistance on the ground level, and we'll have this lady with us."

The kid was right. Ronan accepted the blood, letting it pour down his throat. The power seized his lungs, and he coughed. His head jerked back. Mini-detonations occurred within him, sparking nearly painfully. Healing cells spread out in every direction and began to repair the damage to his body. Quickly. "Thank you."

Garrett nodded, healing his wrist. Then he looked at the quiet woman on the bed. "The Kurjan was here with her for a while. We'll have to check her for trackers just in case."

"Trackers?"

"Yeah. Little devices that can be put on a person so they can be traced. Usually right under the skin." Garrett studied Grace. "I can barely sense her. She's Enhanced, but there's nothing else there. Right?"

Ronan's heart sank. "Yes. A Kurjan gave her a small amount of blood the other day in order to draw my mate here, and it appeared to have helped. Temporarily."

Garrett lifted a dark eyebrow. "More than a little would kill her."

That was the problem, now, wasn't it? Ronan eyed her. She was the only family his mate had on earth. Yet even he couldn't save her. Being Enhanced wasn't enough to give her the necessary strength to survive his blood. "Science has advanced admirably since I've been gone," he mused.

Garrett wiped soot off his chin. "Not that much."

Yet there had to be a way. For Faith, he'd do anything.

CHAPTER TWENTY-TWO

Faith finished settling Grace into a makeshift hospital room in the mountainous haven. Oddly enough, the surrounding rock held a sense of peace. With only the glow of the monitor lighting the room, veins of copper, silver, and zinc created interesting patterns on the wall and ceiling. A plush blue rug covered the floor.

Ronan appeared in the doorway, an ultra-soft blanket in his big hands. She jolted, her breath quickening. Emotions jumbled inside her until she couldn't find any words. Their intense foreplay would've probably resulted in mind-blowing sex. Then the guy had turned all alpha male on her, and she still kind of wanted to kick him in the face. But he'd saved her sister and had risked his life to do so. "Hi," she said lamely.

He studied her from head to toe. "Hi."

A warmth spread out in her belly. Just from his appearing in the door. Okay. Maybe because he had tough-guy bruises across his jaw that he'd earned rescuing Grace. "Are you all right?" Faith asked.

"Yes. Nearly healed." He glanced down at the blanket. "I saw this in a store on the way to the airstrip in Denver and thought she'd like it." Moving quietly, he stepped inside and handed the luxurious knit over. "I had Garrett go inside to purchase it for me."

Faith took the soft material, absurdly touched. "That was kind of you."

He shrugged, his thick hair wet and curling over his collar after his shower. He'd changed into another dark T-shirt and faded jeans that had probably been Benny's. "I didn't get any blood on it."

She spread the blanket over her sister. "This is lovely."

"Good." He turned on one massive boot and headed toward the door.

"Ronan," she said quietly, waiting until he turned around. If the Cyst leader had truly thrown a grenade into Grace's room, Ronan had been telling the truth about them and the Kurjans. He'd saved Grace from their enemies. "Thank you for bringing my sister here."

He nodded. "We've been explaining to Garrett and Logan about the Seven. Ivar said he told you everything?"

"Yes." But she wasn't telling *them* everything now, was she? So far, none of the immortals had guessed that Grace had the birthmark, and apparently she didn't give off any Key vibes in her coma. "What did they say?"

Ronan's eyes darkened, and he held out a hand. "Why don't you come join the conversation?"

She faltered and then accepted his hand, unsurprised by the jolt up her arm when their skin touched. Perhaps these newest immortals would know of something to help Grace. Man, she felt off-center. How could she not be?

He led her through the labyrinth of tunnels, all well-lit and airy, to a sprawling conference room she hadn't realized existed. Benny and Ivar sat on one side of the table, while Garrett and Logan faced them. Faith had met the newcomers when they'd brought in Grace.

All four males stood.

Ivar tugged down his shirt. "I showed them the marking on our backs."

Garrett and Logan wore identical expressions of…nothing.

Ronan pulled out a chair at the head of the table for her, waiting until she sat before yanking another one over. The other males sat.

His warmth washed over her, somewhat comforting and yet also sparking a response from her. Perhaps she should get her adrenal system evaluated, because adrenaline kept ripping through her. Perhaps it was anxiety. She mentally rolled her eyes at herself. Or was it because the most dangerous and sexiest vampire in the world wanted to mate her, and her body was all in for that idea? Her mind was not. She concentrated on the matter at hand. "Thank you all for saving Grace."

Unconcerned nods happened around the table.

So getting bombed and fighting to the death was a normal Tuesday for these guys. Nice to know.

Garrett finished a grape energy drink and crumpled the can. He focused on Ronan. "You need two more members for the Seven."

Faith blinked. "Wait a minute. After what? An hour of explanation, you're on board with this concept? You believe it all? Without any proof but the tattoo on the back?"

Garrett frowned.

Logan elbowed him. "Human," he whispered, plenty loud for everyone to hear.

Garrett's face cleared. "Oh yeah. I forgot." He smiled, and the sight was so charming, Faith could swear she heard women sighing from miles away. "My uncle can teleport, and he does so by jumping dimensions. My dad can lift a hand and stop the motor function of any attacker. I have an aunt who's a mental demon hunter, two aunts who are powerful witches and can throw a fireball at your head if you swear in their presence—"

"Unless they're swearing themselves at the time," Logan interjected.

Garrett snorted. "True. My older sister met Logan's brother in a dream world during their childhood, and now they're mated and have a kid. This tattoo and prison stuff and dimensions? Lady, it's a regular week for us."

Ronan went stiff. Hard as a rock next to her. Her heart started pounding and she turned her head. "Ronan?" Her voice came out a little too soft.

"Dream world?" he asked, his chin lowering. "Your siblings met each other in a dream world. Is it still there?"

Garrett's hard jaw went slack. "Oh, God."

"Shit," Logan agreed. He wiped his hand across his eyes. "No. His sister basically drew a Kurjan bomb from this dimension into it, and it exploded. Seven years ago. It's gone."

Ivar breathed out. "Guess we know how your world shattered."

Ronan nodded. "Yeah. I'll talk to Garrett's family at a later date—much later. It doesn't matter how or why...just that it shattered. Without my sphere, Quade's and Ulric's will eventually fail as well. That's a fact."

"If that world shattered more than seven years ago, where have you been in the meantime?" Logan asked.

Ronan shrugged. "Apparently under rocks and then in a coma."

"Huh." Garrett tapped his fingers on the long stone table. "Is that why you can't heal yourself yet? Did you do some type of damage internally? Some injury, maybe, to your blood itself?"

Faith held up a finger. "Wait a minute." She sifted through the facts and everything she'd learned. Turning, she faced Ivar. "You said the Seven are bonded in blood and bone. That you took each other's blood and forged not only stronger bodies, but a connection."

"Yes," Ivar said, his brow furrowing. "Why?"

She leaned in as she warmed to the topic. "Are you and Benny as strong as you were before? Years ago?"

Benny shuffled on the chair. "Well, no. But we haven't fought for a while, so I just figured I was rusty."

Ivar's expression darkened. "As did I."

Okay. All of this was new information, but if everything they said was true, then there were logical connections to make. "You're bonded in blood and bone, and that gave you strength. But three of your members have died, and you've only replaced one. Adare is missing, and Ronan is healing from catastrophic injuries."

Ronan sat back, turning his head to face her as realization dawned in his expression. "So you're saying..."

She nodded. "I'm saying you created a situation where you need seven to reach your full power. Maybe you require an entire seven before you can even completely heal, Ronan. If Quade is alive and comes out of the shield world, he'll need everyone at full strength." She leaned further forward, thinking rapidly. "Ivar, you were right. It is always about the blood."

Benny paled just a little. "There's more." He cleared his throat. "When Jacer and then Igor died, it was before Ivar became one of the Seven. I *felt* their deaths. Their pain and then their disappearance."

Faith just stared at him. How was that possible? That type of a connection? Was it the same with mates? Something must happen at a cellular level...even deeper. Was there truly a soul level? This was a new area of science, and she wanted to know more. Understand more. Answer some of the largest questions in the universe.

Ronan twirled the damaged purple can around in his hands. "Interesting."

Logan glanced at Garrett. "Are we in agreement that Ulric will manage to get back into this world sometime in the future?"

"Yes," Ronan answered for everyone.

"And you're sure he has the ability to kill all Enhanced females?" Garrett asked, looking suddenly much older. "Even mated ones like my mom and sister?"

Ronan exhaled. "Yes. The power is in his blood, but spreading it..."

"Would be simple," Logan said, leaning back and crossing his arms. "Science has progressed to a point where spreading a contagion is easy. I'm assuming he's had followers through the years preparing for his return?"

"Of course," Ivar said, his blue eyes burning.

"Well." Garrett's shoulders went back. "I guess we have no choice, because you need two more members of the Seven."

"No," Ronan said. "You must've missed the part about how a large percentage of warriors we tried to indoctrinate burned alive in front of us. The risk is mammoth. No way will both of you survive."

Logan's nostrils flared. "I'm assuming Kayrs and Kyllwood blood has an edge, considering we both have ancestors who were part of the Seven. But I need to know. Am I here because I'm your choice, or am I here because I'm Garrett's best friend?"

Garrett glanced sideways. "You're the best fighter I've ever seen. Dude."

Ivar's chin lowered just a little. "You're here because you are a warrior and a great one. We'd choose you before either of your brothers. Zane is busy leading the demon nation and Sam has another destiny. One only whispered about, and I won't tell you if you're not part of the Seven, so don't ask."

"They're not going to be part of the Seven," Ronan said in a low growl. He looked down at the can Garrett had crumpled. "What is yellow number two?"

"Who cares? Joining the Seven is our decision," Garrett said evenly. "It sounds like we don't have a lot of time to waste here. I'm in."

Logan met Ronan's gaze evenly. "As am I."

Ronan shoved away from the table, standing. "Did you not hear the part when I said you will most likely die during the ritual?"

"Yeah, I heard you." Garrett also pushed away from the table. "How long do you need to find a couple of witches to do it?"

"We don't need witches," Ivar said as Benny remained silent. "It's just us now."

Logan also stood. "Good. Then Garrett and I are heading home for a day to somehow say good-bye without letting anybody know why. Just in case one of us doesn't make it."

Ronan shook his head.

"It isn't your decision," Benny repeated. "It's theirs and they've made it." He stood and faced the younger warriors. "You have two days. In that time, Ivar will hunt down a physicist who can help us determine when the other shields will fall."

Faith shivered from the tension in the room. "Why can't you just create another shield?"

Ronan shook his head. "The three were bonded together. It was the only way."

Yeah, that made an odd kind of sense.

Ronan stood and faced the younger warriors. "This is your decision, but I'd ask you to think it through during your time away. With your families. Hope will need protection, and you can do that without being part of the Seven. You cannot shield her if you're dead."

Neither Garrett nor Logan twitched. Not an inch.

Man, these guys were tough. Faith stood, wondering how she could help. "I'd like to see any records you have of the ritual. Maybe as a doctor, I can do something to help ensure success. Or at least diminish the pain you talked about, Ivar."

"No problem," Benny said easily. "I have a bunch of notes we all took way back when. I'll dig them out for you."

Ronan settled a proprietary arm around her waist, and she didn't push him away. "Benny? We must go find Adare," he said. "To perform the ritual, we'll need everyone."

"I'm tracking him down as we speak," Ivar said, grimacing. "As soon as I find him, we'll have to go and get him."

"Good." Ronan glanced down at Faith. "Maybe he's close by. Please tell me we don't have to fly."

Ivar grinned. "I'm sure we'll definitely have to fly."

Ronan sighed. "Very well."

Benny looked around at the gathered group. "At least now we have a game plan. Find Adare, kill Omar before he can take any more of the Enhanced, save the ones he's already taken, fill the Seven, discover if the shield and prison world have collapsed... and prepare for a new war."

"After Adare, killing Omar is paramount," Ronan said softly. "He murdered my brother. For that alone, he'll die."

His tone shot chills down Faith's back.

Ivar's eyebrows rose. "If we find Omar, we need to infiltrate his camp. Discover just how prepared they are for Ulric's return. The Cyst have been silent for one thousand years. Hidden. Even during the last war, they didn't participate, and the Kurjans lost. They let their own people lose a war...just to stay hidden. We must glean information about them. It's imperative."

"It's good to have a plan," Benny said, his gaze darkening. "We have to save any Enhanced Omar has captured. Time is moving too quickly now. It always does."

"Amen," Ronan said. "I'll be ready to go tomorrow morning to find our brother Adare. For now, Faith and I have much to discuss."

She blinked. "We do?"

His chin firmed, and he moved for the door, giving her no choice but to go with him. "Absolutely. It's time we reached a shared understanding."

CHAPTER TWENTY-THREE

Garrett Kayrs kept the helicopter low and near the mountains, his hands easy on the throttle. The moon shone down, giving him plenty of light. Ivar had dropped him and Logan off in Vegas, and they'd quickly made their way to their own transportation.

Logan was normally quiet, but tonight his silence had weight.

"You think it's a bad idea?" Garrett asked through the headset.

"No." Logan reached up and clicked a couple of buttons, turning the helicopter into stealth mode. He'd been tweaking it for the last five years. "I just figured we had more time before destiny kicked either of us in the balls."

Nicely put. "You're a brother to me," Garrett said. "The only one I have."

Logan had two other brothers, and they were close. "We've been brothers since the first punch between us." He twisted a dial on the dash, and all of the interior lights changed to more muted colors. "Which is probably why I should do this and you shouldn't."

There it was. Garrett had been waiting for Logan and his voice of reason. "Let me have it."

"You're heir to the throne. King of the Realm," Logan said, twisting to look out the window at the white-capped mountains down below. "You can't be one of the Seven as well as the king."

Garrett made a flight adjustment and then leveled out. "Dage and Emma just had a kid. He can be king if Dage ever steps down."

Logan shook his head. "You've been tapped, and you know it. The Realm doesn't go by succession, not really, and you're the heir. Have been since you almost had to take over during the last war. You feel it. You have to know it."

That's why his fucking shoulders always felt heavy. "Maybe, but it'll be thousands of years in the future. I can do both. It's called multitasking."

Logan snorted. "Fine. The ritual is dangerous. One or both of us might not survive, and Hope needs protection. Somebody who knows what the hell is happening."

"It feels right, Logan," Garrett said, starting his descent to the field in Idaho. "When they were talking about the Seven and the duties. I sensed something, like I knew it already. Knew what it felt like to earn that marking."

Logan let out a frustrated growl. "As did I. I also need to know what they were saying about my brother Sam. He's always been a soldier and a badass. Destiny? I don't think so."

Garrett eyed the landing circle. "The only way we can be on the inside and protect everyone is to take part in the ritual. We're stronger together, brother. Always have been and always will be." He set the helicopter on the wet grass and quickly powered down.

Several buildings, surrounded the landing pod and private airstrip, sat dark in the night. The moon shone down, illuminating a powerful figure leaning against the closest building.

Garrett's chest compressed. "Ah, fuck." He removed his helmet and exited the copter as Logan did the same.

They moved forward, cut each other a look, and then kept walking.

Garrett felt like a kid again as he approached. "Hi."

Dage Kayrs, King of the Realm, pushed away from the building. At nearly four hundred years old, he had intelligent silver eyes, thick dark hair, and muscles cut from steel. He looked thirty and moved like a panther, dangerous and sure. "I take it you've had an interesting couple of days?"

Garrett barely kept from shuffling his feet. "I lost at blackjack, but Logan hit a jackpot on the high-end slots."

Dage lifted one eyebrow. Slowly and with complete control, showing absolutely no emotion.

Logan somehow stood straighter next to Garrett, who was at full attention. It was like facing some drill sergeant or something. "I later lost the winnings on craps."

Dage tilted his head less than a centimeter.

Heat flowed into Garrett's face, but he didn't blink. Still, he couldn't help speaking. "What do you know?"

"Not everything," Dage admitted, looking more thoughtful than pissed. "It's interesting. I usually do know all details, but apparently in this situation, I'm *just* the king."

Huh. Now that was out of the ordinary. Seriously so. "I've never heard you say that," Garrett murmured. Dage was usually rolling his eyes and reminding everyone, sometimes rather loudly, that he was the king and knew it all. "So. What do you know?"

"Not as much as I'm going to." Dage smiled then, and the sight wasn't pleasant. Or promising. "Right?"

A lump settled in Garrett's throat. His allegiance was to family and always had been. But Ronan. He was family too, right? "You're going to have to trust us." What did Dage know? Anything about the Seven?

Dage watched him carefully. "I do trust you, but I don't know all the facts here, and something's telling me I don't know enough of them. I do have a satellite photo taken from Denver of a Kurjan with white hair who doesn't look quite right. And the universe feels…different to me. A balance has changed."

It was up to Ronan to tell Dage about himself, and Garrett was going to work on making that happen. But for now, there was no reason he couldn't tell his uncle about the Cyst. "Apparently the Kurjans have a monk-like, creepy fighting force we didn't know about."

Dage leaned back. "Extraordinary. The effort that must've gone into keeping that secret, especially from me, is impressive." He motioned the younger immortals toward the door of the hangar. "Let's see how much of the truth I can get out of you."

Garrett paused and then turned toward the door with Logan at his side. "Sounds like fun."

Dage's laugh didn't inspire confidence.

Okay. Garrett had a decision to make and right now. If he was going to be part of the Seven, he had to adhere to their vows. But the Cyst were another matter. Maybe Dage would be appeased with intel on them.

Yeah. Right.

* * * *

Faith led the way into her bedroom, the heat from Ronan's body warming her back. Even without looking, she'd know he was the person behind her. There was a force to his personality...to his presence. She hadn't noticed that with the other males. Did she feel him so completely because he was a vampire and he'd been inside her for way too brief of a time? Or was it more? Why was she so off-balance? Clearing her throat, she turned to face him. "What did you want to discuss?"

He stopped, dominating the entire doorway. "I like your intelligence," he said, his voice silky warm like heated chocolate. Yet in his eyes, a warning lurked. A deep and dark glint that sped up her heart rate and jittered through her abdomen.

She shivered beneath his gaze. "Thank you."

"You need to use it to protect yourself." He didn't move, but somehow seemed to overwhelm the entire room.

What was he getting at? "I fully intend to use my brain as always."

"Your brain," he murmured. "Use all of it."

Irritation clawed up her throat and she grew still. Focused on him. Was he insulting her? "I. Am."

"You're. Not." He crossed his arms, and the sleek muscles bunched in an unconscious show of power. "You're one of the

Enhanced. The Kurjans and the Cyst know this crucial fact." He tilted his head to the side, the sight oddly threatening.

"I'm not that Enhanced," she protested, wanting to step back but unwilling to give him an edge.

His eyes shifted to all blue. A deep, penetrating, unfathomable blue. "Don't lie to me." His voice reached between them, the tempered quietness all danger. A low threat made all the more frightening by the softness of his tone. "Ever."

Her head spun for a second. What was happening to her? Now her feet felt cemented in place. "I'm not lying."

"You are." Arrogance was stamped hard on his fierce face. "Tell me. Now."

Her jaw firmed while her nostrils flared. She faced him directly, warning ticking down her back. Her gift, or whatever it was, was none of his business. And *nobody* told her what to do. "No." Her voice came out breathless.

His chin lifted. Anger was etched in the hard line of his jaw, and a swell of raw heat vibrated toward her. "Faith." One word. A warning. A challenge?

"Ronan," she returned, her legs shaking. But she'd never admit it. Her abdomen clenched, and her body tingled from her toes to her breasts. The tension in the room was making it hard to breathe. This was so outside her experience.

Only a slight uptick in his lip showed he'd heard her. "As I was saying, your enhancement is known."

"So what?" Asking the question didn't admit anything.

His brow furrowed. "Even if you were just one of the Enhanced, they'd come for you. But as my mate, there's a bounty on your head right now. They will not stop. Ever."

Icicles clacked down her back, quelling the odd tingling of arousal. "I can take care of myself."

He came at her fast. She retreated, her legs going into instant motion. Within seconds, she landed in the pink chair, bouncing twice. He reached her, planting both hands on the chair arms and leaning toward her, his face mere inches from hers. "Is this how?" he asked silkily.

Her throat went dry. Completely. What was happening? This wasn't normal. None of this—especially not the way her body was reacting—was normal. Every cell flashed to full burn. Her sex softened and ached.

He breathed in. Deep. The blue in his eyes morphed to sizzling green, making him look like a predator. For the first time. "I can smell you. Hot and sweet. Wanting and needing." Then he leaned even closer. "Mine."

Vulnerability prickled through her. How could he know she was getting turned on when it made no sense? None at all. "You seem to have come into your own," she said, sarcasm heavy in her voice.

"I'm getting there," he agreed. "Now. Show me."

Her fingers closed into a fist. She was a well-educated woman, and she'd aced her physics class. In a physical contest with Ronan, she wouldn't come out on top. "I don't like this side of you," she said, her body stiffening, her mind scrambling.

"Show me how you can take care of yourself." His voice was a low rumble that slid inside her skin, beneath the muscle, and warmed her nerves as if he belonged right there. "The Cyst will hunt you. They will never stop. They will come and come...and they've been training for centuries to fight. Show me, Faith. Show me how you can protect yourself."

"Fuck you," she snapped, at a loss.

His mouth tightened. "You are sadly lacking in discipline."

Her breath heated and her ears burned. Temper swept her. She struck out, slapping him squarely on his left cheek.

He did nothing to dodge the blow. Her hand landed and the sound was deafening. Pain ricocheted through her wrist and up her arm, tingling in her elbow. His face was made of pure stone.

Ronan remained solidly in place. "Is that it?" he asked, his tone mildly polite.

She couldn't breathe. Her lungs just up and stopped trying. The intensity of his gaze shivered over her skin and probed deep, swirling and stealing her control. Fear and desire mingled with jagged edges, energizing her, tightening her nipples. "This isn't me," she whispered. Not once had she been attracted to the dark side. To danger or to loss of control. She did not know him. Not really. What exactly was Ronan Kayrs capable of? "You're different."

The arrogance remained. "No. I'm exactly who I've always been. I tried to be different. Tried to ease you into this reality. Into accepting who you are. But we're out of time and frankly, I'm out of patience."

"Meaning what?" With him looming over her, there was nowhere to go.

He breathed in, expanding his wide chest. "You need to mate. To gain immortality and make you unavailable."

Mate. He wanted to mate. She laughed, the sound high and nervous. "Not a chance."

"Really." He lifted his right palm, showing the Kayrs marking. The bold K surrounded by wild knots and lines. Beautiful and strong. "This says otherwise."

"In your world, not mine," she said, shifting on the chair. If she angled her kick just right, she could nail him in the testicles. He needed to learn not to mess with her.

"If your foot lifts an inch, I'm going to paddle your backside," he said, his tone pleasant.

Her leg froze. Her gaze slashed to his. "You're threatening me?" How dare he.

"Yes." Then he waited. Oh, so patiently.

This was beyond her realm of experience. When she told somebody to do something, they did it. She was a doctor, for Pete's sake. "Get back, Ronan." She put every ounce of command she could into her voice.

"Make me, Doc. Show me how strong you are." Blue mingled with the green in his stunning eyes. "Or kick me. Please."

Her heart hammered into her rib cage and her body coiled into one tight wire. Every ounce of her wanted to kick him. To show him she wasn't afraid and that she could control the situation. That she could control her body and this insane reaction to him. That she didn't want him as badly as she did…because that was crazy. Apeman alpha assholes weren't for her. She ate them for breakfast.

Keeping her gaze, his body seemingly relaxed, he pressed his hand forward onto her clavicle above her shirt. Skin to skin. His rough…hers soft. Heat flashed into her, boiling her blood. Desire slashed her, unrelenting and with claws.

She pressed her lips together to keep from whimpering. Her teeth ached, but she tightened her jaw, meeting his gaze with her last inch of stubbornness.

"I am going to mate you, Faith Cooper," he said, the heat from his palm burning right through her skin to her heart.

She swallowed. "I thought that took sex and a good bite." Her voice quavered on the last.

"It does."

CHAPTER TWENTY-FOUR

Duty yanked Ronan in every direction, but this was more important. Faith was his mate, and she'd always take precedence. Over every duty, every calling, every war. They had to reach a mutual understanding. Now. The second he'd pressed his marking to her flesh, the beast inside him had roared wide awake. Fierce. Ready.

She looked at him, the pupils in her amber eyes wide. Expressions crossed her face in rapid succession—confusion, irritation, calculation, desire. Her leg tensed as if she was preparing to kick him.

"I will spank you," he reminded her, his palm itching to teach her a lesson. Just once. Not to cross him. The idea of her over his knee, her arse bare, made his body tight with a red-hot exploding lust.

"That's battery," she retorted, her stubborn chin lifting even more.

He ran through the dictionary he'd read online. "As is kicking somebody."

She pressed her lips together. Tight.

Beneath the desire, beneath the confusion, was something twisted. Fear. "You don't have to be afraid of me," he said, wanting to strip her naked and soothe her at the same time. This woman had him tied up in knots, and he'd only known her a short time. Dreaming about her for centuries didn't come close to the reality of her. She was kind and giving with a hard shell she'd donned to survive.

She coughed. "You just threatened bodily harm."

He frowned. "A spanking doesn't count."

"Would you stop saying that word?" she exploded, her face flushing a pretty pink.

Amusement caught him, despite his arousal, and he grinned. He wasn't the only one seeing erotic images in his mind. He'd bet his last quid she'd never surrendered to anybody. Ever. "I promise you'd like it. At the end, anyway. After you learned your lesson."

Her blush intensified. "My lesson," she muttered.

Teasing her was much more fun than he would've imagined. "Yes. Oh, my sweet Doc. You will submit, and you'll enjoy doing it."

Her pupils widened and she glared. Her foot twitched visibly. Oh, she wanted to kick him. Bad. He could see it.

This woman, this mate; she was unique. Even trapped in the overly-bright pink chair, so much smaller than he, she faced him bravely. With no escape, no chance of winning a physical altercation, she still spat fire. She brought out a possessiveness in him that was very much expected in his species. This need to be tender, to calm her, was not. "I'm not a male one kicks, Doc." He also wasn't one to give a warning more than once.

"You need to be kicked," she muttered, grasping his wrist and shoving his hand off her flesh.

He pulled back, and the marking burned painfully. Deep and sharp. He eyed the partial K imprint left on her delicate collarbone. His marking. Satisfaction with an edge filled his chest. Oh, the mark would fade in a minute. This time. "The logical conclusion for an educated woman like yourself is to mate me. Protect yourself."

"Yeah. Right." Sitting in the chair with her dark hair pulled back, she looked fragile. Heart-shaped face, soft eyes, petite body. Even in jeans and a light blue blouse, her curves made his mouth water with the need to explore and protect. To keep her safe. To know her better. To learn everything about her while she trusted him.

Then her tone caught him. He delved deeper, scrutinizing her. "You're afraid of me." Sure. That was to be expected. He was a vampire from another time with powers she couldn't match. But...there was more. Oh, the sweetheart. "Little girl raised by an elderly aunt. You took care of her and your sister." So much responsibility at a young age, and yet she was all heart. "You take in raggedy, damaged cats. I saw them."

She leaned back in the chair. "Ronan. Enough of this." A tremor ran through her words.

He pressed his palm against the chair arm again, trying to ease some of the demanding pain. His marking wanted to be transferred and now. "You were in control after losing your parents—when you had no control. Then you became a doctor. Somebody in charge."

"I am in charge." Her nostrils flared, but her gaze darted around the room.

Ah. There it was. "You're not only afraid because I take your control," he mused. "You're terrified because you like it."

Her eyes flared. Hot and defiant. "Bullshit."

Yeah. She'd protested instantly and out of fear. How could he get her to trust him? There wasn't enough time to court her. To be gentle. "Afraid to let somebody else take care of you? Or afraid to lose them once you let down your guard and trust?" he asked.

She crossed her arms and pulled up her legs, setting her feet on the edge of the chair. "Whatever."

His heart hurt for her. Sweet little girl who'd never really had a childhood. Hadn't ever had a chance to let somebody shield her. He *was* a fucking shield, and she would learn to trust him. To let him handle the darkness in life and keep her protected. "Then you lost your sister." That must've been devastating. What he wouldn't give to have been there for her that day.

"She isn't lost," Faith snapped. "In fact, the Kurjans have offered to help her. I can get her back, and I will."

But Ronan knew that even being enhanced wasn't enough to survive the kind of coma Grace had suffered. "The Kurjans can't help Grace. It's a trick. Besides, you aren't going to see any of them." While he might not be on the best footing with his mate, no way in hell would he allow her to put herself in danger with the Kurjans.

"That's not your decision," she countered, glaring at him.

The sweet scent of her desire was going to kill him. The madder she became, the stronger her scent. In his dreams, when he'd just caught glimpses of her, she had seemed so soft. Gentle and pliable. He liked the real woman even better. "I never thought I'd have to tame you," he said thoughtfully.

She gasped. "Oh, just try it, buddy." Her voice went low. Throaty.

The tone shivered down his spine to land hard in his balls. Now, that was an invitation. He grasped her throat and pulled her toward him, setting his mouth over hers.

She sucked in air.

He kissed her, molding his lips to her softness. She tasted of fine wine and woman. Her hands slapped against his chest and pushed, but her mouth moved beneath his. Her tongue swept inside his mouth first, and a roaring filled his ears. The need to take. To make her his.

She kissed him back, her sharp nails curling into his chest.

He went deeper, leaning into her, pushing her head back against the chair. The world narrowed to this small woman, who was devastating him with her mouth. With her acceptance. She was all passion, and soon, she'd be all his.

She shifted. It took nearly two seconds for the pain to hit his groin. Shock jerked him back. She'd *kicked* him?

"Faith," he growled.

She blinked twice, desire and temper still mingling in her beautiful eyes. Her lips were rosy, and arousal had turned her cheeks from pink to a pretty red.

But anger had beat desire, apparently—and challenge was there too. She was definitely throwing down a gauntlet. Had she not believed him? Had his gentleness toward her, his uncertainty in this world, given her the idea that he wouldn't keep his word?

Fury grasped him so quickly his lungs heated. "All right. Lesson it is." He grabbed her arms and hauled her from the chair.

"No." She fought him, twisting and turning, slippery as an oiled pig.

He manacled an arm around her waist, trapping both her arms and lifting her off her feet. He looked around. The bed would be a good place.

She kicked her feet, striking his knees, but this time he was ready for her.

"You're a brat," he muttered, striding toward the big bed, holding her tight to keep from shaking her like a rag doll. "Let's see if you want to kick me after not being able to sit for a week."

She shook her shoulders, trying to dislodge his hold. "Screw you, dickhead. Let me go."

Oh. He was going to actually enjoy this.

A sharp knock sounded on the door. He pivoted, and her feet swung around. "What?" he barked.

She let loose a litany of curses that was rather impressive while trying to free her arms. Her rear shimmied against his groin, and as she fought, his arm brushed the undersides of her breasts. A glance down confirmed her nipples were hard as little rocks beneath that shirt.

Ivar opened the door, his eyebrows rising. "I hate to interrupt."

"Then don't," Ronan said shortly, turning back to the bed. He needed to sit before getting her into place. There was a fine line between an erotic spanking and a punishing one, and he was skirting that line right now.

Faith struggled. "Put me down, you Neanderthal."

Ivar cleared his throat. "What the hell are you doing?"

"Disciplining my mate," Ronan said. "Go away."

"You jackass," Faith said, her butt moving against his groin again during the struggle.

His cock pulsed painfully against his jeans, and he fought a groan. Then he looked over his shoulder. "Why are you still here?"

Ivar's lips twitched, but he wisely didn't smile. "I found Adare. We have to go if we want to catch him. Right now."

Holy damn it. Every muscle in Ronan's body tensed and then clenched to rock. He really had to go. He exhaled and set Faith on her feet.

"Hah," she unwisely said, the sound full of triumph.

He swung then, his hand solidly connecting with her backside. She yelped and turned around, both hands going to her ass.

"We're not finished with this, mate," he said, turning and stalking toward the door.

"You're right—we're not," she retorted.

He bit back a grin. "Get some sleep while I'm gone." He moved into the hallway, shutting the door. The woman was going to be the death of him. But never, in his very long life, had he felt so alive. God, he wanted her. All of her. And he'd have her. For the first time since he'd returned, his life was starting to make sense and he was beginning to feel like himself again. "Let's go," he said.

CHAPTER TWENTY-FIVE

After a two-hour helicopter ride, Ronan's temper and arousal had finally abated. Ivar had wisely stayed quiet on the ride, flying the death machine, letting Ronan calm himself. The helicopter set down in a field surrounded by trees. Rain splattered heavily against the windshield. "Where are we?" Ronan asked.

"Dead fucking in the middle of nowhere," Ivar said easily, powering down the copter. "Adare wanders from place to place, performing menial work for cash and then moving on. He's drunk most of the time."

Ronan stiffened. It took a ridiculous amount of alcohol to truly intoxicate an immortal. Adare was on a destructive path. Made sense after all of his losses, but enough was enough. "You haven't invested his holdings?"

"Sure, I have." Ivar's deep blue eyes sizzled with irritation. "Fucker won't use his money. He's punishing himself for…everything."

Ronan pushed thoughts of his sexy mate to the back of his mind and concentrated. "How many times have you seen him over the centuries?"

Ivar sighed. "I've tracked him through the years, and I've sought him out several times a century. I can't bring him in if he doesn't want to come in. Keeping him prisoner makes no sense. I've argued with him, I've drunk with him, I've tried to console him. But he's a stubborn bastard, as you know."

Ronan pushed open his door and jumped to the wet ground. Rain bore down, wetting his clothes and cheeks. He tilted his face up, feeling the refreshing chill. "I missed this."

Ivar crossed in front of the helicopter and joined him. "No rain in the shield?"

"No. Sunlight, darkness, water, and wild game, plus vegetation to eat." Ronan opened his eyes. "Water wasn't a renewable resource, so I figured I'd only have a thousand more years or so. Guess I was wrong."

Ivar smacked him on the back. "I'm glad you've returned. Hopefully Adare will now see the light."

Ronan nodded and glanced around the clearing. Energy signatures came from the west, so he strode through the wet grass and between trees on a barely-there trail. Ivar followed, his steps silent. Ivar stalked as stealthily as his brother had—sure and quiet. The Vikings knew how to hunt. "Have you hunted anybody in a while?" Ronan asked.

"Sure. In the last war, we helped the Realm when they weren't looking. I assume Dage knew about us, but he didn't get in the way." Ivar pointed to the right when the trail forked. "There's a dive bar about a mile away."

Ronan followed the trail, taking in the scent of the forest. Wet grass, wild pine, animals not too far away. He'd missed this as well. But he'd missed his friends most of all. He'd give anything to have Jacer still on earth. There was a hole in his heart where his brother should be. He'd mourn later and properly—probably with more vodka. For now, Adare.

They emerged at an already muddy parking lot with dented trucks, a few rusty cars, and a line of motorcycles near the door.

Ronan breathed in and settled himself, reaching out to see who was around. Many humans and one vampire-demon hybrid. No other immortals. Adare was an almost-even balance between vamp and demon, which made him rare. And a bit odd. He had characteristics of both.

"You ready?" Ivar asked, striding toward the door, his size-sixteen boots squishing in the mud. Rain drenched his hair, darkening the thick strands.

Ronan nodded and proceeded across the lot, clomping up the battered wooden steps. Heat and the smell of bodies slammed into him when he opened the door, and he strode inside, glancing around. The bar was up front with a grizzly older guy behind it. Several people sat at battered barstools or at tables scattered throughout. Music blared from somewhere. Dart games and two pool tables could be glimpsed past an archway to the left.

He stepped inside and paused as something crunched beneath his boots, looking down. "Huh."

"Peanut shells," Ivar said, turning right. "Adds ambience."

Interesting. Ronan avoided making eye contact with a woman wearing a red skirt that looked like plastic and was short enough he could see blue satin covering her female parts. Her shirt was white, her brassiere blue, and her makeup liberally applied. The smell of her rose perfume, even across the bar, made him want to sneeze.

"The biggest threat might not be the rednecks," Ivar muttered, launching himself into motion. "Let's get this over with."

Ronan cracked multiple peanut shells as he followed his friend, reaching the archway and then pausing as Ivar slid to the side.

The Highlander was leaning over the pool table, lining up his shot, as big as ever. His black hair was long, to his shoulders, and was carelessly held back at his nape. Scruff covered his wide jaw, and if possible, he looked even broader than before. A huge bulk of sleek muscle and strength. Two women perched on barstools near him, giggling and not wearing near enough clothing for the weather.

The balls clicked together as he shot, putting two in the corner pocket. Then he stiffened. Slowly, he stood, his gaze scanning the room.

The second it landed on Ronan, his dark eyes flared. Not just dark. Adare had the black eyes of a demon but without the white-blond hair. His chin lifted. A myriad of emotions crossed his hard face, finally settling into polite lines.

Ronan's temper, still smoldering from the scuffle with Faith, started to burn.

Adare handed his pool stick to one of the women, not looking, and then came around the pool table. "Ronan." His voice wasn't quite the mangled tone of a purebred demon, but the hoarseness gave away his heritage—as did the still-discernible Scottish accent.

"Adare." Ronan lifted an eyebrow. Adare had never been overly emotional, but Ronan had expected a little more from him. Maybe even a masculine hug with a slap to the back. Welcome-home type of thing. "What the fuck, man?"

Adare straightened to his full height, making them eye-to-eye at six-foot-six. "The shield must've failed." Based on his tone, he could've been talking about the size of the trees outside.

"Nothing gets by you, huh?" Ronan drawled.

Adare's lips tightened into almost a smile. "I'm quick that way." He glanced at Ivar. "I figured you'd be making a visit sometime soon. Last time I saw you, you were wearing bell-bottoms."

"I looked good," Ivar returned, his gaze on a couple near the back door, his shoulders going back. Whatever he was seeing, he wasn't liking. "Though I never could quite master disco."

Adare reached out and planted a hand on Ronan's shoulder. "I'm glad you're alive, brother." Then he stepped back. "Now go away."

Ronan stepped forward. "No. The Sphere I guarded has fallen. We don't know if the other one and the prison have yet, but they will. We have work to do, and Omar is kidnapping Enhanced women from around the globe."

"Good luck with that," Adare said.

Ivar stiffened. "Give me a minute before you two start fighting." He prowled toward the couple.

Ronan turned. The human male looked around twenty-five, with bloodshot eyes and a weapon beneath his coat. He had his hand around the female's arm. The female was a pretty girl in jeans and a white sweater. Blue eyes, brown hair, youthful skin.

Adare turned to watch as well.

Ivar reached them and instantly grasped the male's hand, twisting. The human winced and released the girl.

"How old are you, darlin'?" Ivar asked the girl, adopting a Southern accent. Ronan could discern it with his vampire hearing. Easily.

She shuffled her feet, looking down.

Ivar sighed. "You're not in trouble. Just tell me the truth."

The kid swallowed. "Sixteen. I connected with Jeremy online, and this is the first time we've met. He wants me to go to his trailer, but I told my mom I was studying with a friend and would be home, and…I don't want to go. But then he grabbed my arm."

Ivar was partially turned, and when he smiled, the sight was bone-chilling. "Did you drive here?"

The girl nodded, tears filling her eyes.

"Okay, sweetheart. You can go home now. The storm is getting worse, so wear your seat belt and go straight there. Tell your mom about this—I think you should come clean," Ivar said, his gaze now on Jeremy. "No more meeting guys online and driving to bars by yourself."

"Yeah. I won't." The girl clutched her purse to her chest and all but ran through the bar and out the front door. A lesson well learned without her getting hurt. Good.

Ivar grabbed a phone out of Jeremy's back pocket and scrolled through. He winced and then growled. "Looks like you make a practice of picking up underaged girls. Is this naked one drugged?" He held out the phone to Jeremy.

"Fuck you," Jeremy said, shrugging free.

Ivar sighed and looked at Ronan. "Give me a minute." He grabbed Jeremy by the throat and shoved him out the back door into the rain. It closed with a loud bang.

Adare sighed. "If you don't want to clean up a mess, you might want to stop him."

Ronan frowned. "Why? The human deserves a beating."

Adare barely smiled. "Ivar has hot buttons that are triggered by violated females. He isn't just going to hit the human."

They couldn't call attention to themselves. Ronan rushed to the door and ran outside into the rain just in time to see Ivar rip open the human's throat with one hand. "Ivar," he muttered.

Ivar held the man by the lapels and looked over. "He's a pedophile. Go back and have a drink with Adare. I'll make sure the body is never found." He hefted the human over his shoulder and strode into the woods.

Ronan shook his head. Benny was the crazy one. There could only be one. His thoughts reeling, he prowled back into the bar where Adare was waiting in the same place. "He killed the human," Ronan whispered. "Is he always this reckless?"

Adare shrugged. "He's still a'savin' stray cats."

"His oath was to defend and shield," Ronan said quietly. "As was yours."

Adare laughed now, the sound grating. Pained. "Yet I fucking failed. Now I'm just living."

Ronan gestured at the scene around them. "You call this living? Spending time in dive bars and copulating with women who are unaware of proper dress mores?"

Adare leaned in, his breath smelling like mint and tequila. A lot of it. "Since they won't be wearing their clothing for long, I don't give a shit about proper."

"You never did," Ronan said, trying to hold on to his temper with both hands. "I've been gone a long time, but I felt the deaths of Jacer, Igor, and Zylo. I didn't know who had been stricken down, but I knew I'd lost brothers. I'm sorry you were here and had to grieve without me."

"We took an oath. Death was assured," Adare said, a vein bulging in his neck.

"I'm sorry about your potential mate—"

Adare twisted and shoved Ronan up against the wall. His eyes blazed. "Donn'a talk about her. She wasn't a potential. She was my mate."

Ronan drew in air, his arms vibrating with the instinct to fight. But this was his brother. And the pain in his eyes, in his voice, could be felt. The idea of Ronan losing Faith, after just meeting her, after this short time with her, slashed through his heart like a dual-bladed sword. So he truly couldn't imagine what Adare had gone through. Was still apparently going through. "All right. But I'm very sorry for your loss."

Adare shifted then, and Ronan saw the punch coming. He braced for it but didn't lift a hand to block. Pain exploded in his right cheekbone, slamming through his entire skull. Stars flashed hot and bright behind his eyes, but he remained standing. Hands at his sides.

"Are you afraid to fight me?" Adare asked, stepping back, his chest heaving.

"No," Ronan said simply. "You are my brother. Feel free to hit away until you feel better. Then we can stop this nonsense and go fight Omar before he kidnaps and kills hundreds of innocent females."

Adare snarled. "Fine." He drew back and shot a punch to Ronan's gut.

A couple of lower ribs broke and Ronan gasped, but he didn't move otherwise. Yeah, that hurt. He sent healing cells to the jagged edges, and they moved sluggishly. Here he'd thought he was getting better.

"I will beat you dead," Adare snapped, his hands in fists, frustration darkening his skin.

"Meh." Ronan's brain started to swell against his skull. "I'm hard to kill. Brother."

Adare glared for a moment, and people scattered away from the pool tables. Then his shoulders slumped. "Fine." He turned away. "I'll find another fight."

It hit Ronan then. Ivar and Benny had probably reacted much as he had—with sympathy and an effort to bring Adare back into the fold. The need to offer comfort for such a painful loss was as natural as breathing. "Adare."

"Fuck off."

There it was. The comfort and soft words weren't helping. Adare was a Highlander, a powerful being even before the bonding. His heritage was in land and loss. In power and strength. What did he *need*? "Has nobody given you a good fight?"

Adare stilled and then partially turned, looking every inch the predator he'd always been. Stark desolation and a dark hunger glimmered in his eyes. "No." The growl was pained.

Oh. Well, then. Ronan smiled and flexed his right hand. His brother needed his help, and it wasn't for comfort. Just because he couldn't heal himself as quickly as before didn't mean he couldn't cause some damage in somebody else. "I see. How about I give you a fight, a good one, and if I knock your ass out, you come home?"

Adare straightened. His proud heritage was evident in the harsh cut of his cheekbones. The expression of deadly warriors from years gone by crossed his face. Anticipation lit his eyes. "Deal."

Ronan swung, hard and fast.

CHAPTER TWENTY-SIX

After only a few hours of restless sleep, Faith dressed in clothing somebody, probably Ivar, had left by the bed and went to check on her sister. She held Grace's hand in the makeshift hospital room while sitting in another bright pink chair. There was a similar electric blue one on the other side of the bed.

She'd turned Grace several times to avoid bedsores. It was shocking that Grace had never had one sore and her body was healthy. Much healthier than one would expect. But now her blood pressure was dropping a bit and Faith was concerned. She rested her cheek on the pillow, took a deep breath, and tried to feel her sister's mind. She probed, imagining she could, but nothing. She opened her eyes. "Come back, Gracie," she murmured.

Nothing. Her sister remained somewhere else. For the first time, Faith let herself look at the situation objectively. There was no brain activity. When Grace had been taken off life support, she should've passed on.

But she lived.

Without any illness, without bedsores, without any more complications. She hadn't even lost that much weight. Not nearly as much as she should have after being in a coma for so long. Even her muscle tone was still present—barely.

Was it the key birthmark? Faith closed her eyes and daydreamed.

She and Grace had been Christmas shopping in Denver. Bright lights glowed from storefronts, and the snow fell gently all around them.

"One more picture," Grace said, dropping to a crouch on the icy sidewalk for a different angle. She kept catching shoppers and their brightly-lit packages with her lens. "Oh, this is going to be a good one." She stood, and the snow fell all around her dark hair.

Faith shook her head. "Listen. We have to hurry up. I need to get back to work."

A couple of young men ambled over, snow dusting their overcoats. "We're sorry to bother you," the first one said, his power tie evident above his lapel.

Grace grinned. "Now, how could you bother anybody?" With her light green coat, she looked like a fairy princess.

The first guy had blond hair and dark brown eyes, while the other one was a redhead with green eyes. Dressed professionally with nice shoes and clean-cut faces. Faith guessed they were in their mid-twenties.

"I'm Dirk, and this is John," the blond said, his smile charming. They were slightly dorky but kind of cute.

Grace balanced on her thick boots. "Grace and Faith."

"Really?" Dirk asked, his eyes twinkling.

"Yes," Faith sighed. "It's true." She glanced at her watch. "What did you gentlemen need?"

John grinned, his gaze running over her long trench coat. "Ladies to have eggnog with. Of course."

Grace laughed. "As it so happens, we're eggnog-loving ladies." She winked at her sister. "Come on. You have time."

Faith eyed the handsome men. "I guess I could take a moment."

Heavy footsteps sounded down the hall, yanking her right back into the present and away from that long-ago evening. They'd just had a drink and then had gone their separate ways. She wondered what John and Dirk were doing today.

Probably not hiding in a mountain.

Faith sat up, keeping her sister's hand. Her butt still tingled a little from the smack. Was Ronan back? Butterflies swept through her abdomen.

Benjamin Reese soon entered the room, munching on a sugar cookie. "Did you eat dinner?"

"I'm not hungry." She relaxed. "Has Ronan returned?"

"Nope." Benny eyed her sister and walked more quietly toward the blue chair to sit. He had metallic eyes, long dark hair, a broad jaw, and a barrel of a chest. When he sat in the chair, it groaned in protest. The guy had to be at least six-foot-seven. "She's a pretty one."

Faith smiled. "Yeah. You should see her eyes. They're hazel—green and brown. Truly stunning."

Benny perched on the seat as if afraid he'd break it. "She must be a strong little thing to have lasted this long in a coma."

"She is," Faith murmured, wondering again.

Benny glanced at the arm of the chair. "I wonder if Ivar got a deal on these or if he really thinks they're fashionable?" He grimaced.

Faith grinned. "I don't know. The pink one in my room is just as bad."

Benny grimaced. "Pink? I have a bright yellow one with green canaries on it in my room. If I had a woman in there, I don't think I could get it up with those little bastards looking at me." He glanced up, red crossing his rugged cheekbones. "Pardon my badass language."

God, he was likable. A little nutty, but tough and likable. "I'd do anything to save my sister, Benny," Faith murmured.

He nodded. "I get that. But if you're thinking the Kurjans can help her because they gave her a little blood, you're wrong. They're bad, we're good, and nothin' is gonna wake up your sister. I'm sorry."

Okay. Not so likable. Faith cleared her throat. "Let's talk about something else. Tell me about these Keys."

He shrugged a wide shoulder. "You know the story. They're powerful; the only way we'll ever stop Ulric for good. We just have to find them."

"Do they know? About their powers?" she asked, trying to sound just mildly interested.

He pursed his lips in thought. "I don't know. You'd think the information would be passed down through the family lines, but I can see it being hidden as well, since the Keys have been hunted by the Cyst for centuries. Now that Omar is gathering the Enhanced, let's just hope he hasn't found any of the Keys."

Well, at least one of them was safe right here. "Why does Omar want the Enhanced?"

Benny leaned forward. "For a couple of reasons. One, they can mate Kurjans. Two…I'm thinking there's another ritual to be performed when Ulric comes back." He winced.

That could not be good. For now, Faith had to concentrate on her sister. "You're saying there might be a Key out there who has no clue whatsoever that she's a Key. Wouldn't there be some way she would know?" Faith asked.

Benny's gaze narrowed on Faith. "Did you know you were one of the Enhanced? Honestly?"

"I'm still not sure I'm one," Faith retorted.

Benny chuckled. "Yes, you are. Why are you being so stubborn about it? I mean, I understand the mating dance you all are doing, but come on. I heard you talking to your sister. Felt the change in the air."

"Mating dance?" Faith choked out.

Benny grinned. "Yeah. The 'I don't feel what I'm feeling' bulloney. And 'I don't believe in mating, even though I know deep down it's true.'" He stretched out his legs and crossed his ankles, revealing the bottom of truly humongous boots. "All that stuff you're thinking and feeling. I've seen it before."

She frowned. Why was it so difficult to get angry with him? Maybe because he just wouldn't care. Benny had an unconcerned air about him that seemed to go bone-deep. "You're a troublemaker and a rogue."

"So they say," he replied agreeably. "I have been known to steal a ruby or two from a dragon."

She waited for the punch line. Wait a minute. "There are dragons?"

"Yep. Just another shifter—like wolves, felines, and bears." He sighed and read the blipping monitor behind her. "How long you been able to get inside people's heads?"

"No." She held up a hand. "I'm not a mind reader or anything."

His eyes twinkled. "Good thing. How awful would that be? Knowing what everyone thought."

She smiled. "I agree." Breathing out, she searched for the right words. "I can't get into minds. But sometimes, with a coma patient, I can sense them. Can feel some spark of life in their brains, and somehow stimulate it." She shrugged. "I can't explain it any better than that."

"Sounds like a cross between an empath, a psychic, and a mind reader," Benny said matter-of-factly.

She made a mild sound of agreement. "Maybe."

"How come you wouldn't tell Ronan that?" he asked.

She shifted in her seat on her slightly tender butt. "He was being a jerk."

"Methinks you protest too much," Benny said, scratching his chin. "Or maybe that's part of the dance. Hell if I know."

She didn't have a response for him. Plus, while she'd never admit it, she couldn't stop thinking about Ronan. Was he okay flying? Where was he? Was it safe? He still couldn't heal himself as he ought to be able to. She missed him. "Um, all right."

"Can you get into your sister's brain?" Benny asked, his voice going soft.

Tears pricked the back of her eyes. "No." But she hadn't given up hope. "Enough about me, Benny. Tell me why you became one of the Seven."

"They needed me." His grin widened. "Of course."

Of course. While he was certainly congenial, there was an undercurrent of danger about him. An edge. "What happens when you find the Keys?" she asked.

"We protect them until it's time for them to do the job," he said simply.

"What if they don't want to be a Key? Would you force them?" She again tried to sound merely curious.

He eyed her. "Yes."

Good to know. She liked that he gave her the truth, although the fact that Grace would have no options was distressing. "Why don't you have a mate, Benny?"

He mock shuddered. "Can you imagine how mean a woman would have to be in order to put up with me? The thought scares me outta my boots."

Movement sounded down the hallway.

"Your boyfriend is back," Benny whispered.

She cut him a look.

Two seconds later, Ronan filled the doorway. Faith gasped, instinctively moving to him. He had a black eye, split lip, and a cut across his temple. His shirt was in tatters and his knuckles appeared broken. "What happened to you?"

He smiled, showing a gap in his front teeth. "I brought Adare home."

Benny stood and loped over. "Does he look like you?"

"Nah. I'm more handsome," Ronan said with a slight lisp, watching Faith out of his good eye. "Come make me feel better, Doc."

She slipped a shoulder beneath his. "My goodness. Can't you heal yourself?"

"I am," he mumbled, letting her turn him toward her bedroom, but not allowing any of his weight to rest on her. "My abilities are slower than usual right now but shall soon strengthen."

She rested her hand on his ribs, nodding at his quick intake of breath. "You and Adare fought?"

"Yeah," Ronin said. A snap sounded. "One rib back in place," he said with satisfaction.

"Why did you fight?" She pushed open her door and helped him inside. Well, sort of. She just kind of led him.

Ronan released her and moved over to sit on the bed. "He needed to hit and get hit. Tons of grief, lots of guilt, a bucketload of anger. I'm his brother. So we hit each other." The cut above Ronan's temple began to mend. Then his eye cleared up, leaving only a light purple mark.

"You are getting better," she mused. How could she get her hands on those healing cells? Certainly they could be used to help humans. Her mind boggled at the possibilities.

"Stop looking at me like that," he said, his voice strengthening now.

"Like what?" she asked guilelessly.

He snorted. "Like I'm a specimen on one of your modern slides. I'm not a piece of meat, you know."

She grinned. "You really have been studying current vernacular."

"Every chance I get. Siri and I are making a lot of headway." His chin lowered and he sat there, looking perfectly healed. With the ripped shirt and scuffed-up jeans, he held an edge of danger that made her heart thrum to life. "So. How about us? Have we made any headway?"

She blinked. "I, ah…"

"I believe I owe you a spanking."

* * * *

Ronan barely kept his amusement in check as Faith blushed a very enticing red.

"I'd rather we didn't fight," she said, rather primly. "As I see it, we're even. I kicked you once, and you retaliated. Once."

There was a certain logic to her thinking. But he wasn't going to let her off the hook that easy. It was too much fun to tease her. "I'm not sure I agree to those terms," he said, patting the bed beside him. "Why don't you come talk me into it?"

"Seriously, Ronan." Her eyes darkened with amusement. "You were just in a pretty serious bar fight. Are you sure you're even up to talking?"

He paused. Was she flirting with him? He studied her. Pursed lips, increased heart rate, faster breathing. Even her head was tilted in a cute way. His chest warmed and filled. The sexiest, smartest, and most stubborn woman in the world was flirting with him. "Oh, I think I can manage to get it up."

A slight grin played on her mouth at his double entendre. "I missed you while you were gone last night."

The sentiment surprised him before filling him with her sweetness and trust. "Ah, Doc." It seemed she'd discovered the perfect way to disarm him. Her willingness to share her feelings made him feel almost whole again. "I missed you too. Have for centuries." He grinned.

She faltered. "I don't understand this mating stuff, and I definitely can take care of myself."

He rested his hands between his knees. "All right?"

"But I like you, and I'm attracted to you." She swallowed as if admitting the truth hurt. "I think it's silly to pretend otherwise."

If she got any goddamn cuter, he'd lose it and tackle her right to the floor. But her uncertainty required reassurance. "I like you, and I'm attracted to you as well," he said carefully. "If anything happened to you, I'd lose my soul." Probably too much information to share. But if she was going to be honest, so was he. "Thus, I have to protect you. Someday I hope you'll understand."

Her scent wafted toward him. Wildflower sweet and all her. She was getting aroused. "You know things have changed in the world, right? We're equals. Period."

"We can be as equal as you want," he replied. "Hell. You can be in charge, lady. Except when it comes to safety, battle, wars, the Kurjans, or the Cyst. Then I'm in charge."

She huffed out a really adorable sigh. "No. You don't get to decide who's in charge when."

Sure he did. He was the vampire, the warrior, and a shield from the Seven. "Why don't we both do what we're best at?" he asked, very reasonably. "You be the doctor and dispense medicine, and I'll be the soldier and handle the fights. Fair enough?"

"I won't be told what to do."

Man, she was stubborn. Their sons would be a pain in his ass, he was sure. He couldn't wait to meet them. "I shall try very hard to couch my orders in the form of a request."

Lines appeared on her normally smooth forehead. "You're not getting me."

"But I'd like to," he replied silkily. "Now come over here."

CHAPTER TWENTY-SEVEN

When Ronan's voice got all deep and liquid like that, her abdomen clenched. Her lungs struggled to properly function, and a throbbing began between her thighs. She tried to think clinically about physical attraction, but her mind just kind of fuzzed. "I think I'll stay right here." She had to force the words out.

"Don't tell me I scare you," he rumbled.

She met his deep blue gaze. Someday, maybe she'd be able to determine his mood from his eye color since it changed so often. She shook her head. Where had that thought come from? "You don't scare me."

He smiled.

Her body flushed hot.

Most guys sitting on a purple bedspread would look somewhat harmless. Not Ronan. An alertness rolled from him, full of tension and promise. An impish part of her, one she never indulged, had her winking. "You want me? Come and get—ack."

He moved faster than she could see, and she found herself flat on her back on the bed, a vampire trapping her in place. His masculine scent washed over her and she breathed him in.

She shook her head, spreading her hair out on the pillow. "How? I didn't see you move."

"My power is coming back. Fast reflexes and all of that," he said, brushing hair back from her face. The simple touch stole her breath. Then he rolled over onto his back. "Want to try again?"

"Yes." She bounded up and made it to the doorway before turning around. He was still flat on his back. "Okay, now—"

This time she bounced once on the bed before he covered her. She laughed, happiness bubbling through her. "Talk about fast."

"What's my reward?" He leaned in and nibbled across her jaw, keeping his weight off her with his elbows.

"One kiss," she said, out of breath.

He leaned up. "Fair enough." Then he pulled her to her feet.

She blinked, uncertain. "What?"

"I'm preparing for my kiss." His fingers trailed across her collarbone and down the front of her shirt, freeing each button. With infinite gentleness, he pushed aside the material and glided it to the floor. His eyes flared at her plain cotton bra. "Beautiful."

She shook her head. "No. It's just a bra."

Only his gaze lifted, the look intense. "Not the bra. You." He swept his hands down her arms and then up her back, touching every inch, setting her skin on fire. He released the bra and it too disappeared to the floor somewhere. "Perfect."

She'd never felt perfect. But with his gaze, with his words, she did feel beautiful. She glanced over her shoulder at the bed, her legs feeling weak. If they had to stop this time, she'd actually die. "Shouldn't we hurry?"

"No." Almost reverently, he reached out and palmed her breasts. "We went too fast the other night and didn't even get to finish. I'm savoring my kiss this time." His hands were dark against her pale breasts, and his touch firm. Strong and yet gentle. Then he leaned in, laving her collarbone. "Not a kiss yet," he murmured, his mouth hot on her skin.

Her nerves zinged to life, raw and hot. She leaned into him, reaching up to tangle her fingers in his thick hair. He licked down her chest and closed his lips over a nipple.

Her knees wobbled. Electricity streaked to her core, and she arched against him, tightening her grip on his hair.

He groaned around her nipple and suckled while he palmed her other breast.

Excitement pulsed in her body, sending desire flowing through her veins. Needy and edged with demand. Every tug on her nipples zinged down to torment her clit. She ached, empty and wanting. "Ronan," she murmured, letting go of his hair to tug his shirt over his head. He gave a sound of protest and released her breast, helping her.

Then he dropped to his knees. A powerful male, ripped chest, abs tight with tension. He reached for her jeans and unclasped the button. Then slowly, way too slowly, he released the zipper.

She grasped the waist and shoved them down, trying to kick them off.

He smiled. "You're going to need to learn patience." Then he flipped her around.

"Hey," she protested, her hair swinging into her face.

His thumbs slid into the sides of her panties, rendering her speechless. Then he slowly pulled them down, a hum of what sounded like appreciation tumbling from him as she stepped free. Nobody had ever made her feel like this. Worshipped and safe. Protected and wanted. He traced a slightly painful spot across her left buttock. "I bruised you."

She glanced over her shoulder. "I hope I didn't bruise you." Her voice had gone throaty.

"No." His voice lowered to a wild huskiness. He cupped her ass, his hands big and strong. Then, drawing out the anticipation, he turned her around.

"What are you doing?" she asked.

"Getting ready for my kiss," he said, his gaze on her sex.

Vulnerability left her nervous. She reached for him, to pull him up so she could finally get that kiss. A quick shove caught her by surprise, and she landed on the bed, giving a startled laugh. She sobered when she realized he was still on his knees. Right. There. She leaned toward him, going for his shoulders.

His smile was all male. Blatantly so. He grasped her wrists and set them outside her thighs. Then he planted one hand on her abdomen and pushed her until she lay on the bed, her legs over the side. Her body pulsed with need, but this was too intimate. She'd wanted a fast night with him to finally take this edge off. "Ronan," she started.

"I didn't say where I was going to kiss you." His breath brushed her clit.

Her core clenched and throbbed. She closed her eyes on a moan.

"God, you're beautiful." He licked along her thigh, nipping with enough pressure to send her senses spiraling. Then he pressed her thighs open, exposing her to him. For several heartbeats, he just stared. Then he spread her with his thumbs.

She was wet and desperate for more. Going on instinct, she reached for him.

Faster than ever, he manacled both wrists in one hand and yanked her torso halfway up. "Patience. Remember?" Holding her in place, he inserted one finger inside her wet folds.

She gasped, her lungs filling, her chest heating. Her sex tightened around him. Needing more.

"You're tight and wet. For me." Arrogance, male and powerful, was stamped on his face. Hunger glittered in his eyes. "Are you going to be patient?"

At that second, she'd agree to being from Mars. "Yes," she whispered.

"Good." He slid another finger in, fucking her slowly. It was too much. She moved against him, trying to get more pressure.

He stopped.

She stilled.

"Patience. Do not move." He waited as she watched him, her eyes wide and her body on fire. Then he stroked inside her again and twisted his thumb over her clit.

She arched, giving a soft cry. Ripples spread out from her clit, going deep, making her crave him.

His smile was predatory. "Good. Now lie back, and if you move, I'm not only going to stop. I'm going to give you that spanking you escaped earlier." He released her wrists, and she fell back onto the bed.

He opened her more, his shoulders shoving her thighs apart.

Then he leaned in and licked her, sliding his tongue through her folds and sucking on her clit. She bit her lip and tensed, trying not to move. He couldn't stop. Ever. Her thighs trembled against his shoulders.

He released her clit and licked her again, his fingers twisting while his mouth showed no mercy. Within minutes, she was thrashing and mumbling incoherently, trying her best to remain still. Heat swept her entire body, making even her ears burn.

Coils of electricity lashed her inner walls. He chuckled against her clit, and she felt the vibrations up to her breasts. His fingers twisted again, and he nipped her clit. Hard.

She flew into an orgasm, crying out his name, arching into his mouth. Sparks flashed in the corners of her vision, and she rode the shock waves, tears burning in the back of her eyes. She'd had no idea she could feel like this. Finally, she came down, her fingers relaxing on the bedspread.

He removed his fingers and then placed a very soft kiss on her oversensitive clit. "There's my kiss," he murmured. Then he stood and kicked out of his jeans, his erection clearly defined beneath the boxers.

Swooping, he lifted her and set her beneath the bedclothes, climbing in behind her. He wrapped her in warmth after switching off the light next to the bed. They were plunged into darkness.

She blinked. "Ronan? What about you?" That definitely wasn't a huge banana against her backside.

His lips wandered lazily across her ear, and he settled her closer into him. "I must heal a cracked pelvis and three still-cracked ribs.

Give me an hour or so, and we are finally going to consummate this relationship. On my life, we're having sex. Finally."

Cracked pelvis? They weren't ever going to have sex, damn it. Even though she'd orgasmed, she felt empty. She needed more, but the poor guy was injured. She should help him, so she started to move.

"Stay." The arm around her waist was harder than steel.

"I didn't know you were hurt," she protested.

He snuggled his face into her hair, breathing deeply. "I'll be fine. Tasting you was all I wanted."

There was the sweetness she'd seen in him the day he wore those silly tennis shoes. She'd never felt so satisfied or safe. That was interesting. Rarely in her previous life had she truly felt unsafe. But in his arms, beneath the earth, snuggled close? The sense of being protected filled her, giving her a peace she hadn't known she lacked.

"You're thinking too hard," he mumbled.

"I talked to Benny, and he thinks I'm a cross between an empath, a psychic, and a mind reader," she whispered, wanting to share something, anything, with him.

He kissed the top of her head. "That's why you talk with coma patients? You can get into their heads?"

"Kind of. I see images or sparks. But I don't read minds."

"Thank goodness." His breath brushed her hair, and his amusement tickled her. "What else?"

She stared into the darkness. This whole trust thing was difficult. Should she tell him about Grace being a Key? Ronan's allegiance had to be to the Seven. He'd taken the whole vow and had that immortal marking. Would he force Grace as Benny had said he would? But what if they could save Grace? Maybe since she was a Key, she had more power than just an Enhanced. Could she be healed?

Ronan's breathing deepened as he slipped into sleep.

She cuddled closer into his warmth. Perhaps she'd figure out a way to trust Ronan, save Grace, and keep Grace from being a Key.

If it was a secret, then she could never be forced to do anything. Even by immortals.

Her eyelids fluttered shut and she started to fall into sleep.

A blaring alarm jerked her wide awake. Red track lights lit up the floor.

Ronan pulled her from the bed, grabbed his shirt off the floor, and ran for the doorway. Before they made it, he yanked the shirt over her head. Then he slid out before her, keeping a hand on her stomach to hold her behind him. The muscles down his back vibrated.

"Large force coming." Ivar was out in the hall. "Come on."

Another towering male jogged past them, this one with black hair tied at his nape. Ronan looked back down the hallway and set her in front of him, protecting her from behind. "We are never going to have sex, damn it. Run."

She launched into a run, her heart pounding. Her bare feet slapped the hard stone as she tried to keep up with the warriors in front of her. Ivar took a sharp left and Faith followed. Ivar stood in the middle of what looked like a depot with a copious number of weapons. He handed her a green gun. "Point and shoot." She gulped, her mind spinning. The gun was heavy and cold in her hand.

The rock wall slid shut behind Ronan. "What the hell happened?" he growled.

Ivar tossed a bulletproof vest at him, and he pulled it over his head. "I don't know. Best guess? They already knew about this place. Guess those tracks we found were legit. Or...they followed us from the bar."

"Shit," the unknown guy said with a Scottish accent. "It's my fault. They were probably watching me."

Ronan jerked his head toward the guy and made introductions. "Adare, Faith. Faith, Adare." Then he gently pulled a vest over her chest, wrapping Velcro to keep it in place. "Her feet are bare."

Ivar tossed him a pair of cargo pants from a shelf and pointed to flak boots on the bottom. "The smallest I have are size fifteen."

Ronan pulled on the pants and jumped into boots, lacing them up. "I'll carry her."

She shook her head. "It's fine. The stone doesn't hurt my feet." She'd be much safer with Ronan firing freely. "What about Grace?" She turned toward the nonexistent doorway.

It slid open, and Benny stood there with Grace in his arms, along with her nutrient-rich liquid and saline bags. He was dressed in jeans with no shirt, showing his barrel of a chest. "Here. Take her."

Adare backed away. "Hell, no. That's a human."

"Yeah," Benny snarled. "You won't break her, dumbass. Just hold her for a minute."

Adare frowned, looking at Grace like she was a dirty cat or something. Yet he took her from Benny, making her look even more fragile against his size. "Suit up and hurry."

Benny moved toward the cargo pants.

As the door closed behind him, an explosion rocked the entire mountain.

CHAPTER TWENTY-EIGHT

Small rocks rained down from the ceiling. Ronan reached for another pair of the black cargo pants and bent. "Step."

Faith moved nearer her sister, reaching for her.

Ronan manacled her calf and set her foot into the pants. "Faith. Obey." There wasn't time to be gentle.

She faltered and then stepped into them, and he drew them up, pulling the belt as tight as he could. Then he crouched and rolled the pants up several times. They were way too big for her.

He stood. "What kind of force?"

Ivar grimaced and tossed a knife toward Benny, who tucked it in a sheath at his calf. "At least three helicopters came into view five minutes ago. They've obviously landed."

"I'm fuckin' sorry about this," Adare whispered tersely. "I knew I shouldn't come back in."

"I didn't see them, either," Ronan said. "Do you want me to take her?" He gestured to Grace.

"Yes," Adare said, moving to hand her over.

Benny stepped between them. "Ronan, you need your hands free to defend your mate. Adare, stop being a pussy and carry the human. You don't know the grounds as well as Ivar and I do."

Adare growled and glared down at the fragile woman in his arms. She was in a hospital gown, with the twin plastic bags on her chest. He cocked his head to the side. "Then hurry up. Let's go."

Ronan shook his head. Adare had always disliked humans, and weakness repulsed him. A female in a coma would just piss him off. But he'd have to deal with it so the rest of them could fight. Ivar was correct. Ronan needed his hands free to protect his mate. He took another gun. "Ivar? I'm assuming there's a way out?"

Ivar planted his hand on the opposite wall, and it slid open to reveal a dark tunnel lit by red lights on the floor. "Follow closely, because I have several bombs planted along the way. At the end there's transport waiting."

Ronan nodded. "You take point. Then Adare carrying Grace, then Benny, then Faith, and I'll take up the rear. In case they come from another direction."

"Good plan." Ivar looked around his depot. "Fuck. I liked this place." Then he turned and started running down the tunnel.

Another explosion echoed, and this time, sharp shards of rock slashed from the ceiling. Ronan pivoted, tucking Faith into his body and shielding her. He moved for Grace, but Adare had already wrapped himself over her before leaping into the tunnel.

Fury lit Ronan that they were being attacked. That he'd led somebody back to a safe place—the place he'd put his mate. If she wasn't there, he'd stay and fight. Maybe Omar was with the group. With a growl, he nudged Faith toward the tunnel. "Run after Benny, sweetheart. If your feet hurt, tell me. I can carry you."

She looked at him, her face pale and her eyes wide. But she nodded and turned, moving into a jog despite the too-big pants and her bare feet. The gun looked too large for her hand, but she held it, moving quickly.

The tunnel turned into a labyrinth. Ivar led them in what seemed like circles for nearly thirty minutes. The group stayed silent, and more explosions rocked the mountain behind and above them. Finally, they emerged into a gulley of sorts. Rain slashed down and thunder bellowed in the distance.

Ivar ran toward a stand of trees and stopped right before he reached it, tugging off some type of sheet that had masked another helicopter. This one was dark and silent, shaped sleekly. How marvelous to be able to hide a helicopter.

Ronan swept Faith up on the way to protect her feet from the pinecones and other stickers in the grass. He sat in the back of the helicopter with her on his lap next to Adare and Grace.

Benny jumped into the pilot's seat with Ivar next to him. "This is a modified design I may have stolen from the Realm," Benny said easily as he punched the buttons. "We don't need helmets to talk, and we can go into stealth mode." He lifted three red levers toward the middle. "And that's not all."

Something pinged against the helicopter.

Ronan reacted instantly, shoving Faith down and covering her. His window blew open and something pierced his shoulder. He growled and pointed into the darkness.

Three Cyst ran out of the trees, their pale skin glowing even under the cloud cover. They fired continuously.

Ronan leaned out and fired the gun, hitting one Cyst in the forehead. Blood spurted and the monster fell back into a tree. Ronan glanced down at his wrists. These new weapons were handy. Taking aim, he fired toward the second soldier, who was weaving back and forth.

The helicopter lifted into the sky.

Adare leaned out the other side, firing rapidly.

Benny turned the copter to face the Cyst.

"What are you doing?" Ronan growled.

"Watch this." Benny pressed one of the red levers, and smoke billowed from the side of the chopper. Something shot at the Cyst and exploded. "Rockets."

Ronan stared at the scorched earth. Holy shit.

"That's nothing," Ivar said, punching up something on his phone. "Give me a minute."

Benny turned the helicopter and started rising.

Ronan reached for Faith, pulling her onto his lap. She cuddled right in, for once not fighting him. He pressed his thumb lightly to her jugular, where her pulse beat too quickly. "Take a few deep breaths." He tried to keep his voice calm when he wanted to completely blow his temper. How dare the Cyst attack? He'd put his mate in danger, and there was no excuse for that. He pressed her head beneath his chin, holding her tight.

She trembled and curled up on his lap, her nose against his neck. Her knees rose and the sight of her bare feet hit him square in the gut. Slowly, he turned his head to see Adare holding Grace carelessly, staring out the window.

Now Ronan knew. Now he understood why Adare had been so destroyed. So lost. Probably still was. Ronan hadn't mated Faith yet, hadn't even completed the sex act, but even so, if he lost her, he'd be empty.

Ivar cleared his voice. "And out your left window, you'll see a nice burning campfire."

Ronan frowned and turned toward the window.

Ivar tapped his phone.

The earth rumbled. Ronan stiffened, listening. Then the entire mountain exploded. Fire soared high and bright, smoke billowing up around it.

"Fuckers don't like fire," Benny said congenially, banking a hard left.

Ronan relaxed, holding his mate. He'd get her new clothing and definitely some socks. "Please tell me we have a secondary location."

Ivar turned toward him and winced. "Kind of. It's a bit rougher than this one, but it'll have to do." He sighed. "But we definitely need to check the perimeter. I don't know if the Kurjans followed you guys from the bar or if they discovered our holdings years ago and have just been waiting to attack."

Ronan sighed and settled his chin on Faith's head. Her trembling had stopped. He looked at Adare. The last thing Ronan needed was Adare taking responsibility for this attack and disappearing to drink himself into oblivion again. "This wasn't your fault."

"Maybe." Adare hadn't stopped staring out the window. "But it probably is."

Ronan looked down at the motionless woman. "Is she okay?"

Adare frowned and looked down at Grace as if he couldn't wait to be rid of her. He paused and then stilled, tilting his head. "There's something..." Obviously careful not to jostle her, he slowly tugged down the left side of her gown. The shape of a key was clearly outlined on Grace's smooth skin. Above her heart, but below her clavicle.

Adare turned toward Ronan, his eyebrows slashing down. "Did you know?"

Faith stiffened and slowly lifted her head, turning to see her sister and the marking. She bit her lip.

"No," Ronan said, emotions battering him harder than a hurricane. "*I* did not know."

* * * *

Faith didn't have any words. She looked at Grace, Adare, and then braved a glance at Ronan's face. Solid rock. No emotion. That wasn't good. The adrenaline in her body dissipated, and she shivered. Ronan palmed her entire head and pressed her face back to his neck, his other arm holding her securely.

His heated body warmed her, and the scent of male and the woods filled her. She didn't have the energy to fight him—or explain. There was a good reason she hadn't confided in him, and she probably would've told him after she'd worked it all through in her mind. That was true. Time hadn't exactly been on their side. She tried to lift her head, not really surprised when he kept her in place. "Ronan—"

"Later." His breath brushed her hair.

Any time *not* right now worked for her. She let her body relax and absorb his warmth. The helicopter hummed quietly, and every once in a while, they dipped low enough for rain to slash against the window.

Even though she'd hurt his feelings, and she could sense he was mad, she was secure. Safe. What was it about him? About them? As a logical and educated woman, she questioned everything. Yet she'd never been able to explain her ability with coma patients, and she sure couldn't explain her feelings for this man. *Male.* For this immortal, protective, kind...male.

When he'd touched the marking to her neck, it had felt right. As if finally, after years of being alone, she'd finally found home.

How crazy was that?

Even more surprising, her body yearned for that marking to be permanent. Being mostly immortal would be incredible. Just think of the good she could do and the advances in science she could see.

To say nothing of an eternity with Ronan Kayrs. The idea made her both crave and hesitate. He was just...so much.

And she couldn't forget the fact that he needed her. That in mating her, he'd regain his strength. Perhaps he'd also regain it if they rebuilt the full Seven, but her instincts told her Benny had been correct. She could help heal Ronan and help him get ready for the coming battle with Ulric. If she was going to mate Ronan, or if she was even just considering it, she had to believe him about his enemies. Plus, she'd just seen the Cyst attack them. They were the bad guys. She had to trust him.

He'd earned that trust by saving her and her sister.

Finally, they started descending.

"Where are we?" Adare asked.

"Secondary headquarters, which is not up to snuff. Rocky Mountains, much farther north in Wyoming." Benny set the helicopter down with a soft bump. "They won't expect us to stay in the same mountain range."

Good point. Faith lifted her head, and this time, Ronan let her. She shivered, looking outside at the wild rainstorm. Two jeeps were parked beneath a large tarp, barely visible in the storm. A barely discernible road, more like a trail, led between two massive pine trees. "Where exactly are we?" she whispered.

"An hour outside of Northtown," Benny said.

"We'll get you some socks," Ronan said, peering out at the trees surrounding them. "I take it there's a tunnel entrance around here somewhere?" He shifted Faith on his lap and stuck his gun into a harness at his thigh. "How far is it?"

Ivar pointed toward an odd-shaped rock outcropping. "We're at the end of one of the escape tunnels. Wait here, and I'll run and open it. We don't have sensors on the doors yet, so we are definitely unprotected. We'll have to work around the clock securing the place." He stepped into the storm, and the wind plastered his cargo pants to his thighs. He dodged through the rain and pressed his hand to the rock. A hole opened up.

Faith sighed. Then she looked at her sister. "We need to get her a blanket before we take her in. That gown isn't enough."

Adare looked down, frowning. "Humans." He pulled his vest over his head with one hand and dropped it by his feet. Then he tugged his shirt off the same way. The cotton garment was big enough he could almost wrap Grace in it. "I'll keep her dry. Just tell me where I can set her down." His voice was low and hoarse.

Faith bit her lip. She didn't know this guy. Before she could question him, Ronan opened the door and jumped out, running gracefully toward the rock. He held her against him, hunched over her, protecting her from the storm. Within seconds, they were back inside the earth.

Adare appeared right behind them, securely holding Grace. Ivar pressed a button on the stone wall, and lights appeared strung along the ceiling. Temporary mining lights.

"We'll get you all settled, and then Benny and I will cover the helicopter and start the computers." Ivar moved forward, shaking water from his hair.

Faith pushed against Ronan. "I can walk."

"Be quiet." He followed Ivar, with Adare behind them. His hold was gentle but firm, and his steps quick. Before long, they reached another set of bedrooms—these decorated in muted pastel colors.

Faith wanted to be amused that Ivar had gone with different decorating schemes for the different mountains, but she couldn't drum up any humor.

They all moved into the first bedroom, which had a light pink bedspread, matching chair, and antique white dresser. Adare set Grace beneath the covers and looked around for a place to put her food and saline bags. "She probably doesn't need the saline," he mused.

Ronan set Faith on her feet, and her stupid borrowed cargo pants fell to the floor. She kicked them out of the way since Ronan's T-shirt covered her almost to her knees. She pushed the pink chair over and took the bags from Adare to place gently on the seat. "Sure, she does."

Adare looked at her, looked at Grace, and then turned on his heavy boot and left the room. The Scottish guy was kind of a dick.

Faith bit her lip. Gathering her courage, she focused on Ronan.

He nodded. "I know why you didn't tell me."

There were a lot of reasons, most of them time-related. "I'm sure I would have," she said softly.

His eyes had softened with a glow she couldn't quite read. "This doesn't change anything." He paused and then stood firm. What had gone through his head?

"I thought that since she was one of the Keys, maybe she could… you know, be mated," Faith said.

The sympathy in Ronan's face nearly dropped her to her knees. "No, Faith. Sometimes we can force the marking, but no way would anybody mate a woman in a coma." He reached out and pushed a piece of hair out of her eyes. "I'm truly sorry."

She swallowed over a lump in her throat. "You can't be sure."

"I am." He sighed. "Take your time and get your sister comfortable. Then try and sleep. Dawn should arrive in a few minutes, but you could sleep for a few hours."

She faltered. "What about you?"

His gaze, even tired, pierced through her. "I will return when I know this location is secure. We can talk later." His tone hinted that he'd moved past reconnaissance and creating lines of communication with his strategy. Going on attack, no-holds-barred...was next.

There was so much to think about, and even now, she wanted to go to him and snuggle right into his chest. She had never felt like this in her entire life. "Okay," she murmured.

"Right now, I'll go and get the layout of this place in case we're attacked again." He rubbed a hand over his forehead. "Which seems likely, the way things have been going." Then he turned and prowled down the hallway, quickly disappearing.

He hadn't even tried to kiss her good-bye.

CHAPTER TWENTY-NINE

Ronan finished scouting the entire facility around noontime. He stalked through the tunnels toward the main control room. This stone was rougher against his boots, and the lights weren't nearly as bright.

He emerged into a room with half the screens and computers as the control room that had just been blown to hell. Equipment was jumbled haphazardly in one corner, and computers still tilted in the box in another. Ivar sat at a long table, studying a screen on the wall. Pictures of twenty people were lined up on it. "Who are they?" Ronan asked.

Ivar didn't turn. "Top human physics experts of the day." He kicked out a chair next to him, and it rolled a foot. A drink can and a magazine with some guy holding a rose on the cover sat to his right.

"What is that?" Ronan asked.

"Benny and I have a bet on who the next dater will choose on the television show," Ivar said absently. "*Dater* is a show where people date and then the guy chooses one woman. It's called reality TV."

Ronan blinked. "What's real about that?" Had his friends lost their damn minds in this new world? He shook his head.

Ivar shrugged. "Ben thinks it's going to be this woman called Carla, but she's just a wench. No way will Jason pick her."

Okay. They'd lost it. Ronan went to the chair and sat, reaching for the can, which was cool and smooth in his hand. He'd seen Ivar drink a few of these. "What is phosphoric acid, natural flavor, taurine, caffeine, and glucuronolactone?"

"Nobody really knows," Ivar said, staring at the screen.

Ronan set the can down. "Why would you put that into your body? None of the ingredients sounds like anything we should eat." His brothers had been sissified a little bit.

"Tastes good," Ivar muttered.

Ronan shook his head, pulling a keyboard toward himself. "You've done a thorough job with this secondary location."

"I needed more time." Ivar tapped several keys and ten of the faces on the big screen disappeared. "I've already talked to our immortal physicists, and the sad fact is that the humans might have knowledge we've missed." He typed again and three faces remained: Two men and one woman. "These three are working in interesting fields." More keys clacked and only one face remained.

"Pretty," Ronan mused. The woman had thick black hair, deep blue eyes, and a pointed chin. Her hands were up as if the photograph had been taken while she was giving a lecture.

Ivar nodded. "Meet Victory Rashad."

"Victoria?" Ronan asked.

"No. Victory. She signs her emails Vicki." Ivar stared thoughtfully at the picture. "She's a theoretical physicist working in cosmology and particle physics."

"Interesting. Smart woman. What else?" Ronan asked, leaning forward.

Ivar pulled up a list of bullet points on the screen right in front of him. "I had a friend bump into her as she was leaving a yoga studio. He sensed her Enhancement."

Ronan studied Ivar. "Enhanced? Interesting."

"Isn't it, though?" Ivar's voice deepened. "Her research includes extra dimensions of space, elementary particles, and fundamental forces."

"Okay." It all sounded like it might apply. Ronan leaned to the side so he could see the screen and keep reading. "She's at Harvard, studying supersymmetry, cosmology of extra dimensions, and dark matter." Along with several other sciences Ronan hadn't heard of. Or at least, he hadn't heard of the human labels for such. "You think she might be able to help?"

"There's only one way to find out," Ivar said, pushing away from the table. "Garrett and Logan are an hour out. They've decided to do the ritual. You okay with that?"

Emotions jumbled inside Ronan. His longing to know the two males, his fear for the young immortals' lives, the necessity of making the Seven strong again. Finally, he settled his thoughts. "I am. They're old enough, they're seasoned, and they have the right to find their own callings." Even if it resulted in their deaths.

"Odds are, only one of them will survive the bonding."

Ronan exhaled. "I'm aware of that fact." Yet he and his brother had survived; so had one of Logan's ancestors. Perhaps their blood would help. If not, he'd regret this decision. Without question. "We don't have much choice."

"Agreed. Your strength isn't going to fully recover until we're Seven again. Same with the rest of us."

Speaking of which. Ronan glanced toward the quiet hallway. "Where is everyone?"

"Benny is running around like crazy to get security measures in place, and Adare took the jeep into town just moments after we arrived. He said he'd bring a list of supplies back later today, including a sketch pad for your lady." Ivar turned back to the woman's face on the wall screen.

Ronan frowned. "He's been gone for hours?"

"Yeah. I'm sure he wanted to find a bar and a couple of willing bodies before going shopping." Ivar shrugged. "We all deal in different ways." Then he coughed. "You're not dealing at all."

"I am," Ronan muttered.

Ivar stretched his legs out beneath the table. "We should talk—"

"No." Ronan stood, setting his chair back in place. "We'll talk about Grace later. I have to think the situation through first." His chest hurt and his temples pounded. A Key in a coma was useless to them. Now it was obvious why Grace hadn't passed on after being hurt. The Key markings in her blood had kept her alive, but it wasn't enough. There was no way to heal her. "We don't have to make a decision right now."

"Soon," Ivar murmured. "For now, you should go make things right with your mate. If she's been sleeping all day, perhaps she'll be in a good mood and listen to your dumb ass."

Ronan frowned. "You're giving me female advice?"

"Good point." Ivar's lip twisted in a half-grin. "Forget I said anything."

Ronan rolled his shoulders, trying to dispel some of the tightness. "Why haven't you mated in all these years, Ivar?"

Ivar shook his head and exhaled. "When? I've been tracking the Kurjans and the Cyst. Also following Adare while attempting to bring him back in every few decades. Plus, trying to find the Keys, locate Enhanced women, and invest all of our holdings so we'll have funds in the future."

Ronan winced. "That does sound like a lot." Ivar had been forced into the leadership position, it appeared.

Ivar snorted. "Not to mention there have been several wars we've assisted in ending, without letting anybody know we existed." He ground a palm into his right eye. "And then there's Benny. Benjamin Henry Reese."

Ronan swallowed. "Right. So. He's still crazier than hell?"

Ivar sighed and dropped his hand, turning to face Ronan. "I've never thought Ben was crazy. Just wild and dangerous. If there's a good adventure in store, he's there. But if anybody crosses him or his family...let's just say I've done cleanup more than a few times through the centuries."

Ronan needed to step up and add some stability to the Seven. It was his job. "And you've been searching for the dimension for the final ritual—or rather for the keeper of the ritual."

"I found him ten years ago," Ivar said. "I haven't approached because I've been waiting for the Lock."

"You've found her," Ronan reminded him. "You've done your job."

"Yeah. Imagine my delight when I discovered she was both a Kayrs and a Kyllwood." Ivar winced. "Not to mention a prophet. Getting her into place in time is going to be nearly impossible."

But it had to be done. "Having Logan and Garrett on the Seven should help."

"Really?" Ivar asked mildly.

Ronan's spine snapped to attention. "Yes. Why?"

Ivar shook his head. "Just looking at all the angles. Those two would be in the best position to prevent our using the Lock. She is their niece."

"She's my niece too." Ronan tucked his thumbs in the waist of his cargo pants. "She's the Lock, she'll do her job, and we'll protect her."

Ivar turned and stood, facing him. "Take a minute, Ro. Seriously. We don't know that she'll survive the ritual. She's the fucking Lock. We know the ritual, and we understand how to make it happen, but we don't have one damn clue what happens next. Sacrifice might be necessary. You know that. We've *done* that. Remember why we're a secret?"

Yeah. The idea still made him nauseous. Ronan held up a hand. "Then we research more. We figure out what happens at the ritual. We need to find the dimension still. Or world. Or bubble. Whatever it is, we don't know how to find it and don't have a Keeper."

"We'll approach Sam Kyllwood about that once we get Logan in place. Either as one of the Seven, or..."

Or dead, if Logan didn't survive the bonding. Ronan pivoted. "I'm done with this conversation. We have more to figure out before getting to work." He strode for the hallway, his chest heavy. There were too many uncertainties, and time wasn't on his side.

Not at all. The shield had broken centuries before it should have. Perhaps millennia before. That couldn't be good.

His footsteps were heavy as he moved through the rough tunnels, slowly making his way back to Grace's room.

Faith sat on the bed, her eyes closed, her hand over Grace's head. He paused in the doorway. "Have you slept?"

"Yes. I awoke around noon, according to the old-fashioned alarm clock I found in the dresser next to my bed." Faith opened her eyes. "I've been here for a couple of hours. I can't reach her."

Ronan nodded. "I know." The hurt in his mate's eyes was like a punch to the gut. "I could give her blood, and you might be able to reach her briefly, but then she'll pass on." Grace wasn't his mate. If she was, then maybe there'd be some way to save her, since he had a marking on his hand. But he could bring her back briefly before his blood killed her.

Faith's eyes filled. "I won't accept that. There has to be a way to save her. She's a Key."

Which meant even if she came out of the coma, her life would still be at risk. Ronan couldn't find a word to say.

Faith pushed herself up from the bed and stood next to it, looking small and vulnerable. "There are so many things I never got to tell her. Moments we haven't shared yet." She swallowed, her eyes fathomless in the dim light. "I've been thinking about this since you left me to sleep. I don't want regrets with you."

His heart started beating faster.

She cleared her throat. "There's something between us, and it's big. I feel things I've never felt, and I trust you somehow in a way I've never trusted anybody." She shuffled her bare feet on the stone. "I can promise I'll try with you, and I think I can help during the bonding ritual and in the battles coming up. I'm a good doctor."

Was she saying what he thought she was saying? His body tensed to rock. Hope flared in his chest, hot and bright.

"And I would like to live for a thousand years or maybe more," she whispered. "With you, Ronan."

* * * *

In front of Faith's eyes, Ronan changed. His eyes darkened and his chest widened. "Are you sure?" he asked, his voice a raw rumble.

She swallowed. "Yes." Not once in her life had she wavered from a path once she'd chosen it. "I don't know what will happen with us, and I'm not giving up on finding a cure for Grace, but this I want." She went to him, over the bare stone floor, her feet chilling. "I trust you."

He reached for her, drawing her near. This close, his eyes were pure aqua—a perfect mixture of green and blue. "I want you, Faith. I vow I'll keep you safe in this life and the next." He lifted her easily against his chest and began moving farther down the hallway.

It struck her then. His vow of protection. In his mind, that was the most valuable thing he had to give. To promise. She placed her hand over his chest, right above his heart. What about love? Did she love him? It was the closest she'd ever come with anybody, but it sure wasn't peaceful and easy like she'd imagined it would be. Could he love her? Forever would give her plenty of time to find out. Maybe finally they could have sex. She almost laughed at the hysteria that bubbled up in her.

He dropped his head and kissed her, his mouth going deep, and his arms tightening around her. Cool air brushed her as they entered another room, and he kicked the door shut behind him.

Her nerves pulsed and her body hummed. His tongue swept inside her mouth, claiming her, more insistent than before.

Slowly, he set her on her feet. The cold stone chilled her, but his heated body warmed her.

He tilted her chin, his gaze heated. "I knew you'd be mine from the second I awoke and saw your face in this world. In the real world."

His touch inflamed her, but a warning sounded in her head as if from a far distance.

He reached down and gently pulled his T-shirt off her, baring her. "God, you're beautiful."

She'd never felt so beautiful before. "Your chest is beyond amazing." Her fingers tangled in his shirt, and she rose up on her toes to tug it over his head. She flattened her hands across his muscled pecs and her breath quickened.

His fingers tangled in her hair, and he drew her head back. His fangs slid down, lethal and graceful.

She caught her breath. Leaning in, he scraped them along her neck in an erotic tease that shot right to her clit. He licked her jugular and his free hand fell to the back of her waist, bending her into his hard erection.

Her head fell back as she let him hold her up. Then she turned, revealing her neck. Her lungs stuttered and she held her breath.

"Very nice," he murmured, his lips moving against her skin.

She felt so out of control, but there was nothing to do. Except wait.

He placed a very gentle kiss on her neck, nipping her collarbone. She jumped. He chuckled, sweeping his hand over the thin material covering her butt. "I'm not going to bite you until I'm inside you."

Her abdomen contracted, and her thighs dampened. "Ronan—"

A sharp rap on the door had her jerking against him, her eyelids opening. Oh, this could not be happening. Not right now. It just couldn't be.

"What?" Ronan growled, his hand still flattened across her ass.

"We've had movement," Ivar said through the door, his voice weary. "Omar raided a village up in Alaska and got at least two Enhanced. I'm trying to trace him now via satellite. I need your help." His boot steps echoed away and then went silent.

Faith gave a nervous giggle. Then she winced. "I do not giggle. Ever."

Ronan released her and bent to retrieve the shirt he'd put on her in the last hideaway. His grin was pained. "I just heard you giggle." Gently, his hands sure, he drew the material over her head. "I'm sorry about this. I'm starting to believe we will never have sex. It isn't going to happen." Frustration laced his tone.

Her body ached and yearned, and her head was fuzzy. "I give up. We have to stop putting our bodies in this position." She looked around at the room, noting the purple bedspread and perfectly matching chair. There was an antique bed table that looked like a twin to the one in her former room. Apparently Ivar hadn't had time to get rugs yet. "Can I help?"

Ronan cupped her chin and leaned in for a quick kiss. "No. Try to get a little more sleep before dinnertime." His eyes darkened. "We're mating tonight. So you're going to need it."

With that warning, he turned and exited the room.

She touched her still tingling mouth. Was she crazy? Had the last few days of new revelations and danger thrown her decision-making process out of whack? Her body ached as if she'd fallen down a rocky mountain. Yeah, she wanted him. He was smart and sexy and immortal. But the way things were going, they'd never mate.

His tone when he'd said *mine* had held a possessiveness in it that had made her pause. Just a little.

Maybe she should think this through.

CHAPTER THIRTY

Ronan ignored his raging cock and tried to calm his body down as he entered the computer room. Benny and Ivar sat at different consoles, each typing furiously with shot glasses next to them.

Ronan made a beeline for the vodka bottle next to Benny, lifted it, and drank rapidly. The hard liquor hit his stomach and spread out with a nice chill, yet did nothing to quell the fiery desire still pummeling his veins. He finished and wiped off his mouth. "Where's Adare?"

"He'd better return before dark," Ivar said, leaning back from the computer and holding out a hand. When Ronan handed over the bottle, he poured a shot and downed it. Then he kicked the same chair as earlier toward Ronan. "I have satellite feeds coming up in about ten minutes. Benny is sending out notices to known Enhanced that they're in danger. Omar is making a move right now."

Fuck. Ronan wiped a hand over his eyes. "How well-known were the Enhanced he took?"

Benny pivoted in his chair, his entire face frowning. "We knew they were potential descendants, but as far as these notes show, they had no clue they were Enhanced. Probably had special little gifts like your mate, but didn't know how or why."

Ronan dropped into the chair. "We need Adare here to plan."

"Let him roam," Benny countered. "We'll bring him in when it's time to fight. He's too restless to help with this right now."

After losing his potential mate, who wouldn't be? Ronan's entire body ached. "Did you ever meet his mate?"

"Potential mate," Benny retorted, pouring another shot for Ronan. He lifted a broad shoulder, his gaze concerned. "And yeah, I met her. She was a feline shifter. Tough as hell. The only type of woman he's ever pursued."

Ronan tipped back the drink and let it warm a path down his throat to his gut. "You didn't like her?"

Benny shrugged. "Didn't see it. Didn't seem them." He downed a shot. "But what do I know about mates?"

What did any of them know? Ronan thought he'd been earning Faith's trust, but she hadn't told him about her sister being a Key.

Ivar poured three more shots. "We have a few minutes while the searches run." He glanced at the two of them. "I guess we should talk about it."

"No," Ronan said shortly.

"Grace is a Key, Ronan." Benny lifted his glass and waited for the other two to do the same. "At least one Key isn't in Omar's hands."

They drank.

Ronan set down his glass, spinning it in his fingers. "Whatever you're going to say, don't." It wasn't like he had a problem connecting the dots. He wanted to mate Faith before he had to think about her sister. "I mean it."

Ivar leaned back. "We have a duty as the Seven."

"To do what?" Ronan burst out. "Kill an innocent woman? Are you fucking serious?"

Benny eyed Ivar. "She wouldn't be alive if she wasn't a Key. But we need her standing for the ritual—she has to be conscious to take part in the entire thing. We require much more than just her blood. You know that."

"Says who?" Ronan asked, his gut churning as if he'd eaten the poisonous wilder berries that had grown outside his childhood home.

"Maybe her blood will be enough. Take a little, do the ritual, there you go." The idea even sounded lame to his ears.

Benny rubbed his hand across his eyes. "That won't work and you know it. Your centuries of realigning rocks to control magnetic fields is proof enough. If that hadn't been necessary, we could've just made a prison world and left Ulric in it. Blood, bone, and action. The ritual must be performed by the Keys and the Lock—consciously." He dropped his head to his chest, obviously thinking hard. "I don't see how anybody could mate her. Even if they did, she might not awaken."

Ronan grimaced. "Nobody is mating an unconscious woman. Even if somebody could force the brand on their hand, there's no way."

"You have a brand," Ivar said quietly, his blue gaze intense.

Ronan's shoulders went back. Heat slashed through him. "Are you jesting?"

Ivar swallowed. "I hate suggesting it, I really do. But would your mate prefer for her sister to die or be mated to you?"

Ronan coughed out a strangled laugh. "I don't think there's much question on that score. She'd want me to save her sister. Somehow without sex, of course." The idea was sickening. How could he mate anyone other than Faith? And how could he mate a woman in a coma? It was impossible.

Ivar grimaced. "Sounds like a mess."

Ronan nodded. "The marking appeared because of Faith. I didn't force it." That meant it would never pass to anybody else. There were stories of brands appearing and then disappearing, only to appear centuries later with another potential mate. But this was Faith. She was his only and he knew it. "Even if I tried, this marking won't transfer to anybody but Faith." He knew it as sure as he knew his own name.

"Then Grace has to pass on so another Key will be born," Ivar said, his voice hoarser than usual. "I hate myself for even saying that."

Ronan's brain hurt, but no worse than his heart. Not even close.

Something rustled by the doorway. He paused, turning. The scent of his mate was close. Then the sound of her moving away. "Well, fuck."

Ivar winced. "I'm sorry. I didn't hear her."

Yeah. Three of them immortal with superior senses, and they hadn't heard one small human woman. Their topic of discussion had obviously messed with their heads. "I don't know how we're going to fix this, and right now I don't care. But we are not allowing Grace to die," Ronan said.

"Are you going after her?" Benny asked.

Ronan sighed and looked at the empty hallway. "No. She knows I won't allow her sister to be harmed. I've let you two shoulder the burden too much. I need to help you find Omar." He'd let Faith get some sleep and work things out on her own. Right now, he didn't have any helpful words for her.

Benny poured three more shots. "We have to find the other Keys. That at least gives us a little time."

Time could only help. Ronan held up his glass.

The other two did the same.

Nobody spoke. No toast came to mind.

Benny sighed. "I can't think of how we'd be more fucked than we are right now."

Yeah. Ronan tipped back his drink, barely registering the alcohol. Now, that was an accurate toast.

* * * *

Faith lay on her sister's bed, her mind spinning. It was past dinnertime, but she wasn't hungry at all. They couldn't kill Grace. Oh, they could stop the feeding IV, and that would end her life. Probably. Would a Key die from starvation?

So far the only person to have given her any hope for Grace was the Kurjan leader. Dayne had even given her sister a little of his blood. What if he actually could help Grace? There was a chance that the Kurjan scientists had gone beyond the Seven and what they knew. They were good fighters, and their technology was impressive.

But the innovations she'd seen had been for war. Not for healing.

What if the Kurjans had focused their efforts on science? The Seven wouldn't know a damn thing about it. And here she'd been about to mate Ronan. Betrayal burned like acid inside her.

"Faith," Ronan said from the doorway.

Faith donned a calm expression and turned, eyeing him. He'd thrown on a black T-shirt and still wore the cargo pants he'd had on before. The shirt she'd borrowed from him covered her to her thighs, so who cared? Though her feet were still cold. "What?"

He held a bunch of clothing. "Come with me. We need to talk."

Her throat closed. "I'm not leaving Grace." Not for a second would she allow anybody to get past her to hurt her sister.

"I give you my word that nothing will happen to her." He didn't waver.

"Tonight, you mean," Faith said, sitting up. She'd heard plenty, and she no longer trusted any of them. Their mission was centuries old and probably had far-reaching consequences. At least they thought it did. Her mission was quite simple: to protect her baby sister. Period.

He didn't respond to that.

Yeah. That's what she'd thought. "I've changed my mind. We are not mating." What had she been thinking?

"Yes, we are. Like it or not." His tone brooked no argument.

"Is that where you are in your grand strategy?" she snapped.

"Yes."

She sighed. "Go away, Ronan."

"No. Come here, or I'll come and get you." He was immovable in the doorway. Hard and fierce. A true warrior. "I vow your sister is safe. But we have much to discuss, and not a lot of time to do it."

She glared. Fine. She pushed herself up and winced as her foot protested.

He was instantly by her side. "What's wrong? Did I miss an injury earlier?"

Yeah, because they'd been too busy getting ready to have hot and passionate sex. Again. "Nothing is wrong." She brushed by him, barely biting back a startled yelp when he shifted the clothing to his other arm and swept her up. He lifted her high against his chest and strode from the room. "Don't you ever get tired?" she snapped.

"Yes. I'm tired now. And I need to sleep to heal some of these injuries." He entered the bedroom where she'd tried to sleep earlier. "Yet you and I must talk first." He set her down on the bed and put the pile of clothing next to her.

"Fine. Say what you want to say." She was so tired her eyes hurt. In fact, her entire body felt like it had been through a cement mixer. Or a bailer.

He knelt and examined her feet. His gaze hardened. "You're injured."

"Just cuts and scrapes."

He leaned in, brushing his fingers across an injury. "This looks painful."

She sucked in air. Somehow, she had to get out of there. "What are those clothes?"

"Adare returned an hour ago with them. There are shoes beneath the jeans and a sketch pad for you to draw on."

She refused to be touched. When had Adare returned? Did that mean she could go right out to the jeep and just drive away? The security wasn't full force here yet.

Perhaps she could get her hands on a phone and call Dayne. He'd given her his number, and right now, he was her only chance at saving Grace. Truth be told, she didn't trust Dayne either. But maybe she could negotiate. Though the Cyst soldiers who'd attacked the mountain hadn't been there for tea. Could she broker a deal with a dangerous immortal?

What choice did she have?

The Seven's solution was to end Grace's life to let another Key be born. Oh, Ronan had protested, but even he hadn't seen another way out. "I'd like to go to the store for supplies," she said. "Some ointments and medical supplies."

"We can fetch anything you might need," Ronan said. "You will stay here and be safe."

Safe? Right. Like Grace was safe? "I heard your conversation."

"I'm well aware of that." His fangs slid down, and he slashed them into his wrist.

She paused and then started to back away, scooting herself across the bed with her elbows. Her skin chilled.

He pulled her back and pressed his wrist to her mouth. "Drink."

"No." She tried to move away, but he cupped the back of her head and held her still. Then he ground his wrist against her mouth, and she gasped, trying to dislodge him. Fire swept inside like a drug, going right through her tongue and sending her senses spinning. Delicious. She sucked harder, taking more of the elixir into her system.

Her energy soared. Blood popped in her veins and her feet mended. She felt like she was ten years old again with no aches. No pains.

He gently removed his wrist. Before her eyes, his wound closed. She couldn't help but lick her lips.

His eyes flashed. "Better?"

"Wh—what was that?" she asked, her body igniting to a slow burn. Her thighs ached and her nipples hardened to diamonds. Her clit throbbed in perfect time with her heartbeat.

His nostrils flared. "You're my mate. My blood can heal you to a certain point even though we haven't mated. Once we have, I'll be able to take away any pain you experience."

She leaned back, trying to focus even though she was precariously close to orgasm just from taking his blood. Man, she needed sex. Just once. Jeez. "I'm not mating you." Was he insane? The bastard was considering killing her sister for some prophesy that might not even be real. "It's not happening."

He leaned in, his hands on either side of her thighs, trapping her in place. "You've already made up your mind. You said yes. That's the end of the discussion."

She remained perfectly still. "Not a chance."

Arrogance lit his expression. "You'll eat those words." He leaned even closer, his lips hovering right above hers, his eyes boring into her. His hand covered her bare thigh.

Her body clenched with hunger. In just the T-shirt and panties, she should feel vulnerable. But she didn't. She *hungered*. What was wrong with her? She couldn't think.

He nipped her lip and brushed his knuckles lightly across her clit.

Electricity zinged through her lower half. Her entire body jerked. She gasped, her eyes widening on him. "Don't stop," she whispered. This felt way too good.

He smiled, the expression primitive. Then he did it again.

She exploded into an orgasm, crying out. He kissed her hard and swallowed her cry, his knuckles continuing to tap, prolonging the waves until she was spent. The waves pummeled her, taking everything she had.

Then he lifted his head.

She gaped at him, stunned.

He stood. "We will absolutely continue when I'm back around midnight. By tomorrow morning, you'll wear my mark."

CHAPTER THIRTY-ONE

Ronan followed Ivar down through steep tunnels, winding and pivoting until they were deep in the earth. Heat surrounded him, irritating his skin. Sweat rolled down his forehead and matted his shirt to his chest.

Ivar turned right, leading him into a round chamber. "Witch allies created a force field here with an inter-dimensional cross to protect us from the heat." He wiped sweat off his brow. "Believe it or not, without it we would pass out or even die from the fumes and fire."

His ears rang and heaviness filled his body. Ronan cleared his throat and scrutinized the round chamber. A circle was in the middle of a circle, and as he watched, the stone floor there brightened. "Nice job." He fought a chill as he remembered his bonding.

Ivar nodded. "It's ready, and so are we. We can't wait any longer."

"When will Garrett and Logan arrive?" Just saying their names hurt. The idea of one of those young immortals seizing up and dying during the ritual made bile rise in his throat. He'd seen it happen and it had looked excruciating.

"They'll touch down tomorrow afternoon," Ivar said.

Ronan prowled around to see the sharpened blades set at seven points around the outer circle. The Seven marking, the one on his back, was etched into each knife handle. They somehow glinted in the dim room. He could still feel the cut. But that was nothing compared to the pain of the bones in his torso bonding together into a shield. "We can't even tell them what to expect," he murmured. "There are no words."

"I thought I'd go with *devastating and unreal pain,*" Ivar said, his voice hoarse. "But you're right. That doesn't come close to explaining it."

"No." Ronan turned from the blade. Was he making a mistake in allowing the ritual to go forward? What was his alternative?

"If you're mated by the time we do the ceremony, you'll be stronger," Ivar said. "You know you will." He moved around the other side of the circle, dropping to his haunches to examine one of the knives. "Though I don't suppose that's a reason to mate."

"I'm not mating just for strength," Ronan countered. "She must be protected and she's...mine." He glanced down at the marking that still burned on his palm. "It's that simple."

Ivar snorted and stood, turning at the last minute. "Tell me you used better words than that."

Ronan frowned. "Excuse me?"

Ivar rolled his eyes. "You know, the flowery shit. Eternal love and multiple orgasms. Those kinds of promises."

He'd just given her an orgasm. Sure, he'd been making a point, and she hadn't been able to fight it, but still. "Faith is a scientist. I don't think the fate and love poetry appeals to her."

"God, you're a moron," Ivar said, sliding his hands in his pockets.

Ronan's head jerked. Temper pricked the back of his heated neck. "Fuck you."

"No. Fuck her," Ivar retorted. "After you give her the love talk. Any asshole can give an orgasm. A woman, even a scientist, is going to want reassurance that you love her." He shook his head. "Dumbass."

Love? It was a four-letter word that didn't come close to explaining his feelings for Faith Cooper. Even before he'd met her, he'd felt her in his soul. Did she really need those words? Could he even find the right words? What he felt was absolute and true. He looked at Ivar, this new brother he already trusted with his life. "I hadn't thought about all of that."

"You might need to alter your grand strategy just a little bit." Ivar moved toward a back crevice. "Help me get the torches in place. These flashlights won't do for the ritual."

"Of course." Ronan walked around the circle again.

Ivar handed him a torch. "It should take us about an hour or so to get this place completely ready. During that time, I can help you figure out the right words to say before you see her again."

"Right. Like you know how to woo a woman." Ronan moved over to place the torch in a hole already bored into the rock. Now, he just had to figure out what to say to Faith. Good thing he had at least an hour to come up with something good. Love? There was a hell of a lot more to it than that. She was everything.

He would try the flowery words. For her.

But in the end, she would be his. Period.

* * * *

Comfy in her big bed, Hope Kayrs-Kyllwood snuggled with her bunny. Paxton had given it to her yesterday because the bunny's soft eyes had looked lonely. Pax had used the small amount of money he'd earned by washing cars to buy it.

He was her very best friend. Him and Libby. Someday they'd all build houses and live next to each other with their families around. Maybe not his father. But everyone else.

The air around her whispered secrets and she listened, comfortable with her safety. Her daddy was both a vampire and a demon, while her mama was magical. They both could fight off a hundred bad guys. A million bad guys.

When it came down to it, and someday it would, those million didn't count.

There was just one bad guy to worry about.

How she knew that at seven years old didn't matter. None of the weird questions did. She was usually careful not to tell anyone the things she knew. Sometimes, she couldn't help it, so she told. Then the grown-ups listened and nodded, acting like she was normal.

She knew better.

Their eyes always told another story. They worried about her. About the things she knew. So it was better not to tell them.

A mama who worried didn't have time to bake. And Hope's mama made the best chocolate-chip cookies in the entire Realm. She also shot an arrow better than most warriors.

Hope grinned, knowing she'd get more cookies tomorrow. She slipped into sleep, instantly finding her dream world. It had been weeks since she'd seen her friend, and she hoped he wasn't mad at her.

She found him sitting on a rock near the ocean, kicking his foot and scattering sand. Her tummy felt funny. "Hi, Drake."

He turned, his eyes a dark green with a purple ring. So pretty. "Hi. Are you still sick?"

"No." She hopped up by him on the rock and looked around. "I think our ocean is blue, right?" This one was light pink.

"I've never seen it, but I think so," Drake said, stretching his neck back to look up at the two suns. "This feels so good."

She patted his hand on the rock. "You can't go outside, can you?" Maybe someday somebody super-smart like Hope's mama could create a pill or something so the Kurjans can go into the sun. Then they'd all get along, probably.

"Not yet," Drake said. "But I can last out there longer than a grown-up. Most kids my age can."

Wouldn't it be awesome to see Drake in the sunlight and show him her house by the lake? "Are you still working on stuff?" Maybe he'd tell her about his job. A boy with a job was pretty cool. Drake was cool. She kicked out her feet like he did. Maybe he'd think she was cool. What could she say? She didn't work yet. "I learned how to grapple yesterday." Well, kind of.

Drake looked back at her. "You did?"

"Yeah." Her chest puffed out. "I practiced really hard and almost threw Libby over my head." Nobody could throw Libby, though. Feline shifters were very strong.

"That's great." He smiled, his teeth a bright white. "Our females don't train or fight. It's cool that you do."

Cool. Yep. He'd said it. Cool. She grinned. "Where do you live, Drake?"

He looked back over the wide sea. "Where do you live?"

She wasn't supposed to tell anybody. He probably wasn't, either. Why couldn't all the grown-ups just get along? "Do you have a favorite TV show?"

"Not really, but I like the wilderness ones. You know, where the humans go out and try to survive? Those are funny." He twisted his feet, looking at the sand covering them. "Definitely I don't watch cartoons."

She loved cartoons. Especially the ones with bunnies or bears. "How come?"

"They're for babies." He snorted.

Oh. She and Libby watched the bunny stories after school every day, and then when Pax got there, they turned to the bear stories. Pax was nice, but he could also lift heavy stuff. That wasn't babyish. "My friend Pax likes bear cartoons." Maybe Drake had never seen a good cartoon.

Drake scratched his chin. "It's okay for girls to like cartoons."

Now, wait a minute. "Pax is a boy." And girls were just as tough as boys. "It's okay for anybody to like cartoons," she blurted, her cheeks getting warm.

Drake was silent for a minute. "Okay. I'm sorry." He reached out and held her hand. "Don't be mad."

"I'm not." The Kurjans probably didn't have good television shows. There was so much she didn't know about him, but they couldn't talk about jobs or families or homes. "What do you wanna be when you grow up?"

"The leader," he said, shrugging. "Like my dad. It'll be my job." He glanced sideways at her. "Since you have the prophesy mark on your neck, do you have to be a prophet?"

"No," she said softly. "My mama said I can be anything I want."

Drake was quiet for a minute. "Is your mama right?"

Hope rubbed her free hand down her purple jeans. "No."

He nodded. "That's what I thought." He cleared his throat. "Have you heard of the Seven?"

Heard of them? No. But she'd dreamed about them. They were part of the change that was in the air all around her. "Have you?" she asked.

"Yeah. They're warriors from a long time ago who don't know things have changed. They're trying to hurt my family." His face turned red. "They have to be stopped."

"Or just told that things have changed," Hope said, taking her hand out of his.

His big chest moved when he breathed. "That's a good idea." He turned to her, his eyes more purple than green, making him look super-tough. "Do you know where they are?"

"No," she said, honestly. She really didn't know.

"Oh." His shoulders slumped. "How about the bubbles? Have they all popped?"

She bit her lip. Nobody knew about the bubbles or the worlds that were kinda like this one. But Drake was her friend, and he just wanted to make things better. "Just the first one has popped. The second will be next, and then the middle one."

He turned and grasped her arms, his fingers not hurting her at all. "Are you sure?"

She nodded, her eyes widening on him.

"Do you know when?"

She shook her head.

He slowly relaxed. "Remember when you told me that we were gonna change the world?"

"Yeah." It was the first time they'd met.

"Do you know how?"

She shook her head.

He smiled, and his eyes turned back to the green. "Me, neither. But I think the bubbles are where we have to start."

"Okay." She looked back at the pink ocean. Now she and Drake had a job together.

Cool.

CHAPTER THIRTY-TWO

Faith took a quick shower to cool her still-raging body and then braided her hair before jumping into a pair of new jeans and a white sweater. The tennis shoes were new and also white. They were a mite too big, but with socks on, she could make them work. Damn, she missed her boots and lip gloss. When could she return to a normal life? Ever?

She took a deep breath and strode into the hallway, adrenaline filling her bloodstream.

Raised voices made her stop cold. Ivar and Benny were arguing in the computer room. Loudly.

"We can't just kill an innocent human," Ivar snarled.

"Agreed. But we're talking the lives of thousands. Enhanced women. We need a live Key," Benny countered. "Sacrifice has always been the way. Our way."

"I know." Ivar's voice was low with pain.

Oh, God. Even if she trusted Ronan, he was outnumbered by the other three. If they wanted Grace dead, could he defend her? Against his vow and his brothers?

She had to protect Grace. As quiet as she could, she turned and ran back down the corridor. There was one chance to get out of there, and she had to take it.

When Ronan returned around midnight, she'd be gone. She couldn't take a chance with Grace's life. Even if Ronan didn't want to kill her, there were three other vampire-demon hybrids to worry about. They had all taken vows as the Seven, and sacrificing one human probably wouldn't even make them blink.

They might argue and hate the fact, but they obviously hadn't found another solution.

How was she going to get Grace out of there? She crossed into Grace's room and stopped cold at seeing Adare on the fragile pink chair, stripping a weapon. "What are you doing?" Panic heated up Faith's throat, and she rushed toward her sister, feeling for a pulse. Steady and strong.

Adare didn't twitch. "Ivar pretty much ordered me to keep watch."

"So you're cleaning your weapon?" Faith snapped.

Adare shrugged, slipping the clip into place. "I have important things to do."

"She is important." Faith took several deep breaths to calm herself. Grace was okay. Well, in a coma with saline and food drips, but at least breathing on her own.

Adare sprawled in the chair, his legs out, his ankles crossed. In the dim light, his eyes were dark and unreadable. "That Key is important to you," he said, his voice oddly hoarse, even for these growly men.

"She's not a Key," Faith said, fighting the urge to cross around the bed and step between them. "She can't be."

He lifted a shoulder that looked solid enough to move a mountain. "She is a Key. The marking is true."

"What is wrong with your voice?" Faith asked, unable to help herself.

His dark eyebrows rose. "Nothing." He studied her. "Oh. Yeah. You're new to this. Demons have raw vocal cords. Some people call them mangled, which they are not. But I seem to have inherited that characteristic, even though I'm only half demon." He shrugged. "Same with the black eyes. But I do have a secondary color like other vampires."

"What color?" Faith asked. How did the color change work? Did vampires have genes like the chameleon? How fascinating.

"That's a private matter, darlin.' And I'm more Highlander than either demon or vampire. That's important." He softened the rebuke with a smile, transforming his face from deadly to just mildly terrifying. "How'd your sister get into a coma?" His hoarse voice sounded almost bored now.

Faith kept her hand on her sister's shoulder. "A burglar."

Silence ticked for a moment. Adare cocked his head to the side. "You don't sound certain of that."

She swallowed. "They've never caught the guy." She didn't need to go into details with Adare, since he obviously wanted nothing to do with humans.

Adare studied the woman on the bed. "We will find who harmed her."

The vow sent chills down Faith's back. With her wet braid, she wished for a heavier sweater. "Adare? Why do you care?"

He didn't look away from her sister. "I don't, but you're the mate of my brother. Nobody hurts you or yours without inviting death."

Those should be comforting words. They weren't.

He studied Grace. "To still be alive, she must have impressive strength. For a human."

There was no way he'd let Faith leave with Grace. The hybrid was totally ruining her plan. But maybe she could go scout an escape route. What she needed was a wheelchair for Grace, but maybe she could find something else that would serve the purpose. A dolly, perhaps? "If you're going to sit with her, I'll run and grab something to eat."

Adare nodded, his gaze returning to his weapon. "Can she hear us?"

Faith paused. "There's research that says coma victims can hear those around them. Especially family members. I don't know if she can hear us," Faith said softly, "but I talk to her every chance I get and recite poems, just in case. She loved poetry."

"Humph." He looked up. "Benny is supposed to relieve me. He'd better be on time."

Yeah. The Highlander really was kind of a dick. She turned and moved as quietly as she could back down the dimly-lit hallway, hoping he thought she was going to her bedroom before getting something to eat.

She kept going past her bedroom, hurrying through the tunnels. Hopefully Ivar hadn't had time to put locks on the door or sensors or whatever else he had in mind.

She'd look around, find a good way to escape, and return for her sister. Adare would be back to work soon. Or she'd tell him to go back to work and let her sister rest. Would he fall for that? Finally, she reached the opening in the rocks.

Wind and rain pelted in along with darkness. There was no smooth rock wall to move. Excellent.

She rushed into the rain and ran over to the nearest jeep. It was a battered two-door convertible with a plastic top in place. She yanked open the door and scrambled around, finding the keys on the seat. Relief blasted her. Okay. All she had to do was figure out a way to bring Grace safely out here, and then they could escape.

Lightning zapped into the forest, and she jumped. The smell of ozone filled her nose.

Wow. That was close. Thunder ripped across the night as if in agreement. She swallowed and wiped rain off her face before shutting the door, the keys in her free hand. Lightning illuminated the clouds above her, turning them a grayish purple. The forest spread out, dark and deep.

She hustled around the jeep, her tennis shoes sinking in the wet grass. Lightning flashed again, lighting up the small clearing. She headed for the entrance and stopped cold.

Ronan emerged from the rock, his gaze meeting hers instantly.

Her heart stuttered. She paused out of pure instinct. Every nerve in her body flickered in panic, and her knees tensed with the urge to flee.

Lightning flashed again, fully illuminating him.

Fury. Raw and angry, it crossed his fierce cheekbones. He crooked a finger at her in a come-here gesture. She glanced down at the keys in her hand.

His growl vibrated through the storm, stronger than the rain. He sounded like a wild animal. A predator on the hunt. The sound sent chills down her back. If she went back in, she'd never get the chance to save Grace.

In a heartbeat, she made up her mind.

She had to run.

* * * *

Rage burned hot and deep in Ronan's chest, and he tried to calm it. Faith was standing in the middle of a powerful storm, putting herself in danger. There had to be a good reason.

She glanced down at her hand.

Something glinted dully.

The second he realized she held the keys to the vehicle, his body settled. His mind cleared. And his fury intensified, his heartbeat tuning in to the wild weather.

"Come here, Faith," he said over the storm. He owed her the chance. "If I have to chase you, you won't like it." He was a predator by nature, and when prey fled, predators had no choice but to pursue. The fact that she had put herself in danger from the storm pissed him off as much as the realization that she had planned to run.

From him.

That was an error she would not repeat.

The scent of the storm, pine and ozone, filled him along with the savagery of Mother Nature. He breathed in the elements, his senses sharpening. "Now," he said.

She looked behind him at the opening in the rock, and then hesitated. Rain poured over her delicate features, and she blinked.

The water and wind molded her white sweater to her full breasts, and her nipples hardened before his eyes.

His breath heated. Energy cascaded down his back, over his skin. His cock started to throb and the muscles in his thighs shifted, tensing to run. Her scent wafted through the rain, digging deep inside him, settling against his beast. The animal at his core that was ready for her. To claim her. "Faith." His voice came out almost garbled this time.

Emotion after emotion chased themselves across her face, and then she settled. Stilled. Her brown eyes appeared like wild honey, full of intelligence and spirit. Just like the storm around them. "I thought you'd be busy for a while," she yelled.

Interesting line of defense. Deflection. "I'm never too busy for you." He'd never spoken truer words. Apparently, he was having difficulty explaining her position in his life. In his heart. Why was it so hard for this modern woman to see what was right in front of her?

It wasn't as if he was hard to miss.

The wind pummeled them and she staggered, but remained on her feet. He could shelter her, if she'd just let him. "Faith. Stop fighting this." Stop fighting him, damn it.

"I have things to do that don't involve you," she said, her voice rising to beat the wind.

Again, the reality in which that might be true no longer existed. "Everything about you involves me," he said— reasonably, he thought.

She shook her head, that tight braid spraying water. "That's not how life works."

"Considering I've lived many more years than you, perhaps you should trust me on how life works." What was it with current society and its complete disregard for the lessons of the past? For history? For a reality not caught up in smartphones and just this minute. There was so much more around them. "Even you can feel this. Feel us," he said.

"I feel what I choose to feel." She slid in the mud and righted herself, looking around.

How ridiculous was that statement? He grinned, his fangs no doubt glinting.

She met his gaze again, indecision crossing her wet cheekbones. He saw the moment she decided on a path.

Her legs tightened. She drew in a breath and pivoted in the wet grass, turning to flee.

The beast inside him howled in anticipation. Only slightly increasing his normal speed, he reached her before she could open the door of the vehicle.

Careful not to touch her, he plucked the keys right out of her hand. She gasped and whirled around, her wet braid hitting him in the chest.

Fast as a whip, he reached out and released the tie on her braid. The wind took care of the rest, loosening the entire mass to blow around her face. She looked like a descending angel. He then took two steps back, twirling the keys in his hand. The rain pummeled them, but he paid no heed. "Where are you going?" he asked.

Her chest panted and she gulped. Her eyes had widened, probably unconsciously, but her head was up and her gaze direct. God, she was magnificent. Even her stubborn chin was held at a strong angle. "It's none of your business." She had to raise her voice over the rampaging wind.

"That's where you're wrong." He had no need to change his voice, as he was one with the storm. For the first time in too long, he felt his power. His true strength. So he took another step back, giving her the freedom to make the smart decision. The safe one for her. "Go back inside, Faith. We'll forget about this."

She wiped rain out of her eyes, still facing him so bravely. For a moment, she apparently thought the situation through. "No."

No. She'd said no. He studied her, trying to delve into that brilliant mind of hers. Sparks shot from her eyes. Anger and challenge. Without a question, she was challenging him.

As if reading his thoughts, as if wanting without a doubt to make sure he understood, she pressed her hands to her hips. With her small shoes in the mud and her hair wet and plastered to her face, she was the most gorgeous thing he'd seen in his very long life. And she was challenging him.

So things hadn't changed as much as he'd feared. There was still…this. If he wanted her, wanted the honor of protecting her, of building a life with her, he had to earn it. Did she even understand what she was doing? Oh, she was one of the Enhanced, and this defiance probably came instinctively. But she couldn't know, she *couldn't* comprehend, the primitive beast at his core.

She took a step toward him, her hands closing into fists.

There would never be a more fitting mate for him. He lowered his chin. "You have two choices, Doc. Behave yourself and go back inside. I'll deal with you then."

"Or?" It was as close to a growl as she'd ever be able to make.

He let his fangs flash. "Or you could run. But Faith, you won't get far." Anticipation lit him on fire. The choice was hers.

Red filled her cheeks and her eyes glowed. Then she smiled, the sight bold. "Think you can catch me?"

His shoulders went back. "Yes."

"Then let's make it interesting," she said through the pounding rain.

His muscles bunched and the leash he kept on himself stretched tight and thin. What type of game was she playing? "Interesting?"

"Yes." If the woman had had a gauntlet, she would've thrown it right at his head. "First, you give me your word no harm will come to my sister. That we will take her and hide her if your brothers decide to end her life. Period."

Power vibrated down his back. That was an easy vow. "I promise. Second?"

She smiled, her chin lowering. "You give me the count of twenty. If you don't catch me in one minute, you let Grace and me go. Where we want and when. I'll call you when I choose to involve you."

He liked this wild side of her. A lot. "If I catch you, I mate you," he rumbled, his fangs retracting through sheer force of will. "What say you?"

She sucked in a deep breath of air, filling her chest. In the middle of the storm, beneath the raging clouds, she truly was magnificent. "You have a deal."

CHAPTER THIRTY-THREE

Faith turned in the mud and ran down the road. What the hell was she doing? Every part of her had wanted to challenge him. She started counting in her head. *One. Two. Three.*

The rain hammered down, while the wind beat against her. But she was a runner, always had been, and she could outlast him for a minute.

Then she could get her sister free. And she'd call Ronan on her terms. Make him bring her flowers or something. *Seven. Eight. Nine.*

She turned and dodged between two pine trees, heading off the main road. Her breath panted in her ears and her blood rushed through her veins. Desire beat at her and a part of her, one she didn't much like, wanted him to catch her.

But he'd have to fucking earn it.

Fifteen. Sixteen.

She took another turn, this time between a couple of blue spruce with wide reaches. She had to duck and turn sideways. Ronan wouldn't make it. Then she chose another narrow set of trees and barreled between them.

Power sang in her veins as she ran. Stronger and better than ever before. It must've been the blood he'd given her.

Had that infusion caused her to act recklessly in making this deal?

She'd never felt so alive.

Twenty.

She increased her speed. He'd be coming after her now. She started counting down from sixty in the back of her mind.

Her shoes slipped in the mud and she windmilled, catching her balance and not missing a breath. Her feet landed with the pulse of the storm and she ducked her head, going faster. Thirty seconds down. Thirty to go.

She dodged a quick left between more trees, bounding over a series of bushes. Then she turned again.

Ronan stood beside a sweeping cedar tree, blocking the way down a narrow trail.

Twenty seconds to go.

She skidded to a halt and pivoted, rushing for another rocky trail.

He caught her from behind with an arm around her waist, lifting her high and swinging her around like she weighed absolutely nothing.

Before she could catch her breath, he had her up against the rough bark of a tree, and his mouth was on hers. He kissed her hard and fast, his mouth unrelenting. Her head swam, and her mouth was kissing him back before she could think.

Need rippled through her, so intense she clawed his shirt, trying to get closer.

He bit her bottom lip and released her, letting her slide down his impossibly hard body. Lightning burst above them and she jumped. She breathed out hard, her gaze focusing on him.

The vampire was every bit as ferocious as the storm whipping around them. His eyes were a hard blue, his jaw a devastating line. His soaked shirt emphasized the raw and deadly strength in his immense chest. The muscles in his arms bunched and jumped as if he, and he alone, held himself in check. "I caught you in time." The words were clear.

She couldn't move. Her body ached and deep down, she felt him. Needed him. They could save Grace together. This…this was for Faith. He was for her. "I know."

Satisfaction mixed with arrogance as the rain slid over the hard planes of his face. "Good." He ducked his head and she found herself over his shoulder, her forehead resting against the hard ridges of the back of his rib cage.

He moved easily, gracefully—at home in the forest. Her brain awoke seconds later and she started to struggle, her legs kicking out. He responded by securing one arm against her legs, pressing them to his body.

She punched his legs as hard as she could, but he didn't falter in his strides. Not even a little. Lightning sparked again, and then thunder cracked from every direction.

Before she knew it, they were back inside the rock. If she'd expected him to put her down, she was wrong.

They reached her bedroom, and he paused.

She lifted her head to see Adare coming out of Grace's room.

He lifted an eyebrow. "Everything okay?"

She swallowed, feeling slightly ridiculous being soaking wet and over Ronan's massive shoulder.

Ronan shoved the door open. "It will be. Don't interrupt us unless the fucking mountain is being blown up." He paused. "Forget that. Even if the mountain is blowing up, stay away." He stepped inside and kicked the door shut, leaving a boot print this time.

The world tilted as he dropped his head and put her on her feet. A second later, her white sweater flew across the room. Her lungs just up and left her body, refusing to even bother working. What had she done? Challenging an immortal warrior had felt so good. Now, vulnerability swept over her along with a need—a craving—too painful to be considered arousal. It was so much more.

The look on his timeless face was indescribable. A primitive combination of intent, power, and...danger. A warning and a promise. He reached for the button of her rain-soaked jeans. She trembled, unable to break his gaze.

The scientist in her urged her to back away, seek self-protection. The woman... Well, now. The most primal part of her, the deep femininity she'd kept locked away for so long, awoke. She stretched and roared.

Her jeans hit her ankles and caught on her sopping tennis shoes.

Without a moment's hesitation, Ronan slid sideways, wrapped an arm around her waist, and spun her head over heels. When she landed, her wet hair swinging wildly, her legs and feet were bare. Her lips parted and she wobbled on suddenly unsteady legs.

His easy grace in the move should've surprised her, but the logical doctor inside her had already realized she'd underestimated the strength he possessed.

He was more powerful than any storm. Somebody, some thing, totally out of her realm of experience.

And she'd challenged him. For this. For her.

He reached for her face and even desperately in need, she flinched.

His eyes flickered and then softened. Gently, he pushed damp hair away from her cheekbone, caressing down to cup her chin, his touch spreading tingles through her body. "Don't fear me." His words were a command more than a reassurance, and his grip firm rather than soothing.

She'd be a fool not to fear him a little. "I don't think you'd harm me." Physically, anyway. But she was a smart woman, and this was a male you respected. If they mated, it wouldn't be what she'd planned when she'd thought about settling down with a man. For one thing, he wasn't a man. This edge, this inhuman aspect of him, was more animalistic than civilized. She could sense it.

His head ducked and he took her lips, coaxing.

She breathed into him, opening, taking him in. He tasted like the storm. Wild and free, passion lurking beneath the surface.

Finishing the kiss too soon, he leaned back, his hand still in control of her chin. "Don't ever run from me again."

She blinked, the words taking a beat to sink in. "I'd do anything to save my sister." His grip kept her from backing away to make her point. "Even scary as hell, this feels right. But you have to promise my sister is safe."

That veil drew down over his eyes for a moment, and then they cleared. "I give you my word—I'll never harm your sister."

That wasn't quite good enough. She opened her mouth to protest, but he lifted her up, his lips on hers. He kissed her hard and deep, his hands cupping her butt. Fire lashed her, and she wrapped her legs around his waist, pressing her aching core against him.

He growled and set her on the bed. Then he stood back and yanked off his wet clothing.

Everything inside her settled. He was perfect. Hard muscles, long lines, sleek angles.

Her many years of education hadn't taught her about this. A hunger, a primitive instinct, flowed through her. Inside her. She was hot and wet—ready. Not being one to wait, she reached for him. While she'd always been cautious about anything she didn't fully understand, she banished all concerns. Nothing mattered but right here and right now.

He dropped his head to her neck, kissing and nipping.

Manacling his arms, she pulled him back, falling onto the bed. The second his dick rubbed against her clit, electricity zapped through her, and she gasped. "Now, Ronan." She couldn't wait. Not a second. They'd been interrupted way too many times. This time they had to complete the act.

He kissed her, taking over, pressing inside her with deliberate slowness. Never had anything in her entire life felt so good. She widened her thighs, kissing him back, scraping her nails along the incredible planes of his chest and around his rib cage.

With one final, hard push, he was imbedded inside her. Pain and pleasure mixed. He was so big—so full. Yet somehow gentle as he withdrew and pushed back in. It was too much. Nerves flared and sparked. He increased his speed and reached between them, plucking her clit.

She arched and cried out, thrown into an orgasm out of nowhere. It bore down on her and she exploded, panting through the deliciousness. He continued to thrust until she went limp.

A sigh escaped her. She reached up and pushed his damp hair away from his face.

His eyes had changed to a burnished gold. No green, no blue... just darkened gold.

She gasped.

His gaze was beyond intense. He was still rock-hard inside her, and his biceps visibly undulated above her. Slowly, he withdrew from her. She gave a sound of protest. Then he levered himself up on his knees, grasped her hips, and flipped her onto her stomach.

She landed with a surprised moan. He grabbed her hips and pulled her up to her hands and knees. His powerful thighs bracketed the back of hers.

Warning trilled through her, but he reached between her legs and palmed her sex. Tingling warmth radiated from it and she shut her eyes, need climbing in her again. Sharp and real. His hand moved and his dick pushed inside her again, this time going even deeper.

She dropped her head, baring her neck. From head to toe, she vibrated in anticipation. Of what, she wasn't certain. He reached around her and palmed her neck, pulling her up and elongating her back. She swallowed, barely, unable to move.

Then he started to thrust. Harder than before, deeper than she'd thought was possible. He hit a spot inside her, and wings of pleasure flew out in every direction, careening her into an orgasm that had her whimpering at the end.

But he didn't stop.

Faster and harder, he took her. All of her. In total control, his body behind her, his hands on her. He was everywhere.

She started to climb again, her body taken over by forces she could barely comprehend.

His five-o'clock shadow scratched her shoulder. Then his lips. The hand on her hip shifted to her lower back. She tensed, her eyes closing, her breath panting.

He struck deep, his fangs piercing through muscle and tissue to embed in bone. Agony took her. She screamed, fighting, but he held her tight.

Hammering harder, he held on. The pain was excruciating, but gradually, the need in her body began to overtake even that. The feeling of him inside her sent her toward a fall she'd never survive.

Yet he continued to power into her. "Faith. Come now."

As if her entire being had just been waiting for his words, she detonated. Her eyes closed and brilliant light flashed hot and bright. Inside her, he swelled even more. Then a piercing pain, one much hotter than in her shoulder, spread across her lower back.

It catapulted her into another orgasm that stopped her breath. She rode out the waves, her mouth open in a silent scream, pleasure so intense inside her she'd never be the same. With a soft sob, she went limp.

He ground against her and came, his low groan vibrating throughout her body.

Then. Silence.

She opened her eyes and blinked several times. His fangs were still inside her shoulder, and his cock was still inside her core. Her heart rate sped up even more, probably to a dangerous level.

His fangs retracted and he licked the wound. A healing balm spread across her shoulder. The pain dissipated. "I'll always take care of you, Doc." His voice was a low rumble. Then he withdrew and she winced, feeling tender and somehow empty.

He turned her around and flattened himself over her in a huge mass of protection. Balancing on his elbows to keep from crushing her, he kissed her so gently, tears gathered in her eyes.

She swallowed. "Your eyes. They're a dark gold."

"Yeah." He kissed her again, the glowing eyes making him look even more primitive than usual. "Are you all right?"

She ran her hands over his thick chest. Her mind was blown and her body was on fire. She couldn't grasp a thought. Not a one. What had just happened. "Are you?"

His gaze was tender and his jaw firm. "Yes. I'm finally whole."

CHAPTER THIRTY-FOUR

A sense of possession flowed through him as he stared down at Faith's lovely face. Her eyes had turned the color of dark honey, sweet and dreamy. Her lips were rosy and her nipples were still hard beneath his chest. He wanted to find the right words for her, but there were so many, he couldn't grasp just one. "You're beautiful," he said.

Her smile was lopsided and unguarded. Incredibly cute. Her hands on his chest were serving to arouse him again. "Am I immortal?" Curiosity and a little wariness filled those eyes.

He grinned, amusement taking him by surprise. "Not yet." He'd read some current reports from the Realm scientists the previous night. "It'll take a little while for your chromosomal pairs to increase to those of a mate." Before she could ask more questions, he kissed her. Then he leaned back. "You can study all the data we have on it. Vampires have thirty pairs and demons thirty-two. As a hybrid, I probably have thirty-one." He didn't really care about chromosomes.

Her eyebrows drew down very slightly. "So compared to vampires, humans are like, what? Plants compared to humans?"

He loved how her mind worked. "Sure." Why not? "I'll get you all the data." The brand on his hand no longer throbbed, and he lifted his arm to look at his palm. The marking would remain, dark and full. But it had stopped hurting. He'd branded her lower back and his hand was so big he'd spanned the entire width. "Do you feel any different?"

She pursed her lips, obviously thinking. "I feel warm. Kind of bubbly, like my blood is popping. An adrenaline rush of sorts, but that could just be post-climax."

Yeah. He loved her analytical brain. "Forget the 'post' part. We're just getting started." He'd never get enough of her.

A knock sounded on the door. Not a chance. No way. "Go the fuck away," he bellowed.

"Sorry, mate," Benny said, not sounding sorry in the least. "The earth isn't just moving in there."

Ronan snarled. "I'll kill him. Just slice off his entire head and rid the world of a lunatic."

"I can't be killed, buddy," Benny said cheerfully, his voice slightly muffled through the door. "Logan and Garrett are back, and Ivar wants to harness the storm to do the ritual. We have two hours before dawn arrives."

Yeah, it was the perfect time for the ritual. "We need to get our own damn mountain." Ronan sighed. "I'm sorry."

She blinked, rather sleepily. "That's okay." Then she yawned.

Mating did take a toll. The woman should sleep for hours. He kissed her again. "We'll be several miles beneath here. It's not safe for you there." He brushed his knuckles across her pink cheek. "You're to stay either in here or in Grace's room. But I want you to get several hours of sleep first. You're changing on a cellular level."

Her eyelids snapped open. "You're not going to start issuing orders just because we mated."

Of course he was. Time was ticking down, and the need to perform the ritual was pulling at him. But he'd be unreachable during the interim, and he had to know she was safe. "Promise me, Faith. You'll stay here." If she wouldn't make the promise, he'd have to lock her in somehow. He truly didn't want to start his matehood by pissing her off. "I have to concentrate on the ritual, and I can't be worrying that you'll put yourself in danger again."

She sighed, her eyelids half-closing. "Fine. I promise I'll stay here until your ritual is concluded."

It wasn't much, but it was enough for now. "Good. I didn't want to have to bind you."

Her head snapped back. "You're joking."

He nipped her lip and stood, searching for his clothing. "This should take no more than two hours."

She partially sat up, her pink nipples enticing him. "What does it entail? Is it dangerous?"

His heart warmed. "Are you worried about me?"

"Yes," she said simply.

Every once in a while, she showed a sweetness that kicked his legs out from under him. "It is dangerous, but I will be fine." At the moment, he could take on a legion of attackers and win. His blood was changing too. For the better. "Please sleep." He found the clothing Adare had brought back for him in the corner and quickly yanked on faded jeans and a black T-shirt. After giving her a quick kiss on the forehead, he strode for the door.

Benny waited outside, amusement sparkling in his eyes. "Have a good night?"

Ronan breathed in and shut the door, instantly sobering. Strength, new and vital, rushed through his veins. "We have to make sure they understand what's about to happen. Which of them is bonding tonight?"

"Dunno." Benny lost the amusement and started down the hallway, turning into the kitchen area next to the control room. Even though there were stools set strategically along the counter, nobody sat.

The tension in the room prickled over Ronan's skin.

Adare and Ivar stood near the stove, tall and broad. Logan and Garrett, their hair wet from the storm, were near the marvelous invention of a microwave.

"We waited for you," Ivar said.

Ronan nodded. "All right. The actual ritual takes a couple of hours, but the bonding process takes more than twenty-four hours. It's excruciating and you might not make it. We'll do everything we can to help you, but odds are, you'll die." He wouldn't tame his words for them. They had to know the chance they were taking.

"Understood," Garrett said, his gaze determined.

"We're ready," Logan said, the world in his green eyes. That kid had seen some shit.

Ronan hesitated.

"There's no backing out once we begin," Adare murmured, his eyes bloodshot. Was he still intoxicated?

Ronan gave a short nod. "Did you say good-bye to everyone you needed to?"

The males nodded.

"All right. Who's enduring the ritual this morning?" he asked.

Garrett's chin lifted. "We both are."

"No," Benny said. "We can only do one at a time. It's physically impossible to do otherwise. Decide who goes."

Garrett and Logan exchanged a look. With a shrug, Logan drew a silver coin from his pocket and spun it into the air. "Call it."

"Heads," Garrett said.

Logan caught the coin, spun it, and slapped it on the table with a hard smack. His hand remained over it. "I want to go first."

"So do I," Garrett said.

Man, these young vampire-demons were tough. An odd pride filled Ronan. "Lift your hand."

Logan lifted his hand, and the coin had a man's head on it. "Fuck."

Garrett stepped forward. "Let's get this done."

* * * *

Garrett Kayrs settled his mind and tried to relax his shoulders. He had planned to fight to be the one to go through the ritual. Logan wouldn't admit it, but he was still sporting a couple of injuries from a run-in they had with a squad of werewolves the previous week. Oh, he was a tough bastard, but top form was probably needed for this ritual.

The tension from the immortals around him was starting to give him a headache. "Let's go," Garrett said.

Ronan's hard face gave nothing away, but his eyes burned a deep aqua.

Family.

It was there in every angle and line. Garrett could see his father in Ronan's jaw, his uncle in Ronan's gaze, and even his niece in the arch of Ronan's eyebrows. "I can do this," he said.

"I know," Ronan said, turning for the door. "If anything goes wrong, we share blood. I'll be the one to bring you back, regardless of the cost."

"Cost?" Garrett asked, striding behind him.

Nobody answered.

Logan fell into step.

Benny clapped Logan on the shoulder. "You can come down to the bottom level, but you can't enter the chamber. The energy will kill you if you're not part of the ritual. Stay close right outside. We're going to need your blood."

"You can have it." Frustration crossed Logan's face.

Ronan glanced back at Garrett. "Follow me in a second, and don't worry if your skin feels like it's boiling off." Then he disappeared, followed by Ivar, Benny, and Adare.

The quiet of the kitchen ticked.

Garrett paused. "Lo—"

Logan held up a hand, his green eyes burning. "Let me do this first. See if we can survive it. Maybe this ritual won't work like it did before." He clapped a hand on Garrett's shoulder. "My mama has three sons. Yours only has one. Let me do this."

"I love you, man," Garrett said, going for flip and completely missing it. He sobered. "You're my best friend and my brother." There wasn't anything on earth Garrett wouldn't do for Logan. Including risking his life first. "I won the toss." A part of him, one that he probably got from his father, believed in fate. That things happened for a reason, and that he had a destiny to fulfill. This was the first step. He just knew it.

"G, we're family. I can't let you die," Logan said, his lip twisting.

"I won't die," Garrett said, trying to sound sure. "But just in case—"

"Don't say it."

Garrett cleared his throat. "Take care of my family. Help my sister and my folks. My dad is tough, but he'll be the one who needs you. Even more than my mom." His throat burned. "And protect Hope."

Logan's eyes burned. "Don't fucking die. If you do, I'm going to find that wolf shifter who dumped you last year and mate her. We'll name every kid we create G-dog."

Garrett coughed. "Fair enough." He grabbed Logan and yanked him in for a hard hug. Logan clapped him on the back. Then they turned and all but jogged to the stone stairwell down into the earth. Garrett followed steps, winding around, and soon sweat soaked his shirt. Finally, they reached a small pocket with a crevice big enough to slide through sideways.

Logan paused right outside and put his back to the wall, sweat rolling down his face. "Stay tough, G," he whispered.

Garrett nodded. Taking a moment for a quick prayer, he let power rush through his veins. Then he shoved through the opening, which quickly shut behind him. Torches lit the rough rock walls, and the air was so hot it blurred. The four males were positioned around an inner circle, their shirts off.

Garrett ripped his over his head without being asked. Then he moved past Ronan to the area in the middle of the circle.

Power and something ancient surrounded him. The air shimmered with the sense of foreign dimensions, shifting time. The very laws of physics were stretched, contorted. Yet the moment was real and on fire. His body chilled and then heated.

Going on pure instinct, he turned and faced Ronan directly.

"We share blood," Ronan said, his voice echoing off the chamber walls. The words were apparently meant as a reassurance, so Garrett nodded. "When the bonding starts, send your mind elsewhere. You'll see things—places—you never imagined. You'll see the stream of time. Please look for my brother. Try to see if Quade's shield has shattered yet."

"I will." Garrett set his feet, looking down to see the outline of his circle. The black demarcation began to lighten and then glow a fiery red. Looking closer, he could see it was actual fire. Lava? His boots began to bubble, the leather melting away.

A haze surrounded him, and the immortals wavered behind it.

A myriad of sights and sounds assaulted him. Unknown and unfamiliar. Was this a different dimension? One dimension crossing another? His skin pricked, and the cells inside his body began to pull apart with a feeling like sharp knives. What if the ritual couldn't be performed in this time?

His vocal cords stretched inside his throat, snapping and then mending. He panicked and tried to escape the circle. His body refused to move. He remained completely in place. At the realization, he settled and calmed. There was no way out. He was Garrett fucking Kayrs, and he'd survive this. He could survive anything.

Silver glinted. He lowered his chin to focus. Ronan held a sharp blade in his hands. He sliced his palm, and the smell of blood wafted through the haze. Pain slashed through Garrett's palm and he looked down, seeing an identical cut. Ronan stepped closer and held out his arm with the hand down, dripping blood onto the earth. Garrett's arm moved on its own, and he held out his hand, catching Ronan's blood.

Ronan said something, and clouds began to swirl throughout the rapidly-heating chamber. It had been hot before, but this was merciless. Ronan's words were lost in the haze. Part of the ritual Garrett couldn't hear. Then Ronan moved to the right.

An earthquake rocked the entire chamber, creating small fissures in the ground.

Adare came into view, a slightly different knife in his hand. He cut himself and pain again ripped across Garrett's palm. He looked down to see the cut was diagonal to the first one. This time, he held out his hand before Adare offered the blood. Adare's arm came through the mist, hand down, and he dropped blood onto Garrett's already bloody hand.

Warmth flared.

Garrett performed the same acts with Ivar and Benny until he was facing Ronan again, blood from all four immortals mingling with his own on his left hand.

Going on instinct, he drank a full swallow. Agony burned down his throat.

The blood on his hand bubbled, turned black, and singed beneath his skin. He caught his breath, gasping, dropping to his knees. His ribs heated and glowed through his skin. Unimaginable pain, something too deep to even *be* pain, overtook him.

He screamed.

CHAPTER THIRTY-FIVE

Faith finished dressing after a relaxing shower and then went to check on her sister. She moved Grace around, stretching her limbs, marveling at her muscle tone. Grace hadn't atrophied at all. It had to be the Key marking.

She leaned in, remembering when she and Grace had told each other everything after a date. Heck. They'd told each other everything before a date. She so missed those times. Her stomach growled. Faith pressed a hand to it. She was starving. "I've got to get some food. Oh, and I mated Ronan," she whispered to Grace. "I'll be back to explain later."

Then the monitor caught her eye. Oh God. She ran forward and double-checked the cuff around Grace's arm.

Then she took the blood pressure again.

Low. Definitely too low. This was terrible.

Panicking, she turned and ran down the hallway, yelling Ronan's name. She had to find him. Reaching the computer room, she realized it was empty. Where were they? Time was running out for Grace. Right now.

Ivar's phone caught her eye near the computer. She grabbed it and ran down to the other conference room. Where the hell was the entryway to go below the earth?

She couldn't find it. Okay. She'd check on Grace.

Swallowing, she ran back to Grace's room. Her sister had paled even more, and her vitals had all slowed.

Faith bit back a sob. She glanced at the phone in her hand. Damn it. It was a long shot, but she scrolled through Ivar's phone, looking for Ronan's number. Oh yeah. He didn't have a phone yet. So she pressed the speed dial for Adare and then Benny, only getting voice mail. They probably couldn't get service so deep in the earth.

There was only one other person to call.

Okay. This was crazy. Faith's hands trembled. Ronan was going to kill her for this.

She looked at the innocuous device. Biting her lip, she quickly dialed Dayne's number before she could chicken out.

"Dayne," he answered, his voice absentminded.

"Dayne? It's Faith Cooper," she whispered, sitting on the pale pink chair.

He was quiet for a moment. "Are you all right?" His voice quieted as well.

Was she? "I—I don't know." She looked at her motionless sister on the bed. "I mean, I am, but my sister is not."

"I can come get you if you need protection," Dayne said. "Just say the word. Drake and I will find you."

She winced. Betraying Ronan really wasn't an option. "Please tell me how you awoke Grace." She swallowed, her body shaking. "Please."

"Okay." Movement sounded. "I don't really understand the science, but I'll put on somebody who does." His footsteps echoed through the line and then there was the sound of a door opening. "Dr. Maple? Could you explain the procedure we used on Grace Cooper to her sister, who's also a doctor? She should understand your mumbo jumbo."

How dangerous could a guy be who used the term *mumbo jumbo*?

A click echoed, and a woman's face came up on the screen. Long blond hair, intelligent green eyes, pointed chin, and very pale skin. "Yes. Hello?"

Faith pressed a button, engaging the camera. "Hello. I'm Dr. Cooper."

"Oh. Hi. I'm Yvonne Maple, a surgeon with the Kurjan nation." The woman smiled, her gaze intense.

A surgeon? "Are you a Kurjan?" Faith asked, her mind reeling.

"Yep." The woman's eyes changed from green to purple and then back. A couple of rather dainty-looking fangs slid down from her mouth and then retracted.

Holy crap on a cracker. A female Kurjan. A beautiful one, actually. Unless this was all staged, which was certainly possible.

The woman moved, and lab equipment showed behind her. She was wearing a blue blouse with a white lab coat over it. "Before we begin, do you mind taking your sister's blood pressure for me?"

"I already did, and it's incredibly low. Let me check again." Grabbing the cuff and her stethoscope, she did so, her heart dropping. "Gracie, you have hypotension," she whispered, her head reeling. "You're eighty over twenty." Much worse than just hours before. Whatever the reason, Grace's condition was worsening. Without question.

She looked back at the phone. "She has hypotension."

Yvonne frowned. "I was afraid of that. What's your understanding of the H-cells?"

Faith blew out air. "Zero understanding." What the heck was an H-cell?

Dr. Maple nodded. "Ah. Okay." She turned to the side. "Why are we sharing intel with a human?"

"She needs help." Dayne's voice came easily over the line.

Dr. Maple focused on the phone again, her brows creased. "I don't like this, but all right. H-cells are the healing cells that immortal species use to heal themselves. We've been working for decades on a way to use those cells to help humans, although we aren't ready to share yet. We certainly aren't prepared to go public with our existence." The last was said as a warning.

Faith stood up, her blood pumping furiously. Could these people help her sister? "So you used them on Grace?"

"No." Maple shook her head. "We just gave her a minute amount of Dayne's blood. Any more without an HT injection would've killed her." She winced. "In fact, has there been any uptick in her blood pressure?"

"No. It keeps decreasing."

"How unfortunate." Maple shook her head and blond wisps went flying. "I told them it was a bad idea. Even a small amount of Dayne's powerful blood is too much for a human, especially a weakened one. Her heart is going to give out soon."

Faith rushed over to her sister and placed a hand on her sister's shoulder. "How soon?" The change in blood pressure was indicative that Maple was telling the truth.

"Just a few hours," Maple said, her eyes soft. "But I can save her."

"With an HT injection," Faith said slowly. "What exactly is that?"

Maple turned to the side, apparently getting permission to continue. "It's a serum that took me fifty years to develop. It mutates human antibodies in order to bind them to the immortal H-cells from Kurjan blood and lets them perform their job."

"You can save humans?" Faith breathed, hope smashing into her.

Maple bit her lip. "Yes and no. We've had positive results in Enhanced females only—no regular humans. It's a fast healing—within twenty-four hours." She rubbed her chin. "Then the H-cells are absorbed into the body and just disappear. I haven't been able to make the transfer long-term." Her eyebrows lowered again.

"But during the active phase—they cure the Enhanced female?" Faith asked.

Maple nodded. "Yeah. But the goal is to increase longevity and quality of life. Not just heal an injury."

"You can save my sister?" Faith asked.

"If we get an injection into her in time," Maple said, drawing back from the camera. "Usually we would have performed the injection by now." She glanced down at her watch. "You have a very short window, and then there's nothing I can do."

Oh, God. Faith's mind reeled. "Why don't the vampires know about this? Or the demons?"

Maple snorted, making her look like a cute little elf. "Vampires? Right. They're interested in strategy and defense—not science. We have a horrible history of atrocities on both sides. Kurjans aren't innocent by any means. But we've tried to improve and learn. The vampires...have not."

Faith couldn't possibly care less who knew the most about science or who was good or even bad. Her sister was what mattered. Period.

Grace's systolic pressure dropped a couple more millimeters in HG on the monitor.

Faith stopped breathing. If she didn't do something, her sister was going to die. "Would you give me the serum?" she asked.

Dr. Maple drew back from the camera. "No." Her voice rose. "I need to administer the injection and monitor results. You don't know anything about the process." She leaned in closer to the camera. "I'm two hundred years old, Dr. Cooper. You don't have near the experience I do."

"Nevertheless, I'm a leading expert on comas," Faith countered, her stomach tilting. "You seem legit and Dayne appears reasonable, but I'm not bringing my sister to you." She trusted Ronan and definitely didn't trust these folks. She couldn't take that chance with Grace's life. "Please tell me the ingredients of the serum, and I'll keep you informed."

Maple coughed, incredulousness crossing her face. "You can't go out to Target and buy these ingredients. Some of it I created from Kurjan blood cells, and we don't share Kurjan blood with humans. Ever."

That made sense. Faith's mind reeled.

Dayne suddenly appeared on the screen. "It's my fault that your sister is dying. I shouldn't have given her my blood, but I thought it was the only way to get your attention." Lines fanned out from his odd greenish-purple eyes. "Tell me where to bring the serum, and I'll come alone. I'll give it to you and leave."

Faith swallowed, watching Grace's monitors. Her diastolic number dropped again. There just wasn't time. "No. Dr. Maple comes alone. I'm in Wyoming and can meet you outside the town hall in Northtown." There had to be a town hall, right?

Dayne glanced down, probably at his watch. "She can be there in an hour and a half via helicopter." His mouth firmed into a white line. "We're having a bit of a...well, internal struggle here."

"Oh. Because of the Cyst attacking the Seven?" Faith asked, sarcasm nearly burning her tongue.

His gaze hardened. "Yes. There are a couple members of the Cyst who've gone rogue. Apparently some long-standing feud between Omar and Ronan Kayrs." Dayne exhaled heavily, his gaze earnest. "I'm taking care of it and removing Omar from his position. But I'm getting some backlash, so let's just keep this conversation and plan to ourselves?"

Like she'd tell the Cyst. "I have to trust you, Dayne. But if you cross me, you'll regret it." Yeah, probably an empty threat when dealing with an immortal. And she was lying. No way did she trust any of these people.

Grace's pressure dropped again.

Time was definitely running out.

There wasn't a choice.

Dayne's chin dropped. With his pale, angled features, he looked like a hero from a science fiction movie. "I won't harm you, Faith Cooper. And I'd like to save your sister."

She nodded. "I'll meet Maple in an hour."

The screen went blank. She wanted to see Maple in person. Dr. Maple was a female Kurjan. They actually existed.

Faith rushed into the hallway and ran to the control room, looking frantically around for the entrance to the chamber. She had to find Ronan. Going alone to meet any Kurjan was crazy.

Only smooth rock wall met her gaze. She pounded on the wall, but nothing happened.

Fine. Okay. She could handle this. Grabbing a piece of paper, she quickly scrawled out a note for Ronan.

Ronan,

Grace's blood pressure is dropping dangerously low, and I'm meeting a Dr. Maple (Kurjan female) in Northtown for a serum of H-cells to save her. She says she has a cure. It's probably a trap. Well, I'd say seventy percent trap. Maybe eighty. Hell. I don't know. I'm purposefully walking into a trap, but it's my only option right now. My hope is to grab the cure and run. I'm sorry.

I've taken Ivar's phone, and I've made sure the GPS is recording. You can track me the second you come up from the chamber. I'm also armed and will hide the jeep in town before the meet. Come when you can. If it is a trap, and if I can't run with the cure, I'll hold on until you get there. I promise.

Faith.

She read the note quickly. Should she put *Love*? No. Jeez. She drew in an X and an O above her name.

If she could find the entrance down to the ritual chamber, she'd search them out and request backup. But what if they tried to stop her?

But there wasn't time to even find Ronan and argue about it right now.

She ran to the armory and equipped herself the best she could.

Then she hustled to Grace's room and nearly stopped breathing upon seeing that Grace's pressure had dropped again on both measurements.

She kissed Grace on the forehead. Then she turned and ran down the stone hallway, into another gloom-filled rainy day. All of her options were bad ones right now.

Allowing her sister to die was not one of them.

CHAPTER THIRTY-SIX

The heat was unbearable. Ronan widened his stance as an unholy force swirled around the four immortals, trying to knock them to the ground. Invisible, razor-sharp knives attacked his flesh from every direction, and he invited the pain in, fighting the pull of gravity.

He. Would. Not. Fall.

The rock walls around them began to glow, first neon blue and then blood-red.

Garrett had gone silent in the middle of the circles, his body contorting in agony. His fangs had pierced his lips, and blood poured down his chin to drop into nothing. The ground below his feet wasn't visible in this dimension. The way he was moving, it could be made of needles. His pain swelled through the hot chamber, palpable to all of them.

Ronan had been the first to bind, so he'd been through this ritual numerous times.

Yet there was no way to remember the sheer horror of it. Every time was different. The dimensions accessed during the ritual had to be hell worlds. There was no other explanation.

A series of earthquakes assaulted them, and a huge rift appeared in the stone wall, showing a vein of silver.

His skin felt like it was being turned inside out and burned with hot pokers. And it would be a thousand times worse for Garrett. It was impossible even to know what dimension he was in and how bad it was for his body. The bonding happened in different pockets every time.

All were beyond hell.

Adare, Benny, and Ivar remained standing, barely visible through the haze swirling around.

Ronan felt them. Their spirits and their strength. Each one recognizable as a brother. They'd bonded together, they'd fought together, and someday they'd be reunited in the beyond together. But today was to live. To struggle and accept a new brother, no matter what it took.

Ronan tried to speak, but the heat and force seized his vocal cords. *Come on, Garrett. Fight.*

Garrett continued contorting, his eyes open and still that sizzling gray. He screamed again, the sound tortured. Then his eyes morphed into a wild gold color—his tertiary color. A bright strip encircled the gold, making him look like a primitive animal.

He dropped to a knee and blood splashed up. The liquid covered his lower chin and his entire chest.

Ronan tried to move toward him, but the haze held him back. There was no crossing into the other plane. Garrett had to fight his way back himself.

Garrett partially turned, his head dropping. Sweat and blood slid over his face and down his neck.

Fire spread across his back, and he arched, his pain slicing across dimensions. One by one, his ribs turned red, then orange, and finally black as they were bound to each other. Then the spaces between filled in, more solid than any surface ever created.

His head hung down, his hair in wet tendrils.

Ronan's back and torso pounded in time with the changes, the agony of the bonding causing his lungs to seize and stop for a moment. His heart sped up until he became light-headed, and the invisible knives continued to cut. He glanced down to see blood pooled all around his feet.

His blood.

The stone accepted his offering, which flowed toward the center and to Garrett. Blood streamed from the other immortals toward Garrett as well, all mixing together and hopefully strengthening him. Helping him to heal from the agony his body was currently enduring.

So many hadn't healed. Garrett had to survive this.

Another earthquake hit and a fissure opened in the floor, revealing churning lava. It didn't seem possible, but the air became even hotter.

Was the shield between dimensions weakening? Had they made a mistake with the ritual? Ronan had said his words and given his blood, just like before. But had things changed somehow?

Ronan's knees weakened and he tightened them. Time stopped having any meaning. An hour passed, maybe two. He felt it the second Garrett was fully bonded, his torso becoming a shield nobody could penetrate. His heart, lungs, and vital organs would never be pierced, taken out, or burned. Even his spinal column was now impenetrable.

The haze disappeared. The pain wafted away from Ronan.

Ronan breathed out, his chest working again. "Garrett? You have to fight," he called out, hoping his voice would reach from one dimension to another.

Garrett appeared motionless, his eyes open but not seeing.

Ivar moved toward Ronan, a million cuts on his skin slowly beginning to mend. His feet were covered in blood still. "It's up to Garrett now."

Ronan tried to swallow through his parched lips. "I know." If Garrett survived the remainder of the ritual, he'd find his way back to this dimension and time, needing medical assistance and a copious amount of blood. If he didn't survive, the portal would spit back his corpse. "I wish I could go in there with him." He moved forward, and an invisible force threw him back against the rock wall.

His shoulders hit first and pain ripped down his spine. He shook his head to dispel the flashing stars behind his eyes as he landed back on his feet. "Fucking portal."

"The sad fact is that we don't even know what it is," Ivar snarled. "The ritual works, and we performed it as we were taught, but we still don't understand it all."

Some things in life were incomprehensible. This might be one of them, or perhaps their science just hadn't reached the correct understanding yet. Regardless, comprehending what was happening was far less important than surviving it. "He's strong. He'll survive," Ronan said, hoping to hell he spoke the truth.

Logan slipped through the crevice, sweat pooling across his gray T-shirt. His eyes widened upon seeing Garrett, and he lunged for the circle.

The portal threw him up high, and he hit the rock wall with a loud bang. Sharp shards rained down, and Ronan ducked his head to protect his eyes.

Logan dropped to land on his ass, sending more rocks scattering.

Ronan hauled him up by the arm. "You okay?"

Logan shook his head like a dog with a face full of water. "What the fuck was that?" he growled, his gaze returning to Garrett.

"Don't exactly know," Ronan admitted, his entire body feeling like it had been crushed beneath the sea for decades. "But there's no way you're getting inside."

Logan tugged down his shirt. "What's wrong with him?"

Ronan turned to look at the motionless Garrett. Horror still filled his eyes. "His body has bonded. Now his mind, or his spirit, has to survive the process. He's somewhere else right now." There was no other way to explain it. "We'll have fresh blood and medication for him, but we can't help him until he fights his way back here."

Logan swallowed. "There has to be a way to get to him."

"There isn't," Adare said flatly. "Believe me. We've tried countless times before with other potentials."

Ronan focused on the younger immortal. "What are you doing in here, anyway? If you had come in ten minutes earlier, you would've been torn apart."

"We told you to stay out," Ivar snapped.

Logan tore his gaze from Garrett and handed Ronan a soaking wet piece of paper. "Your mate left to meet the head of the Kurjan nation and get a cure for her sister."

The words hit Ronan harder than the force had earlier. "What?" He took the paper and quickly read the note.

Logan shoved his damp hair away from his forehead. "I ran upstairs for the medicine so it would be on hand and saw the note. She took one of the Jeeps." Regret glimmered in his green eyes. "I'm sorry. I didn't even think I had to watch her."

Neither had Ronan. They'd mated, for God's sake. He turned back to the vulnerable vampire in the center of the circles. "I'll kill her." After he saved her ass from the Kurjans. "Why would she do this?" He stared down at the paper. To save her sister. She didn't trust him to do it. Grace wouldn't die—she was a Key. Why had Faith trusted the Kurjans anyway?

Logan wiped his face. "They said they have a cure. She must've believed them."

A cure. A fucking cure from the Kurjans. So much heat surrounded Ronan that it was a miracle fire could still be ignited from within. "How could she?"

The chamber remained silent.

Finally, Ivar spoke. "You have to go, Ronan."

Conflicting allegiances pulled at Ronan from every side. Duty and rage tore him apart. "She's my mate."

Adare nodded. "Go. We'll cover Garrett when he comes out. We've got this."

Ronan shook his head. "We share a bloodline. My blood will help him." But he had to save his mate.

"We all share a bloodline," Benny said, his voice a low rasp and his lips cracked from the heat. "If he makes it out before you return, I promise we'll save him."

The unspoken words lingered in the air. If Garrett hadn't made it out before Ronan's return, then he never would. The impossibility of the situation landed so hard on Ronan's shoulders that he could barely stand. How could Faith do this to him? Even though he hadn't explained the ritual to her, surely she understood how difficult it was. And how important.

"She's trying to save her sister," Ivar said quickly, burn marks beginning to fade from his face. "You'd do the same for one of us. Even if it risked your life."

Yeah, but his mate didn't get to risk hers. Ever. "I'll be back as soon as I can." He moved toward the crevice and shoved through, almost welcoming the sharp cut of the rocks.

Ivar appeared next to him on the other side, coming up behind him.

"What are you doing?" Ronan asked, stopping.

Ivar planted a broad hand on his shoulder. "This is the Kurjans. You need backup."

"No. Garrett requires more help." Ronan tried to push him away.

"There's enough help in there. I've got your back, brother."

An earthquake shook the mountain and rocks began to fall. Ronan shoved Ivar toward the stairs and followed him, falling hard. The earth shook for several seconds.

"We knew this would happen," Ivar wheezed. "The ritual messes with the earth itself."

Ronan turned and looked at the crevice. It was gone. Completely. A mountain of rocks covered the spot where the entrance had been. "Fuck."

Ivar dusted himself off and stood, his gaze on the cave-in. "They're on their own now. They'll make it out."

"I hope so."

Ivar shoved him aside and started running up the stairs.

Ronan settled himself. He'd lost more than half his blood in the ceremony, and his vision was still fuzzy. Yet anger helped focus everything.

Fury propelled him as he followed his brother to suit up for war.

CHAPTER THIRTY-SEVEN

After a quick stop at a pharmacy, Faith waited in a cute coffee shop across the street from the Northtown city hall. Rain splattered down on the stately brick building. Even though it was only April, greenery flourished in planters set around the building. A few people were out in the rain holding brightly colored umbrellas.

Several shops lined the street, with the courthouse next to the city hall.

Nothing out of the ordinary could be seen. Since the Kurjans couldn't venture into the sun, could they appear when the cloud cover was so heavy? She hadn't thought to ask.

Her hands trembled around the mug holding her green tea. Ronan was going to be furious with her, and a sliver of her felt bad for leaving.

But if he had a sister, he'd do the same thing.

Sure, she was taking a risk. But she had a knife in her sock, a green gun that harmed immortals at her back beneath her sweater, and Ivar's phone nicely hidden inside her tennis shoe. If she had to shoot Yvonne Maple, she'd do it.

A woman came into view, walking down the sidewalk. In a moment her features became discernible. Dr. Maple. Faith swallowed. She actually hadn't expected the doctor to come by herself. The clouds shifted and the sun shone down.

Faith jumped up to yell a warning and then paused. The sun shone directly on the doctor's blond hair, and she tilted her head up, smiling.

So the sun didn't harm them any longer...or the good doctor had been faking her species.

Then, she pointed her umbrella down and shook it out, tying the strap around it. She opened the door to the coffee shop, and the bell above it tinkled merrily. Catching Faith's eye, she strode around a gumball machine and reached the table. "Hello, Dr. Cooper." She held out a hand.

Faith shook hands and then gestured to the other wooden chair. "Please, sit." This was all so crazily bizarre. This close, the woman looked incredibly young.

Dr. Maple removed her trench coat and set it on the chair before sitting. "A helicopter dropped me right outside of town." She wore casual jeans, high-end boots, and a green sweater that brought out the stunning color of her eyes. "Is it just me, or does this feel like a James Bond movie?"

Faith chuckled, adrenaline still flooding through her. Was this woman full of it? "It really does. Dr. Maple, you can withstand sunlight?"

Dr. Maple blinked and then smiled. "Call me Yvonne, and of course we can. Only the poor Cyst can't because of their genetic mutation. Did Ronan Kayrs tell you otherwise?"

"Yes," Faith whispered.

"A thousand years is a long time to be gone," Yvonne said. "The world has changed, whether the Seven like it or not. Whether they've even discovered it has or not." She reached out to pat Faith's hand, her nails painted a pretty pink. "This has to be so bewildering for you."

Faith nodded. "You have no idea." Was this a trick? "I have so many questions." Could they save other coma victims?

"I'm sure." Amusement curved Yvonne's pink lips.

"How do you know about the Seven? According to Dayne, Ronan is the bad guy." Which wasn't true. There might be a lot of new advances and uncertainty, but that much Faith knew. Ronan was a good man. Rather, male. Even if he had been gone a thousand years and had no clue how everything had changed.

Yvonne tapped her nails on the table. "Our history pegs him as a killer of the Cyst. He killed many of our people to begin the ritual. You know that's why the Seven are secret, right?"

Faith stiffened. None of the Seven would explain why they were shrouded in secrecy. Had they used Kurjan dark rituals to create their brotherhood? Was it possible? They surely wouldn't want that information getting out. "No. Ulric killed the Enhanced women to bond himself."

Yvonne shrugged. "Bonding takes blood. The Butcher used Cyst blood when he created the ritual for the Seven. Ask him."

So much violence, no matter whom you believed. The knife was comforting in Faith's boot. "Where is the serum?"

Yvonne reached into a large purse and brought out a rectangular box. "Here. I suggest three milliliters tonight and three tomorrow night. It'll help regulate her heart rate and blood pressure until her body takes over again."

"What about the coma?" Faith accepted the box.

Yvonne nodded. "Another three milliliters the third day should mimic Dayne's blood and bring her back for you, without the side effects." She paused. "The most serious of which is death, actually. I really hope this works."

"As do I." Faith kept an eye outside the window, but only the rain was visible. "Let's just see what we have here, shall we?" She reached into the bag on her seat and drew out hydrogen peroxide, a small mirror, a cotton swab, and an eyedropper.

Yvonne leaned over the table. "What do you have?"

Shouldn't the woman know the answer to that? Faith lifted her head. "Let's see those fangs of yours now."

"I can't show them in public." Yvonne rolled her eyes and lifted a hand. A young waiter hurried over, his eyes overly bright. "Could I get a caramel mocha?"

The kid nodded and almost tripped getting back to the counter.

Faith opened the box and drew out the vial, using the syringe to take just a little bit of its contents.

"So much for trust." Yvonne's chin lowered.

Faith ignored her and dropped several dots of blood onto the cheap mirror. Then she took the eyedropper and filled it with hydrogen peroxide. She paused and took a breath. "Right?"

Yvonne threw her head back. "Stop that."

"No." Faith dropped the peroxide on the red dots.

Nothing.

Not a bubble.

Her stomach sank. It wasn't blood. She stood and studied this beautiful woman who had lied to her. This was definitely a trap. No movement showed outside the restaurant. She'd hidden the Jeep several blocks away.

"We're forbidden by law to give blood," Yvonne said evenly.

Faith looked frantically around. "This is a trap." Shit. She'd known it would be, but that small chance of saving her sister had made the risk worth it.

"You're going to want to come nicely with me. There are a lot of humans around." Yvonne waved a hand and drew a gun out of her purse. "Not that I care."

Heat exploded down Faith's esophagus. She jumped up, overturning the table onto Yvonne. The woman shrieked.

Faith leaped up and ran for the door. She had to get out of there. Was the cloud cover enough to protect the Kurjans? If not, she had a very limited time to run. Turning, she walked crisply out of the café and into the rain. She rushed down the sidewalk, dropping the box and serum in a garbage can several storefronts down from the café. Panic assailed her and she ducked her chin.

No way had Dr. Maple come alone. Chills swept down Faith's arms, but she couldn't see the threat as she ran for where she'd hidden the jeep. Fear made breathing difficult. Were they waiting for her to lead them to Ronan and the Seven?

She couldn't go in that direction.

Her hair grew damp and started to curl, so she brushed it out of her face. She jumped in the Jeep and drove around town, needing to get to Grace, but wanting to make sure she wasn't followed.

If she didn't return for Grace, would the Seven harm her? Even if they didn't, she only had a matter of hours left to live.

She paused at a stop sign and closed her eyes. For now, Faith had to get rid of the Jeep and lie low. The Kurjans had to be somewhere close.

They surely wouldn't attack in town, right? A series of helicopters, all black, descended above her.

Her breath stopped. God. Would they fire at innocent humans? What should she do? She planted her foot on the accelerator and drove as fast as she could away from town and in the opposite direction of the mountain headquarters. Her legs trembling, she pulled into the parking lot of a national forest. She ditched the Jeep, running through the rain toward what looked like a fairly hidden trail.

One helicopter circled around to face her. Panic hit her and she stopped running. It fired rockets into the now empty Jeep, and fire blew up.

She screamed and turned to run into the forest for cover. The Kurjans were firing into a park frequented by humans? That was crazy. What happened to their staying off the radar? Her hand fumbled when she drew her gun from her waist. She'd been as careful and untrusting as possible, and they'd still found her.

Oh, God. What had she done?

* * * *

Tracking Faith via GPS, Ronan took a sharp turn down toward the national forest just as three attack helicopters came into view. "Shit." The first chopper shot rockets into the mountain, throwing fire and debris high into the rainy sky. A tree flew in front of the jeep and he turned quickly, smashing into a bur oak tree.

Ivar yelled as he was thrown through the windshield.

Ronan leaped from the vehicle and rounded it in time to help Ivar from the ground. Cuts and scratches marred Ivar's hard-planed face. He shook his head and glass flew from his short hair. "Jesus Christ, Ro."

"Sorry." Ronan leaned to look past the downed tree and saw Faith's jeep. It was a mass of burning metal. His body settled and his mind focused. She'd run into the forest.

Ivar glared at the fire bursting from the trees nearer the town side. One helicopter veered off and turned south. "It won't take them long to find our headquarters now that they're so close. They could bring the entire mountain down on our brothers."

Ronan looked up at the sky just as the second helicopter fired in their direction. Bullets pounded up from the dirt road. He grabbed Ivar's arm and shoved him toward the forest, running after him. "Take cover," he yelled, sliding on the wet foliage.

Ivar leaped into motion, leading the way along an animal trail. Vikings were usually excellent trackers, and he was proof of that.

"Faith ran into the forest," Ronan yelled through the rain.

Ivar made a sharp right turn. "We'll find her," he yelled back, increasing his speed. The cut muscles down his back shifted as he ran faster than any panther.

More explosions ripped through the day miles away and Ronan growled. Was it possible to bring down an entire mountain? The force shields were strong, but so were today's weapons. He had to get back to his brothers—after he found his mate.

A break in the trees showed the second helicopter and it aimed again, firing down.

Branches and leaves pinged all over, and a small pine tree all but exploded. The entire forest smelled of pine and fire. He tried to focus his senses and scent his mate, but the other smells were too overpowering.

They hadn't been mated long enough to communicate telepathically, yet he could sense her fear. Deep and in the center of his chest.

He forced his legs to keep moving, as did Ivar. They were weakened by blood loss and needed time and food to repair themselves. He slipped again, catching himself at the last second and continuing on. Where was Faith?

A Cyst soldier came out of nowhere and charged.

Ronan pivoted and kicked the bastard in the gut before taking him down to the wet ground. His phone and the only way to track Faith spun out of control, dropping over a ledge. Fucking asshole. The cloud cover would allow them some time in the daylight.

The Cyst punched up, hitting Ronan directly in the throat.

His larynx shattered and he punched down as hard as he could, using his remaining strength to render the bastard unconscious. Ronan didn't have the power to yank out his throat or heart, so he kicked the enemy to the side, staggering to his feet.

Ivar finished off another Cyst, stabbing a knife into the white-faced monster's throat. It wouldn't kill him, but he'd be of no danger for the time being.

Ronan stumbled toward Ivar, reaching out a hand. "Brother?" he mouthed, unable to speak yet.

Ivar took his hand and stood, so pale his lips appeared blue. "We're not in fighting shape."

There was no choice. Ronan rolled his neck and forced healing cells to his damaged larynx. This, at least, he could now do. His injury began to repair itself, so he took the lead, going deeper into the trees.

The forest sloped down, and he moved swiftly around rocks and fallen trees as the helicopter continued to pummel them. The second one tracked him and Ivar, always visible between the sweeping tree branches.

It was the third helicopter that concerned him.

Finally, they reached another ledge. He stopped running in time to keep from falling over and caught Ivar a second later. They peered over the edge to a gulley below. The other helicopter had set down, and Cyst soldiers had fanned out around it, all fully armed.

"I'd give my fortune for a gun," Ivar wheezed, leaning against a tree.

Ronan tried to straighten out his right arm, but it wouldn't comply. Had he broken it when fighting the Cyst soldier? He didn't even remember. Pain was a constant in his body right now, so it all melded together. "I'd rather have a sword," he said. That was, if he could lift one.

"We'll have to go south to get down there," Ivar said, straightening.

Ronan tracked the possible route. To the south, there was a slope along the mountain that would allow them to reach the helicopter. But he wasn't looking for the Cyst. "We need to find Faith before they do."

Ivar stilled. "Brother, it's too late." He pointed toward the outer trees to the north.

Ronan's heart stopped.

CHAPTER THIRTY-EIGHT

Faith skidded around a corner and smashed right into a solid male body. Hope flared for a second until she lifted her head. It wasn't Ronan.

The Cyst soldier stood just under seven feet tall with the one strip of white hair braided down his back. This one had a white goatee that blended into his pale skin, and his eyes were a deep, dark purple. He grabbed her arm before she could fall on her butt and then quickly smacked the gun out of her hand. It spun into a stand of sticker bushes.

She struggled. "Listen. I just met with your doctor. You're on the wrong side here."

He pivoted and started dragging her down the rocky slope. "There's only one side." His voice was low and gravelly.

Her feet slipped on the wet weeds, and she fought harder.

He continued downward without a hitch in his stride. His extra-long black boots obviously had traction that hugged the terrain, while her tennis shoes did nothing but glide as he pulled her. She punched him in the ribs with her good arm, and he grunted but kept moving.

They emerged into a clearing where a helicopter waited.

Adrenaline tore through Faith's veins, and she began to really fight, kicking and punching.

With a sigh, the soldier wrapped an arm around her waist and hoisted her, carrying her at his side like a wayward toddler. Her arms and legs hung down on either side of his arm, kicking uselessly. "How tall are you, anyway?" she snapped, twisting so she could kick his thigh.

He didn't answer, instead tossing her into the helicopter. She landed hard and bounced on the seat. A roar filled the day. She turned to see Ronan up on a high ledge, rage crossing his expression. She had to get to him. She bunched her muscles to attack, scrambling toward the door.

"I wouldn't." Dr. Yvonne Maple sat across from her with a silver gun pointed at Faith's head. "I have no problem shooting you."

Faith caught her breath and stilled before pushing rain-soaked hair away from her face. "You're insane."

"Just determined." Yvonne's smile lacked the charm of earlier. "Though so are you. I hadn't expected the homemade test for blood. Very smart."

One Cyst soldier leaned in. "We have two missing and probably down."

Yvonne sighed. "Have the second helicopter pick them up and then provide protection on our way home. The third can finish demolishing the headquarters you just found."

"No," Faith said, tightening her muscles to strike. The knife was still in her sock.

Yvonne lifted her aim. "Tie her up, would you? This gun is getting heavy."

The soldier jumped inside, grabbed zip ties from his back pocket, and quickly secured Faith to the seat. She fought him, kicking and nearly biting him, but his movements didn't slow.

"They're so much stronger and faster than we are," Yvonne said, almost conversationally. "Fighting him just makes you look silly."

The Cyst soldier exited the craft and shut the door. The engines whirred to life. Faith tried to move her hands and failed. "We?" she asked softly.

Yvonne scoffed. "Yeah. I'm human, dumbass."

"I figured, since you wouldn't show me in the café." Faith's shoulders slumped as they lifted high into the air. "The fangs and the eyes?"

"Kurjan inventions," Yvonne said, her green eyes filled with glee. "You're much smarter than we expected. Didn't trust us at all, did you?"

"Just enough to meet you," Faith admitted.

"I guess you would take any chance to save your sister," Yvonne murmured. "I understand that. Willing to risk your life for her?"

"Obviously," Faith muttered.

Yvonne's patrician nostrils flared. "And the lives of the Seven. That's ballsy, bitch."

Faith met her gaze levelly, refusing to show any weakness. "The Seven will be fine. They're immortal." She hoped they were okay. She hadn't considered the threat to them. Not really.

Yvonne's pupils narrowed in the dimming light. "I did enjoy wearing the fangs. I'd like to see if I could have them permanently attached."

The woman was crazy. "What was in the serum, anyway? Saline?"

Yvonne gave a hard smile, the sight oddly garish in her beautiful face. "Food coloring and enough morphine to kill her." She picked lint off her pants. "If you got away from us and we had to attack the mountain, it was easier to just make sure the Key was dead."

Faith stiffened.

Yvonne rolled her eyes. "Come on. Omar was in the hospital room with your sister for some time. We've known she was a Key since that day, and we've been planning accordingly."

Anger flowed through Faith so quickly her ears rang. Then she calmed. The only way out of this was by using her brain. "You'll never get her."

"Again, we don't care. The mountain is about to completely collapse, and she'll be dead. Another Key will be created." Yvonne crossed her legs and eyed her fashionable boots. "You know, I've found that smart girls like you are easy to fool. To tempt."

Faith blinked. "Excuse me?"

"The whole scientist thing. You can convince yourself of anything with talk of genetics, logic, and time. Like how the Kurjans evolved to be—what was it? Diplomats and scientists?" Yvonne laughed. "While the Seven are definitely out of touch, they know an enemy when they see one. Yet you disregarded their experience because of science and what you took as proof."

Faith swallowed. That was exactly what she'd done.

"Trust and faith are proven by time, you know?" Yvonne's eyes gleamed. "Your name is Faith too. That's just funny."

"How old are you, anyway?" Faith asked, caught by the woman's tone.

"Twenty-two," Yvonne said, setting the gun in her monstrous purse. "The perfect age to become mated."

Ah. Faith rolled her eyes. "They promised you immortality if you helped them." The girl was lost. "You must see they're not on the level. You can get out now. Help me, and I'll get you to safety."

Yvonne smiled again. "You don't understand. I'm the Intended. The. Intended."

Faith unobtrusively tried to twist her left wrist free. Pain cut into her skin. "I don't know what that means."

Yvonne sighed. "Every few decades, an Intended is born for Ulric. The Superior. It's my turn, and let me tell you, I'm not dying alone and unmated. This is going to happen. He's going to be free, and you're not going to mess with my destiny." Her chin lowered and her glare burned. "Neither are the Seven. The mountain falling on them might not kill them, but it'll put them out of commission for a hundred years or so. Digging out should take some time." Her voice ended on a purr.

The helicopter banked a hard left and Faith gasped. Her heart rate speeded up. "Where are we going, anyway?"

"One of our safe zones," Yvonne said. "I think Dayne wants to make sure you're not a Key before he kills you."

Faith shook her head. "You're nuts and I'm not a Key. I won't be used to draw Ronan out."

"Nobody wants to draw Ronan anywhere," Yvonne said, unconcerned. "I saw him bellowing for you from that cliff too. We've studied dossiers on the Seven and what they look like. He's bigger than I expected. If he makes it back to the mountain, he'll die. If he doesn't, the Cyst soldiers will find him, and he'll...die. Either way, he's done."

Faith's chest ached. "No. He can take on any of your soldiers." She had to believe that. He was an immortal, and one of the Seven. But what toll had the ritual taken on him? Had he been able to finish it before coming after her?

What about Garrett? If anything happened to him because of Faith, she'd never forgive herself. She'd been as smart and cautious as she could while taking this risk, but she hadn't factored in the immortals. They were immortal, for Pete's sake. The helicopter took another turn and rose higher.

Where were they going?

* * * *

Ronan started to run down the trail to save Faith, but Ivar grabbed him, twisting.

"What the hell?" Ronan shoved his friend.

Ivar shook his head, blood dripping from his cracked lip. "It's too late. Let's get back to headquarters and we can trace her. Trust me."

The helicopter rose into the sky, quickly disappearing in the thick clouds.

Ronan growled, deep and low. An emptiness filled his chest, shocking in its vastness. He pivoted and started running back to the second Jeep. He drove wildly through town and up their mountain, where his heart stopped. The helicopter above them fired down into the trees, and the path ahead exploded.

Heat blew into him. "Get out. We'll run."

They both jumped from the vehicle.

Ronan fell back and waited a beat. "They have to turn around or they'll crash right into the mountain. Go now." Giving it everything he had, he lowered his chin and ran through the fire, ignoring the pain pounding throughout his body. Ivar kept pace, no doubt also in agony.

They cleared the forest and reached the parking area outside headquarters. The third helicopter had disappeared, but he could hear it in the clouds. The thing was coming back.

"The second one peeled off—probably to grab their wounded," Ivar wheezed. "Come on. We have to take care of this asshole."

Ronan ducked his head and followed Ivar into the rock opening, jumping over a series of boulders that had dropped from the ceiling. The devastation was breath-stealing.

Ivar pushed by him, running for the armory.

Something whizzed behind Ronan, and he leaped forward to tackle Ivar to the ground. A rocket sailed over their heads, landing in the computer room. "Shit," he muttered, rolling his brother into the nearest room.

The rocket exploded, shooting chairs, computers, and fire through the hallway.

A ringing echoed between Ronan's ears. He shoved to his feet, taking Ivar with him. "You okay?"

"Fuck, no," Ivar said, his expression grim. "We have to take that bastard out before he levels this entire mountain on top of our brothers. Come on." He jumped into the decimated hallway and ducked and dodged through rock and debris to reach the armory. Once there, he limped to the corner and grabbed a long black square–looking thing. "Watch this."

Another rocket detonated close, and knives flew out from the cabinet. One sliced through the side of Ivar's neck.

His eyes bugged and he dropped to his knees.

"Ivar," Ronan bellowed, going for his brother. He helped him down and looked at the wound. "Heal that." He slashed open his wrist and shoved it against Ivar's mouth. His healing cells had only just returned, but something was better than nothing.

Ivar took a couple pulls and then shoved him away, holding up a hand. "I've got this," he croaked. "Take the rocket."

Ronan paused and then grabbed the rocket.

"Put it on your shoulder," Ivar whispered.

Ronan plugged the thing on his shoulder. It shouldn't bother him, but in his current state, the device caused strain.

"Other way," Ivar hissed.

Damn it. Ronan tilted it around, checked it out, and nodded. "I've got it." He flicked open the lever. "Heal your neck. Then find the others. We have to evacuate before the Kurjans send another force." It would probably be a matter of minutes.

Ivar pressed a hand to his bleeding neck and yanked himself up by using one of the battered lockers. "I'll go now."

Fuck, he was tough.

Ronan turned and carried the rocket through the hallway, alternating between sliding across rocks, ducking under pilings, and plowing through others. Finally, he reached the opening.

The sound of the helicopter echoed down.

He stepped outside into the rainy day and looked up. Nothing. Just angry storm clouds. So he closed his eyes and opened his senses. All of them. The whir of the craft rose over the sound of the rain. To the left. It was circling to attack again.

He put his fingers on the switch.

The helicopter dropped fast, rockets pointed at the mountain.

Ronan hit the lever, and a rocket shot out. The weapon bounced against his shoulder and pain ricocheted down his arm.

A second later, the missile hit the helicopter and detonated. Fire blew out of the windows in every direction. Ronan didn't wait to see it fall. He turned and hustled back through the complete disaster of a headquarters and reached the crater that used to be the control room.

The wall slid open, and Logan barreled through with Garrett over his shoulder.

Ronan coughed in the debris-filled air and moved. "He made it?"

"No," Benny said grimly, his shoulder beneath Adare's arm as he helped him move behind Logan. The side of Adare's face had caved in, and rock shards poked out. "One of the explosions tore him out of whatever dimension he was in."

Ronan's hand went to his chest. The pain was unbearable. "He's dead?" Not the young Kayrs.

"No," Logan said shortly, ducking beneath a beam. "He's not gonna die."

Ah, shit. Nobody had ever come back without finishing the bonding. They either came back bonded or dead. The process had not once been interrupted in the past. Ronan exchanged a look with Benny. This wasn't good.

Benny coughed out blood. "Nothin' we can do about it right now. Let's get us all out of here. Did they hit our helicopter?"

"No," Ivar said, limping in from the hallway with Grace in his arms and a tablet in his hand. "The helicopter is secure beneath the rock outcropping to the south. They couldn't see it from the air."

Ronan reached for the woman.

"I've got her balanced, and she's breathing fine," Ivar said.

Okay. Ronan moved for Garrett.

Logan shook his head. "I've got him. You need to replenish your blood supply."

That was the truth.

Ronan moved a series of rocks out of the way so Logan and Ivar could pass. "Ivar. Is your phone still active?" The idea of Faith in the hands of the Cyst chilled him to his soul.

Ivar jumped across a series of mangled computers, easily protecting the human female. "I don't know, and we have nothing here that works. Once we get to a safe house, I can find her if the GPS is still on. I promise."

Ronan nodded, helping Adare through the hallway.

Adare coughed, blood dribbling from his mouth. "I need a vacation."

"You've been on one for centuries," Ivar shot back, tripping over a burning purple chair and quickly regaining his balance.

Adare snorted.

Ronan eyed the rain outside. God, he hoped Faith was all right. The Kurjans would be able to sense she'd mated, so she'd be of no use to them as a potential mate. He had to get to her before they harmed her. Fear took him, chilling his blood. What the hell had she been thinking?

When he found her, it'd be wrong to kill her. Probably.

CHAPTER THIRTY-NINE

Faith's headache turned to a migraine as they finally touched down on what looked like a farm. It was dusk, and soon night would fall. Her fear for Ronan had grown.

Was he okay? He had to be. But could even an immortal like Ronan survive a helicopter rocket or a mountain falling on him?

Her heart hurt and her body ached. So many feelings bombarded her at once, it was hard to concentrate on just one. Ronan filled her mind. Images of him. His touch. The way her body had changed and warmed when he'd marked her.

He was everything.

Love. It was too fast, and it didn't make sense, but she needed him. He had to have survived. A Cyst soldier opened the door of the helicopter and reached in to cut her ties, pulling her back into the present. She had to get out of here and find Ronan. If the GPS on the phone was still working, maybe he'd find her. Blood flowed back into her wrists, and the numb tingling quickly turned to pain.

She winced and followed Yvonne onto a pristine asphalt landing pad to look around. There had to be a time when she could grab the knife from her sock.

Two armed Kurjans, tall and broad, guarded a sprawling ranch house made of wood beams and square stones. The day was overcast and they kept their backs flat to the building, shielded by an overhanging shingled roof. "Can they truly not go into the sun?" she asked, her mind fuzzing.

Yvonne ignored her, looking up at the clouds. "It's going to storm again. Let's get you inside so I can return home."

"Where's home, bitch?" Faith snapped.

Yvonne glanced over her shoulder. "That's irrelevant." She strode down a newly cemented path to the front door.

Faith studied the area. Where could she run? Several metal buildings that looked like barns dotted the property, making her think it was a working farm. Rolling fields sprawled in two directions, surrounded by trees and forests that led to imposing mountains in the distance. "Where are we?"

"A farm no longer needed by its human owners," Yvonne said, pushing open the door.

Screaming sounded from the nearest barn.

Faith whirled around to face the building. "What is that?"

"The last person who refused to work with us," Yvonne said, unconcerned. "The Cyst are true masters at gleaning information. Well, and torture."

Faith's feet froze. The phone was under one—was the battery still working? She looked frantically around.

Yvonne sighed. "We borrowed the place as a satellite operation once Omar found your sister in Denver. There's nowhere for you to run. It's too bad your sister wears the mark and you do not."

This was all about Grace. "You really want those Keys," she muttered, stepping inside a home that had once probably been cozy. Before the Kurjans had removed all the furniture and created a large command center with several computers and wall screens in the living room. Several Kurjans worked at computers and didn't even bother looking up.

"Well, yes," Yvonne said.

"Why?" Faith asked. "If one dies, another takes her place."

The biggest white-faced monster imaginable came around the wall to what looked like a kitchen. "For the ritual, of course."

Faith stopped cold. He was at least six-foot-eight with one of those freaky braids and a chest broader than a golf cart. His eyes were a weird purple-red mix. He wore an all-black uniform with just one silver star above his heart. "Ritual?" Her voice shook.

He polished off what looked like a roast-beef sandwich and gave a half-bow to Yvonne. "My queen."

Yvonne smiled. "Omar. It is good to see you."

The name stopped Faith's heart. This was Ronan's enemy? "Aren't the Cyst supposed to be the spiritual leaders of the Kurjans?" This guy looked like he could bench-press a truck and still eat another sandwich.

His eyes gleamed. "We are, but we're also their most elite fighting force."

Faith's stomach turned over. "What ritual?" She was getting so tired of rituals. All of them.

"Three Keys and death," Omar said simply. "All three women must die at one moment, and then no more will be born. The threat is over forever."

Yvonne smiled. "I have business elsewhere. I'll take the helicopter. Be well, Omar."

"And you, my queen," Omar said politely.

Yvonne turned to Faith, her eyes sparkling like a young coed on her first date. "I won't see you again. But look at the bright side. You'll be reunited with your sister soon. In the afterlife or whatever happens next."

Shock and anger smashed into Faith. She swung without thinking, punching the blonde right in the cheek. Yvonne cried out and flew back into the wall. Her hair cascaded wildly around her head.

"My queen," Omar hissed, reaching for her arm to steady her. "Are you all right?"

Fury darkened her pale skin as she shrugged him off. "I'm fine." She kicked straight up, her boot hitting Faith beneath the chin. Pain ignited in Faith's skull and she staggered back a step, shock filling her chest. She grabbed her chin as the agony spread down her neck to her shoulders.

Yvonne straightened her coat. "I've been training to fight since the Kurjans found me. You're lucky I didn't break your neck."

Faith's fingers clenched into a fist, and she stepped toward the blonde. "Oh yeah? Why don't you try again?"

"Enough of this," came a low voice from the left. "Ladies. Act like ladies."

Faith turned to see Dayne emerge from what looked like a gentleman's study. He was long and lean in black slacks and a blue button-down shirt with the sleeves rolled up. "Yvonne, you're needed at headquarters and your lab to finish the experiments." He nodded at Omar. "Bring the human into the office."

Yvonne smiled. "You're not the only one with medical knowledge here." She chuckled.

Faith tugged her shirt back into place and followed Dayne without being grabbed by Omar. She swept by Yvonne as if she didn't exist, because she no longer did. Dayne had just basically given her an order, and he hadn't used the "my queen" language. There was no doubt the Kurjan, and not Yvonne or Omar, was in charge. Here, anyway.

The room held a desk with a couple of leather chairs. Mounted bear and elk heads adorned one wall over a fireplace. Another chair, this one sturdy wood, sat in the corner with shackles at the arms and legs.

Darkened blood marred the wooden floor beneath it.

Faith breathed out, her eyes widening.

Omar shoved her into one of the guest chairs. "We won't use that on you," he said, his voice gravelly.

Surprised, she looked over her shoulder at him.

He smiled harshly. "There's a table in the barn I prefer to use. Having you on your back makes everything so much more...accessible."

Her stomach tightened. Fear pricked along her skin. But she turned away from him as if he didn't matter and focused on Dayne, who stood on the other side of the desk, watching the interchange without expression. "He's crazy."

Dayne shrugged. "He relaxes by torturing human women. You're safe, since you're Enhanced. We have other uses for you."

She needed to throw up. "Where's your kid?" she asked as flippantly as she could.

Dayne's odd gaze wandered her face. "At headquarters, far from here. He's just a child. I like to shield him from the harsher side of this business. For now, anyway."

Omar ran his hand down her hair. "Soft," he murmured.

She yanked her head away from him. "Dayne. What do you want?"

He lowered his chin and frowned. "I'm getting vibrations."

"Me too," Omar growled, dragging Faith's sweater to the side. "Bite marks." He leaned over and reached for the bottom of her sweater.

Faith fought him, struggling, but he drew it over her head, partially pulling her up at the same time. Then he forced her over the desk, facedown. "Look at that marking," he snarled.

Vulnerability shot through Faith, and she struggled, but he held her down easily. Tears gathered in her eyes, and she kicked out, hitting the chair. It moved a couple of feet, but she couldn't break his hold.

Finally, he yanked her up, moved the chair, and shoved her back into it. She crossed her arms over her white bra, her skin prickling from the cool air. She fought to keep from crying.

"You mated a Seven," Dayne said thoughtfully.

She reached back for her sweater, but Omar threw it across the room. "That means she's fair game to me." Anticipation darkened his voice. The cashmere landed in the pool of blood, quickly soaking it up. The sight settled her.

She was a neuroscientist. Fear could freeze a person, or it could focus them. She was smart and strong. There had to be a way for her to get free.

Dayne sat across from her and steepled his long fingers beneath his pale chin. "You were kept alive for the limited purpose of becoming a mate to a Kurjan. Now that's impossible." His gaze raked her face. "What is your enhancement, anyway? I've had research conducted on you, and you're very young to hold the position you hold in the hospital. Can you somehow heal people?"

"Sure," she said. Would that keep her alive until she could escape?

"Injuries?" Dayne asked and then held up a hand before she could lie again. "Before you answer, please know that I have a couple of human prisoners and will go cut one for you to heal if you say you can."

She pressed her lips together, her chest filling. She couldn't let anybody else be hurt. "I can't heal injuries. I can get inside a coma patient's mind and help him or her find a way back to consciousness. It's why I went into neurology."

"Useless to us," Omar said, causing her to jump.

Dayne nodded. "Agreed." He looked up at Omar. "Is the Key dead?"

Faith gasped. Grace couldn't be dead.

"We're waiting for confirmation," Omar said. "We lost touch with Air Unit Three and have sent reinforcements. There should be word in about an hour."

The third helicopter? Had the Seven somehow brought it down? If they'd escaped the mountain, could they trace her with the phone in her shoe? Was it still on? God, she hoped they'd somehow gotten out. Faith cleared her mind to focus. One thing at a time. Even if she grabbed her knife, she could only stab Omar. Dayne would be on her before she could get to him. "You guys have blown up two mountains lately. Surely the humans are on notice."

Dayne's dark eyebrows rose. This close, she could see glints of red in them that matched the ends of his black hair. "The humans think a couple of forest fires have sprung up from lightning."

"Oh." She tried another tack. "Listen. Before, you said there was a chance for peace. Why don't we actually see if that can happen?" Diplomacy was her only option at the moment.

His smile revealed abnormally sharp canines. "I agree with the prime directive, killing all Enhanced females."

She paused, her mind reeling. It was difficult to concentrate with the pain in her face and head, not to mention the fact that she was sitting there in her bra and jeans. "All of them?"

"Yes. They weaken the bloodlines." Dayne glanced at an expensive-looking watch.

Bloodlines? She shook her head. "What about your current mates? Future mates?"

"We have plans in place to protect our mates." His smile widened slightly. "As well as a limited number of unmated females."

Oh. She grimaced. "Seriously? You're keeping an Enhanced female farm somewhere?"

He sobered. "I do not like that analogy. But yes, while the Seven and the Realm have spent the last thousand years preparing for war and searching for peace, we've been strategizing. Securing only the most powerful of Enhanced females for our future. They will not be touched by the hell Ulric unleashes."

Where were the women? "Are the women here?" she asked, trying to remember the layout of the barns. She'd have to help them get free before escaping herself.

"No," Omar said shortly.

She leaned back in the chair and angled herself to the side in case she had a chance to go for the knife. "The Seven thought you were kidnapping Enhanced women to re-create the ritual of Ulric."

Dayne scoffed. "That ritual can't be duplicated. Ever."

"It was a onetime occurrence," Omar agreed from behind her.

She glanced toward him, trying to understand. In her world, knowledge led to power and right now, she had none. "You're in charge of the Cyst?"

"No. I'm a general," he replied.

She looked back at Dayne, her body shaking a little from the chill. Did these guys not feel the cold? "So there isn't a power struggle in the Kurjan nation."

"Not at all." Dayne stood. "I have to get back to headquarters. Omar, call in with news about the Seven and our missing copter the second you get it."

"Affirmative," Omar said.

Dayne turned to her. "I'm sorry, Dr. Cooper. Since you've mated an immortal and your Enhanced ability only assists humans, you're of no use to me." He nodded at Omar. "You can take her. Have fun."

"Thank you." Omar grabbed her arms and hauled her up and over the back of the chair.

Panic seized her and she screamed.

CHAPTER FORTY

Ronan stood in the great room of Adare's lake retreat in the middle of nowhere. He owned the entire valley and lake between two large mountain ranges in western Montana. The log home had several bedrooms, bathrooms, and modern conveniences. But the office was just an office and the computer a regular computer. No command center or satellite feeds.

Ivar typed away on the computer, grumbling about mountain headquarters and the time necessary to create and protect them. He leaned over the keyboard, attempting to locate the GPS on his phone. Hopefully Faith had kept possession of the device somehow.

Benny sat on a wide sofa in front of the fire, his head bent as he tried to heal the burn wounds down his back. "Has anybody checked on the patients?"

Logan emerged from Garrett's room, fire burning in his green eyes. "Garrett is out cold and unreachable—no healing activity. It's like he's not really here. Grace is still in a coma and her blood pressure has dropped more. She doesn't have much time left." The young immortal wiped his hands down jeans so faded they were nearly white. "Adare is still unconscious, but I can feel healing in the air, so he's mending."

They were a fucking mess.

Ronan wiped a hand over his pounding forehead. Where was Faith? The idea of her in Omar's hands clenched his hands into fists. If she was harmed, Ronan would feel it in his soul. He'd loved her before he'd even met her, and once he had finally touched her, she was even better than he'd dreamed. Why hadn't he expressed those feelings to her?

If she died, she'd never know.

"I've got her." Ivar emerged from the office, his voice still raspy and a long red line across his throat. He hadn't healed completely. "I traced the phone to a farming community near Boise. It'll take less than an hour to get there."

Ronan nodded. "Benny, stay here and heal. Ivar, you and Logan protect the home and watch the vitals of the patients. I'll bring Faith back."

Benny lifted his head, one of his eyes still too swollen to see. "You can't go by yourself. I'll go with you."

Ivar strode for the door. "I'm going. My neck is better than your face, and I have the tracking information. Plus, I fly faster and lower than you do." He didn't even bother to look back at Ronan. "And Ro, you don't know how to fly, brother."

He had been planning on winging it.

"Wait." Benny shifted and drew a sheathed knife from his back pocket to toss to Ronan. "Most of our weapons were destroyed."

"Thanks." Ronan tucked the knife at his calf and checked his gun. Only three bullets left. "They'll know we're coming," he warned Ivar as he followed him outside in the cool early evening and ran for the helicopter.

"Maybe. They might not have confirmation on their downed copter," Ivar said, jumping inside.

Ronan walked around the front and opened the door, sliding in and wincing as his ankle protested. He had an hour to heal himself.

Ivar powered up the craft, and soon they were rising into the air and banking left. "Ronan, you need to prepare yourself. The Kurjans have no reason to keep her alive." Ivar's voice dropped and regret filled it. "Just in case."

Faith was alive. She had to be. "I love her, Ivar." Saying the words out loud helped, somehow. "She's brilliant, became a doctor to help people. Then when she discovered her gift, she tried to help more people and focus on coma victims."

"I like her too," Ivar said, adjusting buttons on the dash.

"She's a sweetheart too. Saves cats and dogs. And neighbors." Ronan rubbed his chest. Now he had to save her.

Ivar lowered the craft beneath the clouds and skimmed treetops. They sped along as darkness began to take over. The clouds kept the moon hidden, so the forest looked fathomless below. "Sounds like her heart gets in the way of her head."

"Agreed," Ronan said, trying to keep his temper at bay. "She left safety for a slim chance of saving her sister."

"You would've done the same for one of us."

Ronan glanced out the window. "Yes, but I'm not a vulnerable human, now am I?"

"No."

They made the rest of the trip in silence, each trying to heal their wounds before getting new ones. Finally, Ivar spoke again. "I brought up a Google map of the area, and the farm has several outbuildings. There are only two of us, Ronan. The odds aren't good."

Ronan turned and looked at the male who had become his brother. "Agreed. You should head back."

"Nope." Ivar lowered the craft into an incredibly small area between several trees. "I flew low enough they probably didn't detect us. We're about a half-mile out from the farm and will have to run." He powered down the helicopter and turned to face Ronan. "We're together, Ro. Always."

Brothers. Yeah. Gratitude warmed Ronan's chest, reminding him that he wasn't alone. No longer. He was no longer condemned to isolation.

He had a life to live again. Opening his door, he stepped out onto leafy ground cover. The forest was silent around him, the wildlife no doubt quiet after the helicopter had dropped. He tuned in his senses, finding no threats near.

Ivar pointed a direction and Ronan nodded, leading the way through trees and over bushes. There were no human trails, but the deer and elk had left a couple of routes for him.

Soon he reached the edge of the forest and surveyed the farm. The house was dark, yet lights illuminated two of the barns.

Ivar came up on his side and Ronan lifted a hand to stop him. Troops of Cyst soldiers were finishing loading up a couple of helicopters, climbing inside. The two aircraft quickly lifted into the air.

God, he hoped Faith hadn't been in one of those.

Two other helicopters remained, quiet and waiting their turn to take off, over to the south. A Kurjan soldier patrolled next to them. Damn it. Night had fallen, which meant the monsters could walk freely.

Ivar jerked his head. "Let's take him out first," he whispered.

Ronan nodded. "You go from the east, and I'll approach from the west. Be careful, brother." Then he settled himself into battle mode.

The helicopters could probably hold six passengers each. That meant at least twelve on the ground.

The odds were less than good. To use the vernacular of the day...they sucked.

* * * *

Faith huddled in the corner of the barn, her shoulder aching from constantly twisting. Omar had left her there an hour ago, telling her that anticipation of an event was almost as good as the actual moment. He'd shackled her wrists to rings in the wall with twist ties, making sure she faced the heavy wood table in the center.

She couldn't tear her eyes away.

Iron shackles had been placed along the entire length, and blood had darkened the wood to a reddish-black. Hay covered the floor, dyed red by more blood. The place smelled like copper, pain, and death.

She'd managed to grasp the knife and had cut through the binding of her right hand by twisting her shoulder in an unnatural and painful way.

The sound of helicopters starting and then flying away came through the slightly open doors. Thunder rolled in the distance. If Omar had gotten most of his troops off, he'd be back soon. Her breath heated and she partially turned to try to saw through the other tie. It was made of a material much sturdier than most plastics, and her wrist was already tired.

She had to get out of there before he returned.

Biting her lip, she sawed as hard as she could. The material finally started to break. She cut harder and the individual strings in the odd plastic peeled away. One final slice, and she was free.

She jumped to her feet and wobbled when her legs cramped. Ouch. She kicked them out, stretching her neck. Her tennis shoes slid in the wet hay, but she maneuvered around the table of death to the door. The old wood scratched her hand as she slowly slid it open.

The night air chilled her bare skin, but she ignored it, searching for the best route to the forest. There she'd find cover.

"Well. Nicely done." Omar yanked open the door and pushed her several feet back. "Knife, huh? We didn't even search you for that." He closed the door and leaned back against it. "I'm impressed."

She couldn't breathe. Okay. Settle and focus. She retreated another step and gripped the knife handle tightly in her hand. She'd never stabbed anybody, and she wasn't exactly trained in hand-to-hand. So there would be just one chance at this.

She was a doctor and understood anatomy exceedingly well. The Cyst's body didn't seem that different from a human's, and she formulated her best chance to harm him. Cutting into flesh wasn't difficult. She could kill this asshole.

He shoved his shirtsleeves up his pale forearms, his eyes gleaming a bright purple now. "Did you know we actually get stronger during the night?"

She shook her head. "I don't know anything about you except that you're a sadistic, psychotic killer."

His fangs dropped, oddly yellow. Not white like Ronan's. "Sadism is in the eye of the beholder, Dr. Cooper." He tilted his head to the side, studying her. "As an Enhanced, can you feel your death coming? Is vision one of your gifts?"

"Can you feel yours?" she snapped, angling to the side. The walls in this horrific room were new, so if there was a back door, it was hidden somewhere. She'd have to go through him to get outside.

"You're cute. I like you." He watched her like a bird of prey eyeing a rodent. "I strive to be fair in my dealings. So here is your deal. Drop the knife and get up on the table like a good girl, and I'll let you die the third time you ask."

Her mouth dried up like she'd swallowed sand. Lightning cracked outside, and she jumped.

He smiled. "Or you can fight me, and I'll make this last for days. While I should return to headquarters, sometimes a soldier just needs some 'me time.' I'm due a vacation." The sarcasm showed just how twisted he was.

She settled her stance. There was no way she was getting on that table, so she darted around it, putting the gruesome device between them.

The skies opened up and rain slashed down, spilling inside.

He shoved off from the door. "Interesting." He feinted left and then right, pausing to laugh when she tensed and tried to go the other way.

Physics and elementary geometry dictated he could only go one way, so she settled her feet, waiting to see whether it would be left or right.

He came right over the table at her. Instead of ducking or trying to get out of the way, she brought up the knife, aiming true.

The blade pierced his right eye and he shrieked.

She ducked as he went over her head and then put her shoulder to the table, rolling over to the other side. Her feet had barely touched the bloody hay before she'd bounded out the door and into the rain.

The wind whipped into her, but she turned and ran as hard as she could for the nearest stand of trees.

Omar's bellow filled the night. He crashed through the doors behind her, but she didn't pause in her flight.

Oh God, Oh God, Oh God. Her feet slapped the dirt road and kicked up dust and now mud. She had to get away from him. She could feel him behind her, coming at her fast. The trees were too far. She wasn't going to make it.

Out of nowhere, a massive force careened out of the darkness. Ronan! He hit Omar and the sound of the two immortals clashing was louder than the thunder still roaring across the sky.

She gulped and turned around, sliding in the mud.

The two males grappled across the earth, throwing punches so rapidly their figures were just a blur. But the glint of a knife showed. Her knife! Omar lifted his arm and brought the blade down into Ronan's shoulder, just above his shield.

Ronan bellowed and punched out.

Faith ran forward and jumped on Omar's back, trying to jerk him away from Ronan.

Omar twisted and threw her hard. She landed in the mud and rolled end over end, mud flying from her hair. She planted her hands in the mud and pushed herself to stand.

Ronan leaped to his feet just as Omar did the same.

Omar smiled. "This is almost as much fun as cutting her to pieces." Faster than a thought, he drew a gun from his jacket and pointed at her, firing.

"No!" Ronan leaped across the space and took the bullets to his chest, falling to the side and throwing mud in every direction.

She gasped and dropped, grabbing him. "Ronan." Oh God. No.

He immediately stood, pushing her behind him. "Bullets can't hurt my chest, Doc."

Oh yeah. The shield.

Omar charged in a fierce tackle.

Ronan's shoulder hit her and she flew through the air, straight for a tree. Ivar jumped in front of her, blood on his face, and rolled in her midair to land on top of him on the ground. It was like hitting a brick wall.

He stood and helped her up.

Ronan rolled to his feet as Omar did the same, the two circling like ravenous dogs. "Get her out of the way. If it looks like I'm struggling, take her to the helicopter. Now," Ronan ordered.

"No—" Faith protested just as Ivar swept her up and moved toward the forest, turning at the last second to watch the fight.

Twin war cries echoed through the night.

CHAPTER FORTY-ONE

Ronan calmed his inner beast as Ivar got Faith away from the danger. She was okay. When he'd seen her running from Omar in her bra and jeans, he'd almost lost his mind. But she wasn't bleeding and nothing appeared broken.

Omar, on the other hand, was missing an eye. "Looks like my woman kicked your ass," Ronan said, his boots sure in the mud as the rain pummeled them.

Omar snarled, revealing sharp canines. His empty eye socket was bleeding. It took weeks to replace an entire eyeball, and it hurt like hell. "She'll regret it. After I kill you, I'll do nothing else until I hunt that bitch down."

"That's never going to happen." Ronan tuned his senses into the surrounding area. He and Ivar had taken out six soldiers, one at a time. He couldn't sense any other Kurjan or Cyst.

Omar removed a knife from his belt and lifted it, crouching and circling. "We'll see."

Ronan yanked the knife out of his neck. An inch lower, and the strike wouldn't have even scratched him. Without question, Omar had been training to fight the Seven. He'd known right where to place the blade. "Where are the Enhanced women you've taken?"

Omar feinted left. "You'll never find them."

It was his job to find them. "I will, and I think you know that." Ronan flipped the knife to his left hand since his right shoulder was weakening.

Omar watched the movement with his good eye. "You know you can't win. We've trained for over a thousand years. Xeno has created a Cyst army that will decimate any enemy." He moved slightly to the right, his shoulders tightening.

Xeno was still alive? "I figured the Realm had taken him out." The leader of the Cyst was truly crazy and always had been.

"The Realm doesn't know we exist." Omar charged, knife going low and punch going high.

Ronan blocked the knife with his own blade, twisting sideways. The punch hit him right in the temple, and his head rocked back. His vision blurred, so he kicked straight up and nailed Omar in the neck. The soldier stumbled several feet back.

Ronan took precious moments to regain his footing, centering himself. He was back.

The pain from the bonding, the agony of the shield breaking, the fear for his mate's safety, all melted away. He pulled the elements in, using the strength of the oncoming storm to increase his own. Power, pure and real, finally flowed through his veins.

The branding mark on his right hand pulsed in perfect time with the scars of the Seven on his left. All in harmony. His woman was safe and his enemy stood right before him.

Omar came at him with a wild roar, his knife up and his fangs down.

Ronan grabbed him by the shoulders and threw him, his fangs slashing across the Cyst's throat. Blood spurted over Ronan's neck, burning like fiery ashes. He dropped to the ground and used the strength of the entire universe—all the universes—to punch through Omar's neck to the muddy ground below.

Bones, cartilage, and finally the earth impacted his hand, shooting sparks of pain up his entire arm.

Omar's remaining eye bugged out and he clutched at his throat.

Ronan back flipped to his feet and brought his boot down with all force, severing the remaining tendons in Omar's neck.

The soldier gasped in death as his head slowly rolled away in the mud.

Ronan panted.

He stood straighter in the pouring rain, blood washing down his chest, and his fangs bared. He turned to see Faith in Ivar's arms. All color had left her delicate face, and her eyes were a shocked deep brown.

It was good she'd seen the killer inside him. As her mate, he wouldn't hide any part of himself from her. Ever.

He tugged his shirt over his head while moving toward her and then quickly pulled the wet material over her head. Then he took her from Ivar and began striding through the forest. "Did they hurt you?" He needed confirmation more than his next breath.

"No," she said, feeling way too fragile in his arms. "I fought until you got here. I'm fine."

The crazy noise in his head abated. She was all right. Thank God. "Good."

She wiped rain off his chin. "Did everyone make it out of the mountain?" She seemed to hold her breath.

"Yes. Adare was hurt, Grace's blood pressure is still decreasing, and Garrett is in some in-between state we've never seen before." There was no way to soften any of the truth. He increased his stride through the dripping trees. They had to get out of there before Kurjan reinforcements returned for their downed comrades.

The rain and wind continued to punish them as they reached the helicopter. Ronan put Faith in the rear seat and sat next to her, leaning his head back. Now that the fight was over, his body pulsed in one continuous line of complete pain. The flight back should take over an hour, and he needed the time to replenish his strength.

"Ronan—" Faith started.

He held up a hand without opening his eyes or lifting his head. "Silence."

"But—"

"Faith," he said, still not moving. "I don't want to hear a word from you." Now that he knew she was unharmed, his temper was beginning to stir, and he needed to heal himself. "Be silent until we reach Adare's cabin. One more word and I'll gag you." He meant every damn word. "I'll deal with you later tonight."

Her irritated huff did nothing to soothe his beast.

So be it.

* * * *

Aches and pains made themselves known in Faith's body on the flight through the clouds. Her temper joined in at Ronan's treatment. Sure, she'd made a mistake. But he didn't get to tell her what to do. Even so, she let him heal himself in silence the entire trip.

Odd tingles filled the air around her. Was that him healing? Fascinating.

Ivar was also quiet as he flew through the storm, his gaze remaining forward the entire time.

Jeez. Was everyone mad at her?

She hunched her shoulders and ignored both males, saying a prayer for her sister, Garrett, and Adare. Then she threw one in for herself as well. Ronan was seriously pissed.

The image of him standing in the rain, fangs down, after he'd punched a hole through an immortal Cyst would never leave her mind. He was deadly and otherworldly. And he'd come to save her. He'd put himself in danger and fought to the death.

For her.

Even though she was bristling at his words, her heart filled. He'd come for her. A part of her had believed he would. She wanted to reach for his hand, to touch him. But she definitely didn't want to stop his healing.

Or be gagged.

She cut him a look at that thought. His head was back, his wet hair falling to his collar and starting to curl. The lights from the dash played over the shockingly hard planes of his face, highlighting his stubborn jaw.

God, she loved him. All of him. It was so much more intense than she would've ever imagined. He wasn't the slightly goofy lost guy she'd first met. He was a predator, and probably the most dangerous one out there.

That realization aroused both fascination and unease.

The helicopter started to descend, and he turned his head, opening his stunning eyes. The blue and green had mixed together to glitter in the dim light.

She swallowed.

They touched the ground with a small bounce.

Ronan opened the door and reached for her, sweeping her up and slightly ducking his torso over her. The rain slashed sideways, helped by the mournful wind. They wound down a trail through pine trees and emerged by a large cabin in front of a darkened lake. Ronan stomped up the steps and opened the door. Warmth slid across her face.

Benny lowered the gun he'd had pointed toward them. "Just making sure."

Ronan set her down. "Status?" he asked.

Benny's eyes sobered, green and black mixing in them. He rubbed a hand across the scruff on his jaw. "Adare is awake and healing. No change in Garrett or Grace. Both are the same as when you left."

Ronan pointed toward a room next to the wide stone fireplace. "Go be with your sister. I'll deal with you later."

She whirled on him. "Deal with me? *Deal* with me?" Her voice was shrill, but she didn't care. He did not get to speak to her like that. "I was trying to save my sister, you buffoon. Don't you get that?"

He leaned in, his face a hard threat. "No. If there was a way to save your sister, I would've fucking done it. Now go while you still can."

Oh. He did not. Her entire body shook with anger and unshed tears. He was wrong. On every level. "There is a way to save her. I'll find it."

His eyes softened a fraction. "Sweetheart. I'm sorry. There's no way to save Grace."

"I think there is," Adare said, limping from the room next to Grace's and leaning heavily against the side of the fireplace.

Faith partially turned. One side of his face was covered in a deep purple bruise, and his temple looked concaved. "What do you mean?" she asked.

He winced and held his right hand up, palm out. "This appeared when I held Grace in the helicopter the other day." A perfect C was visible in the middle of jagged Celtic knots. Different from Ronan's, but looking just as beautifully deadly. "It's never appeared before. Not even when..." His voice trailed off.

A mating mark? Naturally occurring instead of being forced? Was it possible? She tried to think. "Why didn't you say anything?" Faith breathed.

His eyes flared. "I didn't think we'd be attacked or that you'd venture out on your own to deal with the Kurjans."

"Amen," Ronan muttered beneath his breath.

Faith cut him a look.

Adare straightened. "I was working it through in my mind."

"You want to mate her?" Faith asked, hope rushing into her.

"No," Adare said bluntly. Then he exhaled. "But I will. I hadn't planned on ever mating, so I'll do this to save your sister. But that's all it is."

Ronan glanced at Faith and then back at Adare, his eyebrows slashing down. "You're not—I mean, you can't..." he whispered.

Adare winced. "God, no. Not a chance." He looked at his palm. "I've been thinking about this. She's a Key, which is why she's still alive. She must have power we can't see. While a bite alone wouldn't have completed the mating, maybe the fact that this marking appeared on its own, without being forced, will."

Faith moved a step toward him. "We give her your blood, you bite her, and then you mark her?" It was a huge decision to make for her sister, but the alternative was death.

Adare nodded and glanced over his shoulder. "You have to decide now. Her blood pressure has dropped to nearly zero."

Faith faltered.

Ronan placed a hand on her arm, warm and somehow soothing. "There's no time to waffle. You know your sister. What would she want?"

Her vibrant, fun, daredevil of a sister? "She'd want to live," Faith whispered.

"All right." Ronan took her hand. "Success is still improbable. You understand?"

"Yes." She gripped his fingers. They could fight later. She walked toward Adare, her throat closing. "Thank you."

He nodded and gestured her inside the room.

Grace lay on a queen-sized bed, covered with a plush blue blanket. Her saline and food bags were gone. They must not have been able to get them in time. Her lips were blue and an unhealthy tinge covered her face.

Faith reached her and released Ronan to grasp Grace's hand between two of hers. She closed her eyes and once again tried to press into Grace's mind.

Nothing. Just quiet.

Faith opened her eyes. "Okay." She looked over her shoulder at Adare.

The bad-boy vampire faltered and then his fangs slid free. "This is better than a syringe." He slashed his wrist and then moved to sit on the bed, holding the blood to Grace's mouth. Then he tilted her head and gently pried her lips open, allowing the blood to slide down her throat.

Color bloomed in her face.

Faith caught her breath. Was it working?

Adare reached beneath Grace and partially lifted her. "Let me have her."

Letting go was the hardest thing Faith had ever done. Adare lifted Grace to cradle her in his lap. He gingerly pushed her hair away from her neck, his other hand beneath Grace's shirt in the back. Fast as a whip, he struck.

His fangs pierced Grace's neck.

Grace stiffened, her body tightening.

Faith moved to her, but Ronan pulled her back.

Grace slowly relaxed in Adare's arms. Then she sighed, her eyelids remaining shut.

Adare removed his fangs and licked the wound until it closed. He set her back on the bed and placed the blanket over her. "It's done."

Faith pushed her sister's hair away from her face. "What happens now?"

"She wakes up or she doesn't." Adare dropped into a paisley chair next to the bed. "It'll be fast, either way."

Ronan walked behind Faith and pressed a hand to her shoulder. She leaned into his strength, her stomach churning. "Grace?"

Her sister didn't move.

The room remained silent. At least fifteen minutes passed.

Adare's chin dropped to his chest. "It didn't work."

Pain flowed through Faith. Tears gathered in her eyes.

Suddenly, Grace sat up with a harsh gasp, her eyes opening wide. "Grace?" Faith grasped her shoulders.

Grace turned toward her. "Faith?" She looked around the room until her gaze landed on Adare; she smiled. "Man, I'm tired." Her eyelids closed and she went limp.

"No," Adare said, moving to the bed.

"Wait." Faith settled her sister back down, her heart thundering. "Look." Grace's eyes were moving beneath her eyelids. "She's in REM sleep. Out of the coma."

Adare sat back down. "Oh. How long will she sleep?"

Faith was almost overcome, she was so happy. "Probably days. But she's sleeping. It's good." This was happening. It was real. She sat back. It was all about blood, wasn't it?

Wait a minute. Blood. A thought occurred to her, and she had to ask the question: "The reason the Seven is a secret. Did you use Cyst blood to create the ritual?"

Ronan removed his hand from her shoulder. "Yes. We broke every law out there to do it, and if discovered, even our own people might hunt us down." Regret and determination hardened his voice.

She paused, breathing in and ignoring the tension in the room. "If you're caught?"

Ronan shrugged. "Depends. If it's just our people, we might be spared. If other immortal species, especially the witches, discover we violated life and the laws of physics in such a manner? Execution for us."

She didn't care what had happened to make him so strong, but she needed to understand better. "What laws did you break?"

He studied her for a moment, while Adare remained silent. "During the original ritual, when Ulric killed the Enhanced women, a proven and mystical number of Cyst members were involved. Seven of them. They took in Enhanced blood, and then their blood was used in Ulric's ceremony."

Adare growled. "The Enhanced blood they drank was that of their own mates."

Her stomach rolled. "These seven allowed their own mates to be killed?"

"Yes," Adare whispered.

She shook her head, her chest aching. "What did you do?"

Ronan's eyes glowed. "We hunted down those seven Cyst and sacrificed them in our ritual. We used their blood and their bones to make us stronger."

Her throat closed. "This ritual requires sacrifice." No wonder it was illegal, as well as being against the laws of physics and morality.

"Originally," Ronan said. "Now the blood of the remaining Seven is enough to perform the ritual when we lose somebody." He rolled his neck, his gaze tortured. "We crossed to the dark side, without question."

She sighed. So they had the Kurjans, Cysts, and maybe their own people to fear. This new world was fraught with enemies. "Thank you for explaining."

Ronan nodded. "I will never keep secrets from you. Stay with your sister as long as you want. Then we will talk." With that, he left the room.

CHAPTER FORTY-TWO

Ronan finished scouting the property in the rain, looking for weaknesses. They were everywhere. Adare had never intended for his retreat to be used by anybody else. Well after midnight, Ronan prowled inside the warm house. The living room remained empty, so he kicked off his wet boots and strode toward the bedrooms. Faith remained in Grace's, still holding her hand. "How is she?" he asked, keeping his voice low since Adare was sleeping in the chair, his long limbs overwhelming it.

Faith looked up, her eyes tired. She'd changed into an overlarge sweater that had to be Adare's. "Sleeping." Her mouth curved into a sweet smile. "A normal dream cycle."

Ronan forced a smile. That truly was phenomenal news. Unfortunately, his walk had done nothing to tamp down his temper. "I'd like to see you in a few minutes." Without waiting for her response, he exited the room and walked into Garrett's bedroom.

This one was slightly bigger, with a king-sized bed. The younger Kayrs sprawled over it, his stillness unnatural. Logan sat in a leather chair on one side of the bed, and Ivar sat on the other. Benny snored over in the far corner, sitting on the floor with his back to the wall and his long legs extended.

Ronan tried to reach out to Garrett with his senses. "Anything?"

"Convulsions," Ivar said wearily. "We used morphine on him for a while."

Logan exhaled. "Then phenobarbital. That helped a little bit. Now he's somewhere else again."

Ronan swallowed over a lump in his throat.

Faith appeared at his side. "Phenobarbital?" she asked, her voice shaking.

"Yeah," Ivar said, grinding his palm into his eye. "Even when the bonding goes right, convulsions are pretty normal afterward. The phenobarbital has elements in it we had to create ourselves before, so we stocked up."

Ronan looked down at her. "Why?"

She moved past him and looked down at the pale immortal. "Maybe what Garrett is experiencing is like a coma." She placed her hand on his head and closed her eyes.

Ronan caught his breath. Was it possible? Could she help Garrett?

Her shoulders slumped and she stepped away. "He's not in a coma. There's plenty of activity in his head, but he's not... well, here." She turned. "I'm sorry." She faltered and turned pale.

"You need sleep, Doc," Ronan said, shoving his temper away. "We can talk tomorrow."

Ivar leaned back in the chair. "The master bedroom is on the other side of the kitchen. Adare said to tell you to take it. I think we're all in place for the night."

Ronan reached for his mate's hand and drew her from the room. He'd get her settled in, and then he'd go scout the property again. Her well-being came before his irritation, and the woman definitely needed sleep. Her body was probably still processing the mating, not to mention the ordeal of being kidnapped.

Which never would have happened had she just obeyed him. He growled low. "Have you eaten?"

"Yes. You?"

"Yes." He'd grabbed a bagel before going on patrol. He led her past the kitchen and found the wide doorway to the master bedroom, which had been decorated in blues and tans like the rest of the house. The bed was extra-large and looked comfortable. His blood started to burn. "Get some sleep. I'll check on you later."

She yanked on his hand. "If we're going to fight, I'd rather just get to it."

He paused. "No, you wouldn't." Maybe he'd go for a run and burn off some of this energy.

She released him and put her hands on her hips, glaring with all her might. "Listen. If you want to fight, let's do it. I'm sorry I left to meet the Kurjan doctor, but she seemed somewhat believable on the phone, and I couldn't get to you under the ground. I tried."

"I don't give a holy fuck how believable she was on the phone," he ground out, his good intentions two clicks away from deserting him. "I told you there were no female Kurjans. I also told you that the Kurjans and Cyst were enemies of ours. Finally, and this is the one you are going to want to remember in the future, I told you to stay put."

"I took precautions and didn't trust any of those people." Her honey-brown eyes blazed and her lips thinned. "Besides, I don't answer to you."

He moved into her then, unable to help himself. His body sprang wide-awake and his blood started to pound. "That's where you're wrong, sweetheart. In this new world where we are gearing up for a war you can't even imagine, for a danger that's unbelievable, you do answer to me. Every damn time."

She shoved him in the chest and he took a step back. Pink flushed across her face. Her chest panted. Anger glimmered in her eyes along with something else: Challenge and desire. "Not a chance, immortal boy. I don't answer to anybody. Never have and never will."

He loved a good challenge. Especially in the form of a sexy brunette. This one needed a lesson. "Faith, I'm giving you one chance here." Last time he'd done that, she'd tried to take his head off.

She rolled her eyes.

He almost grabbed her. Almost. She was definitely challenging him, and he wasn't in full control. Hadn't been since he'd seen her, wearing only her bra and jeans, running from a monster. "Get your ass in that bed and go to sleep."

She stared at him, her lips a pretty pink. "No."

* * * *

She wasn't afraid of him. Faith faced Ronan, having to look up more than a foot. The vampire had stormed an enemy camp to save her like some avenging warrior from days gone by. The reality of that shot power through her. Power and something else.

Desire. Raw and primitive.

His nostrils flared and tension poured from him, overtaking the air. "Faith." A low rumble.

"What?" she challenged, not moving an inch. For the first time in her entire adult life, she felt free. Wild and protected. She was smart enough to know that freedom came from him. From being mated to him—tied to him on a level she could barely comprehend. But her instincts were good. And this male, this deadly immortal, needed to be himself with her. When he didn't answer, she sighed. "If you're done threatening me, I'm going to go sit with my sister."

"You need to sleep." His teeth clenched. The roped muscles up his arms visibly tightened.

"Nope." Poor vampire-demon immortal deadly hybrid. She bit her lip. "Ronan?"

He moved then, the snapping of his control confirmed by another growl. He lifted her by the arms with no effort, raising her until they were face-to-face. "Why are you challenging me?"

Because he needed it. Whether he understood or not, they had to get things settled between them. Him coddling her and hiding his nature wasn't fair. His raw strength shot desire through her veins. Her panties dampened. "Because you're boring me," she murmured. Just how far was too far with him?

His expression smoothed out. Those otherworldly eyes morphed from green to blue and then the deep gold.

Her breath caught. Instinct warned her to flee, as if she could, but his eyes fascinated her.

Easily holding her aloft, he tilted his head to the side. Studying her. "You know, I don't think you've taken me seriously since the very beginning." His gaze turned thoughtful while his jaw remained determined. "Must've been the shoes."

Those ridiculous shoes. "I take you seriously," she murmured, aiming for just a bit of self-preservation. "I saw you destroy Omar."

"Yes." His tone remained gritty—almost hoarse. "Yet you don't fear me."

Her eyebrows rose. "That's good, right? We're mated." Her heart hammered against her rib cage.

"There's a fine line between fear and respect, Faith Cooper. I've been avoiding one result while sacrificing the other."

She cleared her throat, trying to concentrate. Her entire body was on fire and the marking on her lower back, his marking, pounded through her lower half. "Put me down, Ronan."

"No."

She planted her hands on his arms and pushed down. It was like trying to shove a steel beam. "Seriously. Don't be a dick."

"There it is." He leaned in until his nose was almost touching hers. "New rules for Faith. One, no swearing. Two, no mistrusting. Three, you fucking stay where I tell you to stay."

"You just swore," she returned, leaning in until their noses did touch.

He nodded. "Yes. I swear and fight the wars. You do not." His breath brushed her lips.

She leaned in and kissed him, indulging herself.

He paused, his eyes darkening. "A lesson it is, then." He swooped in and kissed her, taking over. Finally. She kissed him back, putting every emotion she had into it. He spun her like he had before, removing her borrowed sweater. Her bra and panties flew across the room a second later.

She tugged on his shirt, needing to feel all of that smooth, hard muscle. He ducked so she could take it off.

Then he moved and she found herself on the bed, facing the painting on the wall. "Hey."

His big hand caressed down her back and over her marking. Sparks flew through her body as if firecrackers lived inside her skin. She gasped and arched, her abdomen rippling. She tried to turn around, to see him, but he held her in place.

His fingers found her. Hot and wet—way too needy. She may have mewled. His thumb ran across her clit and her thighs trembled. The sound of his zipper releasing rasped through the air. So that's where his other hand had gone. Then the press of his thighs against hers caught her awareness.

He was perfect.

His fingers continued to play and he leaned over her, his breath hot on her ear. "There are a lot of ways to teach a lesson, sweet girl."

She blinked. Words. Was he saying words? "Hmmm."

He palmed her sex. All the feeling rushed right to where his hand held her. A sharp crack filled the air a second before she realized he'd slapped her ass. Pain spread out, heated and sharp. She arched her back. "Ronan."

Crack. More heat. His fingers continued to torture her, keeping her right on the edge. She moved against him, sweat dotting her forehead. Three rapid slaps hit her butt, almost sending her into an orgasm.

His fingers prevented that.

Her body rioted, needing more. She gasped, riding his fingers. God, she was so close. He palmed her again and she dropped her head, gasping his name.

He released her.

She caught her breath, waiting in place. Was he finally—
Smack.

He slapped straight up, hitting her clit with unerring accuracy.

She cried out, an orgasm starting. He pinched her clit, stopping the progression.

"No," she gasped.

He bit her earlobe, the sensation of pain melding with all the other. "Make no mistake, Faith. This is just step one in taming you." To emphasize his words, he slapped her clit again. The words should piss her off, but all she could think about was that orgasm drawing near.

He licked the shell of her ear and she trembled. So much need.

"Say the words, Faith. You will not swear." He teased her clit again.

She bit her lip. "No damn swearing." Who the hell needed to swear? "And I'll trust you." She'd already decided that one on her own.

"I'll take the trust. Maybe forget about the swearing." He slipped a finger in her, brushing against her G-spot. Her body jerked in hunger. "The important rule is number three. Stay where I put you."

That one was tougher. She liked her—he pinched her clit. "Okay," she moaned. "I'll stay, you know, there." Wherever the fuck *there* was. She didn't care. Not anymore. He could go off and fight all the Kurjans he wanted. She was out of the intrigue game. "Ronan."

He grasped her hips and shoved inside her with one hard push. Pain and pleasure mixed together until she couldn't tell them apart and didn't care about trying. He powered into her and she shut her eyes, ecstasy taking her over. She started to climb again, her entire body throbbing as he hammered harder.

Then he stopped.

Ah, man. Her head dropped. "Ronan," she gasped. He was the only thing in the universe.

His fingers dug into her hips and his cock pulsed inside her. Stopping had obviously cost him. He nipped her ear again, his fang running along the edge. "One more thing, Faith."

"Anything."

The hard slap to her ass shocked her eyelids open. Tremors started deep inside her. "You're mine. I want the words. Now." He slapped her again.

The primitive words should've bothered her. At least a little. But in this new world, with how she felt, they made sense. "I'm yours, Ronan. Always will be."

His breath caught behind her. She smiled, even in pain.

Then he tightened his hold and thrust into her, increasing his speed. "I'm yours, too, Doc. I promise." He went deeper than before, taking everything she had and making her feel completely safe for the first time ever.

She cried out his name as she broke.

CHAPTER FORTY-THREE

Ronan awoke slowly, feeling better than he had since returning to this earth. He reached for his mate and then frowned at finding her side of the bed empty. The sound of her breathing caught his attention. He turned to find her in the chair, watching him, her gaze unreadable.

She'd put on his T-shirt from the day before, but her scent wafted around him. "Faith?" he asked, partially sitting up.

She smiled, her lips a pretty pink and her brown eyes clear. "Morning."

He sat all the way up and studied her. Curls cascaded down with her hair free. She was the most stunning woman in the world. "Are you all right?" He might've been too rough on her the night before.

She nodded and drew her knees up so she could hold them. "Yes. I wanted to tell you that I do trust you." She pushed hair away from her face. "Even without a damn orgasm looming." Her grin brightened the entire room, and her trust brightened places in him he'd feared would always be dark. Who cared if she swore so long as she trusted him? Damn, she was cute.

He opened his mouth to speak and a sharp rap echoed on the door. "What?"

Ivar poked his head in. "The kid is doing worse. More convulsions, and he's not coming out of it. Do we call his family or not?"

Ronan shoved himself from the bed, uncaring of his nudity. Should they call Garrett's family? The Seven was supposed to be a secret.

Faith bounded to her feet. "How long does he have?" she asked, obviously going into doctor mode.

Ivar shook his head. "Not long. He's too pale and his heart rate has slowed."

She bit her lip. "It's crazy, but..."

"What?" Ronan dragged his jeans on, his heart heavy. "We're at crazy. What do you think?"

She pushed her hair away from her face. "What if we use the phenobarbital to put him into a coma? If it's a last chance, I can try to reach him."

Ronan paused. He thought it through. "Is there any danger to you?"

She shrugged. "I don't see how. But if we do this and it doesn't work, he'll die."

"He's dying anyway," Ronan said grimly, grabbing her hand. "Let's see what you can do, Doc." His heart beat rapidly as he led her to Garrett's bedroom. Even though he'd been warned, he wasn't prepared. The young immortal was deathly pale and his chest was barely moving. "Shit."

Logan remained at the bed, looking almost as bad. "We have to call his parents. Talen and Cara need to be here." Pain filled the male's voice.

"We have an idea," Ronan said, reaching for the nearest syringe and filling it. "How much?"

Faith gave him the directions, explaining to Logan what they were doing. "I'm just guessing, since he's a vampire. It's ten times the amount to take out a human." She paused, looking at Logan. "I know Ronan is his family, but so are you. Is this what you want?"

Logan nodded, his gaze desperate. "It's our only chance."

She injected Garrett, and his body slumped almost instantly. Then she took the chair next to him and laid her head on the bed, holding his shoulder. She exhaled and her body went still. Then, silence.

Ronan moved toward her. "Faith?"

She didn't answer. He ran a hand down her hair, reassuring himself that she was all right. Had it been a mistake to let her go in? He eyed the silent immortal on the bed.

This had better work.

* * * *

Faith opened all her senses and eased inside Garrett's head. This was so much easier than it had ever been before. Was it because she'd mated Ronan and was becoming immortal? Perhaps her gift would increase, and she could help even more people.

"Garrett?" She reached out with her mind.

Lights flashed around her, and she found herself on a rocky hill with fire all around. Holy crap, this was new. She'd never actually seen anything before inside someone else's head. She'd only been able to whisper encouragement. "Garrett?" she called again.

The vampire jumped out of the fire and rolled, his clothes smoldering. "Faith?" He looked around wildly. "What the hell are you doing here?"

She faltered. Even the heat felt real. "I'm here to take you back."

His chin dropped. "Great. Which way?"

She looked around, panic making her feet twitch. "I don't know." Then she looked up, and her brain seized. "What the—?" Three suns bore down on them.

Garrett moved closer and pinched her bicep.

"Ouch," she said, yanking her arm back. "Why?"

He frowned. "Figured you weren't real."

"I am, but we're not really here," she said, not understanding any of this.

Garrett sighed. "I know. I figure something interrupted the bonding ceremony, and my body went into one dimension while the rest of me went in another."

That made as much sense as anything. "How do we get back?"

He winced. "I've learned a lot in the hours I've been here—most of it by accident and just experimenting. We can move from dimension to dimension by creating an invisible door and walking through. The problem is, some of the dimensions try to kill you." He looked around. "Can you get back by yourself?"

She closed her eyes and tried to return to the bedroom. The heat continued to bombard her. "No." Her eyelids opened and her eyes widened. She was stuck here. In this odd dimension. Her knees wobbled and her stomach flipped over.

"Then our bodies will die," Garrett said grimly. "I don't know about you, but I'd rather keep traveling through dimensions just in case we find a good one." He moved toward her and stood by her side. "Let me go first, and if it looks okay, come behind me."

This was crazy. Totally nuts. "Okay?"

He swept his hand out, and several portals opened. "Pick one."

She pointed to the middle one and then followed him through. This world was full of ice and snow. Something howled in the distance and the hair rose along her neck. Garrett opened more portals. "You've been doing this for days?" she asked.

He nodded. "I figure it's like teleporting in slow-motion. But who the hell knows."

They went through about fifteen dimensions and barely escaped something that looked like a rabid Snuffleupagus. Garrett was definitely weakening and Faith's legs were starting to ache. She swept her arm and opened a series of portals.

"Garrett!" Somebody called from the far left opening.

Garrett's eyes widened. He hesitated and moved through it. Faith scrambled to follow. She landed on a beach next to a pink ocean.

An adorable little girl stood in the sand, tapping her white sandal. The girl from the screen: Hope. Little Hope Kayrs-Kyllwood. Her pretty blue eyes were anxious, and she shook her head, crossing her arms. "Uncle Garrett. What are you *doing*?"

Garrett paused and then grabbed the little girl for a hug. "Hope." He leaned back, horror crossing his face. "Are you stuck here too?

Oh God." He held her close and looked around frantically. "Don't worry, sweetie. We'll get you out of here."

Hope sighed. "Oh, Uncle Garrett. Boys are so dumb."

Faith coughed and tried to sound reassuring. How was any of this possible? "Hope? I'm Faith."

The girl smiled. "I know." She looked back at her uncle, settling comfortably in his arms. "This hasta be a secret. Just like you being a Seven."

Garrett straightened. "Wait a minute. How do you know—"

Hope rolled her eyes. "I know lotsa stuff. Probably more than you." She leaned in and pressed one little finger to her pink lips. "We hafta keep secrets."

Garrett shook his head. "I can't keep secrets from your mom."

"You hafta. For a while." The girl swept her hand out, and a sparkly portal opened. "That will get you home, but it's gonna be hard. You hafta go."

Garrett looked around. "Can you get out?"

"Yes. Hurry up. Mama is bringing me ice cream." The girl started to fade right from his arms and then disappeared.

Garrett shook his head, his face slack. "I was not expecting that."

Faith nodded and moved toward him. "I say we go through that portal." If Hope was the Lock, whatever that meant, maybe she had found a way for them to get home.

"We have nothing to lose." Garrett grabbed Faith's hand and leaped through.

* * * *

Ronan shook Faith again, frustration eating through him. He couldn't awaken her. This had been a colossal mistake. It had been nearly five hours, and she hadn't so much as twitched. "Faith. Wake up."

She jumped up with a shriek.

Garrett leaped out of the bed at the same time.

Ronan pivoted, putting Faith behind him. What was happening?

Garrett looked around and dropped to his ass. "Faith?"

She leaned around Ronan, her fingers digging into his ribs. "Was that a fucking brontosaurus?"

So much for the no-swearing. Ronan turned and yanked her into him, his heart feeling like it had left his body for too long. "Are you okay?" He leaned back to study her.

She smiled, the sight beautiful. amber-colored eyes, dark hair, stubborn chin. Smart and steady...and all his. She looked at him, delight in her eyes, her mouth curving in a gentle smile. "I'm starving."

"Me too," Garrett said, standing and hugging first Logan and then Ivar. "Shit, man. That bonding stuff hurts."

Ronan's shoulders sagged. "It surely does." His relief was so great he nearly started babbling. He looked at the young warrior. "Garrett, welcome home." The kid had survived.

Garrett grinned. "Boy, do I have a lot to tell you."

Ronan nodded, his chest filling. "After you eat." He wrapped an arm around Faith's shoulders. If he didn't get her alone for a few moments, his head was going to explode. "We'll return in a few moments." Holding her tight, he led her through the house to their bedroom.

She yawned and trooped alongside him. "I need to check on my sister."

"She's still resting comfortably," Ronan said, shutting the door behind him. "I was starting to think I'd lost you."

She turned to face him, tilting her head back. "The whole experience was crazy. I'm excited to tell you about it." Her nose wrinkled. "Then I want to draw what I saw."

His chest calmed. Faith was safe and right here with him. He pushed the hair away from her face. "I just need a moment. We were interrupted earlier, and I want to make sure you know that I love you." He placed her hand over his chest. "You beat here and always will. Everything I am or will ever be is yours."

Tears filled her eyes. She swallowed. "Ronan. I love you too. I've never trusted anybody like I do you." She leaned up and kissed him, her lips soft and sweet.

He returned her kiss, his body settling. For so long, he'd been alone. But in this miraculous moment, he was home, surrounded by family and friends. There was a war coming, but he had time to prepare. For now, he would work on rebuilding the Seven, planning to save his brother in the Shield, and then protecting the Keys and Enhanced women.

Finally, right here, he was whole. He leaned back and studied his woman. The one who held his soul in her very capable hands. "Immortality won't be long enough to show you how much I love you." He grinned. "But I'll do my best."

Epilogue

The rain pattered gently outside, while Faith snuggled down in the big bed, her back to Ronan's front. His arm was around her, and she played with his long fingers, marveling at his size. "I can't believe I moved through dimensions yesterday," she murmured, feeling warm and safe.

"You get used to it, but I much prefer this dimension," he mumbled, his mouth near her ear.

She shivered, her body slowly awakening. Morning would arrive all too soon and reality would intrude. "I felt you leave last night." Even in her sleep, she had known when he'd slipped from the bed.

"I walked the property. This is not a secure location." He moved against her, ripped muscles shifting against her bare skin. "Benny and Logan will leave this morning to scout out a mountain somewhere. We're running out of ranges."

How scary was that? She stretched against him, and tingles exploded through her. "Did you check on Grace?"

"I did. She's sleeping peacefully."

Tears threatened Faith's eyes, and she let them be. It was a miracle, or rather an immortal gift, and she'd take it. "Was Adare with her?"

"No." Ronan caressed down her arm. "Adare dislikes weakness as much as he does humans. He saved her life because he's my brother and because she's a Key. Don't hope for anything more from him."

Faith sniffed. "Gracie can do better, anyway." As soon as communications were up, she was going to figure out more about the virus that negated mating bonds. Since Grace was essentially out of her coma, she wouldn't be harmed by cutting all ties with the grumpy Adare. "While she heals, I'll need to take a leave of absence from the hospital."

Ronan's palm moved up her arm, the touch gentle. "That would be wise, considering you'll be locked down in a mountain somewhere."

She blinked, noting the shadows on the wall as dawn slowly arrived. "Maybe temporarily, but you understand I have work I love to do, right?" Especially now that she knew there were immortal cells available that could cure people. "I'm a doctor."

"I do understand, and I promise I'll get you back to work as soon as possible." He brushed the hair away from her face and rolled her, landing squarely on top of her. Hardness and heat. "You also realize that you will be immortal soon? That at some point, you will need to disappear from human contact for a time?"

That was so freakin' weird. She traced the amazing angles of his face, marveling at the strength even there. "As long as we're disappearing together, I can do it."

His eyes softened to light aqua. "We'll always be together, Doc."

Man, she loved him. Every stubborn, hard, wounded line. Her feelings didn't make sense after such a short time, but screw that. He was hers, and she was keeping him. "I'll call Louise and the hospital later today with the news about Grace and my sabbatical." She had to introduce Louise and Ronan at some point. They'd get along wonderfully—she just knew it.

He pressed a soft kiss to her forehead. "I will have somebody fetch your felines for you as soon as we find a new headquarters."

There was that sweetness in him. Her entire body flushed and then warmed. "I should probably get up and check on Grace and Garrett." The doctor in her insisted upon it.

He dropped his head, and his mouth wandered up her neck. "Maybe in a few minutes."

Desire swamped her, and she smiled. She'd faced enough loss in life that she knew to take the good moments and squeeze every ounce of pleasure out of them. "I guess there's no hurry. Although didn't Ivar say he was cooking us a Viking breakfast today?" Whatever the heck that was.

"He did, but plans changed." Ronan kissed her, his mouth lazily wandering across hers. "He went hunting one of those physicists we need." A slight edge rode his words.

She paused, her fingers tangling in Ronan's hair. "You sound concerned?"

"No." He pressed kisses along her jawline. "Ivar is the responsible one around here—usually. But he also has little regard for humans—especially those breaking laws. I just hope he uses finesse with the scientist. He might just grab her up."

That didn't seem like Ivar. She opened her mouth to ask a question and Ronan swooped in, kissing her until there were no questions left about anything. Finally, he let her breathe.

She moved restlessly against him. "I can't believe I've found you. No matter what happens next, I love you."

His smile would stay with her forever. "I love you too. And I *knew* I'd find you."

She placed her hand above his heart, her palm warming. "How? How could you know that?"

He leaned in, his feelings for her glowing in his eyes. Promise, possession, protection...and love. "Because, Doc. I always did have Faith."

Read on for an excerpt from Rebecca Zanetti's blazing hot romantic suspense series, The Requisition Force, coming October 2018.

THE HIDDEN
By Rebecca Zanetti

The day he moved in next door, dark clouds covered the sky with the promise of a powerful storm. Pippa watched from her window, the one over the kitchen sink, partially hidden by the cheerful polka-dotted curtains. Yellow dots over a crisp white background—what she figured happy people would use.

He moved box after box after box through the two-stall garage, all by himself, cut muscles bunching in his arms.

Angles and shadows made up his face, more shadows than angles. He didn't smile, and although he didn't frown, his expression had settled into harsh lines.

A guy like him, dangerously handsome, should probably have friends helping.

Yet he didn't. His black truck, dusty yet seemingly well kept, sat alone in the driveway containing the boxes.

She swallowed several times, instinctively knowing he wasn't a man to cross, even if she was a person who crossed others. She was not.

For a while she tried to amuse herself with counting the boxes, and then guessing their weight, and then just studying the man. He appeared to be in his early thirties, maybe just a couple of years older than she.

Thick black hair fell to his collar in unruly waves, giving him an unkempt appearance that hinted nobody took care of him. His shoulders were tense and his body language fluid. She couldn't see his eyes.

The damn wondering would keep her up at night.

But no way, and there was absolutely no way, would she venture outside to appease the beast of curiosity.

The new neighbor stood well over six feet tall, his shoulders broad, his long legs encased in worn and frayed jeans. If a man could be hard all over, head to toe, even in movement, then he was.

He was very much alone as well.

A scar curved in a half-moon shape over his left eye, and some sort of tattoo, a crest of something, decorated his muscled left bicep. She tilted her head, reaching for the curtains to push them aside just a little more.

He paused, an overlarge box held easily in his arms, and turned his head, much like an animal rising to attention.

Green. Those eyes, narrow and suspicious, alert and dangerous, focused directly on her.

She gasped. Her heart thundered. She fell to the floor below the counter. Not to the side, not even in a crouch, she fell flat on her ass on the worn tile floor. Her heart ticking, she wrapped her arms around her shins and rested her chin on her knees.

She bit her lip and held her breath, shutting her eyes.

Nothing.

No sound, no hint of an approaching person, no rap on the door.

After about ten minutes of holding perfectly still, she lifted her head. Another five and she released her legs. Then she rolled up onto her knees and reached for the counter, her fingers curling over.

Taking a deep breath, she pulled herself up to stand, angling to the side of the counter.

He stood at the window, facing her, his chest taking up most of the panes.

Her heart exploded. She screamed, turned, and ran. She cleared the kitchen in three steps and plowed through the living room, smashing into an antique table that had sat in the place for more than two decades.

Pain ratcheted up her leg, and she dropped, making panicked grunting noises as she crawled past the sofa and toward her bedroom. Her hands slapped the polished wooden floor, and she sobbed out, reaching the room and slamming the door.

She scrabbled her legs up to her chest again, her back to the door, and reached up to engage the lock. She rocked back and forth just enough to not make a sound.

The doorbell rang.

Her chest tightened, and her vision fuzzed. Tremors started from her shoulders down to her waist and back up. *Not now. Not now. God, not now.* She took several deep breaths and acknowledged the oncoming panic attack much as Dr. Valentine had taught her. Sometimes letting the panic in actually abated it.

Not this time.

The attack took her full force, pricking sweat along her body. Her arms shook, and her legs went numb. Her breathing panted out, her vision fuzzed, and her heart blasted into motion.

Maybe it really was a heart attack this time.

No. It was only a panic attack.

But it could be. Maybe the doctors had missed something in her tests, and it really was a heart attack. Or maybe a stroke.

She couldn't make it to the phone to dial for help.

Her heart hurt. Her chest really ached. Glancing up at the lock, a flimsy golden thing, she inched away from the door to the bed table on her hands and knees. Jerking open the drawer, she fumbled for a Xanax.

She popped the pill beneath her tongue, letting it quickly absorb. The bitter chalkiness made her gag, but she didn't move until it had dissolved.

A hard rapping sound echoed from the living room.

Shit. He was knocking on the door. Was it locked? Of course it was locked. She always kept it locked. But would a lock, even a really good one, keep a guy like that out?

Hell, no.

She'd been watching him, and he knew it. Maybe he wasn't a guy who wanted to be watched, which was why he was moving his stuff all alone. Worse yet, had he been sent to find her? He had looked so furious. Was he angry?

If so, what could she do?

The online martial arts lessons she'd taken lately ran through her head, but once again, she wondered if one could really learn self-defense by watching videos. Something told her that all the self-defense lessons in the world wouldn't help against that guy.

Oh, why had Mrs. Melonci moved to Florida? Sure, the elderly lady wanted to be closer to her grandchildren, but Cottage Grove was a much better place to live.

The house had sold in less than a week.

Pippa had hoped to watch young children play and frolic in the large-treed backyard, but this guy didn't seem to have a family.

Perhaps he'd bring one in, yet there was something chillingly solitary about him.

Of course, she hadn't set foot outside her house for nearly five years, so maybe family men had changed.

Probably not, though.

He knocked again, the sound somehow stronger and more insistent this time.

She opened the bedroom door and peered around the corner. The front door was visible above the sofa.

He knocked again. "Lady?" Deep and rich, his voice easily carried into her home.

She might have squawked.

"Listen, lady. I...ah, saw you fall and just wanna make sure you're all right. You don't have to answer the door." His tone didn't rise and remained perfectly calm.

She sucked in a deep breath and tried to answer him, but only air came out. Man, she was pathetic. She tapped her head against the doorframe in a sad attempt to self-soothe.

"Um, are you okay?" he asked, hidden by the big door. "I can call for help."

No. Oh, no. She swallowed several times. "I'm all right." Finally, her voice worked. "Honest. It's okay. Don't call for anybody." If she didn't let them in, the authorities would probably break down the door, right? She couldn't have that.

Silence came from the front porch, but no steps echoed. He remained in place.

Her heart continued to thunder against her ribs. She wiped her sweaty palms down her yoga pants. Why wasn't he leaving? "Okay?" she whispered.

"You sure you don't need help?" he called.

Her throat began to close. "I'm sure." *Go away.* Please, he had to go away.

"Okay." Heavy bootsteps clomped across her front porch, and then silence. He was gone.

* * * *

Malcolm West knew the sound of terror, and he knew it well. The woman, whoever she was, had been beyond frightened at seeing him in the window. Damn it. What the hell had he been thinking to approach her house like that?

A fence enclosed their backyards together, and he'd wondered why. Had a family shared the two homes?

He grabbed another box of shit from the truck and hefted it toward the house. Maybe this had been a mistake. He'd purchased the little one-story home sight unseen because of the white clapboard siding, the blue shutters, and the damn name of the town—Cottage Grove. It sounded peaceful.

He'd never truly see peace again, and he knew it.

All of the homes the real estate company had emailed him about had been sad and run-down...until this one. It had been on the market only a few days, and the agent had insisted it wouldn't be for long. After six months of searching desperately for a place to call home, he'd jumped on the sale.

It had been so convenient as to have been fate.

If he believed in fate, which he did not.

He walked through the simple one-story home and dropped the box in the kitchen, looking out at the pine trees beyond the wooden fence. The area had been subdivided into twenty-acre lots, with tons and tons of trees, so he'd figured he wouldn't see any other houses, which had suited him just fine.

Yet his house was next to another, and one fence enclosed their backyards together.

No other homes were even visible.

He sighed and started to turn for the living room when a sound caught his attention. His body automatically went on full alert, and he reached for the Sig nestled at his waist. Had they found him?

"Detective West? Don't shoot. I'm a friendly," came a deep male voice.

Malcolm pulled the gun free, the weight of it in his hand more familiar than his own voice. "Friendlies don't show up uninvited," he said calmly, eyeing the two main exits from the room in case he needed to run.

A guy strode toward him, hands loose at his sides. Probably in his thirties, he had bloodshot brown eyes, dark hair, and graceful movements. His gaze showed he'd seen some shit, and there was a slight tremble in his right arm. Trying to kick a habit, was he?

Malcolm pointed the weapon at the guy's head. "Two seconds."

The man looked at the few boxes set around the room, not seeming to notice the gun. Even with the tremor, he moved like he could fight. "There's nowhere to sit."

"You're not staying." Malcolm could get to the vehicle hidden a mile away within minutes and then take off again. The pretty cottage was a useless dream, and he'd known it the second he'd signed the papers. "I'd hate to ruin the yellow wallpaper." It had flowers on it, and he'd planned to change it anyway.

"Then don't." The guy leaned against the wall and shook out his arm.

"What are you kicking?" Malcolm asked, his voice going low.

The guy winced. "I'm losing some friends."

"Jack, Jose, and Bud?" Mal guessed easily.

"Mainly Jack." Now he eyed the weapon. "Mind putting that down?"

Mal didn't flinch. "Who are you?"

Broad shoulders heaved in an exaggerated sigh. "My name is Angus Force, and I'm here to offer you an opportunity."

"Is that a fact? I don't need a new toaster." Mal slid the gun back into place. "Go away."

"Detective—"

"I'm not a detective any longer, asshole. Get out of my house." Mal could use a good fight, and he was about to give himself what he needed.

"Whoa." Force held up a hand. "Just hear me out. I'm part of a new unit with, ah, the federal government, and we need a guy with your skills."

Heat rushed up Mal's chest. His main skill these days was keeping himself from going ballistic on assholes, and he was about to fail in that. "I'm not interested, Force. Now get the fuck out of my house."

Force shook his head. "I understand you're struggling with the aftereffects of a difficult assignment, but you won. You got the bad guy."

Yeah, but how many people had died? In front of him? Mal's vision started to narrow. "You don't want to be here any longer, Force."

"You think you're the only one with PTSD, dickhead?" Force spat, losing his casual façade.

"No, but I ain't lookin' to bond over it." Sweat rolled down Mal's back. "How'd you find me, anyway?"

Force visibly settled himself. "It's not exactly a coincidence that you bought this house. The only one that came close to what you were looking for." He looked around the old-lady cheerful kitchen. "Though it is sweet."

Mal's fingers closed into a fist. "You set me up."

"Yeah, we did. We need you here." Force gestured around.

Mal's lungs compressed. "Why?"

"Because you're the best undercover cop we've ever seen, and we need that right now. Bad." Mal ran a shaking hand through his hair.

"Why?" Mal asked, already fearing the answer.

"The shut-in next door. She's the key to one of the biggest homegrown threats to our entire country. And here you are." Force's eyes gleamed with the hit.

Well, fuck.

About the Author

New York Times and *USA Today* bestselling author **Rebecca Zanetti** has worked as an art curator, Senate aide, lawyer, college professor, and a hearing examiner—only to culminate it all in stories about alpha males and the women who claim them. She writes contemporary romances, dark paranormal romances, and romantic suspense novels.

Growing up amid the glorious backdrops and winter wonderlands of the Pacific Northwest has given Rebecca fantastic scenery and adventures to weave into her stories. She resides in the wild north with her husband, children, and extended family who inspire her every day—or at the very least, give her plenty of characters to write about.

Please visit Rebecca at: www.rebeccazanetti.com
Facebook: www.facebook.com/RebeccaZanetti.Books
Twitter: www.twitter.com/RebeccaZanetti

Printed in the United States
by Baker & Taylor Publisher Services